On Shakespeare

On Shakespeare
JOHN BELL

First published in 2011

Copyright © John Bell 2011

All rights reserved. No part of this book may be reproduced or transmitted in any form or by any means, electronic or mechanical, including photocopying, recording or by any information storage and retrieval system, without prior permission in writing from the publisher. The Australian *Copyright Act 1968* (the Act) allows a maximum of one chapter or 10 per cent of this book, whichever is the greater, to be photocopied by any educational institution for its educational purposes provided that the educational institution (or body that administers it) has given a remuneration notice to Copyright Agency Limited (CAL) under the Act.

Every effort has been made to contact the copyright holders of material reproduced in this book. In cases where these efforts were unsuccessful, the copyright holders are asked to contact the publisher directly.

Allen & Unwin
Sydney, Melbourne, Auckland, London

83 Alexander Street
Crows Nest NSW 2065
Australia
Phone: (61 2) 8425 0100
Fax: (61 2) 9906 2218
Email: info@allenandunwin.com
Web: www.allenandunwin.com

Cataloguing-in-Publication details are available
from the National Library of Australia
www.trove.nla.gov.au

ISBN 978 1 74237 193 1

Internal design by Lisa White
Index by Geraldine Suter
Set in 11/16.5 pt Minion Pro by Bookhouse, Sydney
Printed and bound in McPherson's Printing Group

10 9 8 7 6 5 4 3 2 1

The paper in this book is FSC certified. FSC promotes environmentally responsible, socially beneficial and economically viable management of the world's forests.

I dedicate this book to lovers of Shakespeare everywhere, and I am most grateful for the expert guidance of my wife Anna, and my editors Catherine Milne and Ali Lavau.

Contents

Author's note		ix
Introduction		xiii
1	The great Globe	1
2	Starting out	11
3	Stratford-upon-Avon	19
4	Shakespeare himself	34
5	An interview with Robert Greene	58
6	Acting Shakespeare	66
7	Directing Shakespeare	98
8	An interview with Ben Jonson	112
9	The Histories	128
10	The Tragedies	170
11	The Comedies	215
12	Shakespeare's books	257
13	The Romans	266
14	A fireside chat with John and Harry	297
15	The sonnets	314
16	*Romeo and Juliet*	332
17	*Troilus and Cressida*	341
18	*Timon of Athens*	349
19	The Romances	356
20	The Bell Shakespeare Company	378
Conclusion		385
Appendix A: What Shakespeare's contemporaries said about him		389
Appendix B: The sequence of the plays		397
Recommended reading		400
Index		401

Author's note

When my publisher suggested I might write something to mark the twentieth anniversary of the Bell Shakespeare Company, I nearly ran a mile.

The last thing the world needed was another book on Shakespeare, I thought. They come at the rate of three a week and so many of them are brilliant! Whether it's the erudition of Stephen Greenblatt and Frank Kermode or the more populist approach of Peter Ackroyd and Bill Bryson, they're all wonderful—what more was there to be said on the subject?

But then I thought of all the knowledge I've picked up over the last fifty years as an actor/director, and the ten years before that as a university and high-school student, the theories and ideas I've read, researched, heard about or been taught by various professors, directors and commentators. And I thought about those many theatregoers who enjoy seeing Shakespeare but have a lot of questions: Did he really write all those plays? How do you remember your lines? Why do you do Shakespeare in modern dress? Is he still relevant? How do you prepare a role? What's it like doing a long run? Should we translate the plays into modern English? Was he a Catholic? Did he believe in ghosts? Was he a feminist? A subversive? On it goes . . .

So this is a response to those sorts of questions based on my personal experience and reflections—the thoughts and reminiscences of a theatrical insider, and an Australian one at that. I have limited my comments to productions I have been involved with or that were especially significant to me. If I were to comment on every Shakespeare performance I have seen, even in the last ten years, that would mean at least one more hefty volume. Some of my musings are, necessarily, conjecture. For instance, I dare to undertake some fictitious 'interviews' with various acquaintances of Shakespeare. This is simply to put my research into dialogue form rather than attempt a scholarly essay. But the facts are as close to the truth as I can ascertain. The one person I could not interview was Shakespeare—because I couldn't hear his voice. The man had a thousand voices, but which one comes closest to his own? Do any of them? How can we ever know?

The more I write of this book, the more aware I become of how much I'm leaving out; the subject of Shakespeare is simply inexhaustible. So this is a book I shall never finish. I'll just stop.

It's not a book for academics or theatre buffs. But I hope it may encourage students and other interested readers to delve further into the complexities of Shakespeare in books weightier and worthier than this.

In the twenty-first century,
Shakespeare at his best is still the
most fun we can have in a theatre.

Michael Wood, *In Search of Shakespeare*

Introduction

I am sitting in a cramped backstage space in Brisbane's intimate Cremorne Theatre during a preview of *Anatomy Titus Fall of Rome: A Shakespeare Commentary*, by Heiner Müller. I'm having trouble writing because my right hand is swathed in bandages, having been 'cut off' by Aaron the Moor.

On stage a battle rages as members of the all-male cast fling blood-soaked copies of Penguin Shakespeare at each other to the strains of a corny MGM fanfare from *Demetrius and the Gladiators*. Shortly I shall enter as mad Titus, wearing a chef's hat and apron, banging a dinner gong and ladling helpings of blood from a big bucket into the cupped hands of my dinner guests in an obscene parody of Holy Communion. 'Where are my sons?' asks the empress Tamora, to which I reply, 'You've just eaten them, you nigger's whore . . . How tastes your scum?'

This is what you might call theatre in the raw. I'm curious to see how many people will walk out.

Titus is a co-production between Bell Shakespeare and the Queensland Theatre Company, and Michael Gow is directing in a way that reflects how much German theatre he has absorbed over the last ten years or so. I've only seen a little myself, but I'm familiar with the territory.

The Cremorne is the smallest of the three theatres in the Queensland Performing Arts Centre. We share the green room and its bar with the other two companies performing here at present. In the larger Playhouse Theatre they are performing David Williamson's gentle, whimsical drama *Travelling North*, and in the largest of the three, the Lyric, *My Fair Lady*. As we slosh down the corridor in our blood-soaked T-shirts and jeans, our heads and hands dripping with gore, we run into the musical's chorus, impeccable in grey toppers and ostrich plumes, tripping upstairs to perform 'Ascot Gavotte'. We grin and wave at each other.

It's not uncommon for ticket-holders to wander into the wrong theatre by mistake. It strikes me that they wouldn't be far into *Titus* before thinking, 'This doesn't look like *My Fair Lady* . . .' And this causes me to ruminate a little on audience expectations and the many different things people require from a night at the theatre.

Most people simply want a good night out, whether it's a toe-tapping musical or taut contemporary drama—something a touch spectacular and not too obfuscating. Throw in a harbour view and a couple of glasses of bubbly and punters are happy to fork out the dollars. Entertainment of this sort is, by definition, reassuring, comfy and fairly predictable. You more or less know the boundaries. Your imagination and assumptions may be challenged a little but you'll always come home to a safe place.

There are other kinds of theatre that are deliberately *not* reassuring or comfy. They aim to disconcert us, shatter our preconceptions, offend our notions of what is appropriate. They want to change the way we think, the way we see the world, the way we define 'art'. These forms of theatre—or painting or music or literature—have a much smaller audience. But it's an audience that is looking for something other than 'entertainment'.

Art can help us towards some resolution of the problems and questions that assail us. In times of trouble and chaos we are drawn to drama

Introduction

that deals with conflict in order to see that conflict aired and somehow resolved. Picasso, for example, challenged our academic notions of form and beauty, and many painters since, like Francis Bacon and Willem de Kooning, have been determined to yank us out of our comfort zone. Theatre of the Absurd challenges our notion of an ordered and meaningful universe, showing us instead a cosmos that is godless and meaningless. We have to find new answers to the questions of who we are and what we are doing here. This kind of theatre has a place too. It may provoke hostility and outrage, but it's important that it exists.

So I'm sitting here backstage, waiting for my entrance, caked in fake blood and taking part in a play that is brutal, nihilistic and offensive according to all criteria of 'good taste'. And it's thrilling. I can sense that the audience is getting off on it: this is not another 'nice night at the theatre'.

But it's Shakespeare, and Shakespeare is classic—revered by academia, taught in schools, quoted by bishops and headmasters, it is the touchstone of English culture and high art.

Is there a discrepancy here? Can Shakespeare be respectable high art and at the same time fodder for theatre that is grossly offensive, challenging and nihilistic? And why is he the most popular playwright of all time? Why is that popularity still growing? And why have I devoted most of my life to studying and performing his work? Why is it endlessly fascinating?

It has been said many times that Shakespeare is a wonderful guide to the workings of the heart and mind. Philosophers and psychologists have marvelled at his perceptive analysis of human behaviour. Even more striking is the variety of his understanding: how he achieves that mix of good and evil, comedy and tragedy, cruelty and compassion that makes his work so true to life, so close to how we know the world to be. His plays are built on paradoxes—for every winner there is a loser, one man's tragedy is comedy to another. Add to all this the fact that he is not preachy or didactic, nor is he judgmental. This means that the plays are essentially open-ended, capable of various interpretations and, therefore, controversial. There is an ambivalence about the plays that is reflected in the enigmatic nature of their author, all of which causes endless speculation, rival schools of commentary and productions that are wildly different from each other.

Then, of course, there is his language, striking in its originality, in the boldness of his juxtaposition of unlikely words, the range of his metaphor and imagery, the pounding or subtle rhythms of his verse that can stir the blood or soothe the savage beast. With words on a page or actors standing on an empty stage, he can create empires, deserts and magical islands. Like his contemporary Ben Jonson, he is a critic of humanity, but a milder one. He has the compassion of Chekhov but inhabits a much larger universe. He can be as political as Brecht but is more effective because he is not dogmatic. And he can be as satirical as Molière, but more profound, with a romantic, lyrical element that is absent in the work of his French counterpart. Unlike Dickens, he is never sentimental, but he can be equally indignant over injustice. For all his empathy he can be merciless in his assessment of human folly. His work is, as the Polish critic Jan Kott puts it, 'cruel but true'.

As an actor or director you have a special privilege when it comes to working with Shakespeare. When you rehearse you interrogate him, hold a dialogue with him, try to get inside his mind. You embody all those voices he had inside his head. You share the rage he felt when he has Philo exclaim of Antony:

> . . . his captain's heart,
> Which in the scuffles of great fights hath burst
> The buckles on his breast, reneges all temper,
> And is become the bellows and the fan
> To cool a gypsy's lust . . .

Introduction

You can see him curl his lip in contempt as he pens the words of Coriolanus:

> You common cry of curs! whose breath I hate
> As reek o' the rotten fens . . .

You can feel his heart swell with emotion as he has King Harry exclaim:

> We few, we happy few, we band of brothers . . .

And you are swept up in the wave of joy he experienced when he has Rosalind cry:

> O coz, coz, coz, my pretty little coz,
> That thou didst know how many fathom deep I am in love!

Reading a novel, you are on the outside looking in. When you perform Shakespeare, you are his collaborator—you are up there on the stage with him, you enter into his mind and heart and bring his creations to life, give them a body and a voice.

I have said Shakespeare was not didactic, but that doesn't mean we can't learn from him. He can teach us to look at the big picture, to stand back from a situation and see all sides of an argument. He teaches us to be sceptical about received wisdom, men's motives and human institutions. He shows us how history is not made according to some grand design but by fallible people, their follies and ambitions. He encourages us to rejoice in the marvellousness of humankind, to identify with nature, to value the precious brevity of life and to accept the inevitability of the life cycle. He demonstrates a sympathy for the common man and invites us to walk in his shoes awhile. He teaches us to revel in the wonderment of language, the ecstasy of poetry, the power of rhetoric and how it can shape destinies. And he introduces us to the joy of playing, of make-believe, of inhabiting universes of the imagination.

He has opened up vistas for us, and our lives are diminished if we do not venture there.

1

The great Globe

Your mouth is dry. Your chest is tight and your stomach is a knot of tension. For the hundredth time you check that your helmet's on straight and you're carrying the right halberd. You're about to make your entrance on the Globe stage and open the play. You peek through the curtain . . .

Christ, there's a crowd out there, well over two thousand of them, squashed into every nook and cranny. The galleries are crammed and the pit is a seething mass of apprentices and lawyers' clerks pushing and shoving. The din is deafening and the air thick with excitement. It's a hot summer afternoon and you feel the sweat trickling down your back under the heavy jerkin.

They're all here to see the new play, *Hamlet*, by Master Shakespeare. He's hot. His last few shows have smashed box-office records and blown Kit Marlowe out of the water. The racket is getting louder, the mob is becoming impatient—let's get it on, the tension is killing. You peek out through the curtain again—the galleries are full of merchants, businessmen and their wives, lawyers and a fair sprinkling of courtiers, sitting on wooden benches. The galleries are more expensive: sixpence a pop compared with a penny to stand in the pit.

Someone else is peeking through the curtain too . . . Blimey, it's the boss, Master Shakespeare himself. Is he nervous too? No—he's counting the house! Always has a keen eye on the box office.

He's playing 'the Ghost' in this one. He always likes to play the more dignified roles—kings, dukes and so on. He's wearing a rather elaborate suit of armour and a long black cloak. His face is visible under the helmet. He seems pretty chuffed by the size of the house and very calm for a first performance.

He tips you a wink and a pat on the shoulder then goes to take his place. The bookkeeper, prompt copy in hand, gives you the stand-by. You are terrified of forgetting your lines. You've never seen the whole script; they say it's too expensive to run off twenty copies, but the real reason is to stop you nicking it and selling it to a rival company. So all you get are your lines and your cues. At least there's a storyboard pinned up backstage to remind you what scene comes next.

You lick your lips and try to relax your jaw, gripping the halberd tighter than ever. The bookkeeper raises his hand and gives you the go—you're on! You step through the curtain onto the stage of the Globe and you're almost overwhelmed by the sea of faces all around you, staring up from the pit at your feet, peering from the galleries on three sides of you. It's a thrilling moment but the noise is still rumbling. It's your job to shut them up, so you yell in your clearest voice, 'Who's there?' and immediately the noise subsides—you could hear a pin drop. You spin around to confront the guy playing Francisco on the gallery above you, pointing his halberd at your chest:

Francisco: Nay, answer me. Stand and unfold yourself.
Barnardo: Long live the King!

Francisco: Barnardo?
Barnardo: He.

In a few moments, Horatio and Marcellus are on. We all wrap our cloaks around us and act like we're shivering with the cold, and even though it's a summer afternoon and the sky above our heads is a bright blue, the audience is in Denmark and it's midnight. I take my exit and a few moments later a low bell rings from off stage. 'Look where it comes,' says Marcellus in a hoarse whisper and the Ghost paces slowly across the gallery overhead. A lot of this audience believes in ghosts, so we're getting to them. A few older blokes in the pit cross themselves surreptitiously.

The crowd is with us all the way, utterly spellbound, and the scene finishes in a state of excitement, the actors scurrying away from the sinister battlements. As they exit through the door to the left of the stage there is a blare of trumpets, oboes and kettledrums, and the Danish court erupts onto the stage from the right-hand door.

The crowd applauds the spectacle of the brilliantly costumed courtiers and soldiers, and there are loud cheers for Dick Burbage, who's playing Hamlet. He's a great favourite, not just with audiences but with Master Shakespeare himself. He's not a big man, but he's charismatic—alert, quick-witted, agile and very natural. He doesn't seem to be acting at all. He and Ned Alleyn are the two best actors in London, but Ned is more your old-style actor with a great ringing voice; they reckon you can hear him across the Thames.

Time for a small pot of ale before your next entrance; you can't drink water out of the river, it's filthy.

The court has exited, leaving Hamlet on his own with the audience. Peek through the curtain, see how he's doing. The sea of faces is absolutely rapt and somewhat baffled. They knew they were coming to see *Hamlet*, which is an old story about a crazy, vengeful Danish prince. But here is

Burbage being all melancholy and doubt-stricken, telling them that he thinks revenge isn't such a good thing!

Something else is going on here; Hamlet is tapping into something deeper—the doubt and confusion of the audience and the time we're living in. This isn't medieval Denmark—this is England here and now, 1602; an England riven by religious doubt and sectarian hostilities, the new science and Protestant philosophy in a death struggle with ancient Catholic belief and practice. This is an age of terrorism, political assassination, police spies and brutal censorship: 'Something is rotten in the State...' And that's why there are two thousand people crammed into the Globe Theatre this hot summer afternoon in 1602...

Reality check

The scene above is not an attempt at a reconstruction. Rather, it's an impression, a series of sensations that hit me when I stepped through the curtain onto the stage of the new Globe Theatre in London and felt the buzz of what it might have been like back then.

In an age without radio, television or newspapers, the theatre was where people went not only for entertainment, but to see the dilemmas, the controversies, the fundamental issues of the day acted out. Not everyone in the audience would have known how to read and write. But they knew how to listen. Their lives depended on it. In those tense times, you had to be careful what you said in the pulpit—you could be burned at the stake. You had to be careful what you published—you could have your hand chopped off. But in the theatre you could just get away with it. Set your plays somewhere remote in place and time, as Shakespeare frequently did, and you could comment on all manner of corruption and tyranny. You could say, 'Something is rotten in the State...'—as long as you added: 'of Denmark.'

The great Globe

On the day in 2005 when I visited the new London Globe, there was no sea of faces—the place was virtually empty, except for us, a small group of Australian actors. But I could imagine the place crammed with eager spectators and how 'in your face' they would be.

This Globe is much smaller than the original, which could accommodate close to three thousand. And it's not yet as gaudy, though eventually it will be, when they finish painting the interior. Research suggests that the Globe was painted throughout in bright colours, wood emulating marble, with vivid tapestries. But the sensation of being on that stage, in that space, was revelatory and informative.

In 2005 the Bell Shakespeare Company was invited to take *The Comedy of Errors* to the Bath Shakespeare Festival, to perform in the beautiful Georgian Theatre Royal. On the way we had a few days in London and managed to score a tour of the Globe. The management and the artistic director, Mark Rylance, were hospitable and indulgent and allowed us to play on the stage. We ran the last scene of *Comedy of Errors* and were warmly applauded by a tourist party who arrived on cue.

The main discovery we made was how much you had to play to the audience—they were all around you and above and below; only occasionally could you turn to face your stage partner. And you had to keep on the move, making sure all parts of the house could hear and see you. Those who had seats behind the pillars must have been content to sit and listen. After all, they used to go to 'hear' rather than 'see' a play.

Nevertheless, the visuals were pretty spectacular—highly ornamental costumes, some of them specially made, many of them hand-me-downs from wealthy aristocratic patrons. Shakespeare knew the value of spectacle—dances, masques, battles, processions, coronations—and he kept the musicians busy.

There was virtually no attempt at authenticity in costume. That obsession with keeping things 'in period' didn't happen until the nineteenth century with the conjunction of archaeology, medievalism and the picture-frame stage. If you have a picture frame you have to put something inside it.

The only surviving visual image we have of an Elizabethan performance was sketched during *Titus Andronicus* and shows the characters in basically contemporary Elizabethan costume—Aaron the Moor is blacked up and one of the actors wears a laurel wreath to give a hint of ancient Rome. But otherwise the plays were performed in what you'd call 'modern dress'. With their talk of clocks and rapiers and 'Popish tricks' these were not ancient Romans but Elizabethan Englishmen and the plays were about themselves.

Sets were either nonexistent or as perfunctory as the costumes. A single tree designated a forest. The actors always told you where they were:

Hang out our banners on the outward walls . . .

This isle is full of noises.

How sweet the moonlight sleeps upon this bank.

The stage itself had a hangover of the old medieval pageants: the ceiling was painted with celestial signs and, in the gallery above, angels and gods appeared. Beneath the stage was hell; devils, ghosts and witches appeared through the trapdoor. Men stood in the middle, between heaven and hell, negotiating with both.

This open, empty, non-specific space made for great speed in performance. You walked out one side and walked in the other—you were somewhere else, from Rome to Egypt in a twinkling. You were wherever you said you were:

What wood is this before us?
The wood of Birnam.

What country, friends, is this?
This is Illyria, lady.

And you could be inside one moment, outside the next, or inside and outside at the same time. Hamlet is inside the castle at the end of the play scene, when Polonius accosts him. Pointing at the open sky above the Globe stage, Hamlet says, 'Do you see yonder cloud that's almost in the shape of a camel?' And the whole audience would have looked up to check it out.

All this mobility of playing was lost in the nineteenth century with the proscenium-arch theatre and curtains constantly being raised and lowered so that sets could be changed around—so unnecessary and so redundant when Shakespeare was painting the scenery for you. What painted set could live up to the words: 'How sweet the moonlight sleeps upon this bank'?

With the audience wrapped around you, the Globe has a curiously intimate feel, something the original shared, despite being so much bigger. You didn't have to shout or declaim to be heard (and, unlike the modern Globe, there were no aircraft overhead). So the action hurtled along, no time lost in scene-changes, the actors speaking quickly and clearly, always on the move. When Shakespeare referred to 'the two hours' traffic of our stage' in the prologue of *Romeo and Juliet* he meant it. Plays started around three in the afternoon and finished at five, no interval.

It would seem to have been Shakespeare's (and others') practice to write out the whole play of his imagination and then cut it down to a performance script two hours long. The stage-keeper would have the original, while the actors' individual parts along with their cues would be copied out and given to them. A script by Shakespeare or Jonson or Marlowe was money in the bank and, since there was no copyright, anybody could put it on. But some actors sold off their individual parts along with a garbled version of as much of the play as they could remember.

When the play was eventually published for sale, once the company had thoroughly exploited it, it was the entire original, not the cut-down performance script, that was published.

We get a good snapshot of Elizabethan actors at work watching the Athenian mechanicals rehearse *Pyramus and Thisbe* in *A Midsummer Night's Dream*. Peter Quince casts the actors, hands them their parts with their cues, then plays director-cum-stage manager. We get another insight when Hamlet (as author) teaches the actors how to play their roles—'Speak the speech, I pray you, as I pronounced it to you'—and launches into a very perceptive critique of what constitutes good and bad acting.

All these thoughts were rattling around my head as I stood on the stage of the new Globe and examined its backstage areas and dressing (attiring) rooms (or 'tiring house', as Shakespeare called them). I had a flashback to one of my earliest Shakespearean raptures, when, as a schoolkid, I saw Laurence Olivier's movie of *Henry V* and decided I was going to be an actor and do Shakespeare for the rest of my life. I fell in love with the whole package—those quaint little medieval sets and knights in armour, the heroic speeches on the battlefield and so on—but what thrilled me most of all was the opening of the movie, set in the Globe Theatre. The film may look a bit quaint sixty years on, but I think Olivier got a pretty good feel of the old Globe—the palpable excitement, the newness of the whole thing, the lively interaction between actors and audience, the thrill of exotic language and flamboyant acting. It seemed to be the best kind of theatre that could be. It was free of affectation and pomposity. It bridged the gap between popular entertainment and 'high art' with nonchalant ease. It was the kind of theatre I wanted to be part of, wanted to create.

Looking back over fifty years I guess that has been a constant in the work I've done, either acting or directing: that desire to make 'high art' accessible and popular. It's also about the importance of conserving something so precious, so inspiring, as well as a strong conviction that

Shakespeare has to be acted—it's of limited value sitting on the library shelf. Director Peter Brook once compared theatre to a piece of coal: you can lecture about it, theorise about it, but it only comes to life when you put a match to it.

The art of writing lines, replies which express a passion with full tone and complete imaginative intensity, and in which you can none the less catch the resonance of its opposite—this is an art which no poet has practiced except the unique poet, Shakespeare.

Søren Kierkegaard in Gross (ed.), *After Shakespeare*

2

Starting out

As a kid I was fortunate enough to have had two English teachers who loved Shakespeare and brought him to life in the classroom. They also marched us off to the cinema to see the Olivier Shakespeare movies—*Hamlet*, *Henry V* and *Richard III*—and to the Maitland town hall to see any touring Shakespeare show. These were severely reduced in scale and the sets and costumes were pretty tacky, but it was great to see actors on stage bringing to life the lines we were struggling over in the classroom.

When I was about to graduate from high school my English teacher informed me and my parents that my destiny was clear—I was to go to university and then become an actor. My parents were rightly apprehensive about the latter, but hoped (in vain) that an arts degree might offer some guarantee against penury.

My four years at Sydney Uni (I took an Honours degree in English) were mainly about growing up and committing the usual youthful indiscretions and doing a lot of acting, in everything from Revue to

Shakespeare—but of course it was the latter which was my main focus and the subject of my rather humdrum thesis.

On leaving Sydney Uni in 1962 I announced my arrival on the theatre scene by hiring the Genesian Theatre in Kent Street for a few nights and presenting a one-man show called *This Sceptr'd Isle*, a quick gallop through Shakespeare's history plays with myself providing the narrative and running commentary, peppered with all the choicest monologues of *Richard II*, *Henry V*, *Richard III* et al., assisted by a few props, cloaks and crowns.

It was a cheeky thing to do but it got a good notice in the *Sydney Morning Herald* and opened an important door for me: I was invited to join the newly formed Old Tote Theatre Company and within a few months found myself playing Hamlet, followed some six months later by Henry V in a circus tent at the Adelaide Festival. It was a dream run, much enhanced by my encounter with Anna Volska, the other 'juvenile' in the company. We fell in love immediately and are still going strong nearly fifty years later.

The downside was that I had peaked too early—where do you go after Henry V and Hamlet? And I had begun to realise my inadequacies. I had never had an acting lesson and had underestimated the vocal strain of playing Henry V eight times a week in a circus tent.

A British Council Scholarship took me to England and the Bristol Old Vic Theatre School in 1964 and gave me the opportunity to nip up to London at weekends and camp outside the Old Vic in Waterloo Road overnight to get tickets to see Olivier perform. I saw his Othello four times and half a dozen other of his late great roles.

But the best was yet to come. I had only been at Bristol Old Vic for a few months when its principal, Nat Brenner, sent me to audition for the Royal Shakespeare Company in Stratford-upon-Avon. This was the beginning of my real apprenticeship over the next five years.

Starting out

I remember very clearly my excitement on first walking into the foyer of the Royal Shakespeare Theatre. Whenever I go back there, I sniff the air and all that excitement comes rushing back to me. But for my first six months in the company I wasn't to set foot on stage. I had been assigned to a new experimental studio group whose task it was to explore new ways of performing Shakespeare under the tutelage of the renowned old French director Michel Saint-Denis.

To this day I cannot figure out the real purpose of that studio group. Maybe the RSC had had a grant or windfall and were obliged to spend it on something; maybe they were stuck with Michel on contract and had to find something for him to do. Anyway, there were ten of us bright young things stuck in this old house on the river, just beyond the church. We were all madly ambitious and desperate to prove ourselves. We did voice and movement classes, a good deal of rather old-fashioned mask work with Michel (that was his specialty) and some verse analysis with John Barton, the ultimate pedagogue. After six months we were drafted into the main company as walk-ons, bit players and understudies. It was not a particularly happy group—too much frustration, too many egos and rivalries, resulting in some heavy drinking and a few punch-ups. I don't know what's happened to most of them forty years on; Frances de la Tour is the only one I see still working. But to be in some of those productions and working with some of those people was the great learning experience of my life. There were flops too—some really shonky productions and a few stodgy ones—but even they taught me something.

The first director I worked with was John Schlesinger, a movie director brought in to direct the little-known *Timon of Athens* with Paul Scofield. I didn't find Schlesinger a pleasant man, maybe because his direction to the extras was: 'You're just heaps of shit . . . sit on the side of the stage and do nothing.' The production was not a good one, but I was able to bask in the aura of Scofield and watch his performance from the wings every moment that I was off stage. His remarkable voice, so mellow, at times so craggy and unpredictable in cadence, was matched by a physical ease and solemnity. It was a joy to listen to him rehearse, testing every phrase over and over, wrestling with its meaning, with torturous slides in pitch and emphasis. He was also one of the most sweet-natured and courteous people I've ever met, possessed of a calm, natural dignity—qualities I associate with our own Ron Haddrick. I had the great pleasure and privilege of working with Scofield later in Peter Hall's *Macbeth* and I understudied him in Gogol's *The Government Inspector*. He had that ability, which you don't come across much these days, to make you aware of the richness and music of language. That musicality goes in and out of favour. At present it doesn't accord with the sort of naturalism we're used to on the screen. But you still get it occasionally in actors who've done the classics. Daniel Day-Lewis for instance, in *There Will Be Blood*, has a vocal presence that is idiosyncratic and disconcerting. It is a major part of that remarkable characterisation.

Ian Richardson was nearing his zenith at this time and epitomised the vocal timbre and articulation that was a hallmark of the RSC. He had a ringing tenor and great command of the architecture of language that resulted in stunning clarity. With him on a bad day, and in lesser actors, it could tip into affectation and a display of technique for its own sake.

His opposite was the physically diminutive Ian Holm, who puzzled everybody by not seeming to act at all, yet he performed heroic roles like Romeo and Henry V with enormous power and heart-rending effect. His apparent nonchalance and introversion were a cloak for an intelligent, carefully wrought technique.

In my time at the RSC I played Rosencrantz in Peter Hall's *Hamlet* with Glenda Jackson giving a strident and forceful Ophelia who seemed pretty dotty well before the Mad Scene. I played alongside the warm and sexy Diana Rigg in a colourful but shallow *Twelfth Night* directed by Clifford Williams. David Warner was a gangling beanpole Aguecheek dressed in garish yellow. (The pay-off came when Aguecheek is told, after months of wooing Olivia, 'Yellow is a colour she can't abide.') Ian Holm (as Malvolio) appeared as a grumpy pint-sized Shakespeare. I'm not sure why—maybe the resemblance was accidental.

Judi Dench was in the company too. I never got the chance to work with her, but I shared a dressing room with her brother Jeffrey for a while. One evening Jeffrey came in from a day's cycling around the Stratford countryside. He had stopped to chat to two old gaffers who were trimming hedges. When asked what they were doing one explained: 'I rough-hew them and he shapes their ends.' Suddenly the line from *Hamlet* sprang out with new significance:

There's a Divinity that shapes our ends,
Rough-hew them how we will.

Who else but a Warwickshire country man would have thought of that image? And how amazing to find the expression still in the vernacular four hundred years later.

As a director, the shabby, shaggy and increasingly eccentric John Barton was awesomely knowledgeable about text, structure and meaning. His productions could be ponderous; I saw the opening night of his *Love's Labour's Lost*, which was a heavy, plodding affair. But by the end of the season, once the actors had digested all the footnotes, and invested it with lightness and buoyancy, it was one of the richest, most multi-layered Shakespeares I've seen. And his *Twelfth Night* with Judi Dench as Viola and Donald Sinden as Malvolio was a precious gem. Australians were lucky that it toured here in 1970.

Peter Hall's preoccupation (which, naturally enough, became my own for some time after) was to stress the timeliness, the political and social relevance of the plays, to rescue them from the glamorous picture-book representations of the previous generation. This approach was widely successful in the *Wars of the Roses* cycle he directed with Barton in the early 1960s.

Looking back on it now, those productions don't seem that radical, but they did then. The costumes were still what you'd call 'period'—i.e. medieval. But they were simplified, toned down in colour, toughened up with leather and metal, broken down with stains and fake mud. Never pretty or romantic. The acting was tough and forceful. Heroics gave way to brutal cynicism.

Hall took something of the same approach with his *Hamlet* in 1966 with relative newcomer David Warner, who had grabbed the headlines with his Henry VI. Hall stressed the black comedy and existentialist elements in the play. Warner's Hamlet, a shambling, pimply, grouchy university student trailing a long scarf, had massive appeal for the under-twenty-fives, who camped outside the theatre in the hope of buying tickets. It's a production that would raise few eyebrows today, but critical reaction at the time was full of outrage. 'No! This will not DO!' bellowed one critic. What a very English way of putting it. Hall's thinking, while modern, was hardly revolutionary. His idea of a contemporary look for *Hamlet* was to put all the courtiers in traditional Tudor garments, but to give them a pinstripe—a whiff of Whitehall. It was an intelligent but very subtle statement.

Peter Brook was the real radical and I don't think his colleagues fully understood or appreciated what he was up to. After the first preview of his groundbreaking *Midsummer Night's Dream* Hall is said to have gone up to him, patted his back in commiseration, and said: 'Well, don't feel bad—you did your best.' I saw a lot of Brook's work while I was in the company—his spectacular *Marat/Sade* at the Aldwych, along with his disturbing anti-Vietnam War piece, *U.S.* At the National I saw his Senecan *Oedipus* with Sir John Gielgud—an austere and classical rendition which erupted at the end with a jazz band cavorting through the audience sporting rubber phalluses and playing 'Yes! We Have No Bananas'.

I got the chance to work with Brook only once, in a staged reading of a piece called *The Investigation,* a transcript of the trials of Nazi war criminals. But in the late 1970s, when my partners and I were running the Nimrod, we brought his company from Paris to Sydney to present *Ubu Roi*, *The Ik* and *Conference of the Birds*. Now in his eighties, Brook is necessarily slowing down a little, but the work that I saw, along with his many writings, remains inspiring and challenging. His work has become increasingly spare and simple as he seeks to answer the question: 'What is the very least I need to create a piece of theatre?' In this regard he learned a lot from his sojourn in Africa, travelling with his small troupe (including Helen Mirren and Bruce Myers) to the most remote villages. Upon arrival, they would spread a carpet on the ground and sit around it. Soon the whole village would have gathered out of curiosity. Then someone would place a random object like a cardboard box or pair of shoes in the middle of the carpet and the actors would improvise a story around it: theatre at its most pure and simple. More recent Brook productions of *Carmen*, *Don Giovanni* and *Hamlet* have all pursued this quest to strip away the accretia, the inessentials, to get to the guts of a piece, its vital motor. Hence Brook continues to be a source of inspiration to me. It's so easy to get caught up in the peripheral things when you're acting or directing—being too literal, falling back on cliché without even realising you're doing it—instead of reinventing the piece in your head, seeing it for the first time.

Towards the end of my time with the RSC, when Anna and I had decided to return to Australia, Peter Hall took over the National and anointed the young Trevor Nunn as his successor at the RSC. Trevor had hitherto been only an assistant director but announced his arrival with a stunning production of *The Revenger's Tragedy* and a cast of young recruits—Patrick Stewart, Ben Kingsley, Alan Howard and Helen Mirren among them. This was the beginning of an exciting new wave at the RSC, with a more abstract and contemporary approach to design and staging. But by this time I was heading for home. I did feel some pangs of loss and regret in leaving England and the RSC—it had been a most extraordinary experience and Australia offered a very uncertain future. In retrospect, it was one of the best decisions I ever made.

3

Stratford-upon-Avon

Let me take you on a walk around Stratford-upon-Avon, Shakespeare's birthplace...

If coming to London from Sydney was a great pilgrimage, then Stratford was the Holy Grail itself. I walked the town for days, hugging myself with delight, seeking out every possible Shakespeare relic and trying to picture the place four hundred years ago. I lived here, in this fine old half-timbered house in High Street, opposite Harvard House and close to New Place. It belonged to Denne Gilkes, the RSC's legendary voice and singing teacher. She must have been in her late seventies then—a large lady with a fine big nose, stumping along with her stick, swathed in a woollen cape and wearing a big shapeless beanie. A couple of us rented rooms in this rambling fifteenth-century house with its low beams, uneven floors and mess of books, cats and manuscripts. I had a casement overlooking the High Street with a leaded window and a rush candle. I had an electric light too, but for obvious reasons I preferred the rush candle.

Anna followed me to England six months after I arrived and when we were married in 1965 we lived for a couple of years with our dear friends

Mike and Hilary Smith in their guesthouse, The White House on the Warwick Road. Our first daughter, Hilary, was born there. Later, when I was given a three-year contract with the RSC, we bought a little house in Bull Street, not far from the Holy Trinity Church. It was a humble enough little Georgian workman's cottage, but I had a lot of fun whitewashing it and getting it ready for the birth of our second daughter, Lucy. This was in Old Town, but if we head back towards the town centre we come to the Market Place, where John Shakespeare plied his trade.

Of course it's changed a lot since Shakespeare walked these streets, but from the eighteenth century people started to realise the town's potential as a tourist Mecca and were a little more wary of demolition and redevelopment than they might otherwise have been. The great actor David Garrick was largely responsible for creating the Stratford mystique that led to a campaign to raise money to preserve the Shakespeare family home in Henley Street.

A few doors up from the Shakespeares' house was the White Lion Inn, now the home of the Birthplace Trust. Across the street and up a bit was the official muck heap. The streets had open drains, and a contemporary woodcut shows a man with his horse and cart shovelling up the muck and conveying it to the muck heap. But as if to underline the primitive hygiene of the town, the same woodcut shows a woman emptying her chamber pot from her upstairs window onto an outraged passerby, while another woman defecates on the street, much to the delight of a greedy pig. John Shakespeare was fined for having a dunghill outside his front door. In constant fear of the plague, the town council vigorously enforced laws governing hygiene, far more successfully than they could hope to do in London.

This is where John Shakespeare brought up his family and conducted his business as a wool merchant and glover. He was a canny and successful businessman—somewhat too canny it seems, because he was fined several times for crooked dealing. He served as a town councillor and rose to the rank of Bailiff, equivalent to Mayor. Stratford, a centre of the Cotswold wool trade, was a busy and significant market town, and John Shakespeare was a prosperous, respected and important citizen—though he was later to fall from grace.

There is no reason to suppose that John and his wife Mary were uneducated or illiterate. They managed their business affairs very efficiently. They signed documents with their 'marks' rather than signatures, but that was commonplace. According to Thomas More, sixty per cent of Tudor England was literate. Look at the artisans in *Midsummer Night's Dream*: they are all given their scripts to learn, even Snug the joiner, who admits he is 'slow of study'.

While he was in office, John Shakespeare enjoyed considerable pomp and ceremony. Every Sunday morning he was escorted with his family by sergeants bearing maces to the Holy Trinity Church to sit in the front pew. He was decked out in his red mayoral robes and wore his alderman's ring, which seems to have impressed itself on young Will's memory; in *Romeo and Juliet* Mercutio describes Queen Mab thus:

> Mercutio: She is the fairies' midwife, and she comes
> In shape no bigger than an agate-stone
> On the fore-finger of an alderman . . .

We can walk from John Shakespeare's house in Henley Street, with its fine little orchard garden out the back, down High Street to the Edward VI Grammar School, still operating and still looking very much as it did in Shakespeare's day, with its half-timbered walls and long low-ceilinged classrooms with desks and benches inscribed with the initials of generations of schoolboys. As Bailiff, John Shakespeare enjoyed the perk of a free education for his sons at this prestigious school and no doubt took advantage of it for William, Gilbert, Richard and Edmund.

One of young William's tutors was a Welshman, Thomas Jenkins. In *The Merry Wives of Windsor* there's a very funny scene of a young scholar called William being given a lesson in Latin grammar by his Welsh tutor, Sir Hugh Evans. It is sometimes claimed that an aristocrat such as Edward de Vere, the 17th Earl of Oxford, was the real author of Shakespeare's plays. It is inconceiveable that any aristocrat could have written such a scene. Shakespeare mimics his tutor's accent to perfection.

The standard of teaching at Stratford's grammar school was very high and the teachers were all Oxford graduates. Students attended classes six days a week from six a.m. to five p.m. They had to study Latin, Greek, grammar, rhetoric and rudimentary science. They had to be very well versed in Virgil, Horace, Ovid, Seneca, Plautus and Plutarch. Students were taught to take a classical source, embellish it, expand upon it or turn it into verse. (This remained Shakespeare's working method as a playwright.) They had to be able to debate in Greek and Latin and perform plays in both languages.

While Stratford's grammar school was undoubtedly one of the best—the headmaster was paid twenty pounds a year, double that of Eton's headmaster—discipline was severe. The master always had his birch rod handy and if you displeased him, he would order some of your stronger classmates to hold you down while he pulled down your breeches and whipped your backside. It's not hard to see why 'the whining schoolboy with his satchel and shining morning face creeps like snail unwillingly to school'.

It is sometimes falsely assumed that girls did not go to school, but that is not so. Witness Helena and Hermia reminiscing over their school days. Girls did not go on to grammar school, but attended petty school with the boys. Every good Protestant girl had to be able to read the Bible and her prayer book.

The family fortunes declined when Shakespeare was in his early teens. John Shakespeare was probably a closet Catholic, loyal to the old religion. He was fined numerous times for not attending Protestant church services, though whether this was because of religious belief or to avoid his creditors is unclear. He lost his position on the town council and his business went downhill. Documents bearing his name and professing his Catholic faith were found hidden in the rafters of his Henley Street house when it was being restored in 1757. John's neighbour, the wool draper George Badger, was deprived of his office as alderman and imprisoned for his Catholicism.

Right next door to the school is the ancient Guild Chapel, which bears on its walls faint impressions of medieval frescoes. It's a pity they're so faint because they look like a pretty lively depiction of the Last Judgment, complete with grinning devils and naked sinners being boiled in oil. About eighty per cent of English medieval religious art was destroyed during the Reformation, including stained-glass windows, missals, frescoes, statuary and paintings. John Shakespeare, as Bailiff, was ordered to paint over the frescoes in the Guild Chapel and destroy all the icons of 'Popery'. This must have taxed his heart sorely and might explain why the frescoes still exist: instead of being obliterated they were simply whitewashed over, so that at some future date they could be restored.

Across the road from the Guild Chapel is the site that should be the greatest Shakespeare shrine of all—New Place, the great house Shakespeare purchased when he made his pile in London. But alas, all that's left is the garden. The house itself was demolished by its cranky and spiteful owner, Reverend Francis Gastrell, in 1759. It is said that he was sick and tired of daytrippers coming to the door and asking to see over the house.

A sketch of New Place survives and shows a very impressive frontage with five gables. We don't know what state the house was in when Shakespeare bought it in 1597 for sixty pounds. It must have been a bit run-down because he spent a good deal on its restoration. It had a prime address, two orchards, two barns and two large gardens. The orchards yielded apples, quinces, pears and cherries and an extensive vineyard. It was no doubt regarded as a grand residence and his purchase of it was an ostentatious statement—the prodigal had returned, a wealthy gentleman with his own coat of arms, to expunge the family's disgrace.

The garden of New Place is one of the most delightful spots in Stratford with its lawns, its little knot garden, herb beds, covered walk and ancient mulberry tree. Legend has it that the man himself planted the original tree, and for a couple of hundred years afterwards bits were nicked off it and made into souvenirs. If all those knick-knacks came from the same mulberry tree, it must have been the size of Windsor Castle.

At the corner of High Street and Sheep Street stood the town stocks, just outside the house of Shakespeare's friend Hamnet Sadler. Sadler and his wife Judith were godparents to Shakespeare's twins, who bore their names.

Not far out of town in Wilmcote is the farmhouse of the family of Mary Arden, Shakespeare's mother. We don't know much about her, except that she could claim connections to gentry. The Ardens were one of the oldest and wealthiest families in the country—the enormous Forest of Arden had all been theirs. But Mary was only a distant relation and by the time of Will's birth the mighty forest was shrinking rapidly, being turned over to pasture as its timber went to feed the ironworks in Birmingham.

Still, this was where Will spent most of his childhood—playing at Robin Hood, lions and tigers, letting his imagination run free and picking up that vast compendium of country lore that distinguishes him from other playwrights. No other author knows as much or makes as many references to the changing seasons, flowers and foliage, animals, birds and insects, rustic folk and their superstitions.

He relives a lot of his childhood in *As You Like It*, that wonderfully dreamy and luxuriant pastoral. Although his source material, *Rosalynde* by Thomas Lodge, is set in the Ardennes in France, Shakespeare quite logically relocates the story to his own Forest of Arden. He retains a few of the French characters but throws in a few English ones, as well as snakes, a lioness, shepherds and outlaws who 'live like the old Robin Hood of England and pass the time fleetingly as they did the Golden world'. This is no real forest—it's the forest of Shakespeare's childhood memories, a nostalgic and idealised Neverland. But Shakespeare the sceptic, the realist, is always just around the corner. He knows that life can't all be idle as a dream, so he lets winter intrude into this pastoral idyll and has the shepherds complain that they are being driven off their holdings. Life can't be perfect.

Like John, Mary Arden's family also had strong ties to the old faith. After the aborted Gunpowder Plot of 1605 there was a vengeful crackdown on Catholics throughout Warwickshire, a Catholic stronghold. Edward Arden, a distant relative, was executed for treason and his head stuck on Tower Bridge. Jesuits, including Edmund Campion, were similarly punished. Some of Shakespeare's tutors at Stratford Grammar had Jesuit connections; Thomas Hunt became a Jesuit and went to Rome, while Thomas Cottam, brother of Shakespeare's tutor John, was executed along with Edmund Campion.

Coming back into town we can visit the house of Thomas Quiney, who married Judith, Shakespeare's younger daughter. Thomas turned out to be a bit of a blackguard, got another woman with child and was forced to do public penance. Shakespeare's disapproval was severe.

And at the other end of town we step into Halls' Croft, the handsome dwelling of Dr John Hall, who married Shakespeare's elder daughter, Susanna. She helped him out in the dispensary which is still part of the house. Hall was known to be something of a Puritan, which would not have endeared him to his father-in-law, but he may have been moderate in his views as there are no recorded tensions between them. In any case, his diaries show that he treated Protestant and Catholic alike, without prejudice.

We can walk west from here for about a mile, along paths that would once have been through fields, until we come to the picturesque house known as Anne Hathaway's cottage. It is a substantial twelve-room house with a thatched roof and one of those enormous walk-in fireplaces that are such a feature of medieval and Renaissance houses. I can't think of anywhere cosier to be on a winter's night than around this fireplace. You would nibble on nuts, apples and comfits, sip your pot of ale or warm wine, and in the flickering firelight listen to all the favourite old tales of family lore or scare each other with stories of witches, ghosts and goblins. In *The Winter's Tale* little Mamillius says:

> A sad tale's best for Winter.
> I have one of sprites and goblins . . .
> I will tell it softly;
> Yond crickets shall not hear it.

Nowhere is an English domestic winter better depicted than in this delightful song from *Love's Labour's Lost* and its image of crab-apples roasting over the fire:

> When icicles hang on the wall,
> And Dick the shepherd blows his nail,
> And Tom bears logs into the hall,
> And milk comes frozen home in pail;
> When blood is nipped, and ways be foul,
> Then nightly sings the staring owl:
> Tu-whit! Tu-whoo! A merry note,
> While greasy Joan doth keel the pot.
>
> When all aloud the wind doth blow,
> And coughing drowns the Parson's saw,
> And birds sit brooding in the snow,
> And Marian's nose looks red and raw;
> When roasted crabs hiss in the bowl,
> Then nightly sings the staring owl;

Stratford-upon-Avon

Tu-whit! Tu-whoo! A merry note,
While greasy Joan doth keel the pot.

The images are so precise and so simple. We feel we know Tom, Dick and Marian—and of course poor greasy Joan scrubbing the pot!

Young Will Shakespeare must have sat by this fireplace on many a long winter evening during his courtship of Anne Hathaway. The Shakespeares and Hathaways had been friends for generations, so there could be no surprise in Will wooing Anne—except for their age difference: he was eighteen and she was twenty-four. And when they married she was six months pregnant.

It may have been a shotgun wedding or maybe it was all above board; the church service was a formality, and a plight-troth or hand-fasting ceremony some time earlier would have been seen as sufficiently binding. Whatever the circumstances, it seems to have been a love-match that lasted both their lifetimes. Shakespeare provided well for his family, made regular trips home from London to Stratford, and the children kept on coming.

Anne died on 6 August 1623, aged sixty-seven, just three months before the *First Folio*—containing thirty-six of Shakespeare's plays—was published. She asked to be buried next to her husband, who had died seven years earlier, and the inscription on her tomb, written by her daughters Susanna and Judith, reads:

Oh Mother, you fed me with the milk from your breasts and you gave me life. Woe is me then that I have to return a tombstone for such gifts! How dearly I yearn for a good angel to remove this stone and release into the light your soul, the image of the body of Christ. But my prayers are to no avail. Come quickly, oh Christ; set free my mother from her prison tomb and let her rise to the stars.

Assuming the marriage was a happy one, it is hard to fathom why Shakespeare left Stratford for London so soon after his wedding. One local legend focuses on Charlecote Manor and its owner, the magistrate Sir Thomas Lucy. The story goes that young Will, caught poaching deer on the estate, later wrote scurrilous verses about Sir Thomas and had to skip town. The story falls apart with the revelation that there were no deer at Charlecote in the late sixteenth century.

The real reason has to be Shakespeare's passion and ambition for the theatre; besides, he had to earn a living to support his growing family. By marrying at eighteen he had barred himself from university or being formally apprenticed to a trade.

Groups of travelling players, including Leicester's, Strange's, Berkeley's and Oxford's, had visited Stratford at least seventeen times during Shakespeare's boyhood. It was a good gig—a wealthy and sizeable town. As Bailiff, John Shakespeare was entitled to free seats—the best in the house—for himself and his family. Performances were in the Guild Hall underneath the schoolroom that exists today, though John Shakespeare was entitled to have a private performance in his home as well.

In 1681 John Aubrey reported of Shakespeare: 'I have been told heretofore by some of the neighbours, that when he was a boy he exercised his father's Trade, but when he killed a calf, he would do it in a high style and make a speech.' This has been misunderstood to mean John Shakespeare was a butcher, which he was not; he was a glover and wool merchant and young Will may well have helped him out. 'Killing the calf' was a popular fairground entertainment—a shadow play performed behind a cloth. The neighbour's anecdote is our first record of Shakespeare as a performer.

Young Will may also have seen performances of the Mystery Plays in Coventry, though these were phased out during the Reformation. When Hamlet talks of a ham actor out-Heroding Herod, it sounds as if Shakespeare had witnessed it—how else would that image spring to mind?

There were other shows, too: every year Stratford hosted the Pageant of St George and the Dragon, attended by much rowdiness and celebration.

We don't know how much theatrical talent or enthusiasm the adolescent Shakespeare displayed, but if he had an inkling of it (and he surely had), there was plenty to encourage it: the stories and poetry he studied at school, the excitement of the political and religious upheavals that were rocking the country, and the regular visits of theatrical troupes from London—colourful, swaggering 'pomping folk', glamorous but slightly disreputable. Their performances in the Guild Hall must have been a highlight of the year in this country town. There is some evidence that during such a visit an actor died and had to be replaced. This may have been the occasion of Shakespeare's recruitment to the Queen's Men—the chance of a lifetime.

Now we come to the riverside, the Avon, flowing under the stone bridge built in 1490 by Sir Hugh Clopton, the man who built New Place. And next to it is a rather ugly red-brick building, often compared to a biscuit factory—the Royal Shakespeare Theatre. It was opened in 1932 to replace the old theatre destroyed by fire. Part of the old theatre is left—Victorian Gothic and a good deal more charming than its replacement. When I was with the company this old wing was used as the rehearsal room. It has since been very successfully transformed into the Swan—a workable version of an indoor Jacobean playhouse. Combined with The Other Place, just up the road, this means the RSC has a good variety of auditoria in the town.

Let's walk along the riverbank. The parklands either side of the river are unspoiled and I recall many a lazy Sunday when we'd hire a rowboat and drift up the Avon, picnicking by the river. Over on the right is the cute little Black Swan Hotel, better known as the Dirty Duck, favourite hangout for actors and celebrity-spotters. And next door to that is a row of quaint cottages frequently rented out to actors who are here for the season. One was occupied by Laurence Olivier and Vivien Leigh when they were here doing *Titus Andronicus*, and it was here that Ralph Richardson gave them one of his famous fireworks displays—inside the house, unfortunately. We pass by The Courtyard Theatre, which started out as a tin shed used for rehearsals and experimental pieces. It is now a temporary home for mainstage productions while the main house undergoes renovation and also a thriving hub of new works—an expansion of the RSC's repertoire. The summer's day is hot and hazy and you breathe in the scent of the wallflowers in the window boxes of the cottages. They are a deep tawny red flecked with old gold and remind me of Beefeaters' livery.

We come at last to the lovely thirteenth-century Holy Trinity Church and walk along the flagstone path through the mossy graves and headstones. There is one gravestone under my feet that I always try to avoid looking at. It bears the name Lucy, who was probably a member of the family of Charlecote Manor. But I inevitably think of my daughter Lucy and the gravestone makes me sad.

There are a number of interesting monuments in the church and some delightfully bawdy medieval carvings on the seats of the choir stalls—robust images of everyday peasant life. But the monument we've come to see is Shakespeare's tombstone and memorial. Every Shakespeare-lover will be familiar with the lines of blunt doggerel on the stone which is set inside the communion rail in front of the altar:

> Good friend, for Jesus' sake forbear
> To dig the dust enclosed here
> Blest be the man who spares these stones
> And curst be he that moves my bones.

I've modernised the spelling but the words still have an odd, chilling, pre-Reformation ring to them. Did Shakespeare write them? He could certainly be as blunt and direct when he wanted to. Or were they inscribed by the sexton or parson? Unlikely—they sound too stern, too personal compared to the more elaborate, formulaic inscriptions on the other graves. Why was Shakespeare so insistent? His message does echo Hamlet's disgust and horror as he watches the gravedigger chucking out bones and skulls to make room for Ophelia:

> That skull had a tongue in it, and could sing once. How the knave jowls it to the ground, as if it were Cain's jawbone, that did the first murder! . . . and now my lady Worm's, chapless and knocked about the mazard with a sexton's spade. Here's fine revolution an we had the trick to see it. Did these bones cost no more the breeding but to play at loggets with 'em? Mine ache to think on it.

Every few years bones were dug up and graves made ready for new occupants. The bones and skulls were kept for a while in the charnel house next to Holy Trinity and Shakespeare as a child must have developed a horrified fascination with the fate of these bones, echoed so strongly in *Hamlet* years later. Juliet expresses a similar horror:

> Or hide me nightly in a charnel-house, o'er-covered quite with dead men's rattling bones, with reeky shanks and yellow chapless skulls . . .

Standing in the graveyard of Holy Trinity you cannot help but make those connections. You can picture that scene in *Hamlet* with the gravediggers at their work, tossing up bones and skulls and carting them off to the charnel house. And beside these graves runs the river where, during Shakespeare's boyhood, a young woman named Kate Hamlet drowned herself. Willow trees line the riverbank. How often did young Will, passing through the graveyard, brood on that scene? 'There is a willow grows aslant a brook that shows his hoar leaves in the glassy stream.'

Next to Shakespeare's gravestone are those of Anne, Susanna and Susanna's husband. It is rather remarkable to see the family interred side by side and in such a place of honour, especially since actors were still regarded as disreputable. Obviously in Stratford Shakespeare's status as a player was outweighed by his status as a poet, a gentleman and a man of property. He may have never performed in Stratford but his reputation as a poet is immortalised in the verses on his memorial set into the wall above the gravestone:

> Stay passenger, why goest thou by so fast,
> Read if thou canst, whom envious Death hath placed
> Within this monument Shakespeare: with whome,
> Quick nature died, whose name doth deck this tomb,
> Far more than cost sith all that he hath writ
> Leaves living art, but page, to serve his wit.

Well, Shakespeare certainly didn't write that—the verse is clumsy—but the meaning is reasonably clear. More elegant is the epigram, in Latin, above it:

> In Judgment a Nestor,
> In genius a Socrates,
> In art a Virgil:
> The earth covers him,
> The people mourn him,
> Olympus has him.

The monument itself is a handsome structure of marble and Cotswold stone with pillars and cherubs surmounted by a skull and the Shakespeare coat of arms. The sculpture of Shakespeare himself is no great work of art and is a source of disappointment to those devotees who long for an edifying and noble portrait. This rather pedestrian sculpture is blank and expressionless, but close enough in likeness to the engraving by Martin Droeshout at the front of the *First Folio*. Obviously the Shakespeare family, who paid for this fairly expensive monument, must have been satisfied enough with the portrait to let it pass. The Droeshout engraving is no great work of art either, but Ben Jonson attests to its being a good likeness. Obviously no artist could capture in paint or plaster the spark of life, the genius, the personality of Shakespeare. So Jonson tactfully and quite rightly advises us to 'look not on his picture, but his book'.

He was a countryman who worked in the city, a teller of English folktales who was equally well-versed in the mythology of ancient Greece and Rome. His mind and world were poised between Catholicism and Protestantism, old feudal ways and new bourgeois ambitions, rational thinking and visceral instinct, faith and scepticism.

Jonathan Bate, *Soul of the Age*

4

Shakespeare himself

Shakespeare's body of work displays a tremendous creative personality, yet the man remains an enigma. This has prompted generations of his admirers to ask: what was Shakespeare like?

'He was a very dark, confused man,' says David Suchet, a fine actor who has performed in many of Shakespeare's plays.

It's an interesting comment and ties in well with one of the presumed portraits of the poet—the so-called Chandos painting, which depicts a rather swarthy, wild-haired but melancholy buccaneer with a gold earring. Nevertheless the features are reasonably similar to the better-authenticated likeness, the engraving in the *First Folio* by Martin Droeshout. It's generally agreed that whether or not the Droeshout ikeness is a good one, the engraving itself is somewhat inept. It was not made during Shakespeare's lifetime so is presumably based on an earlier portrait which has since been lost. It has also been suggested that it depicts Shakespeare in one of his many acting roles. What expression there is suggests an alert mind and a sly sense of humour.

Shakespeare himself

All the surviving accounts of his personality (apart from Robert Greene's bilious attack) describe an amicable, modest, temperate and disciplined artist—'gentle Shakespeare', 'Sweet Mr Shakespeare', 'he would not be debauched', 'he was of an honest, free and open nature', etc. But in the light of David Suchet's comment, does the above estimation seem too bland, too unruffled, for a mind that could conceive and express such volcanic emotions, such despair, black cynicism, heart-rending jealousy and vituperative sexual disgust?

It is true that some geniuses seem to have led fairly uneventful, pedestrian lives: Johann Sebastian Bach, father of a large family, plodding off to work each day and at the end of every week delivering yet another mighty cantata; the urbane, patient, hen-pecked Josef Haydn; the handsome, successful diplomat, Peter Paul Rubens... But more often works of great genius are accompanied by stormy temperaments, bouts of self-doubt, fiery altercations, moodiness and introspection. From where inside himself did Shakespeare dredge up the envy and malignity of Iago, the insane jealousy of Leontes, the sexual revulsion of Lear?

Even in his earliest plays there is a grim humour in his acknowledgment that the heavens are empty, that we inhabit a meaningless universe. To redeem the lives of his two sons, the old Titus Andronicus has just had his hand chopped off. He prays:

> O here I lift this one hand up to heaven,
> And bow this feeble ruin to the earth;
> If any power pity wretched tears,
> To that I call...

Almost immediately his severed hand is returned in mockery, along with the heads of his sons. His reaction:

> If there were reason for these miseries,
> Then into limits could I bind my woes.

This bleak vision of the cosmos is echoed in Gloucester's:

> As flies to wanton boys are we to the gods,
> They kill us for their sport.

It finds its ultimate expression in the most nihilistic statement in all of Shakespeare, spoken by Macbeth:

> Life's but a walking shadow, a poor player
> That struts and frets his hour upon the stage,
> And then is heard no more. It is a tale
> Told by an idiot, full of sound and fury,
> Signifying nothing.

So, is that what Shakespeare believed? You'd be tempted to think so, given the finality and relish of the language.

But against it you have to weigh Hamlet, facing death, who informs us that 'there is providence in the fall of a sparrow' and that 'there is a Divinity that shapes our ends, rough-hew them how we will'.

Did Shakespeare, at various times, subscribe to both of these philosophical points of view? Or should we simply fall back on the reality that before he was a dramatist, Shakespeare was first and foremost and always an actor—if not a great one, certainly one with the most extreme sensibility and such empathy that he was able to imagine himself a fourteen-year-old girl, a crazy old man, a malignant Machiavel or an anguished mass-murderer? I am convinced that only a consummate actor could have written the roles of Hamlet and Richard III.

He didn't have to believe anything—all he had to know was what his characters believed and his imagination would take him there. I think that the best actors are the ones who are most open to suggestion, who allow themselves to be vulnerable, who are willing to access all their emotions without fear, shame or embarrassment, who are prepared to tell the truth about themselves, are non-judgmental and are able to empathise so fully and easily with others that they can take on characters' emotional situations as their own. This is what we strive for; and as you get older, more confident, and learn to let go of inhibitions, affectations, mannerisms and things to hide behind, you become more of an actor, or rather a re-actor, listening to what's happening and letting it carry you where it will. The readiness is all.

This is the acting talent that Shakespeare undoubtedly possessed. The rest is all research. We know that Shakespeare was a prodigious reader. *Titus Andronicus* is a show-off display of his acquaintance with Ovid and classical references. He devoured the histories of Plutarch, Holinshed and Hall, the Geneva Bible, of course, and research material as diverse as *A Geographical History of Africa* for *Othello* and *A Discovery of the Bermudas—Otherwise called the Isle of Divels* for *The Tempest*.

These were the keys that unlocked his imagination. I know from my own experience as an actor how necessary research is to get the motor ticking over. I've played Macbeth twice and Richard III three times and on each occasion have scoured book and film libraries for material on Hitler, Stalin and other murderous psychopaths. For the Bell Shakespeare 1994 production of *Macbeth* my wife and I, who were playing the unholy couple, explored the murky depths of thrill killers and child killers like Ian Brady and Myra Hindley—a very unpleasant experience, but rewarding. I sought expert advice from psychiatrists for both Richard III and Leontes. And I undertook extensive research for Shylock—visiting the homes of various Jewish families, attending religious services, observing and listening to Jewish businessmen, and studying the history of European Jewry.

All of this just helps you feel closer to the character, gives you the confidence to claim some sense of ownership of the role. To this research you add the other ingredients that make up your performance—observations of behaviour from real-life role models or (let's face it) from other performers, and all the emotional memories you can muster plus a very large dollop of imagining *what it would be like* to be that character in that situation. Obviously, the more research you've done, and the closer you are in age, temperament and life experience to your role, the easier the transformation will be.

So, given we know a fair bit about what research Shakespeare did, and given we know he had an extraordinary imagination and capacity for emotional empathy, that leaves the question: 'What did he actually feel?' Let's hazard a few guesses ...

It's a fair guess that he was well acquainted with sexual desire. If you enter into marriage at the age of eighteen with a woman who is six years your senior, and she is pregnant, that smacks of sexual impetuosity.

His plays and poems consistently convey a robust sexuality, frequently bordering on the erotic, as in *Venus and Adonis*, for instance. His sexuality is frank, joyful and ninety per cent heterosexual. It has caused previous generations to blush and excise passages from stage presentations and school textbooks. The sex is frequently bawdy, sometimes downright obscene (some of the brothel scenes in *Measure for Measure* and *Pericles* spring to mind). So it seems pretty clear that Shakespeare enjoyed dirty jokes, that he knew his way around the brothels and enjoyed an active sex life. His wife Anne bore him three children but he was away in London or touring the provinces for a very large percentage of his married life. Scuttlebutt such as John Manningham's anecdote about Shakespeare and Burbage both pursuing the same damsel in the name of Richard III was widely accepted, as was the Poet Laureate William Davenant's claim that he was Shakespeare's bastard. Other women's names were linked with his: the various claimants to be the Dark Lady of the sonnets (including Emilia Bassano, Lucy Negro and Mary Mountjoy, the wife of his landlord in Silver Street, Cripplegate).

Many of the Comedies, poems and songs trumpet the joy of sex, as in this song from *As You Like It*:

> And therefore take the present time
> With a hey and a ho and a hey-nonny-no
> For love is crowned with the prime
> In spring time, in spring time
> The only pretty ring time
> When birds do sing, hey ding-a-ding ding
> Sweet lovers love the spring.

But Shakespeare also has a remarkable facility for expressing sexual disgust. The sonnets run the gamut of desire from flirtation to bawdry to a repudiation of lust:

> The expense of spirit in a waste of shame
> Is lust in action . . .
> All this the world well knows, yet none knows well
> To avoid the heaven that leads men to this hell.

There are also, in the sonnets, expressions of regret for infidelities:

> Alas 'tis true, I have gone here and there,
> And made myself a motley to the view,
> Gored my own thoughts, sold cheap what is most dear,
> Made old offences of affections new . . .

Nowhere is sexual revulsion more graphically depicted than in the mad Lear's raving against women:

> But to the girdle do the gods inherit,
> The rest is all the fiends'.
> There's hell, there's darkness,
> There is the sulphurous pit, burning, scalding, stench, consumption.
> Fie, fie, fie! pah, pah!

But we find an earlier echo of this in Hamlet's repudiation of women in general:

> I have heard of your paintings well enough.
> God hath given you one face, and you make yourselves another.
> You jig, and you amble and you lisp,
> And nickname God's creatures,
> And make your wantonness your ignorance.

Both passages are remarkable not just for their vehemence but for their excess in the given circumstances. Poor Ophelia hardly deserves to be lambasted with this tirade; all she has done is return Hamlet's love letters according to her father's instruction. Hamlet's real target is his mother and her o'er-hasty marriage. He feels jealousy and revulsion (and maybe a touch of envy?) at the thought of her 'seamed sheets', of her 'making love over the nasty sty' and of her lover 'paddling with his damned fingers in thy neck' and calling her 'his mouse'.

Lear's rage at his daughters' ingratitude is aimed not at their hard hearts but their sexual appetites (or, rather, his fantastical imaginings of the same) and their reproductive organs:

> Hear, Nature, hear dear goddess, hear:
> Suspend thy purpose, if thou didst intend
> To make this creature fruitful.
> Into her womb convey sterility . . .

So I think it's fair enough to say that Shakespeare must have personally known something of regret and sexual disgust to tap into such an extremity of feeling.

Given these polarities of sexual delight and revulsion, how about the middle ground of constancy, and contented married life? What does Shakespeare have to say about 'true love'?

Shakespeare himself

I don't think any other writer has written more extensively about love, in all its manifestations, or represented it so iconically. Ask the man in the street to name the world's greatest lovers, and if he doesn't say 'Romeo and Juliet' he will tell you 'Antony and Cleopatra' (via Shakespeare, not Plutarch).

Romeo and Juliet represent sexual romantic love in its rapturous adolescence, virginal (on her part, at least) yet with an instinctive knowingness:

> ... Come, civil night, thou sober-suited matron, all in black,
> And learn me how to lose a winning match play'd for a pair of
>   stainless maidenhoods.
> Hood my unmann'd blood, bating in my cheeks,
> With thy black mantle, till strange love grow bold,
> Think true love acted simple modesty.

Teenage love dares all and knows no bounds:

> I am no pilot, yet wert thou as far
> As that vast shore wash'd with the farthest sea,
> I should adventure for such merchandise.

The rapture of love in middle age is just as excessive, reckless and careless of consequence, as demonstrated by Antony and Cleopatra:

> Let Rome in Tiber melt, and the wide arch
> Of the ranged empire fall! Here is my space.
> Kingdoms are clay; our dungy earth alike
> Feeds beast as man: the nobleness of life
> Is to do thus [*embracing*].

But as well as this robust heterosexual love in youth and middle age, there are many more shades of love in Shakespeare: we see in *Twelfth*

Night the foppish self-indulgence of Orsino, who imagines himself a 'true lover', contrasted with the dumb, pining adoration of Viola, who cannot declare her genuine love for her master. But in her male disguise she is able to comment on Orsino's shallowness:

> We men may say more, swear more, but indeed
> Our shows are more than will: for still we prove
> Much in our vows, but little in our love.

And in the same play, that mad carousel of passion, we have the nerdy, smitten Aguecheek and lonely sexual fantasist Malvolio, the devoted homosexual Antonio pursuing the boy Sebastian, the Sapphic overtones of Olivia's lust for 'Cesario' and Orsino's entanglement with his boy/girl page set against the domesticity of Maria's patient devotion to the reprobate Sir Toby. All of these are observed by the caustic clown Feste, who has seen it all before:

> But when, alas, I came to wive . . .
> By swaggering could I never thrive.

Twelfth Night is something of a compendium of Shakespeare's commentaries on love and in it we find echoes of his narrative poems, his sonnets and pretty well all his plays.

You don't have to be a parent to feel tenderness towards children, but Shakespeare's work is outstanding for its delight in children and the pathos that often attends their young lives. There is nothing to suggest he was anything other than a loving father to his daughters Susanna and Judith and his son Hamnet, who died at the age of eleven. *King John*, written around this time, would seem to reflect the father's grief. Philip the Bastard watches Hubert pick up the body of young Prince Arthur and exclaims:

> How easy dost thou take all England up!
> From forth this morsel of dead royalty,
> The life, the right and truth of all this realm
> Is fled to heaven . . .

Constance, the prince's mother, laments in words that are so graphic, so particular, it's hard to believe they do not stem from personal experience:

> Grief fills the room up of my absent child,
> Lies in his bed, walks up and down with me,
> Puts on his pretty looks, repeats his words,
> Remembers me of all his gracious parts,
> Stuffs out his vacant garments with his form;
> Then have I reason to be fond of grief . . .
> O Lord, my boy, my Arthur, my fair son,
> My life, my joy, my food, my all the world.
> My widow-comfort, and my sorrow's cure!

The children in Shakespeare are usually precocious, which gives him great delight. To modern ears they often seem *too* precocious and need to be played with a deal of charm to offset their smarts. I'm thinking of the younger of the two princes in *Richard III*, little Mamillius in *The Winter's Tale*, Moth in *Love's Labour's Lost* and the young Macduff in *Macbeth*.

The horror of infanticide is a card that Shakespeare plays again and again. If we have any admiration for Richard III or Macbeth, it is extinguished by their murders of children. And in the midst of the battle of Agincourt in *Henry V*, with knights and soldiers being slaughtered in their thousands, the action is brought to a halt while Gower and Fluellen lament the killing of the baggage boys—the ultimate war crime.

Shakespeare's apparent soft-heartedness extends from children to animals, again to an unusual degree. Hunting was a universal pastime in

Shakespeare's England, ranging from the courtly sport of coursing deer, boar and all forms of bird life to the peasants' more needy foraging for fish and conies. Shakespeare, as a country man, was well acquainted with all forms of hunting and trapping wildlife, but he shows no relish for it, nor for the cruel sports of bear- and bull-baiting, which were acted out within earshot of the Globe.

There is a rather remarkable speech by one of the foresters in *As You Like It*, describing a stricken deer:

> Under an oak, whose antique root peeps out
> Upon the brook that brawls along this wood,
> To the which place a poor sequest'red stag
> That from the hunter's aim had ta'en a hurt
> Did come to languish; and indeed, my lord,
> The wretched animal heaved forth such groans
> That their discharge did stretch his leathern coat
> Almost to bursting, and the big round tears
> Coursed one another down his innocent nose
> In piteous chase . . .

As a child Shakespeare must have taken an intense interest in the animals, birds, flowers and plants of his native Warwickshire.

In *Venus and Adonis*, the goddess promises the boy that if he gives her just one kiss, she will stop pestering him:

> Upon this promise did he raise his chin,
> Like a divedapper peering through a wave
> Who, being looked on, ducks as quickly in—
> So offers he to give what she did crave.
> But when her lips were ready for his pay,
> He winks, and turns his lips another way.

Of this passage, René Weis remarks in his book *Shakespeare Revealed*:

> It is one thing to read about the dive-dapper 'peering through a wave,' and ducking in when 'being looked on'—in *Venus and Adonis*—but to spot a little grebe or dive-dapper on a pond or in a still corner of the Avon enhances the imaginative life of the image. The only way Shakespeare could have learnt to keep ducks apart from grebes, to know that one of the dive-dapper's characteristics was its extreme shyness, was through patient bird-watching on the river, through living close to nature in a way that is increasingly rare today (p. 17).

Peter Ackroyd, in his excellent *Shakespeare: The Biography*, expands further on this theme:

> No poet besides Chaucer has celebrated with such sweetness the enchantment of birds, whether it be the lark ascending or the little grebe diving, the plucky wren or the serene swan. He mentions some sixty species in total. He knows, for example, that the martlet builds its nest on exposed walls. Of the singing birds he notices the thrush and the ousel or blackbird. More ominous are the owl and raven, the crow and maggot-pie. He knows them all and has observed their course across the sky. The spectacle of birds in flight entrances him. He cannot bear the thought of their being trapped, or caught, or snared. He loves free energy and movement, as if they were in some instinctive sympathy with his own nature (p. 31).

Shakespeare expresses a great appreciation and knowledge of horses, dogs and flowers. At the end of *Love's Labour's Lost*, the country folk sing of the changing seasons. As the cuckoo and the owl swap roles, spring meadows are decked with daisies, violets, lady smocks and cuckoo-buds.

He knows about grafting and pruning, digging and dunging, in ways that would be foreign to an urban writer or aristocrat. He names over one hundred different plants, most of them the local Warwickshire varieties—the primrose, wallflower, daffodil and cowslip. And he gives them their Warwickshire names: Ophelia's 'crow-flowers' and Lear's 'cuckoo-flowers'; he calls the pansy 'love-in-idleness', the whortleberry 'bilberry' and clover 'honey-stalks'.

Anyone who has puzzled over the following lines from *Cymbeline*:

Golden Lads and Girls all must,
As Chimney-Sweepers, come to dust . . .

must understand that in Stratford the dandelion is called a 'Golden Lad' when it is in bloom. You blow on it, the fluff all flies away and you're left with a bare stalk that resembles a chimney sweep's broom. That's life for you—one moment you're a Golden Lad in full bloom; one breath and you're a dead stalk.

An observant and sensitive country boy, Shakespeare understood the significance of weather in all its diverse aspects—the swift or slow succession of rain, wind and sun, fog and ice, the endless cycle of the seasons—and he translated all of this into a metaphor for the human life cycle and a spiritually charged universe of signs and omens.

Local names and references continually pop up in the plays. In the induction to *The Taming of the Shrew* Sly exclaims:

Am I not Christopher Sly, old Sly's son of Burtonheath . . . Ask Marion Hacket, the fat ale-wife of Wincot, if she know me not.

Wincot is a tiny village south of Stratford and there was a Hacket family there in 1591. Burtonheath is Burton-on-the-Heath, where Shakespeare's relatives lived.

Peto, Bardolph and Fluellen are all names that appear alongside John Shakespeare in a lawsuit, while Shakespeare's school friend and subsequent publisher, Richard Field, gets a special mention. An expert in foreign-language books, Field would often put his own name on the title page in the corresponding language. For instance, he called himself 'Richardo del Campo' in his publication of several Spanish books. Making a joke of this, Shakespeare invents a name in *Cymbeline* for 'a very valiant Briton' who has fought the Roman invaders (Field had printed many books of anti-Catholic propaganda). He calls him 'Richard Du Champ'.

Shakespeare never forgot his country origins. He never attempted to write a 'city comedy' like his contemporaries Ben Jonson, Thomas Dekker, Thomas Middleton or Philip Massinger. The closest he comes to that genre is *The Merry Wives of Windsor*, which is set, significantly, not in London but in a small country town not unlike Stratford-upon-Avon.

There is no doubt he was driven by a considerable personal ambition. His being snubbed by the likes of Greene and other 'University Wits' reminded him that he was considered a rustic who spoke and spelled with a Warwickshire twang. This may help explain his empathy with the outsiders, the marginalised ones: Othello, Caliban, Shylock. Just as Hamlet is more at ease with common soldiers, gravediggers and actors than he is with foppish courtiers like Osric, Shakespeare delights in the warmth and humanity of commoners and country folk who expose the shallowness of their social superiors. We side with the honest artisans attempting to perform *Pyramus and Thisbe* and resent the sarcastic comments of their aristocratic audience. The exercise is repeated at the end of *Love's Labour's Lost*, when the rustic folk put on a show of *The Nine Worthies* for the ladies and gentlemen of the court and have to endure their sneers and jibes. How much of this had Shakespeare the player endured when performing for Their Majesties? You can't help feeling he would much prefer to be in the pub with Falstaff than in the cold and cheerless court of Westminster.

Determined to restore his family's name and fortunes after his father's fall from grace, he worked indefatigably, refusing to mix it with the lads and going home after performances to write for the next day's rehearsals. Between 1600 and 1607 he wrote ten plays, including *Hamlet*, *Othello*, *King Lear*, *Macbeth* and *Antony and Cleopatra*. Most years he produced at least two or three plays, and all this time he was acting, touring, helping to run the Globe and attending to domestic matters in Stratford.

He assiduously courted aristocratic connections and patronage and was determined to achieve a coat of arms—though not for himself, it should be noted, but for his father. The roles he assumed on stage were usually those of kings and dukes, and he wanted to be known as a gentleman. Like Burbage, Heminges, Condell and the rest of his troupe, he was keen to throw off the 'rogue and vagabond' image of the actor and establish his craft as a respectable profession. (The first actor to be knighted was Henry Irving, but that was a couple of hundred years later.) This desire for respectability may have driven his acquisitiveness. He was frugal, prudent and shrewd in his property investments, and was accused of hoarding malt in one of his barns in Stratford in order to force the price up.

He was apparently pleasant and witty company, and obviously enjoyed the society of women. The women in his plays are never sentimentalised or soppy like the heroines of Victorian drama. Early on some of his women are shrews and vixens, like Joan La Pucelle in *Henry VI: Part 1*, Katharina in *The Taming of the Shrew*, Tamora in *Titus Andronicus* and Margaret in *King Henry VI: Part 2*. Then we get the sharp and witty ladies like Beatrice in *Much Ado About Nothing* and the Rosaline of *Love's Labour's Lost*. Next we have the warm-hearted lovely heroines who assume a male disguise—Rosalind in *As You Like It*, Viola in *Twelfth Night* and Portia in *The Merchant of Venice*. And we finish up with heroines who are almost idealised figures of devotion, patience and chastity: *Othello*'s

Desdemona, *Lear*'s Cordelia and *The Winter's Tale*'s Hermione. Looming over them all is that most feminine and complex creation, Cleopatra: irresistible in her wit and sensuality; formidable in her rages, whims and imperiousness.

And then there is a gallery of wonderful character sketches of older women, marvellous creations like Juliet's nurse, Mistress Quickly, Volumnia in *Coriolanus* and the Countess of Roussillon in *All's Well That Ends Well*, great character roles for middle-aged male actors. (The pantomime Dame and men in drag are part of a long and illustrious tradition.)

Shakespeare's love of and fascination with women is evident everywhere. So are some of his dislikes. He has no time for puritans, time-servers, hypocrites, pedants or stuffed shirts. These are the constant butts of his jokes and satire.

The above is a picture of a mature Shakespeare—discreet, industrious, respectable and socially aspirational. His youth may have been a bit wilder. (Is there a hint of this in a speech by the old shepherd in *The Winter's Tale*? 'I would there were no age between ten and three-and-twenty, or that youth would sleep out the rest; for there is nothing in the between but getting wenches with child, wronging the ancientry, stealing, fighting . . .') He certainly learned to govern his youthful impulses, but it's likely that his character contained both the pragmatist and the scapegrace—a Hal and Falstaff in one.

His experience as an actor was of enormous value to his craft as a playwright. He knew that a play is more than just the text; that gesture, silence, significant images could be as eloquent as words. In short, he knew what to leave out . . . He knew what he could leave to the actors. One of the most marvellous moments in *Antony and Cleopatra* occurs towards the very end of the play. Cleopatra has committed suicide and her devoted companion Charmian follows her. A shocked Roman guard discovers her and exclaims:

> What work is here! Charmian, is this well done?

To which the dying Egyptian maid replies:

> It is well done, and fitting for a princess descended of so many royal kings. Ah, soldier! [*Charmian dies*]

That 'Ah, soldier!' is an inspired piece of writing and a gift for any actress. What does she mean? She could mean any number of things:

> Ah, soldier, if only you understood the greatness of Cleopatra and how much I loved her . . .

> Ah, soldier, if only you had witnessed the love affair of these two great spirits . . .

> Ah, soldier, you are young and handsome. What might have been, but now it is too late: I am dying . . .

The actress playing Charmian can make of those words anything she wants and evoke a pathos that goes beyond language.

Charmian was probably played by the young actor Alexander (Sander) Cook, John Heminges' apprentice for whom Shakespeare had written Portia, Rosalind and Olivia. He must have been a wonderful young actor. So was his friend, the small and swarthy Nick Tooley (Burbage's apprentice), who had played the roles of Hermia, Nerissa, Celia and Viola. For him Shakespeare wrote one of his greatest roles, Cleopatra, and gave him the wonderful cadences:

> O, withered is the garland of the war,
> The soldier's pole is fallen! Young boys and girls

Are level now with men. The odds is gone,
And there is nothing left remarkable
Beneath the visiting moon.

But to Sander he entrusted the words:

Ah, soldier!

Shakespeare's greatness is so universally acknowledged and his popularity so entrenched that some people think he's almost too good to be true. Hence the emergence of some ludicrous theories that the plays must have been written by somebody else: theories that betray a woeful ignorance of history and theatrical practice. 'One person cannot have written so many masterpieces,' some exclaim. In fact, Shakespeare's output, compared to that of many artists, is reasonably small. The difference is that nearly *all* of his works are regularly studied and performed, whereas only three or four of those of a playwright as prolific as George Bernard Shaw have survived the test of time.

How to explain the phenomenon of Shakespeare? It's relatively simple. To begin with, we have to accept the fact of his genius, just as we accept the genius of Mozart, Leonardo, Einstein and a few dozen others. But genius in itself is no guarantee of success, as we know:

Many a flower is born to blush unseen
And waste its sweetness on the desert air . . .

The conditions have to be right, and in Shakespeare's case, they could hardly have been more so.

He was born in just the right place at the right time. Elizabethan England was a sturdy mercantile nation with a powerful navy, a thriving middle class, widespread literacy and a strong sense of identity that expressed itself in a bellicose adventurism. Its formidable queen enjoyed an iconic status that rubbed off on many of her acolytes: Raleigh, Drake, Sidney, Leicester and Essex. The New World was being colonised, the French and Dutch held at bay and the Spanish treasure fleets routinely plundered. Having thrown off the yoke of Rome, England had its own national Church headed by its own Blessed Virgin, Elizabeth. Despite the spectres of espionage, trial by torture and repression of religious freedom, it was considered a glorious time to be an Englishman, especially after the defeat of the great Spanish Armada. National pride and patriotic fervour knew no bounds and people eagerly sought expression for them in song, poetry and drama.

The English language, too, was at last coming into its own, despite the efforts of classicists like Francis Bacon to curtail it. The court now spoke English instead of French (though Elizabeth herself was proficient in seven languages, including Hebrew). The Bible had at last been wrenched from the hands of the clergy and translated from Latin, encouraging not only universal readership but personal interpretation. There were rules of grammar to be sure, but as yet no dictionary, so the precise meaning of words was variable, as was their pronunciation. What a word meant, how you spelled it and how you pronounced it depended on where you came from.

Shakespeare spoke and spelled with a Warwickshire accent and uses many words, phrases and references peculiar to his native Stratford. Queen Elizabeth and many of her court spoke with a cockney twang and the actors on the stage of the Globe spoke in a wide variety of dialects; there was no one 'correct' standard accent.

New words were coined with an intoxicating profligacy, Shakespeare himself one of the prime contributors. Public speaking, oratory and preaching were among the most prized and important of a man's attributes, and little wonder: in an age before newspapers, radio or television, the words of town criers and public proclamations could be a matter of life and death. And as for sermons—why, your immortal soul depended on them.

Shakespeare himself

It was a highly litigious age, and boys like Shakespeare were taught at grammar school to argue all sides of an argument—in Latin! Shakespeare was quite a litigant himself (though no more so than most of his contemporaries) and had a shrewd working knowledge of the law. There is some evidence that he may have worked for a short time as a lawyer's clerk, but his familiarity with the law was that of the average Londoner. A good proportion of his audience was made up of lawyers and students of the Inns of the Court, hence the presence of so many legal jokes and references. *Twelfth Night* was performed in the hall of the Middle Temple in 1602 and *The Comedy of Errors* at Gray's Inn in 1594. There was no doubt a chorus of cheers and catcalls from the audience during *Henry VI: Part 2* when Dick the rebel suggests: 'First thing we do, let's kill all the lawyers!'

London was a strident, tough and energetic city. Of its population of one hundred and seventy thousand, half were under the age of twenty. High-spirited apprentices made up ten per cent.

Provincial audiences as well as Londoners had a thirst for pageantry, display and performances, and literacy was widespread enough for everyone to play a part. The honest artisans of Athens put on a play for the Duke's wedding just as the rustics of *Love's Labour's Lost* devise a pageant to entertain the nobility.

All of this amounted to fertile ground for theatre. Now that the Reformation had done away with the Mystery and Miracle plays on biblical themes, theatre turned for its source material to the history chronicles, myths, legends, folktales and depictions of contemporary life. Theatres began to spring up all over London to cater to the hunger for entertainment—and Shakespeare arrived in London just as all this was happening! If he'd come fifty years earlier, he'd have had no theatre to write for, no company of actors to employ him. And some forty years after he died the theatres were all pulled down and theatre disappeared completely during the Ice Age of the puritan Commonwealth. For Shakespeare, as with many a successful career, timing was everything.

The genie was out of the bottle: bawdy, violent, iconoclastic, irreverent, subversive, wildly popular plays were attracting all of London. Courtiers like Essex and Southampton spent most of their leisure time at the theatre, and the Queen herself had her own troupe of players. Rail against it they might, but the Puritan preachers could not check the popularity and proliferation of the theatre. Aristocrats rivalled each other to see who could employ the most popular troupe of actors. Seeing this, the Queen's spymaster Walsingham decided to put the new phenomenon to good use: acting companies were to be used as a propaganda tool; travelling the provinces they would perform plays that celebrated English history and Protestant values that legitimised the Tudor succession and added to the lustre of Gloriana. Besides, having troupes of actors performing in the great country houses could be a very useful source of information. A canny actor could chat up the servants, observe the audience and report back to Walsingham and Secretary Cecil any hints of disloyalty or Catholic sympathies.

For the investors in the new phenomenon, people like James Burbage and Philip Henslowe, building playhouses meant a big risk but huge potential gain. To cover themselves, most theatre proprietors had other investments—they maintained brothels, inns and troupes of bears and other animals for the arena. Eventually most of them became wealthy men. Shakespeare certainly did, as did his friends Heminges and Condell. For Will it sure beat the hell out of glove-making or being a lawyer's clerk or country schoolteacher. This was big money.

And the Elizabethan theatre was exactly the right *kind* of theatre for a man of Shakespeare's particular genius. It was a *writer's* theatre, a theatre of the imagination—an empty space that could become anything you wished through the sheer power of words and images. There was no clutter, no distraction, no smart technology, no directorial spin. It was all up to the writer and his band of actors. And here too Shakespeare had it all pretty much his own way. As a sharer in the Globe, one of its owner-managers, he could use the actors of his choice, mould them into an ensemble and write roles according to their particular talents. That is how great drama is born. Brecht had a similar opportunity and so did Chekhov. But not many playwrights are lucky enough to get their own theatre and permanent company of actors.

He was born into the right family. Had Will Shakespeare been born into a family of farmers, he might never have got his lucky break. Life was not easy for those on the lower rungs of Elizabethan society and the pressure would have been intense for him to become apprenticed to his father's trade or take up a job on the land as soon as he was able. He probably would have gone to 'petty school' along with his sisters, but not on to grammar school. A farmer or artisan would have no use for Ovid and Seneca, Latin, Greek and rhetoric. As long as he could read his Bible and do his sums, that would be education enough. And if he had been born into the aristocracy he would have been destined for the army, the Church or the life of a courtier. He'd have been well taught in the arts of arms and hunting and had private tuition in the classics, but he'd never have known the hurly-burly of the schoolyard or the life of the classroom Shakespeare depicts so accurately in *Merry Wives of Windsor*. He'd never have met a country schoolmaster like Sir Hugh Evans or Holofernes in *Love's Labour's Lost*. Indeed, he'd never have met a Nym, Bardolph, Pistol or Falstaff, a Quince, Bottom, Flute or Starveling. These are the people Shakespeare saw in the streets and shops of Stratford, the pubs and brothels of Cheapside. He might have been an aristocratic poet like Philip Sidney or he might have dabbled in a little entertainment for his fellow courtiers, but he could never have become a playwright.

And that's what Shakespeare was—a hard-working, ambitious professional actor and playwright who toiled hard at his craft day after day, year after year, as Ben Jonson witnessed. As he pushed the boundaries of his craft and skill, his plays became more complex, more demanding for both actors and audience. We travel a long way from the knockabout farce of *The Comedy of Errors* to the bleak and bitter satire of *Troilus and Cressida*, whose thought and language are at times so complex as to be almost indecipherable on first hearing. Shakespeare expected a lot from his audience and he wasn't going to make it easy for them.

He met the right people. Shakespeare was extremely fortunate in his friendship with the Burbage family. There were Burbages in Stratford, but it was James Burbage, of the Queen's Men, who helped to change Shakespeare's life. They met when Shakespeare was an adolescent and the Queen's Men paid regular visits to Stratford. There they were welcomed by the town's Bailiff, John Shakespeare, and gave private performances for him and his family besides their public shows in the Guild Hall. When Shakespeare joined the Queen's Men in his early twenties he renewed his acquaintance with James and his sons Richard and Cuthbert. This was timely. James was now an important entrepreneur, having built London's first custom-made playhouse, The Theatre, and Richard was on the way to becoming the greatest actor of his day. He and Shakespeare inspired each other and Shakespeare wrote some of his greatest roles for him. Without the assurance of Burbage's talent Shakespeare might never have created Richard III, Hamlet, Othello or Lear.

He also maintained his friendship with his schoolmate Richard Field, who had gone to London some years earlier and established a successful publishing business. It was he who published two of Shakespeare's major successes, *Venus and Adonis* and *The Rape of Lucrece*.

Shakespeare seems to have forged close ties with most of his fellow players, especially John Heminges and Henry Condell, who rendered him the greatest service of all by collating and publishing his complete works. Even his testy rival Ben Jonson 'loved the man' and paid generous tribute to him. He made a big impression on aristocratic patrons—the Pembrokes and Henry Wroithsley, Earl of Southampton—and courted their favours. Perhaps most importantly, he earned the approval of Queen Elizabeth and her successor King James, who adopted Shakespeare's company and made them the King's Men as well as Grooms of the Chamber.

He was fortunate in being one of a number of talented writers. Competitive and ambitious in himself, he was nevertheless willing to learn, and gained a great deal by acting in the plays of Marlowe, Kyd, Greene and Jonson. He had great raw material to work with: loads of popular old plays, like *The Famous Victories of Henry V*, *The Troublesome Reign of King John* and *The True History of King Leir*. These were due for an overhaul and the works of Ovid, Seneca and Plutarch were all waiting to be plundered.

He made the most of his opportunities. Having absorbed the classics at school he put them to good use. He had an inquisitive mind and a prodigious memory (developed by rote-learning and his craft as an actor). Thus he was able to recall and quote plays he had seen as a child, including the old Mystery Plays at Coventry. When an opportunity arose to join an acting company he left home and went to London, leaving his wife to bring up their young family. But many a soldier or sailor had to do the same, and he had no future in Stratford. He seems to have made regular visits home and certainly provided for his family very well financially.

He mixed with the right crowd, cultivated the right patrons and learned from his peers and rivals, finally outstripping them. He was a shrewd investor in the theatre business as well as in rural properties.

In short, he was no idealistic poet languishing in an ivory tower but a hands-on, energetic theatre practitioner with a good nose for business and a shrewd eye for the caprices of a fickle and shifting audience.

5

An interview with Robert Greene

After a lot of hassles, I've managed to get an interview with Robert Greene. They tell me he's terminally ill—maybe with only a few days to go—but he has a lot to get off his chest and is willing to talk. Destitute, he has been taken in by a poor shoemaker, Isam, and his kindly wife.

I make my way through the winding stinking streets of Shoreditch. The ways are so narrow that the gables and attics of the houses on opposite sides of the street almost touch each other. Foreign visitors have commented on the cleanliness of London streets. Well, as in any city, that's only true of the tourist beat. Here in Shoreditch it's different. In the perpetual grey drizzle you can sink up to your ankles in the muddy roads; poultry, pigs and calves are slaughtered in the middle of the street, which is littered with garbage, dunghills and dead domestic animals.

They say you can smell London twenty miles away. Open drains run with raw sewage, but thankfully it's September so the flies aren't as thickly clustered as they are in high summer. People are packed close together and the noise of squalling babies, bickering urchins, scolding wives and raucous arguments from the grog shops adds up to a fair old

An interview with Robert Greene

din. Rats are scuttling everywhere, so you look where you put your feet. The air is thick with the stink of piss and shit, unwashed bodies, musty clothes and tobacco. Most of the houses look as if they would collapse from fatigue were they not so propped up and patched together. It's a miserable last home for Robert Greene, one of the so-called University Wits and a successful playwright.

Having found the hovel where he lives, I push aside the front door, which is hanging off its hinges, and peer into the darkness. The windows are boarded up to keep out the weather; the last of the glass is long since gone. I can hear a confusion of voices upstairs—a cursing cantankerous man's voice and the shrill despairing voice of a woman, both competing with the wailing of an infant.

Gingerly I make my way up the creaking staircase and come upon a cramped loft, thick with smoke from a small cooking stove. The few sticks of furniture are draped with wet washing, additional pieces of which are also strung diagonally across the room. Against one wall the invalid is propped up on sweaty pillows on a narrow wooden bed, with his shirt open and a couple of mouldy blankets tossed over his shrunken form. The floor is littered with yellowing papers and tattered books which also spill out of a wooden chest in the corner. A dozen or more empty wine bottles have been kicked into the corner or roll under the bed.

Seeing me in the doorway, the playwright stops his tirade in mid-sentence, stares at me wild-eyed for a moment, then, obviously remembering our appointment, gestures to his companion to pull me up a chair. The woman, looking bedraggled and harassed, gives me a sour look and slumps the bawling baby onto her hip. 'Empty the jordan!' the poet growls, and hands her a steaming chamber pot. I am told that Greene's wife, the long-suffering Dorothea, left him a couple of years back. His current mistress, Em Ball, bore him this child only three months ago and Greene, apparently without any sense of irony, named the boy Fortunatus. The house is widely known as a refuge for all sorts of criminals, led by the pimp, cutpurse and hit man known as 'Cutting' Ball, who is the brother of Greene's mistress.

While the latter studiously ignores me and turns her attention back to whatever it is that's burning on the stove, I help myself to a rickety chair and sit as close to the bed as stink of body odour and bad breath will allow.

I am shocked at Greene's appearance. He's only thirty-two (four years older than Shakespeare) but looks at least fifteen years older, raddled by syphilis, gaunt, and burning with rage and resentment. His long straggly beard is teased into a sharp, greasy point.

'The bastards have all left town,' he rasps. 'All those maggoty fly-blown actors. Whenever the plague hits town the theatres are all closed, so the players pack their bags and piss off to the country where the air is clean. It's all right for some—but what about us who are left behind? They don't give a stuff about us. You certainly find out who your friends are.'

He pauses for a moment to take a hearty swig from the bottle of Rhenish on the floor by the bed, and burps loudly. 'A plague on these pickled herrings!' he splutters, and sinks back for a moment into the pillows.

'So you don't have a high opinion of actors?' I suggest.

'Rotten, thieving, pomping bastards,' he fumes. 'You know what the arseholes do? They get hold of a copy of my play then piss off to some rival theatre company and flog it to them, and there's nothing I can do about it! They play to packed houses, all the money goes to the actors and the management and I get sweet fuck-all!'

'But how do they get hold of the script in the first place?' I ask. 'There's only one copy of the manuscript and that's kept under lock and key as the company's property.'

'That doesn't stop the mongrels,' he sneers. 'They gather up all the bits and pieces, learn what they can by listening backstage—and whatever they can't remember they make up! My God, you should see some of these bastardised versions that get rushed into print—and with the playwright's name on the front to ensure good sales! Arseholes!'

Sensing that this is a sore point and could occupy us for some time, I change tack. 'When you first started writing for the theatre back in the early 1580s, a whole bunch of you from Oxford and Cambridge hit town around the same time, the so-called "University Wits" . . .'

'Yes, well, I don't know who first called us that but you're right, there was a little group of us—Tom Nashe, George Peele, Kit Marlowe, John Lyly, Tom Lodge . . . The theatre scene in London was just starting to take off. Jim Burbage—Richard's old man—had built the first ever playhouse in 1576. Until then plays were put on in the courtyards of the pubs—the Boar's Head in Whitechapel, the Bull in Bishopsgate Street . . . oh, quite a few of them. But the idea of an actual playhouse was something totally new. Burbage called it simply The Theatre and it took off so fast that within a couple of months another one went up just a couple of hundred yards away in an alley called Curtain Close, just off Holywell Lane. Nice theatre, the Curtain. And then Henslowe built the Rose over on Bankside, and then there was the Swan—all good houses, all holding between two and three thousand people.'

Another hearty swig of the Rhenish—he's obviously enjoying recalling the glory days.

'Yes, there was a living to be made, all right. At first some of us put all our efforts into flowery poetry and smart-arse pamphlets—but it soon became clear that theatre was where the money was. So we decided to tackle it head on, give it a touch of class and kick out the grammar-school boys.'

I thought it might be timely to remark that Will Shakespeare and Ben Jonson were grammar-school boys who learned their craft as actors on the stage rather than at university. 'But Will Shakespeare . . .'

The mere mention of Shakespeare's name is enough to launch Master Greene into a paroxysm of rage. 'That bastard!' he yells, thumping the pillows with his fists, trying to sit up. 'Talk about thieving bloody actors taking over our turf—well, he's the worst of the lot! I've spent the last month putting out a pamphlet warning all my colleagues about him. I've got a copy here—let me show it to you.' He rummages in a box of papers on the other side of the bed and flourishes his pamphlet in my face. 'There! I've called it "A Groatsworth of Wit, bought with a million of repentance". It's probably the last bloody thing I'll ever write, but by Christ, I'm not going to go without saying how I feel!'

At this point several pulls at the wine bottle are necessary while he allows me to scan the pamphlet. He pushes his lank hair away from his profusely sweating face and grows more wild-eyed as he fulminates against those actors who have abandoned him. He seems to regard their exhausting slog around the provinces as some sort of extended picnic.

'I warn my colleagues: "Trust them not!" They are just a bunch of leeches and parasites who grow fat on our labours. But *this* one! This Shakespeare. He's not content with that! Listen to what I call him: "an upstart crow beautified with our feathers, that with his tyger's heart wrapt in a player's hide, supposes he is as well able to bombast out a blank verse as the best of you: and being an absolute Johannes Factotum, is in his own conceit the only Shakescene in a country." So there! Up him! I'm quite pleased with that "tyger's heart wrapt in a player's hide" bit because it's a twist on a line from his *Henry VI* where old York abuses Queen Margaret: "O tyger's heart wrapt in a woman's hide."'

'But what do you mean exactly? "An upstart crow beautified with our feathers"?'

'What do I mean? I'll tell you what I bloody well mean! He's a mere pomping actor strutting about in borrowed plumes, like the crow in Aesop's fable, mouthing fine lines he didn't write! What's more, he's a thieving bastard mimicking us and filching our choicest phrases ... But he's only a jack of all trades, not a university man!' He draws breath and adds, gloomily: 'Mind you, being a university man is no guarantee of anything anymore... Look at that sod Marlowe: a fine talent but a fucking atheist! I have a go at him in my pamphlet too!'

(It's worth noting that after Greene's death, the pamphlet's publisher, Henry Chettel, was pressured by influential courtiers to make a cringing apology to Shakespeare: 'because myself have seen his demeanour no less civil than he excellent in the quality he professes. Besides, divers of worship (ie; people of rank) have reported his uprightness of dealing, which argues his honesty and his facetious grace of writing that approves his art.' But he wouldn't apologise to Marlowe.)

The invalid is starting to ramble. He has collapsed back on his pillows and is alternately plucking at his stringy beard, fumbling with the sheets and staring at his fingertips. 'Ah, golden days... the roaring boys. Georgy Peele and Tommy Nashe... a deal of money I made what with *Friar Bacon and Friar Bungay* (that was a funny show)... *Orlando Furioso*... made a deal of money for that turd Henslowe... Where are they now? Where are they now?'

He is barely mumbling; his eyes are shut and his voice is weak. I look around the decrepit room which has fallen strangely quiet; Em Ball has slipped out with little Fortunatus. Master Greene seems to be dozing, so I quietly rise to leave him. But suddenly he starts up, coughing, and grabs my wrist. 'You must tell goodwife Isam to place a garland of bay on my head when I lie in my coffin. I shall go to my grave a laureate, albeit crowned by a shoemaker's wife!... Tell Em to fetch me a penny-pot of malmsey and be good enough to seek out the wife I did abandon, poor Dorothea.' With that he hands me a much-creased letter he had concealed under his pillow.

He sinks back again and I leave the room, aware he must be coming close to the end.

The rain is still drizzling steadily and there is no sign of Em Ball or Fortunatus. The shops and ale houses are crammed full of people taking shelter from the weather, and it seems impossible to seek them out.

I trudge gladly out of Shoreditch and make for dry and warmer lodgings than those of poor dying Greene. On the way I reflect on the likelihood that he was the model (or one of them) for Falstaff. Shakespeare, having got over the 'upstart crow' insult, seems to have used its author for his own raw material, continuing his pilfering habits by modelling his *Winter's Tale* on Greene's *Pandosto*.

And although Shakespeare recovered from Greene's taunt, he never quite forgot it. That phrase 'beautified with our feathers' stuck in his craw. Years later he has Polonius read Hamlet's letter to Ophelia:

> To the celestial, and my soul's idol,
> The most beautified Ophelia—
> That's an ill phrase, a vile phrase;
> 'beautified' is a vile phrase.

Robert Greene was harshly judged by some of his malicious contemporaries. Gabriel Harvey called him, among other things, 'a Ruffian, a Gamester, A Botcher, A Pettifogger, a Cozener, a Railer, a Gay Nothing . . . an Image of Idleness, an Epitome of Fantasticality, a Mirror of Vanity'.

When I am dryly ensconced in my chamber, I take a look at the soggy letter he has pressed into my hand with the request I track down his wife. He is anxious that the good shoemaker Isam should not be out of pocket for his funeral expenses:

'Doll, I charge thee by the love of our youth, and by my soul's rest, that thou wilt see this man paid: for if he and his wife had not succoured me, I had died in the streets.'

Shakespeare, himself an actor and an intelligent man, knew how to express by the means not only of speech, but of exclamation, gesture and the repetition of words, states of mind and developments or changes of feeling taking place in the persons represented.

> Leo Tolstoy, *Shakespeare and the Drama*

6

Acting Shakespeare

> He had only to think of anything in order to become that thing, with all the circumstances belonging to it.
> HAZLITT

Shakespeare redefined the art of acting. Most people, when they think of Shakespearean acting, think of something old-fashioned—actors adopting heroic postures and declaiming in fruity voices. It's the sort of acting Shakespeare himself hated, mocked and roundly criticised, whether it's actors 'out-Heroding Herod' and 'sawing the air' with their arms, or Bottom declaiming:

> The raging rocks and shivering shocks
> Shall break the locks of prison gates;
> And Phoebus' car shall shine from far
> And make or mar the foolish Fates . . .

And then sighing contentedly:

> This was lofty.

When Shakespeare was a boy, professional acting was still in its infancy. The Mystery Plays which he would have seen on the streets of Coventry were performed by amateurs—members of the various trade guilds who produced them. It's here he would have seen some popular amateur ham actor tearing a passion to tatters in the role of King Herod—a role famous for its raging bombast. It was a role hugely popular with audiences (and ham actors, too, of course). When Hamlet warns the actors against out-Heroding Herod, it is no doubt such a performance that Shakespeare is recalling.

He also saw the guild actors (models for the loveable troupe of artisans in *A Midsummer Night's Dream*) playing roles like the Vice, a companion of the Devil and another crowd pleaser. The Vice was the charismatic smiling villain who is very much at the core of Richard III—

> Why, I can smile, and murder whiles I smile,
> And cry 'content' to that which grieves my heart
> And wet my cheeks with artificial tears...

—and in a more sophisticated, enigmatic way, Iago.

The character of the Vice obviously appealed to the boy Shakespeare and in *Twelfth Night* he gives us a thumbnail sketch of the Vice in performance:

> ... like to the old Vice...
> Who, with dagger of lath [wood]
> In his rage and his wrath,
> Cries 'Ah, ha!' to the devil...

Monarchs maintained groups of musicians and sometimes Fools or Jesters. Henry VIII's favourite fool was Will Somers, who served him for twenty years and (like Lear's Fool) became his closest companion, the only man who could keep the King's spirits up when he was ill.

Rag-tag groups of players trudged around the fairgrounds and performed in the various inn yards that were to become the model for England's first professional theatres. But these players were much despised by the civil and church authorities, branded as rogues and vagabonds, frequently whipped out of town and—like murderers and suicides—denied burial in sanctified ground. Their only chance of survival was to attract the protection and patronage of the aristocracy, and gradually the great noblemen began to vie with each other as to who maintained the best troupe of players. Eventually Queen Elizabeth herself weighed in and supported a company known as the Queen's Men. They were obliged to perform at court or some great house whenever required, but were otherwise free to perform in the city or tour the provinces with the Queen's protection.

The actors in these troupes bore little resemblance to the movie and TV stars of today or the polished products of our drama schools, who are buffed and dentally perfect with nicely modulated vowels. Imagine instead a random selection of desperados from all parts of the kingdom, of all shapes and sizes, and all speaking different dialects—some cockney (like the Queen herself), others Northumbrian, Scots or Irish, some from Somerset, some from Wales. There would be no standard pronunciation, or spelling, until Dr Sam Johnson's great dictionary in the eighteenth century. Until then you spoke and spelled according to your fancy and local custom. Even then, there was room for inventiveness. In one speech Shakespeare himself spells the word 'sheriff' eight different ways.

It's no wonder Shakespeare was so fond of punning. Words had a very different meaning depending on who was speaking them and in which dialect. We lose those many shades of ambivalence when accent is standardised. Shakespeare spoke (and spelled) with a Warwickshire accent which it is not difficult for linguists to reconstruct. Consider *Macbeth*'s witches' line: 'Fair is foul and foul is fair.' In 1606 it would have sounded more like 'Fear is fool and fool is fear'. Characters in Shakespeare often misunderstand each other and send up each other's regional accents. Listen to the Englishman Gower and the Welsh Fluellen in *Henry V*:

> *Fluellen:* Ay, he was porn at Monmouth, Captain Gower. What call you the town's name where Alexander the Pig was porn?
>
> *Gower:* Alexander the Great.
>
> *Fluellen:* Why, I pray you, is not 'pig' great? The pig, or the great, or the mighty, or the huge, or the magnanimous, are all one reckonings, save the phrase is a little variations.
>
> *Gower:* I think Alexander the Great was born in Macedon; his father was called Philip of Macedon, as I take it.
>
> *Fluellen:* I think it is in Macedon where Alexander is porn. I tell you, Captain, if you look in the maps of the world, I warrant you shall find, in the comparisons between Macedon and Monmouth, that the situations, look you, is both alike. There is a river in Macedon, and there is also moreover a river at Monmouth—it is called Wye at Monmouth, but it is out of my prains what is the name of the other river; but 'tis all one, 'tis alike as my fingers is to my fingers, and there is salmons in both.

With such a rich stew of regional accents and odd assortment of physical types on stage, the ensemble would appear bizarre to modern eyes and ears. With no universal healthcare, no dental care and pretty basic hygiene, it would not have looked much like your respectable classical theatre troupe today. But it was a very robust one and a young one. Life expectancy in London was thirty-five in the more affluent parishes, twenty-five in the poorer parishes where the actors lived. Shakespeare did pretty well to survive till fifty-two. Given all this youthful energy, the cut-throat competition, the excitement of working on all-new material and the heady success and popularity of the plays, we can never hope to recapture the visceral thrill of the Elizabethan theatre or the amazement of its audience hearing all these plays for the first time, marvelling at new-minted words and wondering how the story was going to end. The extraordinary thing is how today, under such very different conditions, the plays still manage to thrill, entertain, disturb and inspire us.

There were as yet no acting schools, no acting theories or philosophies. Expertise and technique were the fruits of experience. The more gifted, ambitious or charismatic actors led the troupe and passed on their skills to young apprentices. Companies became increasingly close-knit, identifiable and competitive, echoing the rivalries of their patrons. But the acting style, like the scripts they performed, was still rooted in the tradition of the old Mystery and Morality Plays with their stock one-dimensional characters, clichéd mannerisms and simplistic texts.

Once playhouses began to be built and theatre became more lucrative and widely popular, it began to attract the talent of the 'University Wits' and the standard of playwriting lifted significantly. Nashe, Greene, Peele and Marlowe penned lively and exciting poetry in dramas with a mighty sweep and broad appeal. But characterisation still remained conventional, archetypal, one-dimensional.

Shakespeare's earliest plays share this universal defect. Characters in *Henry VI* parts 1 and 2 are largely interchangeable; there are few distinct voices. The rhetoric is powerful and emotional, but everyone tends to talk the same way—it's hard to discern what we now call 'personalities'. And then in Part 3 a distinct solo voice emerges—that of the murderous hunchback Richard, Duke of Gloucester. Shades of the old Vice are still discernible, to be sure, but overriding those is the sense of a fully fledged, living human being. This was one of the first parts written specifically for the twenty-year-old Richard Burbage and the first triumph in what was to become a great partnership. Between them, Shakespeare and Burbage revolutionised the nature of acting. This was in part due to Burbage's natural facility for playing truthfully with a quickness and lightness that was a distinct contrast to Ned Alleyn's booming declamation. Until now, Alleyn had been regarded as the tops. Ben Jonson said of him: 'Others speak, but only thou dost act.' Thomas Nashe said he was the best actor 'since before Christ was born'. But he was limited by the roles he was given. His most famous role was Marlowe's Tamburlaine, who has page after page of thundering rhetoric but no personality. None of Marlowe's characters has any psychological development, any inner life, any spontaneity. And this is the great gap between Marlowe and Shakespeare.

Such was the success of Burbage's Richard III that one of those links was forged between two artists that makes theatre history: think Bertolt Brecht and Kurt Weill, Arthur Miller and Elia Kazan, Rogers and Hammerstein or Gilbert and Sullivan. Together, Shakespeare and Burbage set out to discredit and replace the old-style acting of Ned Alleyn. In what is an almost gratuitous digression, Hamlet gives the travelling players a lecture on acting. Plot-wise, this does not come at a fortuitous moment in the play. We are awaiting the arrival of the court to watch *The Murder of Gonzago*. Hamlet is all wound up because this is the litmus test of Claudius's guilt, an event which will answer his doubts and decide his course of action. The last thing we need right now is a lesson on the art of acting. Sure, Hamlet wants his interpolated speech delivered to effect, but having taught the leading actor of the troupe how to speak it (a somewhat presumptuous act in itself), he then launches into a full-on critique of the craft of acting. Fortunately for us, it's just about the best acting lesson we could ever hope to hear. By giving these lines to Burbage, both the author and the actor are nailing their colours to the mast and repudiating the sort of acting that was too often being acclaimed and accepted as legit:

Speak the speech, I pray you, as I pronounced it to you, trippingly on the tongue . . .
(Deliver the speech, please, as I taught you, lightly and easily.)

But if you mouth it, as many of your players do, I had as lief the town crier spoke my lines . . .
(But if you rant the way many actors do, my lines may as well be yelled out by the town crier.)

Nor do not saw the air too much with your hand, thus, but use all gently . . .
(Don't throw your arms around like this, but do everything with moderation.)

For in the very torrent, tempest, and, as I may say, whirlwind of your passion, you must acquire and beget a temperance that may give it smoothness . . .
(No matter how worked up you're supposed to be, you have to develop both technique and artistic instinct to make your work comprehensible.)

O, it offends me to the soul to hear a robustious periwig-pated fellow tear a passion to tatters, to very rags, to split the ears of the groundlings, who for the most part are capable of nothing but inexplicable dumb-shows and noise . . .
(It makes me sick to hear a bawling actor in makeup tearing a passionate speech to pieces, destroying it, just to impress the slobs in the audience who appreciate nothing but spectacle and noise.)

I would have such a fellow whipped for o'erdoing Termagant. It out-Herods Herod. Pray you avoid it.
(An actor should be whipped for overacting a part like Termagant—that violent character in the Mystery Plays. It's even more over the top than ranting King Herod. Please don't go there.)

Be not too tame neither, but let your own discretion be your tutor . . .
(You mustn't err on the side of being under-powered; develop a sense of just how much energy is required.)

Acting Shakespeare

Suit the word to the action, the action to the word, with this special observance, that you o'erstep not the modesty of nature...
(Make sure your actions are appropriate to what you're saying and be scrupulous about keeping it real.)

For anything so overdone is from the purpose of playing, whose end, both at the first and now, was and is to hold as 'twere the mirror up to nature.
(Because if you overact you're missing the whole point of acting, which always has been, and still is, to accurately reflect reality.)

To show virtue her own feature, scorn her own image, and the very age and body of the time his form and pressure...
(To give us convincing images of goodness, of those things we should despise, and of the times we live in as precisely as the image made by a seal pressed into wax.)

Now this overdone or come tardy off, though it makes the unskilful laugh, cannot but make the judicious grieve, the censure of which one must in your allowance o'erweigh a whole theatre of others.
(Now if you ham it up or are slovenly, you may get a laugh out of the slobs but you're going to really turn off the intelligent theatregoer, and the opinion of one of them is worth a whole theatreful of the other sort.)

O, there be players that I have seen play—and heard others praise, and that highly—not to speak it profanely, that neither having the accent of Christians, nor the gait of Christian, Pagan, or man, have so strutted and bellowed that I have thought some of Nature's journeymen had made men, and not made them well, they imitated humanity so abominably.
(There are certain actors I've seen and heard others raving about—and this may sound heretical—who were so appalling I could only imagine they were made by one of God's apprentices rather than God himself.)

And let those that play your clowns speak no more than is set down for them—for there be of them that will themselves laugh, to set on some quantity of barren spectators to laugh too, though in the meantime some necessary question of the play be then to be considered. That's villainous and shows a most pitiful ambition in the fool that uses it.
(Make your clowns stick to the script and not ad lib or muck about. Some of them pretend to 'corpse', or 'go up', and this always gets a response from the dim-witted in the audience. Meanwhile the play goes out the window. That really is scraping the bottom of the barrel.)

This last salvo seems somewhat irrelevant to the subject in hand and may be a crack at the company clown Will Kemp, just as some of the remarks about audiences must reflect more of Shakespeare's frustration than Hamlet's.

One of the obstacles blocking this new style of naturalistic, lifelike acting was the old style of writing as exemplified by Marlowe. He is justly renowned for his 'mighty line', that pounding iambic pentameter:

Is it not passing brave to be a King and ride in triumph through Persepolis?

Gorgeous stuff, but it can get mighty tedious as it rolls out page after page unrelieved by any variety. It's almost impossible for the actor not to become declamatory. Yet Marlowe shows no interest in experimentation or developing new technique.

By contrast, Shakespeare never stopped experimenting, breaking up the iambic pentameter to make it more natural and psychologically truthful, switching back and forth between verse and prose, inventing an individual voice for each character. Just as he pokes fun at Ned Alleyn in the character of Bottom playing Pyramus, he satirises Marlowe in the role of Pistol (*Henry IV: Part 2* and *Henry V*). Pistol is the swaggering soldier, the cowardly braggart much given to declaiming scraps of verse he has picked up at the theatre:

> ... Shall packhorses and hollow pampered jades of Asia,
> Which cannot go but thirty mile a day,
> Compare with Caesars and with Cannibals,
> And Trojan Greeks? Nay, rather damn them with
> King Cerebus, and let the welkin roar.

This is a wonderfully twisted rendition of one of Tamburlaine's famous speeches:

> Holla ye pampered jades of Asia!
> What, can ye draw but twenty mile a day,
> And have so proud a chariot at your heels.
> And such a coachman as great Tamburlaine ...

In Pistol, Shakespeare is ridiculing Marlowe, Alleyn and that whole tradition of bombastic strutting and fretting that he and Burbage were determined to eradicate.

The acting revolution was not, however, an overnight affair. There was still a generation of actors playing by the old entrenched conventions and many plays other than Shakespeare's were still in the repertoire. For all his freshness, Shakespeare too still observed some of the formal gestures audiences had come to understand. There is much kissing of hands to demonstrate lovesickness (think of Malvolio); kneeling to show submission; lowering the head as a sign of modesty; folding of arms to suggest contemplation or grief. Macduff's pulling his hat down over his brow is another accepted token of grief.

With Burbage, Shakespeare found it possible to explore the inner man as well as play the outward flourishes and conventional symbols of emotion. Richard III may have begun as a variation of the medieval Vice, but unlike that stock character, he is capable of change—of fear, guilt and remorse. This 'internalising' of character reaches its apogee in Hamlet, who reveals himself much more through his soliloquies, his inner self, than by his external actions.

It was written of Burbage:

> Whatever is commendable in the grave orator is most exquisitely perfect in him; for by a full and significant action of body he charms our attention. Sit in a full theatre, and you think you will see so many lines drawn from the circumference of so many ears while the actor is centre . . . for what we see him personate we think truly done before us.

People often spoke of his naturalness, and the liveliness of his 'personation', capable of

> so wholly transforming himself into his part, and putting off himself with his clothes, as never (not so much as in the Tiring-house) assum'd himself again until the play was done . . . never falling in his part when he had done speaking, but with his looks and gestures maintaining it still until the heighth.

He seems to have remained one of Shakespeare's closest friends as well as a colleague. He named his children Juliet, William and Ann. He also seems to have had a robust personality and could be just as violent off stage as he was on.

The close alliance between Burbage, Shakespeare and the rest of the troupe was no doubt born out of Shakespeare's having risen through the ranks, as it were, being an actor himself rather than one of the blow-in 'University Wits' determined to use the stage as a showcase for their erudition. An anonymous play entitled *The Second Return to Parnassus* has two characters named Richard Burbage and Will Kemp. They speak on behalf of all actors, decrying the 'University Wits' who write plays that 'smell too much of that writer Ovid, and talk too much Proserpina and Jupiter'. They praise instead 'our fellow Shakespeare . . . it's a shrewd fellow indeed . . . puts them all down'.

Burbage paved the way for those great actors who reinvent Shakespeare for each new generation. It's always the same pattern: at first they are rejected and criticised for breaking the classical mould, for being too 'natural' and ignoring the 'poetry', for being 'too modern'. Then, little by little, they become the accepted norm, the icon of classical acting, the new breed. Unfortunately, in their later years, many of them are in turn rejected in favour of newcomers more in touch with, and more a true reflection of, the current audience.

In the eighteenth century it was David Garrick who rewrote the rules and had people's hair standing on end with the realism of his acting, whether it was seeing Hamlet's Ghost or recoiling from Macbeth's air-drawn dagger.

In the nineteenth century Edmund Kean was the great revolutionary. Coleridge remarked that watching Kean act was like 'reading Shakespeare by flashes of lightning'. Sometimes Kean was criticised for effects that were regarded as too sensational, too showy for a refined theatre audience. But he certainly knocked the stuffiness out of classical acting and made Shakespeare astonishingly 'modern'.

George Henry Lewes was present at his last performance as Othello in 1832, as he recounts in *On Actors and the Art of Acting*:

> On that very evening, when gout had made it difficult for him to display his accustomed grace, when a drunken hoarseness had ruined the once matchless voice, such was the irresistible pathos—manly, not tearful—which vibrated in his tones and expressed itself in look and gestures, that old men leaned their heads upon their arms and fairly sobbed. It was, one must confess, a patchy performance considered as a whole; some parts were miserably tricky, others misconceived,

others gabbled over in haste to reach the 'points'; but it was irradiated by such flashes that I would again risk broken ribs for the chance of a good place in the pit to see anything like it.

The whole notion of Shakespearean acting being bombastic and 'hammy' is a hangover of the nineteenth century with its huge theatres like Drury Lane and the Lyceum. The theatres of the Restoration period and the eighteenth century were relatively small and intimate. The Elizabethan theatres, although they held up to three thousand people, were also intimate and wrap-around, with the actors in close proximity to the audience; at the Globe, no one was further than fifteen metres from the stage. But the Victorian theatres were vast, and most of the audience remote from the stage. Opera glasses were needed to study the actors' expressions. There had been some degree of class distinction in the earlier theatres, but the nineteenth century saw audiences severely stratified, with the nobs in the stalls and dress circle, the lively riffraff consigned to 'the gods' way up the back.

Moreover, all intimacy was lost by the introduction of the proscenium arch, or picture frame, with its front curtain. The magical simplicity and economy of the Elizabethan stage was jettisoned in favour of massive sets and painted scenery, the more realistic the better (Sir Herbert Beerbohm Tree even had live rabbits hopping around his Forest of Arden). The new gas lighting and, later, electricity meant one could achieve all sorts of marvellous effects.

All of this was, of course, greatly to the detriment of Shakespeare's plays, which had to be severely cut to allow time for all the elaborate scene-changes behind the curtain. But with the revival of medievalism, so beloved of Sir Walter Scott and the Pre-Raphaelites, and the exciting new discoveries in archaeology (especially in Egypt), audiences revelled in the visual extravaganzas—Alexandria, the Capitol, the siege of Harfleur—all brought to life before your eyes, with scores of extras in 'authentic' period costumes, horses, hunting dogs and an orchestra sawing away in the pit.

Charles Kean's production of *Richard II* had a weekly bill of seventy-six pounds, seven shillings for one hundred and thirty-nine extras, thirty-two 'extra ballet', thirteen 'extra ballet girls' and forty children, plus three men to ring church bells. All of the above were employed to stage a spectacular tableau of Bolingbroke's entry into London, which is not in the script.

To compete with all of this the acting had to be pretty BIG, and thus was born a school of acting that gave us, at its best, Sir Donald Wolfit, and at its worst, several generations of ham actors bellowing melodramatically and tearing passions to tatters.

In the twentieth century in England it was undoubtedly Laurence Olivier who took on the mantle of Burbage, Garrick and Kean. Pictures of Kean's Richard III bear an uncanny resemblance to Olivier's personation and he seems deliberately to have set out to emulate Burbage and play all of his roles. He studied Burbage's career closely, and when he was preparing to play Othello, remarked:

> I think Shakespeare and Burbage got drunk together one night and Burbage said, 'I can play anything you write, anything at all.' And Shakespeare said, 'Right, boy, I'll get you.' And then he wrote *Othello*.

This is a testament to the difficulty of playing what Olivier termed the 'monstrous burden' of Othello—a role that has no relief from its consuming rage and intensity. I'd be tempted to put Lear in the same category—and he has to be an octogenarian to boot!

Olivier was not, of course, the only great Shakespearean actor of the twentieth century. Before him others like Gielgud had seamlessly evolved as part of the great tradition and had beaten him to a knighthood—much to Olivier's chagrin, it would seem. But in the tradition of Burbage, Garrick and Kean, Olivier broke the mould, seized the crown and brought

Shakespeare back into the arena of popular mass entertainment through a peculiar modernity of approach. This was noted by Laurence Kitchin when he saw the young Olivier's Henry V at the Old Vic in 1937:

> There sat the king as the prelates got down to expounding his claim to the throne of France and there was I, ready to watch a matinee idol's growing-pains. Having seen [Godfrey] Tearle [a leading Shakespearean actor in the 1930s] and [Ralph] Richardson, I expected to learn nothing new about the part. Sooner or later the legalistic drone would end and Henry would ask, in the stately manner of Tearle, or as near as a classical novice could get to it: 'May I with right and conscience make this claim?' It would, of course, be essential that the claim was just. Any doubt, and Henry would call off the war at once; if the play was not staunchly and reputably patriotic it was nothing. And then I noticed that the king was getting restive... Generations of persecuted schoolboys were being vindicated by a Henry who had no more time for that dreary speech than they. That was the revolution, consolidated when Olivier spoke the enquiry very clear and fast on a rising, hectoring inflection. It was plain that he was going to war anyway. Right and conscience were being given the value they had in 1937 when speeches relative to the international situation were made.

It has been my great pleasure and privilege to see many wonderful performances in Shakespeare over the last few decades, including Olivier's Othello (on stage, not the dreadful film recording); Judi Dench as Viola, Perdita and Lady Macbeth; Ramaz Chkhikvadze as Richard III; David Warner's Henry VI; Peggy Ashcroft's Queen Margaret; Henry Goodman's Shylock; and Ian Holm's Henry V—all original, idiosyncratic and, in their time, definitive.

But 'in their time'... that is part of the cruel nature of theatre, of acting. Great pieces of music, great paintings, great sculptures are somehow fixed in time. They may go in and out of fashion, fall into neglect and then get rediscovered, but acting is of the moment, and begins to date almost while you're watching it. Most of Olivier's screen performances now look quaint and mannered to the younger generation, as do most old movies. Only a handful of performances still hold up, and even then the viewer is conscious of making allowances for old conventions and aesthetics. It's a continual puzzle to me that performances hailed for being so truthful, so realistic, ten years later look false and stilted. What has changed? Are people that different? Have our body language, our intonation patterns, our ways of reacting to fear, bliss or despair changed that radically in such a short time? I doubt it. But our ways of portraying them have. The sets of signals, the artifices, the conventions of acting are in a constant if subtle state of flux. Performers imitate life and then play it back to the viewer. The audience, if it likes what it sees, will either enthusiastically or unconsciously begin to take on the nuances of the performance: this is what it is like to be cool, to be tough, to be sexy, to look successful.

Art imitates life and then life imitates art. We're all familiar with famous movie stars who have managed to capture the zeitgeist and become role models for a generation who ape not only their clothes and hairstyles but their mannerisms, catch-phrases, deportment and gestures.

When it comes to acting Shakespeare today, things are a lot less clear-cut than they were, say, fifty years ago when I first set foot on stage. Back then it was pretty widely accepted in England, Australia and America that there was a definable Shakespeare 'style' appropriate to the Tragedies and the Comedies—a manner of vocal delivery, accent, posture, an attitude to the material that marked it out as 'Shakespeare'. This aesthetic edifice was already beginning to crumble, but there were enough actors, directors, critics and drama teachers of the old school still clinging to the wreckage.

It made acting Shakespeare in Australia quite a schizophrenic experience. Our role models were people like Ron Haddrick, who had recently returned to Australia after spending time with the Shakespeare Memorial

Theatre in Stratford (the predecessor to the Royal Shakespeare Company) where he had played major roles like Tybalt in *Romeo and Juliet* and Horatio to Michael Redgrave's Hamlet. There was also a generation of wonderful radio actors (now almost as extinct as radio drama) like Richard Davies, Alastair Duncan, Nigel Lovell, Lyndall Barbour and Amber May Cecil with wonderfully cultivated and mellifluous voices, especially when they were reading poetry or classical drama. (Of course, it was important to drop those honeyed tones when you were off stage or outside the studio, otherwise people would say you were 'up yourself'.)

So for a young actor coming into the business, it was very much a matter of 'putting on' a voice when you started to act and it's a problem we in Australia still have. Critics and a fair proportion of audiences condemn actors for playing Shakespeare with Australian accents. Unless you sound like a BBC recording you've got it wrong. I admit there are some plays where an Australian accent can be inappropriate—for instance, if you're playing Henry Higgins, an Australian accent would be very confusing, likewise a good deal of Oscar Wilde—but not Shakespeare.

(When we did *Long Day's Journey into Night* (1999, a Bell Shakespeare/ Queensland Theatre Company co-production), the two boys were encouraged to use quite broad Australian accents. There were gains and losses. On the one hand, it helped the characters seem more real and familiar. It relieved that tension where the audience is listening for inconsistencies. It freed up the actors to concentrate on the situation and emotional journey rather than listening to themselves. The losses were in the jarring inconsistencies when place names came up: the play is very site-specific. There are also phrases, instances of vocabulary, cadences and rhythms which are specific to their place and time. In a less domestic and naturalistic piece you might get away with it. But so much American and Irish drama is written almost in dialect. It would seem self-defeating to play David Mamet or Sean O'Casey with Australian voices. Very confusing.)

But Shakespeare does not belong in that realm of naturalism or domesticity except where a specific dialect is called for—like Fluellen or MacMorris in *Henry V*, Sir Hugh Evans and Dr Caius in *Merry Wives of Windsor*. In such cases you simply go for an authentic accent; there's no point shying away from it. It's worth noting that Australian actors can assume American accents with ease and most of our movie stars spend the bulk of their lives being American.

Shakespeare has a universality and timelessness that has seen him adapted into many different languages and cultures, and each has its own way of speaking and acting Shakespeare. Some of the most outstanding productions of Shakespeare in modern times have not been English ones. I'm thinking of the famous Zulu *Macbeth*, with its tom-toms and witch doctors, which came to London in the mid-1960s, the great Georgian *Richard III* with Ramaz Chkhikvadze, Declan Donnellan's *Twelfth Night* with an all-Russian cast, and Kurosawa's *Throne of Blood*, to name but a few. At the Shanghai Shakespeare Festival in 1994 there were eleven Shakespeare productions, each in a different Chinese dialect. The standout success was a Peking Opera version of *Hamlet* entirely sung, danced and choreographed with a blood-curdling Ghost singing in that unique and weird high-pitched voice of the Chinese theatre. The least successful production was a *Henry IV* which tried to reproduce an Anglo-Saxon aesthetic. They had medieval costumes, a Tudor pub, blond wigs and white makeup, along with lots of thigh slapping and tankard clinking. It was a painful lesson, demonstrating the advantages of tapping into your own cultural roots rather than aping someone else's.

But it's harder for *us* in Australia because such a large part of our heritage is an English one. When the Germans, Russians or Japanese hear Shakespeare they hear it in an up-to-date translation, so there is no sense of the archaic. Part of the burden as well as the glory of Shakespeare for us Australians is that we have this still-living and vibrant four-hundred-year-old language which is largely comprehensible but is also riddled with obscure words, different grammar and unfamiliar syntax. Even in his own day Shakespeare's use of language was more complex, more challenging than that of most of his contemporaries. So how do we handle that? Once you get the hang of it, get familiar with it, Shakespeare's language is a source of endless delight, but for an audience coming to it unprepared, for schoolkids puzzling over textbooks, it can be a big hurdle ... Do we translate it, do we cut out the hard bits?

I think theatre practice will see more and more minor surgery taking place—translating individual words or even whole phrases which have lost their currency. Some scholars are currently undertaking major translations of complex plays like *Troilus and Cressida* and have shown me their work. I would be very happy to stage such a version. It would not be a substitute but an alternative, one easier to comprehend in performance. My only stipulation would be that we keep as much of the original as possible and only translate those sections which are baffling on first hearing and which are essential to understand in the context of the whole play. Would you ever want to translate 'To be or not to be ...' or 'Once more unto the breach ...'? I doubt it, but the day may come (language changing as rapidly as it is) when even the most commonplace words and phrases in Shakespeare will be obsolete.

For modern actors working in Australia (and the same thing applies in America, and to some extent even in Britain) archaic text is not the only problem. I come back to the question of voice, of accent: what is appropriate for Shakespeare? I include Britain in this query because there, too, a social revolution inside the theatre has thrown all the cards in the air. It began some time in the 1950s when a new generation of actors like Albert Finney, Peter O'Toole and Richard Harris brought regional accents and energy into London—a sound distinctly different to the cadences of Olivier, Gielgud and Redgrave. It wasn't just the sound but a new class-consciousness and anti-establishment vigour reflected in the writing of people like John Osborne, Arnold Wesker and Harold Pinter—the kind of writing that led a despairing Noël Coward to decide that theatre was dead. Regional British accents are now widely accepted on the English stage whether you're playing the classics or not. And black actors are regularly seen in roles such as Henry V and Hamlet. Thirty years ago that was unimaginable. If such a situation is acceptable in England, why do we find any resistance in Australia?

Let's first dispose of this thing about the Australian accent: *which* Australian accent? There are dozens of them. You don't have to be Henry Higgins to note the many varieties but I'm sure he could pick not only a Queenslander from a South Australian: he could tell you what school you went to and what street you were born in. He could tell if you're a lawyer, a market gardener or a stockbroker, a bus driver, a schoolteacher or a politician (and probably your party and your electorate). Today these differences are rarely a hindrance to social or professional mobility in Australia, but for a country that loudly proclaims its egalitarianism, when the chips are down the old school tie and prestigious address still count for something. So we can still relate to the world of Shakespeare and its various power structures, and decide on the Australian accent of our choice when playing an emperor, a lad-about-town or a gravedigger. Our job is to make our audience feel they *know* these people.

The challenges facing the modern actor when speaking Shakespeare go way beyond accent. When people criticise an actor's 'accent' they are generally meaning something else: a flatness of tone, a lazy diction, a thin sound that fails to express the richness of the language. And this is a charge that can be levelled at actors the world over who are struggling to reconcile the sort of acting generally accepted as appropriate for the movie or TV screen with the heightened language and rhetoric of the classics.

The language employed by writers of film and TV scripts tends to be monosyllabic, a precise reflection of everyday speech relying heavily on cliché and colloquialism. The language of Shakespeare is far more complex. It employs an unfamiliar syntax and a wide-ranging vocabulary that can be erudite, archaic and obscure. It needs a thorough understanding, great clarity of thought, and the vocal technique to sustain and communicate it. Because it is 'unnatural' to modern ears, the actor's job is to make it both heartfelt and comprehensible.

In much modern drama, especially for the screen, silences and facial expressions can be more eloquent than words. A good actor in silent close-up can convey volumes. The subtext and the things left unsaid are often more significant than the dialogue. In Shakespeare there is virtually no subtext. Characters mean what they say and, if they're faking it, they tell you so in an aside. Some actors and directors tie themselves up in knots to wrest perverse meanings from the text. Of course you have to dig beneath the surface of the text to decide why characters say the things they do, but you can be almost a hundred per cent sure they mean what they say. This is particularly so when they are speaking verse. The rhythm of iambic pentameter is the same as the human heartbeat, so when characters speak in blank verse they are speaking, literally, from the heart. You've got to pay more attention when they speak prose, because here the rhythms are broken up and you have more options in phrasing. When people speak prose they are often being tricky, deceitful and jokey. A notable example is the first meeting of Hamlet with Rosencrantz and Guildenstern. The surface banter is undergraduate bawdy humour, but it is a smokescreen for duplicity which Hamlet senses and sets about deconstructing.

In a lot of contemporary writing emotions are disguised (as in life) with an assumed nonchalance, an attitude of 'cool'. For reasons that vary according to circumstances, feelings are repressed, internalised and hidden. Rather than being declared, emotions are often wrung out of people and express themselves in short grabs. No one hides their feelings for long in Shakespeare; they're pretty upfront, and if feelings are momentarily suppressed they burst forth in impassioned and sustained rhetoric. With most film and TV drama, we are watching through a window in the fourth wall. Characters are usually oblivious to our presence and go about their lives as if we (via the camera) are voyeurs. Performances of Shakespeare, on the other hand, benefit enormously by acknowledging and playing directly to the audience. There is no fourth wall. Shakespeare reminds us again and again that we are watching a play, that we are in a theatre and that all the world's a stage. This creates an intimacy, a bonding with the audience, a unique relationship the camera can never achieve. When a live actor eyeballs you and asks you directly, 'What's to become of this?', you get that visceral thrill you experienced when picked on in class. This struck me most forcibly on that occasion when I first stepped onto the stage of the new Globe in London. I was amazed to find how closely the audience is packed all around the stage, gazing up from the pit, staring down from the galleries. It would be pointless to pretend they weren't there. The space demands that everything, as far as possible, is shared with them and all soliloquies are spoken directly to them so that they become, in a sense, colloquies. The play isn't for the actors; it's for the audience.

Because so much of contemporary TV and cinema aims to reproduce everyday life there is a lot of low energy and inconsequential material. Hopefully it has a dramatic pay-off and we can take delight in seeing the trivial, the petty, the domestic bits of life being well observed and truthfully rendered. But in Shakespeare the stakes are always high. Every scene is a little play in itself, with a conflict and a resolution. Every scene deals with a crisis of some magnitude. Energy is always at an optimum, even when you're only standing and watching, because you are partaking in a crisis. You're always poised like a greyhound in the slips, ready to spring into action. And when you do spring into action you need all your energy to sustain you through the demanding rhetoric and ring the changes. Your whole body must be fully engaged whether you're speaking or not. You have to be an active listener. There is no slackness in Shakespeare. People should rarely sit down. Shakespeare works best when everyone's on their feet.

There are no pauses in speaking Shakespeare; leave that to Chekhov and Pinter. Shakespeare dictates very clearly the tempo and dynamic of a scene. If he wants a silence he'll indicate it. Otherwise you think of your reply while the other fellow's speaking and you come in right on cue. Keep the ball in the air. Your *need* to speak must be paramount. If your need to speak isn't strong enough, when you do speak you'll sound phoney or under-powered. And the higher the stakes the more heightened the language and the feelings become. There are no inconsequential scenes in Shakespeare. It's been said that theatre is life without the dull bits. That's especially true of Shakespeare.

When it comes to the worst faults of actors playing Shakespeare, I'd say one of the most widespread is being incomprehensible. This is for a number of reasons but the basic one is laziness. It means the actor hasn't done his homework and hasn't figured out how to communicate meaning, thinking close enough is good enough . . . Even after fifty years of playing Shakespeare and being more familiar with it than many people, I always find it a shock when I go to the theatre; it takes five minutes or so to adjust my ear and brain—especially if it's a play I'm not that well acquainted with. An audience needs time to take in the set, the costumes, figure out who's who and follow the exposition in a language that is foreign to them.

So the actor needs to start by fully understanding and appreciating the text, and this entails a lot of dictionary work. You might have a rough idea what a word means, but look it up nonetheless—and not just in one dictionary but in a range of three or four good ones to compare their different definitions. You need to know not just what the word means now but what it meant four hundred years ago. Has its meaning changed? Where did Shakespeare get it from and what's its origin? Does it have a Latin or Greek root? Did the Danes bring it over or the Normans? Does it derive from the medieval French or is it a good old down-to-earth Anglo-Saxon word? Does this matter? It can certainly be enlightening: consider Macbeth agonising over whether or not to kill King Duncan.

His brain, his conscience, is telling him one thing while his gut is urging him the other way.

He begins with resolve, expressed in Anglo-Saxon monosyllabic hammer blows:

> If it were done when 'tis done, then 'twere well
> It were done quickly . . .

But then his intellect intervenes, and the words become Latinate, polysyllabic:

> . . . If the assassination
> Could trammel up the consequence, and catch
> With his surcease success . . .

The gut takes over again, urging action, with more Anglo-Saxon hammer blows:

> . . . That but this blow
> Might be the be-all and the end-all here,
> But here, upon this bank and shoal of time . . .

Note the sudden change of thought in the middle of the line: 'that but this blow . . .' There's no pause there, no break—the change is instantaneous, which shows a mind in torment, torn this way and that. This is no contemplative piece; it hurtles along at breakneck speed. It's the picture of a man racing against time and wrestling with the terror of damnation. You appreciate this more fully if you know where the language is coming from.

The value of dictionary work was brought home to me in a workshop I did with Lindy Davies. As part of an exercise I was handed a phrase from an old Anglo-Saxon poem—'I am a salmon in a pool'—and instructed to look up the words in the dictionary. I thought this was pretty pointless as

I already had a good idea of what a pool was and what a salmon looked like. The first dictionary definitions I came across weren't much help but another was more expansive: it described how the salmon fights its way upstream until it can find a deep, still pool where it may spawn. Suddenly the phrase sprang to life and I had this image of a gloriously heroic fish flashing silver in the sunlight as it leaps and twists in the thundering snow-white rapids, battling its way against the current until it comes to rest in the calm, cool, green-black serenity of a deep forest pool.

The image is not only an active as opposed to passive one (which makes it much easier to act), but it has a narrative and philosophical implication: I am someone who has battled against the odds and had a tough life, but now I have reached a haven of peace and reflection and I am preparing for the future.

So I think dictionary work and study of the language is invaluable, as is an awareness of its structure and subtleties of phrasing, pitch and cadence. I watch opera singers working on a score and note the precision they bring to bear. Actors could do with more of that, as long as we regard it as illumination and not a rigid formula which has to be lifelessly and technically regurgitated. Just like the opera singer we have to fill that form with spontaneous liveliness.

If you can visualise each image as fully as the salmon in the pool, a poetic speech becomes a necklace of images and you spring from one to the next. You can easily access and bring to life each image because it has been so fully explored and personalised. I am constantly disappointed with actors speaking Shakespeare who have forgotten or failed to notice what extraordinary language they are speaking—what original, bizarre and fantastic images and usages. They rattle it off as if it were commonplace instead of the most astonishing and original invention. And it's not a matter of pressing the voice and the face into service to achieve expression—just the imagination; the rest will follow.

Just as the actor particularises each word in Shakespeare he must particularise each moment. We look at a slab of text on a page and call it 'a speech'. It's not. It's a series of thoughts, impulses, ideas and actions. If you go for more than three or four lines without changing direction you're missing something. And if someone remarks, 'That was a long speech you had,' it means all they noticed was how long you were going on, not what you were saying or doing. If a speech seems long it's because you haven't motivated it or noticed the shifts.

It's not just those who are speaking who have to particularise and motivate each moment they're on stage. If you're on stage you have to ask *why*, just as you ask why you enter and why you exit—and where are you going? You have to justify every moment you're on stage and make it live. I've been astonished, for instance, to see the trial scene in *The Merchant of Venice* played in such a way that when Shylock goes to cut out the heart of Antonio everyone stands around looking helpless! Would you? Wouldn't you yell out, rush in and try to stop him? What stops you? You and the director have to think of *something*, otherwise the moment (which is the climax of the scene) is dead.

This kind of unthinking generalisation is a great enemy of acting Shakespeare. It's like when everyone steps aside to give the leading actor centre stage. Why? It's like acting a noble or a gentleman or a saint rather than a person. It's like acting woe or grief rather than trying to cope.

What do people *really* do when they are grief-stricken, how do they *really* sound? They can do many different things, they can make many different sounds. You have to observe, to choose and particularise, not generalise. (An actor has to be a little callous and detached to note and replicate extreme human behaviour. I think it was Leonardo who remarked that when a man falls from a tower, most people rush to help. The artist is the one who sketches him on the way down.) If you particularise each word and image as well as each moment, you don't have to worry about 'acting', about how you sound or look. The tempo, dynamic and pitch will change with each impulse and change of thought or intention.

Bad actors listen to the sound of their own voices; they sound pompous and affected. They are being grand rather than real.

Bad actors don't think through what they are saying. They trot out remarkable images without discovering them and then inhabiting them.

Bad actors are not really in the moment. They know what's coming next; they shouldn't.

Bad actors play types (a fop, a rustic, an officer) rather than a *particular* fop, rustic or officer.

You can spot bad actors who are dead behind the eyes waiting for their cue. They only act when they are speaking.

Bad actors use stock gestures and postures rather than observing how people really deport themselves. They should spend more time analysing body language—it's an inexhaustible mine of information, and frequently contradicts the words coming out of the mouth.

Bad actors signal to the audience ('I don't know what the fuck it means either' or 'That's a lousy joke, isn't it?'). That's cowardly.

Bad actors let you know it's a bawdy joke—there are two stock gestures for doing this. You've seen them many times.

Bad actors play a characteristic ('I am evil') rather than playing an action.

Bad actors bring their homework on stage and show the audience how hard it is. If you signal to the audience, 'This is really difficult stuff,' they'll agree with you and switch off. Your job is to make it effortless and spontaneous. Leave your homework in the rehearsal room. As long as *you* know what you're talking about, the audience will too. They mightn't get every single word, but they'll understand the intention.

Bad actors break up the verse and make it sound like prose in an attempt to make it more 'real'. In fact it turns it into a jolting ride and makes it harder to follow, besides robbing it of its dynamic and emotive power. The verse structure is a gift, it's a life raft, it will support you and take you on a wild ride.

Observe that the bulk of his work is written in iambic pentameter. Why? Because it's an easy approximation of everyday speech. The iambic rhythm is the same as the human heartbeat and five stresses to a line is close enough to how we use everyday English: 'I think I'll go and make a cup of tea' is perfect iambic pentameter.

Shakespeare didn't invent iambic pentameter but, like the other playwrights of his day, he found it a fluid and flexible means of expression, one taken for granted by audiences. His earliest plays, like the *Henry VI* trilogy, use iambic pentameter in a quite conventional way and the stresses are unambiguous. When you get to a play like *The Merchant of Venice*, the verse form is the same but you can make multiple choices. You can choose which particular word to stress within the format, and interpretation starts to creep in. If you're playing Antonio and you have the first line in the play, you may choose to play him with a vague melancholy and give all five beats an equal stress:

'In sooth I know not why I am so sad.'

Or mildly exasperated:
'In sooth I know not *why* I am so sad.'

Or fed up with being interrogated:
'In sooth I *know* not why I am so sad.'

Or frustrated and longing to break out:
'In sooth I know not why I am so *sad*.'

All the above are legitimate. You can even be a bit perverse and distort the rhythm to make a point. You could be argumentative, as in (hit the first 'I'):

'In sooth *I* know not why I am so sad.'

Or, still argumentative:

'In sooth I *know not* why I am so sad.'

As he goes on, Shakespeare is increasingly experimental, playing with rhythm and metre, dropping into prose and back into verse, striving for psychological truth, playing with vernacular naturalism and creating compelling individuals, each with his or her unique voice.

Hamlet chats to the strolling players in playful prose, then encourages them to perform a piece of blood-and-thunder rhetoric which may be seen as either a homage to or parody of Marlowe. Then they lapse back into conversational prose. But when the players leave Hamlet alone he bursts into an impassioned soliloquy in verse that echoes the performance he has just seen. Does the audience notice that Hamlet has switched from prose to verse? No; all they feel is an emotional gear change. The heightened language, the intensity of the rhythm and metre express Hamlet's frustration, self-disgust and excitement.

One of the best books I know about acting is Declan Donnellan's *The Actor and the Target.* He gives good advice on how to avoid the affectations in voice and gesture that result in hollow performances of Shakespeare. He reminds us not to watch or listen to ourselves, worrying about how we look or sound; think instead of what you are hearing and looking at. Escape self-consciousness by giving your attention to the other—to the target. Before you step on stage ask yourself where you are going and why. What makes your entrance necessary? When you go to speak, remind yourself you have never said this line before, never heard this line before.

A good actor lives 'in the moment'. But a brilliant actor is somehow living *beyond* the moment, thinking and feeling ahead. If you know the play you know what they're going to say next, but when they open their mouths to speak, you feel *anything* might come out, such is their spontaneity. Marlon Brando and Cate Blanchett are actors who do that.

Finding your voice in Shakespeare is one of the biggest challenges. You may have to go through all sorts of twists and turns, but eventually the voice you end up with has to be your own. You need to constantly feed your fantasy life by absorbing plays, movies, books, poems, art galleries and museums. You need to restock your imagination. What first stirs you in a role? What does your intuition tell you? Hang on to that. Question and test it by all means, but don't discard it too quickly—it may be right.

With Shakespeare it's a good idea to know your lines before rehearsals, or at least the major passages. Do all your homework with footnotes and dictionaries and come to rehearsal ready to play. Struggling for lines only holds you back. When I'm directing I have the text pasted on the wall or on a video screen so that actors don't have to carry books around.

How much should you 'feel' the role? Not at all really. It's your job to make the audience feel. You may, in rehearsal, summon up real emotions from your past or events you have witnessed. Once you know what those precise emotions are, you use your craft to reproduce and simulate them. That's why it's called acting. It's pretending. Actors who try to feel real emotions every night are getting in their own way and engaging in self-indulgence rather than acting. There's an old theatre rule that says if *you* cry, the audience won't. It's far more affecting for an audience to see someone struggling to hold back the tears. Acting is all about intuition, acute observation, expert mimicry and the art of manipulating an audience.

That's not to say you can dispense with sincerity. You have to be astute enough to capture the precise emotion and brave enough to reproduce it without generalising, sentimentalising or pulling back from the truth. Even the most unsophisticated audience can pick a phoney. And they want to believe that it's *you* who's going through this. The most successful performances are those where the audience feels it has had an insight into the performer's soul, that a revelation, a kind of public confession has taken place, that something precious, intimate and private has been shared. That's when an audience is grateful for the generosity of the actor, who has done something most of us never dare. There are aspects of Macbeth, Iago or Goneril that are indeed part of ourselves. If we can delve into them and present them in public, an audience will understand that and be grateful for it.

When I'm auditioning actors, what do I look for?

Someone I want to watch, who intrigues me; someone who I think will tell me something.

Someone who has understood the text and made it her own, so that she appears to be making it up as she goes along, not just giving an intelligent recitation.

Someone who has a lively imagination and the flexibility to take direction, to come through a different door.

Someone who is prepared to take risks, has an air of danger; a free spirit who is brave enough to go all the way.

Someone who seems to have a real appreciation of language, its power, nuances, music and colour.

Someone who acts with the whole body, not just from the neck up. He has great physical energy, stamina and a flexible, expressive body.

Someone whose voice is compelling and pleasant to listen to. It has range, colour, expression and flexibility. Accent is immaterial.

Someone who doesn't take herself too seriously but evinces a sense of humour and appears to be a good collaborator and team player. She is not just a show pony.

And talent? Well, if someone has the passion to perform and possesses the above qualities in some degree, the talent will grow. It's like a muscle and develops the more you work it.

The striking peculiarity of Shakespeare's mind was its generic quality, its power of communication with all other minds—so that it contained a universe of thought and feeling within itself, and had no one peculiar bias, or exclusive excellence more than another. He was just like any other man, but that he was like all other men. He was the least of an egoist that it was possible to be. He was nothing in himself; but he was all that others were, or that they could become. He not only had in himself the germs of every faculty and feeling, but he could follow them by anticipation, intuitively, into all their conceivable ramifications, through every change of fortune or conflict of passion, or turn of thought. He had 'a mind reflecting ages past', and present—all the people that ever lived are there. There was no respect of persons with him. His genius shone equally on the evil and on the good, on the wise and the foolish, the monarch and the beggar.

William Hazlitt

7

Directing Shakespeare

When I returned to Australia in 1970 after five years in England, I was a little shocked to find how much the country had changed. There was a nationalism in the air, assertive and at times aggressive. It seemed to go hand in hand with a celebratory materialism resulting from the recent minerals boom. Or maybe I was just meeting the wrong people...

The new Australian plays were identifying the Ocker, the Ugly Australian: a crass, vulgar, drunken loudmouth. He featured in the plays of John Romeril and David Williamson and strutted the stage of Melbourne's Pram Factory.

Suddenly the RSC with its cloaks, crowns, tights and rounded vowels seemed ten thousand miles away, not just in space but in time. I thought, 'If Shakespeare's going to survive in this country, then he has to look and sound more like us.'

Of course I was not the first to think this. Bille Brown, for instance, had played Falstaff in Brisbane in a production of *The Merry Wives of Windsor* directed by Geoffrey Rush as an Australian suburban sitcom. And I played Petruchio in Robin Lovejoy's production of *The Taming of the Shrew* set in the Australian outback for the Old Tote Company. But these were exceptions to standard theatre practice of the time.

I was very conscious in the early years of Bell Shakespeare of trying to shake off any trappings that might identify a production as being 'English' or 'traditional'. I encouraged actors to use their own voices rather than whack on plummy accents. We strove to defy the British cultural hegemony. But this self-conscious Australian-ness was short-lived because it became unnecessary. Productions from Europe and Asia touring to various Australian festivals gave us role models other than a British one and we began to see ourselves as part of a 'global village' with access, via movies, TV, recordings and the internet, to all the best and latest of work across all art forms. We saw that many different approaches to the classics were viable. Besides, the Anglo-Saxon stage tradition was becoming remote as we saw our population demographic change to include more people from all over Asia, Africa and much of Europe. We had to create a theatre for this new audience.

It became apparent that the English no longer held the franchise on Shakespeare. He had become increasingly universal throughout the twentieth century, as witnessed by great productions from Russia, Germany, Eastern Europe and the films of Kozintsev and Kurosawa. We can learn a lot from their example as we go about the business of creating 'our' Shakespeare—not in a self-consciously nationalistic way, but simply by being ourselves and making sure we talk to our audience in ways they will understand.

When the English are good at performing Shakespeare it's because he's in their blood and they get plenty of practice. In Australia we still have not done enough, regularly, over a long stretch of time to make it our own. But we can and we will. In some ways we are lucky to not have the burden and expectations of a long tradition bearing down on us. It leaves us free to be inventive, original and fearless. It's hard enough to take on Hamlet in Australia; how much tougher in London with that long line of Hamlets and Hamlet-experts looking over your shoulder! We are not judged (so much) in comparison to all those who have gone before. It has not been drummed into us that there is a 'correct' way of playing every role. The same applies to directing.

There is no one 'correct' way to direct Shakespeare. When I was starting out as a director, I tried to evolve a method. Now I try to avoid one. Every play has its own needs and its own circumstances. The director's job is to respond to these. Who are you directing the play for? Who is your audience? What talent have you at your disposal? What venue are you performing in? And what is the desired outcome of the exercise?

You might wish to attempt a 'traditional' production, which generally implies period costumes and what you assume is a 'classical' style of acting and speaking.

You might update the costumes and settings, but not the language, or you may rewrite the play in contemporary language.

You might do your own 'cut and paste' job on the text, rearranging scenes and introducing new material. You may decide on a parody approach, a revue skit, or you may create a new work inspired by a speech, character or situation in the original.

All of these are legitimate depending on the circumstances. There is no law against them.

How much reverence should you have for the original text? Again, it's up to you. Shakespeare himself cut his texts for performance, depending on how long a show his audience wanted and how many actors were available.

Different theatre companies have many different approaches and philosophies. In the case of the Bell Shakespeare Company, I urge actors and directors to err on the side of caution. Having established ourselves as the national touring company of Australia for Shakespeare's plays, with a huge commitment to education and school performances, I am aware that for many people we may be their only contact with Shakespeare, so

I feel duty-bound to present as fully as possible the words he wrote and what he meant by them. I have no problem with other companies doing their own spin on the plays, but I see my company having something of a conservationist role in keeping these plays alive.

But that position is by no means inflexible. I was happy to let Barrie Kosky cut and rework *King Lear* to make his own theatrical statement and, as mentioned, I am seriously pursuing some contemporary translations of dense texts like *Troilus and Cressida*. The staging of a modernised version would not invalidate the original, but reawaken interest in it much in the way that modern translations of *The Canterbury Tales* and *Beowulf* have reintroduced those works to a wide general readership. Bell Shakespeare's development arm, Mind's Eye, exists precisely to create new works inspired by Shakespeare's thoughts and scenarios.

But with my own productions I try to be as sparing as possible with cuts and translation. Occasionally a modern word or phrase may be necessary where the original is simply too arcane to be comprehensible. But if the actors know what they're talking about and play a scene with conviction, it's amazing how much an audience will understand. Words which would baffle them on the printed page seem crystal clear in performance. And one way to keep Shakespeare's language alive is by speaking it, not watering it down. As for length, I am very aware that today's audiences have a much shorter attention span than Shakespeare's audience. Here, I think, we can take a hint from Shakespeare's original productions, which had no interval and no scene-changes. The action flowed uninterrupted and the actors spoke and moved quickly about the empty stage. They rarely had time to sit down.

Over the last fifty years or so I've seen a number of stand-out productions of Shakespeare. All have influenced my own aspirations as a director.

Peter Brook's *Midsummer Night's Dream* had a huge impact on the theatre of the 1970s and beyond, especially on Shakespeare. Gone was any illusion of romance or moonlit forest. Brook's play took place inside a stark white box. His actors wore brightly coloured silks; they swung on trapezes and spun plates on sticks—*real* theatrical magic. In contrast, his artisans were solid serious workmen in cardigans and cloth caps. Their performance of *Pyramus and Thisbe* was heartfelt and poignant and helped show up the shallowness of the courtly lovers. The program announced 'Music by Felix Mendelssohn', which struck me as being quite out of place. But this was Brook's little joke at the expense of the 'traditionalists'. Mendelssohn was indeed used, but only once: at the end of the first half Bottom was borne aloft by the fairies making a triumphant entry into fairyland. Mendelssohn's Wedding March blazed out over the speakers while the fairies skimmed paper plates over the stage like a shower of confetti. Brook's theatrical acumen and daring were always underscored by a wicked sense of humour. Michael Bogdanov was Brook's assistant on that production and when I asked him what was the greatest lesson he had learned from Brook he quoted, 'Give them a good show!'

Declan Donnellan directed a beautiful *Twelfth Night* which came to the Sydney Festival in 2005. It was played by an all-male Russian cast and performed in Russian with English subtitles. As with Brook's *Dream* its great virtue was in stripping away preconceptions and generations of production clichés, seeing the play afresh. And, like Brook's *Dream*, it was set in a white, neutral space with few props and no tricksy effects. The actors playing Viola, Olivia and Maria made no attempt to disguise themselves as women or play effeminacy. In fact the actor playing Olivia was completely bald and wore a headscarf for the role. But their observations of female behaviour were so acute as to be a revelation. One suddenly understood the power of Shakespeare's all-male companies. Impersonation was not the point, but observation and comment. The audience was simultaneously distanced and enchanted by the theatricality of it.

The drinking scene had a Russian wildness and earthiness about it—Sir Toby decked Maria when she criticised his behaviour. And Malvolio was no pompous blow-hard, but a sprightly ambitious young butler, just attractive enough to believe that his mistress might have fallen for him. Because the text was a modern Russian translation, the actors spoke easily and naturally without any of the English-speaking actors' constraint to sound (or not sound) 'Shakespearean'.

This *Twelfth Night* was a very different one to John Barton's magical version of the late 1960s. Fully Elizabethan in its setting, costumes and music, Barton's production was steeped in scholarship and a love of the play. It ambled along effortlessly, greatly enhanced by Judi Dench's puppyish schoolboy Cesario and Donald Sinden's magisterial Malvolio. A triumph for the traditionalists.

John Barton was responsible, with Peter Hall, for one of the great RSC successes of the 1960s—an adaptation of the three parts of *Henry VI* and *Richard III* into an epic saga, *The Wars of the Roses*, which was televised internationally. The landmark aspects of this production were similar to those I've mentioned above: a stripping away of sentimental and romantic theatrical conventions in order to show the plays in a new light. This time what was chucked out was the technicolour period sets and costumes, the velvets and ermines, the cloaks and tights, the trains and wimples. This was a production based on the realpolitik of Polish critic Jan Kott's Cold War perspective. In his book *Shakespeare Our Contemporary* Kott asked innocently, 'Who doesn't know what it feels like to be woken by a door-knock at four in the morning?' Hall and Barton realised with a shock that Kott's experiences were closer to Shakespeare's England than were their own cosy Oxbridge existences. Their *Wars of the Roses* was a hard world of hard men—plate-metal walls like some gigantic battleship and heavy iron furniture. The clothes and armour had a medieval toughness and were mud- and blood-splattered, devoid of decoration. After that, history plays would never look pretty again.

The great Georgian production of *Richard III* featuring Ramaz Chkhikvadze predated the RSC version but was informed by the same political scepticism, only this time from behind the Iron Curtain, so it had a lot of extra edge and far greater risk attached for those involved. Less literal and formal than the RSC productions, this *Richard* featured an impressionistic set (somewhat shambolic), a sleazy jazz band, a choric Queen Margaret who acted as narrator/commentator and a sinister Richmond in a long black leather coat who followed Richard about, taking notes and studying his tactics. There were undoubted elements of parody of Soviet leaders and hidden messages that must have thrilled the Georgian audiences. But whatever repressive measures the Soviet censors enforced, Eastern Bloc theatre was still way more experimental than its English counterparts of the time. I first saw the Georgian *Richard III* at the Roundhouse in London. Sitting next to me was an old chum from my RSC days, Clive Swift, who remarked dourly, 'If *we* did this to Shakespeare, they'd crucify us.'

I'll finally mention a production of *The Winter's Tale* by London theatre company Complicite, which in the early 1990s showed Australia yet another kind of Shakespeare. The production was dominated by Simon McBurney as a terrifyingly insane and erratic Leontes. But he showed his clowning skills by doubling as the Young Shepherd. His troupe was a bizarre mix of shapes, sizes and accents which destroyed any audience preconceptions about 'appropriate' casting; and their delivery of the language was likewise idiosyncratic—not the standardised uniformity one expected from, say, the National or RSC.

As with the Georgian *Richard III*, the set was impressionistic and featured a huge wardrobe on which Leontes occasionally perched. The cloaks worn by Leontes and Polixenes were made up of dozens of suit jackets sewn together, as if the two kings were dragging their subjects around on their backs. The whole production had an air of nonchalant freedom occasionally bordering on anarchy that defied the conventional 'well-made' production, and was thus liberating.

My forty-odd years of directing for the stage have taught me a few 'don'ts':

- Don't over-direct. Know when to stop and let the actors have their heads. Micro-managing can destroy initiative.
- Don't demonstrate how to do it—find ways of letting the actor discover it for herself. Evoke a performance, don't prescribe it.
- Don't play favourites—give everyone equal attention and respect. Greet everyone, including the stage crew.
- Don't decide everything in advance; come to rehearsal well prepared but with an open mind and encourage new ideas.
- Don't try to control—don't dictate; collaborate instead.
- Don't destroy actors' confidence. Be constructive in your criticism. Praise where possible.
- Don't panic and rush to lock down solutions. Stay fluid and open to change up to the last minute.
- Don't come to rehearsal with the actors' moves worked out in advance. Let the actors discover them, otherwise they'll never own them. It's sometimes called 'blocking'—and to me that's just what it is, like blocking a drainpipe and stopping the flow.
- Don't lose your temper or cry for help. Your actors will secretly despise you for it. Stay buoyant—you're the leader.
- Don't be too solemn—it's a play, and plays should be playful. If you're doing a tragedy, all the more reason to stay light-hearted: solemnity will bog you down.
- Don't try to force comedy. If it's truthful it will be funny. Go for the truth, not the gags.

Remember that as a director you have a huge responsibility—to your writer, to your cast and to your audience. You have no responsibility to yourself—you are a mere functionary, there to make everyone else look good and make sure everyone has a good time. It's your job to make every actor look his or her best. Their reputation and future employment may depend on it. Your audience may have come a long way and paid good money to see your show. You are ethically obliged to give them the very best you can do (that goes for actors too).

Shakespeare is more interesting than you are. Submit your ego to his and try to do his work justice. You'll never fully succeed. His challenges are too great, his vision too huge for any production to get it in one, but even from halfway up the mountain the view is grand.

Whatever else you succeed in bringing out, it's Shakespeare's *humanity* that carries the day, and it's what audiences delight in.

The most fundamental job of the director is to tell the story. No matter how many times I see *Hamlet* or *Macbeth* (and I know them both by heart), I want to follow the story. How much more the case for people coming to the play for the first time... Sometimes you might need to simplify a complex text to tell the story more clearly. You may have to engage in a little careful cutting and/or translating. That's okay. The audience will understand the play more fully and if they want to study the original it's still sitting intact on the library shelf. When I've directed *Julius Caesar* and *Antony and Cleopatra* I've tried to simplify the complex series of battle scenes at the end of both plays. I think Shakespeare was being a little too faithful to his source material for once, probably knowing that his audience was fully versed in Plutarch and would complain if he distorted history.

It's no use baffling your audience—they soon lose interest. So make sure you spell out the plot as clearly as possible. Signpost the characters' names. After a few weeks' rehearsal we start to take things for granted and forget our audience will be hearing these names and this information for the first time.

As a director you soon learn that casting is seventy-five per cent of the job. With the right actors the play can take wing. With the wrong ones, you're pushing it uphill all the way through rehearsal, being overly grateful for small breakthroughs. But typecasting can make the show dreary and predictable. Having the 'right' actor for a role is not the same thing as typecasting. It's exhilarating to see a role brought to life by an unexpected choice of actor, revealing elements of the character you'd never considered before.

It's unfortunate that most theatres, in Australia at least, are of the proscenium-arch variety. It's not sympathetic to Shakespeare and makes it all the more remote. Shakespeare's plays, like the ancient Greek plays, were written for a very specific space and architecture. In Shakespeare's theatres the actors stood among the audience who surrounded them on three sides. They spoke to them intimately and naturally. There was no 'set' to distract attention. Everyone focused on the actor and the words. Some of the most exciting Shakespeare productions I have seen have recreated these circumstances or at least subverted the tyranny of the picture-frame stage.

When I set out with a designer to create a new production my first priority is to provide a playground for the actors, a space they will find liberating and stimulating. It must serve the actors, not hinder them.

Sometimes you walk into a theatre auditorium, take your seat, look at the set and groan, 'Oh, it's going to be *that* all night . . .' If you must have a set then it should have an element of mystery or surprise, something to stimulate the audience's imagination and expectations.

Rather than clutter up the space, ask your actors how many ways they can use the same prop to mean different things. That's the kind of theatricality audiences enjoy. And do all you can to avoid scene-changes and blackouts—they are just so much dead time. Whenever I set out to design a show I always cast my mind back to the Globe and think about how the play would have first been staged, what elements of that I can incorporate. It solves a lot of problems.

When it comes to costume I like to spend several months before rehearsals start collaborating with the actors and the designer. We explain to the actors the overall concept of the production and its likely setting and then ask them for feedback on how they see their characters.

At our next meeting the designer will show them a range of sketches, photographs and magazine clippings based on their feedback. Little by little we work towards a consensus, so that by the time the costume drawings are finalised, the actors have had maximum input as to how they want to look. The only snag is, of course, that many actors won't 'know' their characters until some time into rehearsals, but meantime the production manager has to have all the costumes completed in time for week five of rehearsals. So one always aims for as much latitude as possible to allow for last-minute changes and adjustments.

The first thing to nut out with the designer is what the costumes are *for*. They can't be merely decorative items to titillate an audience's taste for spectacle or admiration of the designer's taste and wit. The cleverest costumes in the world are absolutely useless unless they convey the audience into the world of the play and help the actors realise their characterisations. At the same time they can't do *too* much of the actor's work for him. Some costumes make such a strong character statement that the actor is redundant: they become the designer's or director's comment on the character, and leave the actor's contribution out of the equation.

Ideally, costumes, or at least reasonable replicas of them, should be got into rehearsals early on. This rarely happens because everybody is racing to meet deadlines. But the sooner an actor can get used to his costume and learn how to work it, the better. Otherwise it's just one more hurdle, one more distraction in the week leading up to opening night.

I count myself lucky that I'm an actor as well as a director because it gives me the opportunity to observe other directors at work. I've learned a lot from working with good directors. Here are just a few examples:

From Peter Hall I learned the potency of identifying the scenarios of the classics with current events and politics.

From John Barton I gained an understanding of the importance of verse structure and the mechanics of Shakespeare's language.

From Steven Berkoff I discovered the thrill of precision of gesture, intonation and physical dynamics.

Michael Bogdanov demonstrated the infinite patience required to get a moment just right.

Liviu Ciulei has a thoroughness and attention to detail I admire. (He took four days to light *The Lower Depths* for the Old Tote. Most lighting sessions are about six hours.)

Barrie Kosky taught me the importance of fun and jokes when you're rehearsing a tragedy.

And from Peter Brook I learned a seemingly endless range of things. No other contemporary director (except perhaps the late Jerzy Grotowski) has undertaken such a serious lifetime's quest to understand the meaning and significance of theatre. His work has always been earmarked by a stripping away of worn-out conventions. Unsentimental and uncompromising, he combines a fierce intelligence with a warm sense of humour and a flair for showmanship. In his many books of theory as well as his landmark productions, he has been one of the most important theatre personalities of the last sixty years.

What are the hardest parts of directing? They include:

- Scheduling: Trying to envisage how many hours to rehearse each scene.
- Keeping everybody working at roughly the same pace. Some will be galloping impatiently ahead, some lagging fearfully behind. I find it useful to begin each day with a quick round-the-circle—'How's it going? How are you all feeling?'—and to finish each week with a longer version of the same so everyone can air frustrations or anxieties.

- Dealing with tricky temperaments. Often they're a disguise for fear and insecurity, and recognising this makes them easier to deal with. Either way it's no use losing your cool.
- Knowing how far to push it if an actor can't realise the moment. When do you let go?

I once read an interview with one of Fellini's film crew. He was asked, 'What's it like working with Maestro Fellini?' He laughed and replied, 'It's not work, it's a holiday!' That's the kind of director I try to be.

He understood his age perfectly, and the depth and profundity of that understanding which continued to draw contemporaries to his plays has ensured that we still read him and see these plays performed today in 'states unborn and accents yet unknown', as he prophetically put it in *Julius Caesar* (III, i, 114). More, perhaps, than any writer before and since, Shakespeare held the keys that opened the hearts and minds of others, even as he kept a lock on what he revealed about himself.

James Shapiro, *1599*

8

An interview with Ben Jonson

> What things have we seen
> Done at the Mermaid!
> Heard words that have been
> So nimble, and so full of subtle flame
> As if that every one (from whence they came)
> Had meant to put his whole wit in a jest——
> And had resolved to live a fool the rest
> Of his dull life.
>
> FROM MASTER FRANCIS BEAUMONT'S LETTER TO BEN JONSON

Ben Jonson has agreed to meet me at the Mermaid before noon. I get a bit lost in the narrow lanes around St Paul's—the pub's address is Bread Street, but the entrance is in Friday Street—so I'm running a bit late, and by the time I get there Mr Jonson is already settled at a table by the window, tucking into a large venison pasty, a pot of ale at his elbow.

It is a crisp spring day, but the light struggles feebly through the heavy leaded glass and the room is thick with smoke as gentlemen with their long clay pipes take their whiffs. A handful of rowdy women are

An interview with Ben Jonson

smoking and drinking along with the men. The floorboards are strewn with sawdust and the air reeks of roasting meat, sweat and tobacco. A sleepy-looking bull terrier lies at Ben's feet with its nose on its paws. A number of other dogs mooch around or scratch themselves or snarl at each other from under the tables.

Jonson shakes hands but doesn't bother to get up. Even sitting down, I can tell he's a big man—broad shoulders, barrel chest and a face like the side of a ham with shrewd eyes and a moody brow. I've been warned that he has a sharp tongue and a quick temper, so I'm going to gang warily.

JB   If I could start by asking you a bit about your early life and how you got into the theatre . . .

BJ   I never knew my father. He died before I was born. A Scotsman. I was put into Westminster Grammar School and I lapped it up: took to the classics like a duck to water, especially Aristotle. So I was more than a bit pissed off when Mother married a master bricklayer and he made me his apprentice. I had no intention of ending up a bloody bricklayer so I enlisted in the army and got shipped off to the Netherlands. Didn't fancy getting my bollocks shot off either, so when I was twenty-two or twenty-three I tried my luck as an actor with Pembroke's company here in London. I wasn't much of an actor but I enjoyed mucking in and helping write the scripts—you know, patching up old plays, writing new scenes here and there, collaborating on new shows. That was a lot of fun, but I got into a shitload of trouble with a piece called *The Isle of Dogs*. The theatre was closed down and I got chucked in prison—the Marshalsea. I was in there about ten weeks, but luckily that old tight-arse Henslowe had lent me four quid, so that saw me through. I was in with Bob Shaw and Gabe Spencer, two of the actors in the show. Things

	didn't go well with me and Gabriel. I killed him in a duel a year later. See that letter T on my thumb?
JB	I had noticed it, yes.
BJ	Well, that stands for Tyburn. They branded that on my thumb as a warning—any more rough stuff, I'd swing for it. I should have been hanged *that* time by rights, but I got off by benefit of clergy.
JB	What does that mean?
BJ	It means I could read a passage from the Bible. If I'd been illiterate they'd have hanged me. [*He grins.*] An arcane law but handy sometimes. They were going to cut off my ears because of *Isle of Dogs*, but someone must have changed their mind. Here, Pug.

He tosses a crust of his pasty to the bull terrier who snaps it up then rests his nose on his paws again with a contented groan.

BJ	Yes, I've been in the nick a couple of times. They locked me up again for *Eastward Ho!* because it had a couple of gags about Scotsmen and po-faced old King Jamie didn't like it. I could have got into trouble when that prick Marston libelled me in *What You Will*. I challenged him to a duel but the cowardly turd wouldn't face me. I tracked him down in the pub and he pulled a pistol on me. So I grabbed it from him and thrashed the bastard with it . . . Hey, Francis, top me up.

He bangs his empty tankard on the table as the spindly pot-boy, Francis, staggers past with an armful of wooden trenchers and pewter pots.

Francis	Anon, sir.
JB	So, tell me how you first met Will Shakespeare . . .

BJ	It was right here in the Mermaid; well, it's the actors' pub . . . most of the bastards spend half their lives in here.

Francis returns and fills the tankard from a large, blackened leather bottle.

Francis	One for you, sir?
JB	No thanks. [*I'm a bit wary of the hygiene conditions.*]
BJ	Yes, he was sitting right there, in that corner by the chimney. The place was full of actors and writers all holding forth and shouting each other down, and he was just sitting there, quietly sipping his ale, looking and listening. Every now and then, whenever he heard a good line or a good quip, he'd take out his tables and jot it down. Hello, I thought, I'm going to have to keep an eye on this one—the silent watchful type, you see. So I was very suspicious at first, because he had this deadly reputation—you know, the new boy wonder, the Next Big Thing. But when I got to know him we became good mates.
JB	What attracted you most?
BJ	His wit. He was smart and very quick, yet subtle with it. He would run circles around anybody in a battle of wits.

I recall the words of Thomas Fuller in his *Worthies of England*:

Many were the wit combats betwixt him and Ben Jonson, which two I behold like a Spanish great Galleon and an English man of War; Master Jonson (like the former) was built for higher learning, solid but slow in his performances. Shakespeare, with the English man of War, lesser in bulk but lighter in sailing, could turn with all tides, tack about and take advantage of all winds, by the quickness of his wit and invention.

Another witness of the Mermaid gab-fests (the anonymous author of *Parnassus*) remarked:

> Our fellow [i.e. fellow actor] Shakespeare puts them all down, ay, and Ben Jonson too. O that Ben Jonson is a pestilent fellow, he brought up Horace giving the Poets a pill, but our fellow Shakespeare hath given him a purge that made him bewray his credit.

Ben takes a swing of ale and resumes:

BJ   But I suppose the thing that sealed our friendship was working together in my play *Every Man in His Humour*. He persuaded the Burbage boys they should put it on at the Globe and then he acted in it.

JB   Was he a good actor?

BJ   Bloody good! You look at my collected works and you'll see his name top of the bill (above Dick Burbage) as one of the principal actors in my comedies as well as my tragedies. He saw to it that they were often revived and taken on tour as well as performed at court, and he always played his old parts.

JB   It was pretty generous of him to be so supportive considering how much you criticised and made fun of him.

BJ   Made fun of him? When?

JB   Well, for instance in *Every Man out of His Humour* when you bring in that character Sogliardo who has newly acquired a coat of arms with the motto 'Not Without Mustard'. Now, that's obviously a crack about Shakespeare getting his coat of arms with the motto 'Not Without Right'.

BJ   Yes, well . . . [*He laughs ruefully, gazing into his pint-pot.*] I thought it was all a bit ridiculous, chasing after a coat of arms and the status of 'gentleman'. The College of

Heralds thought so too and resisted it for a long time: 'He's only a bloody player!' Of course he was trying to restore the family name. Apparently his old man was entitled to it; and it can't have hurt that his mother was a distant relation of his patron, young Southampton.

Do I detect a touch of envy in this glance at Shakespeare's aspiration to gentility? This, after all, is the man who dared to publish his plays, the first to do so, as collected 'Works', much to the derision of the literati: 'Jonson's *works*! They're not literature at all, they're only play scripts!'

JB	Well, apart from that you had a few harsh things to say about his writing. You told William Drummond that Shakespeare 'wanted Art' and when the actors remarked that Shakespeare never blotted a line you said that he should have blotted a thousand!
BJ	Now that's taken out of context and was not meant maliciously. I was just reprimanding them for making a virtue out of what I regard as one of his faults. I've always maintained that he had an excellent fantasy, brave notions and gentle expressions, wherein he flowed with that facility, that sometimes it was necessary he should be stopped. He had a powerful wit but sometimes it ran away with him. But I've always said that he redeemed his vices with his virtues. There was ever more in him to be praised, than to be pardoned.
JB	When you said he 'wanted Art' I presume you meant that he disobeyed the classical rules for playwriting—unity of time and place, for instance—as set down by Aristotle?
BJ	That's right! Those classical rules shouldn't be ignored. My plays follow Aristotle's rule that the action should all happen in the same location and in real time. So what does

Shakespeare do? One minute you're in one place and the next minute you're somewhere else, or it's sixteen years later, or some bloody thing! Now that is not playing by the rules.

JB   But he could observe the unities when he wanted to; even in an early play like *The Comedy of Errors*, let alone one of his last great plays, *The Tempest*.

BJ   Sure, *The Tempest*'s fine, but in the very same year he writes that mouldy tale *Pericles*—one minute you're in Antioch, next thing you're in Ephesus and it's sixteen years later again!

I don't want to break the bad news to Ben, but it's the very fact that Shakespeare either bent or ignored 'the rules' that has ensured his longevity. Jonson's Roman tragedies *Catiline* and *Sejanus* are models of classical propriety but don't stand up against the power and immediacy of *Julius Caesar*. Shakespeare's wide-ranging imagination and flexibility have made him adaptable and translatable to all succeeding generations. And as for overwriting, well, again the sad news for Ben is that even his best works (*Volpone*, *The Alchemist*) seem too loquacious by today's standards and need heavy cutting and a fair bit of translation to work for a modern audience.

JB   Just one last point regarding criticism: you said of Shakespeare that he had 'little Latin and less Greek'. Isn't that a bit unfair, seeing that you had almost identical educations at the grammar schools where Latin and Greek were high on the agenda? He was actually steeped in the Latin classics.

BJ   Now, that's not how I mean it! What I was saying was that he was an original and didn't slavishly imitate the ancients... For Christ's sake! I said that for tragedy he

An interview with Ben Jonson

surpassed Aeschylus, Sophocles and Euripides, for comedy Aristophanes, Terence and Plautus! But he actually took it in good part. At one time I asked him to stand godfather to my boy, young Benjamin. He scratched his head, looked solemn and said, 'Well, Ben, what shall I give him for a christening present? I know! I'll give him a dozen latten spoons and you shall translate them!' Latten is the alloy christening spoons are made of and to 'translate' is to turn base metal into gold ... so he had me there! Here, Francis, top me up!

Francis   Anon, anon, sir!

BJ   C'mon Francis, move your arse—I'm thirsty!

Francis obligingly skitters over with his heavy leather jug.

JB   There's a story going around that Shakespeare didn't write his plays at all and they were written by Christopher Marlowe, who faked his own death and was spirited off to Italy whence he continued to send new plays back to England. After all, the author seems to know Italy pretty well.

Jonson stares at me solemnly.

BJ   That's a good one, that is.

He takes a long swig from his pint-pot then slams it on the table.

BJ   What an absolute heap of steaming horseshit! You put their plays side by side, or, better still, act them aloud: they are chalk and cheese in their styles, their vocabulary—Christ, where do I start? Marlowe never moved: play after play he hammered out the old iambic pentameter, whereas Will was always experimenting, breaking up the metre, inventing new words. No two plays are alike, he's always moving on, from farce to historical epic, to romantic comedy, to tragedy, to fairytale romances—he ran the full gamut. And what about women's roles? Kit couldn't write a female character to save his life. His plays are all about men in some sort of queer relationship: Edward and Gaveston, Barabas and Ithamore, Faust and Mephistopheles . . .

Look at *Faustus*—he brings on Helen of Troy of all people and has her walk across the stage *mute*; he can't think of anything for her to say! Whereas Will has the greatest line-up of women you could hope to see—from Juliet and the divine Rosalind to Lady Macbeth, Cleopatra and Mistress Quickly—what variety! What truth of observation! What brilliant characterisations—now *that* I do envy him.

And all this rubbish about Shakespeare's knowledge of Italy—we *all* set our plays in Italy because that's where all the best stories come from, whether you're talking ancient Rome or the modern novellas about lovers and machiavels and scheming cardinals—Italy is all the rage. But you don't have to go there to write about it! What do we do? We read about it, we do our research like any writer does. Research is fifty per cent of the job. What did Will know about Italy? He writes a piece called *The Merchant of Venice* and never once mentions the canals! He puts sea ports in Milan and Verona and reckons you can catch a ferry from Venice to Padua! Will knew as much about Italy as Pug here. [*He gives the dog a nudge with his foot and Pug responds with a loud yawn.*]

Kit wasn't destined for a long life—he was a crazy bastard, a real tearaway. He and Tom Watson killed Will Bradley in a brawl in Marlowe's own backyard! And then he got involved with Dick Baines and they started counterfeiting money. Kit reckoned he had as much right to make coins as had the Queen of England. But that Baines was a dirty piece of work. He was a government spy and at Kit's inquest he poured shit all over his reputation.

No, the fact about Will and Marlowe is that Will admired Marlowe enormously, was even somewhat in awe of him. When Will first came to London in his early twenties and took up acting he was acting in Marlowe's plays, and mine, and Bob Greene's and a whole heap of others. So he really got to know Marlowe's style well, and a lot of it stuck with him. In his earliest stuff he was quite consciously copying Marlowe (those *Henry VI* plays, for instance) and competing with him. But, of course, as he gained confidence he started to parody him. Look at Ancient Pistol in *Henry V*: he's a complete send-up of Ned Alleyn and Marlowe. He's a swaggering pisspot who's always quoting lines from plays he's seen, most of them parodies of Marlowe.

The rivalry between them was pretty intense. Will's *Richard III* was a riposte to *Tamburlaine*, the overreacher. When Marlowe tried his hand at history chronicle with *Edward II*, Will hit back with *Richard II*. The structure of the two plays is almost identical; so is the theme of a weak, effeminate king overthrown and murdered. Kit cashed in on the anti-Semitic rage sweeping the country after the so-called Lopez conspiracy with his arch-villain Jew, Barabas. So Shakespeare comes back with *The Merchant of Venice* which also has a Jew as the ostensible villain.

But although Shylock's in only five scenes of the play, he's a mighty creation and a disturbing one. So there's this ongoing rivalry between Marlowe and Shakespeare and their two companies, the Admiral's Men versus the Lord Chamberlain's Men. There's no telling where it would have ended up had Kit not been murdered, and my God, was he set up!

Kit's problem was that he got caught up in the spy game. Most of us actors and writers did to some extent. We were the perfect tools for the job—always hanging around the court chatting to the various aristocrats' entourages, performing in the great houses all around the country. You pick up a lot from servants and domestics. So if Master Walsingham or Secretary Cecil says to you, 'Just keep your eyes and ears open. If you hear any rumours of sedition or spot any Romish priests lurking around, give us a nod. There'll be something in it for you,' well, you take notice. You could be on the way to gaining a new patron, or at least earning a bit of favour in high places.

I turned Catholic for a while myself, after I killed Gabe Spencer. Went through a bit of a crisis of conscience. But when the shit hit the fan after Guido Fawkes and his Gunpowder Plot, I recanted quick-smart. I had to drink off a whole cup of communion wine to prove my bona fides. And I was asked to name names of all the Catholics I knew. So I did. I shopped about fifty of them and some were investigated. Well, you know, they were dangerous times. And Kit was right in the thick of it, spying for Walsingham and rooting out Catholics. But he was an erratic bastard, couldn't keep his mouth shut. Used to say out loud that Christ was a poofter, had a thing going with John 'the beloved disciple'. Then he'd suddenly yell out

An interview with Ben Jonson

things like, 'All Protestants are hypocritical asses, and all they that love not tobacco and boys are fools!'

Another time I heard him getting stuck into Moses, saying he was a fraud and that any two-bit conjurer could work better miracles. All this in public, deliberately baiting and outraging people—and this man is supposed to be a spy! You know, the invisible man! Well, Walsingham eventually decided that Kit had outlived his usefulness, that he was becoming an embarrassment. Besides, it was strongly suspected he was a double agent and was moonlighting for the Papists.

So they raided the lodgings of Tom Kyd, the bloke who wrote *The Spanish Tragedy*, a good mate of Kit's. I don't know who tipped them off but they found a lot of papers they labelled as 'lewd libels and blasphemies' and 'vile poetical conceits denying the divinity of Jesus Christ'. Tom and Kit were both arrested. Tom was tortured almost to death, poor bugger. Never recovered. Kit was released, but they had him set up. Just three weeks after he was released, he was invited out to Ma Bull's tavern in Deptford by three right scumbags—Nick Skeres, Bob Poley and Ingram Frizer. All three were on Walsingham's payroll. They had supper and spent the afternoon smoking and drinking and then one of them grabbed Kit from behind while Ingram Frizer stabbed him in the right eye with his own dagger. Went straight into the brain, killed him instantly.

Frizer claimed it was a quarrel over the reckoning and that he'd acted in self-defence. Of course the three of them got off, quietly disappeared, and the whole thing was hushed up. Kit was a very well-known figure, hence all the machinations, but any fool could see through it.

Now, he was killed in 1593, and nearly thirty of Will's plays were written after that date.

I guess Will must have been relieved deep down to have Kit out of the way, because he'd felt Kit breathing down his neck. But he always spoke well of him. Even seven years later, when he wrote *As You Like It*, he mentions Kit a couple of times, probably because it's a pastoral and Kit had described himself as a shepherd in *Hero and Leander*.

Will quotes one of Kit's lines when he says:

Dead shepherd, now I find thy saw of might,
Whoever loved that loved not at first sight?

And then he has the clown say:

When a man's verses cannot be understood...
It strikes a man more dead than a great reckoning in a little room.

Besides being a direct reference to Kit's murder, it's also quoting the first line of *The Jew of Malta*: 'infinite riches in a little room'.

So, yes, I think you could say that Kit's ghost stayed with Will for quite a while after Kit was gone. After all, Will owed Kit a lot. He learned a lot from acting in Kit's plays and Kit sort of paved the way for him with the power of his verse—he set a high benchmark. But the difference in their careers was that Kit was a hellraiser, he couldn't keep out of trouble. Will, on the other hand, was ambitious, competitive and had his eye on the prize. He didn't always go off drinking with the lads after a show, but went home to work all night and would come in next morning with a whole bunch of new scenes to rehearse. He was absolutely focused and kept raising the bar for himself.

When they asked me to write something about him I hammered the point that a good poet's not just born, he's *made*. Writing's not easy, you know; you've got to work at it, slave at it day by day. With a play, you've got to rework it with the actors until it's right. A play's not something you toss off in your spare time—it takes years of hard work and experience. It came easier to Will than to most people; let's face it, he was a genius. But he didn't take that for granted. No, sir, he was a worker ... Almost time for me to be going. Anything else I can tell you?

JB Well, you've told me a lot about Shakespeare the writer, but how about Shakespeare as a person—how did you relate to him?

He looks at me for a moment.

BJ I loved the man. Without actually idolising him, I guess you could say I loved him as much as I loved anyone in my life. He was indeed honest and of an open and free nature.

He hands me a sheet of paper.

BJ If you want any more, you can cast your eye over that. It's what I wrote for the first edition of his plays. You're welcome to keep it ... C'mon, Pug, walkies.

Jonson hoists his frame out of the settle and claps down a fistful of coins on the table. He tosses one to Francis, who catches it in his cap.

I watch him go out into the light of the spring afternoon, then turn my attention to the paper he has given me. The fog of tobacco smoke and meat on the spit is getting thicker all the time but I can make out in his bold, clear hand:

To the memory of my beloved, the author Mr William Shakespeare . . . and what he hath left us . . .
    Soul of the Age! The applause! Delight! The wonder of our stage!

. . . Triumph, my Britain, thou hast one to show
To whom all Scenes of Europe homage owe.
He was not of an age, but for all time!
Sweet Swan of Avon . . .

A generous spirit, I conclude, Ben Jonson. Big heart and big feelings. Not someone you'd want to cross swords with, literally or figuratively. He outlived Shakespeare by twenty years. In 1616, the year Shakespeare died, Ben published his own collected works and received a royal pension of a hundred marks, thus becoming the first (unofficial) Poet Laureate. But he died a poor man.

Daniel Lapaine and Essie Davis as Romeo and Juliet (1993)

Luciano Martucci as Hector, *Troilus + Cressida* (2000)

Michael Craig as Caesar and Christopher Stollery as Mark Antony, *Julius Caesar* (2001)
(PHOTO HEIDRUN LÖHR)

Paula Arundell as Cleopatra, *Antony and Cleopatra* (2001) (PHOTO HEIDRUN LÖHR)

Amy Mathews, Matt Edgerton, Ed Wightman and Briony Williams on the road (2002) (PHOTO BELL SHAKESPEARE)

Blazey Best as Lady Anne and myself as Richard, *Richard III* (2002) (PHOTO HEIDRUN LÖHR)

Leon Ford as Hamlet with Bille Brown as the Gravedigger, *Hamlet* (2003)
(PHOTO HEIDRUN LÖHR)

Christopher Stollery as
Antipholus of Syracuse
with Paul Eastway as
Dromio of Ephesus,
Comedy of Errors (2004)
(PHOTO HEIDRUN LÖHR)

Blazey Best as Adriana and Jody Kennedy as Luciana,
Comedy of Errors (2004) (PHOTO HEIDRUN LÖHR)

Death of Talbot—*Wars of the Roses*—Georgia Adamson as Joan, Peter Lamb as Talbot (2005) (PHOTO HEIDRUN LÖHR)

The Yorkist Brat-pack, *Wars of the Roses*. Darren Gilshenan, Julian Garner, David Davies, Richard Piper (2005) (PHOTO HEIDRUN LÖHR)

David Hynes (Gentleman), Garry Scale (Mistress Overdone), Matthew Moore (Lucio) and Julian Garner (Froth), *Measure for Measure* (2005)
(PHOTO WENDY McDOUGALL)

David Whitney (Macduff), Huw McKinnon (Lennox), Tim Walter (Malcolm), Richard Sydenham (Angus), *Macbeth* (2007)
(PHOTO WENDY McDOUGALL)

Linda Cropper as Lady Macbeth and Sean O'Shea, Macbeth (2007)
(PHOTO WENDY McDOUGALL)

Leeanna Walsman as Desdemona, Wayne Blair as Othello (2007)
(PHOTO WENDY McDOUGALL)

Wayne Blair as Othello (2007)
(PHOTO WENDY McDOUGALL)

Lizzie Schebesta as Ursula, Megan O'Connell as Margaret, Alexandra Fisher as Hero, Tony Llewellyn-Jones as Leonato, Arky Michael as Antonio, Robert Alexander as Friar Francis, Tyran Parke as Balthasar and Blazey Best as Beatrice, *Much Ado About Nothing* (2011) (PHOTO WENDY McDOUGALL)

Toby Schmitz as Benedick and Matthew Walker as Don Pedro, *Much Ado About Nothing* (2011) (PHOTO WENDY McDOUGALL)

Toby Schmitz as Benedick, Blazey Best as Beatrice and Matthew Walker as Don Pedro, *Much Ado About Nothing* (2011) (PHOTO WENDY McDOUGALL)

Saskia Smith (Rosalind), Damien Ryan (Jaques) in *As You Like It* (2008)
(PHOTO WENDY McDOUGALL)

Pippa Grandison, Patrick Brammall, Tim Richards playing at witches in Andy Griffith's *Just Macbeth!* (PHOTO WENDY McDOUGALL)

Robert Alexander and myself in *Titus* (2008)
(PHOTO CRAIG RATCLIFFE)

Bloody but unbowed . . . the cast and crew of *Titus* after a performance (2008)
(PHOTO BELL SHAKESPEARE)

Susan Prior and Melissa Madden Gray in Marion Potts' version of
Venus + Adonis (2008) (PHOTO JEFF BUSBY)

Andrea Demetriades as
Marina in *Pericles* (2009)
(PHOTO WENDY McDOUGALL)

Marcus Graham as Pericles (2009) (PHOTO WENDY McDOUGALL)

Myself as Lear with Peter Carroll as The Fool, *King Lear* (2010)
(PHOTO WENDY McDOUGALL)

After God, Shakespeare created most.

Alexandre Dumas

9

The Histories

Shakespeare's political beliefs are as elusive as his religion, his sexuality and just about everything else about him that matters. Precisely because he was not an apologist for any single position, it has been possible for the plays to be effectively reinterpreted in the light of each successive age. In the four centuries since his death, he has been made the apologist for all sorts of diametrically opposed ideologies, many of them anachronistic—we should not forget that he was writing before the time when toleration and liberal democracy became totemic values.

JONATHAN BATE, *Soul of the Age*

Some of Shakespeare's plays go in and out of fashion. It may take a landmark production or individual's performance to bring a play back into vogue. The four great Tragedies are the most resilient (partly because they offer 'star' vehicles to actors) along with certain of the Comedies. Others (despite their remarkable qualities) will never be in the top ten for the theatre-going public, beloved as they may be among the literati:

plays like *Measure for Measure, Troilus and Cressida* and *Timon of Athens*. Modern audiences can't grapple with them; they are too ambivalent, brooding and unsettling—not a 'feel-good' night at the theatre.

The Histories need constant reinvestigation, especially here in Australia. Native Brits have a headstart because they own the content and know something of the territory. Even if they don't know the history at least the place names are familiar.

For some Australians, still trying to overcome our 'cultural cringe' or disowning a heritage of monarchy and British imperialism, Shakespeare's historical chronicles might be seen as irrelevant and resistible.

'Oh, I can't be doing with those plays!' a lady said to me. 'All those names and all those kings!'

But the Histories are about a lot more than kings and chronicles. They provide political commentary, satire and wry comedy. They have an epic sweep that can be viscerally exciting. They are about treachery, ambition, idealism and dirty deals. Above all, they are about family—fathers and sons, brothers and cousins, wives and lovers. They are packed with great characters, great scenes and great roles for actors. And, most importantly, they are packed with humanity. A production that is dry, pedantic, cold or overly intellectual will confirm an audience's worst fears about history plays. Shakespeare's Histories are emotionally driven: passion, rashness, hate and envy are things we can all relate to. And we can watch in sadness and in horror to see how these primal forces dictate men's actions and shape the course of human affairs. And whether we're talking about medieval England, twentieth-century Europe or contemporary Australia, the patterns and archetypes are disturbingly familiar.

Shakespeare's tragic heroes exist on a higher plane. We can marvel at their sufferings but hardly expect to share their experiences. The people in his history plays inhabit a world much closer to our own. We know these people from everyday experience. The crimes they commit and the mistakes they make are the stuff of the daily press. Forget 'all those names and all those kings'; Shakespeare's Histories are relevant to us in a profound and satisfying way. It is the job of the actor and director to make that plain.

There are ten 'history' plays in all; that is, plays based on actual English history, starting with *King John* then skipping to *Richard II*. From here we run in an unbroken historical sequence through the reigns of Henry IV, Henry V, Henry VI, Edward IV and Richard III. There's another small break, jumping over Henry VII, but we pick up again with *Henry VIII* (or *All Is True*), written by Shakespeare in collaboration with John Fletcher. It's tempting to add *Edward III* to the top of the list. The authorship is disputed but Shakespeare may well have had a hand in it.

I have directed or acted in all of them except *King John* and *Henry VIII*. (I don't know anybody else who's been in those two either.)

Henry IV

I'm very attached to all of the Histories but my firm favourites are both the *Henry IV* plays. They should be seen more often, but I guess the sheer scale of them and the size of cast required puts them out of reach for a lot of theatre companies.

Their crowning glory is Falstaff. It's the only major Shakespeare role I have not played and have a yearning for. But I'm apprehensive about it—I might be totally miscast. Along with Hamlet, Cleopatra and Rosalind, Falstaff is a character of such genius he seems to have invented himself. You can't imagine how any author could have thought him up. It has often been remarked that he seems to have a life independent of the play. He has just dropped in, so to speak. Elizabeth I thought so too. According to legend she liked Falstaff so much she asked Shakespeare to write a play showing the fat knight in love—so Shakespeare whipped up *Merry Wives of Windsor* in a fortnight.

Falstaff is an uncanny mix of cunning and innocence, of largesse and self-interest. He is the father of mirth and carries laughter wherever he goes. Moreover, he realises that he is not only witty in himself but also the cause of wit in other men. Despite his grandiose swagger he has the human failings of gluttony, sloth and cowardice, with which we can all identify. He has a natural dignity that is never swamped by his utter shamelessness. Nothing can subdue his zest for life, and this is his greatest attribute.

We travel a long road with Falstaff and are privy to his many moods, including the pathos of old age and the pain of rejection. His wit has a quicksilver brilliance. He can be disarmingly shrewd and candid. But there is an overweening ambition to Falstaff, a monstrous gulf that cannot be filled. When he hears that the old king is dead and his protégé is now Harry V, he flourishes his fist in the face of all civil authority and invokes a vision of chaos and misrule:

> Let us take any man's horses: the laws of England are at my commandment,
> Blessed are they that have been my friends;
> And woe to my Lord Chief Justice!

Finally Falstaff has to go. But the *Henry IV* plays are stuffed with a multitude of great characters besides Falstaff. There is the enigmatic and fascinating Prince Hal, his low-life sidekicks Poins, Bardolph and Pistol; the fiery and glamorous Hotspur, the mad Welsh wizard Glendower, the deliciously observed Mistress Quickly and Doll Tearsheet, the quirky old country justices Shallow and Silence, the autocratic and guilt-ridden King Henry himself, along with a score of brilliant cameo sketches.

A whole nation is set before us like a vast Brueghel landscape, so populous, so detailed. From the cold and lonely court of Westminster we flee with Hal to the warm, riotous embrace of the Boar's Head Tavern.

We travel from the wild Welsh marches through the countryside of Shrewsbury with Henry's army . . . We go from Northumberland's castle in Warkworth to the streets of Cheapside and Eastcheap, to York and the Archbishop's palace, through a forest in Yorkshire and to Justice Shallow's farm in delightful Gloucestershire, where we come across the pathetic army conscripts Mouldy, Wart, Feeble and Bullcalf.

Shakespeare uses the polarities of the court and the tavern not only to show us the diversity of English life and society but to let the one comment on the other. At Westminster King Henry rules in bitter loneliness. In the tavern Falstaff is king, sitting on his throne with a cushion on his head in mockery of a crown, surrounded by mirth and ribaldry. He conducts a mock interview with his 'son', the prodigal Prince Harry—a travesty of the painful father/son reconciliation scenes to come.

In contrast to the japes of Hal and Falstaff we have the cold-blooded realpolitik of Hal's sibling, Prince John of Lancaster. Having made a peace deal with the rebels, Prince John executes the lot of them with the pious exclamation, 'God, and not we, hath safely fought today.'

Pragmatism runs in the family. On his deathbed Henry laments the fact that his kingdom is factious and rebellious. He shrewdly advises his eldest son to 'busy giddy minds with foreign quarrels', thereby setting the scene for a totally unjustified invasion of France and the creation of a cult of the national hero.

Prince Hal himself is the arch-pragmatist, which makes him easy to play because his motivation is unambiguous. But it can make him difficult to empathise with unless one offsets the ruthless pragmatism with some sterling virtues.

I played Prince Hal in a highly successful production at Sydney's Nimrod Theatre in 1978. It was directed by Richard Wherrett with something resembling a medieval set and costumes. We combined the two parts of *Henry IV* into one fairly long evening accompanied by a 'medieval banquet' in the foyer during interval. Frank Wilson played a raffish Falstaff with a whiff of the Australian racetrack about him. I enjoyed our scenes together as Frank was a natural comedian and song-and-dance man. Comedy and pathos came easily to him, along with a natural insouciance.

Hal's strategy is made clear right from the start. He has observed his father's tactics and found them wanting. King Henry's concept of kingship is aloofness:

> By being seldom seen, I could not stir
> But like a comet I was wondered at . . .

Hal, on the other hand, is determined to get to know his subjects and speak their language:

> I am sworn brother to a leash of drawers [tavern waiters], and can call them all by their Christian names, as Tom, Dick and Francis . . . when I am king of England, I shall command all the good lads in Eastcheap.

This is a strategy he follows through when he is King, all the way to Agincourt. Before that famous battle he again calls his troupes by name—

> Harry the king, Bedford and Exeter,
> Warwick and Talbot, Salisbury and Gloucester

—and assures them that together they make up

> We few, we happy few, we band of brothers.

Hal is an absolute master of spin and supremely conscious of the effect he is having. He is determined that in his youth he will be a popular scapegrace, one of the lads, but when the time comes to assume his kingly responsibilities, he will dump all his old companions and dazzle the world with his reformation:

> So when this loose behaviour I throw off,
> And pay the debt I never promised,
> By how much better than my word I am
> By so much shall I falsify men's hopes;
> And like bright metal on a sullen ground,
> My reformation, glittering o'er my fault,
> Shall show more goodly and attract more eyes
> Than that which hath no foil to set it off.
> I'll so offend to make offence a skill,
> Redeeming time when men least think I will.

This game plan is carried out with calculated efficiency: on the day of Hal's coronation all his old companions are arrested and carted off into obscurity. This behaviour is chilling but is consistent with Hal's subsequent behaviour.

So, in playing him what does the actor look for?

For a start, there is a vulnerability in Hal. He is the eldest son of an iron-willed autocrat with whom he has little in common. One can't help but side with him when he seeks to let loose and have fun with his mates at the Boar's Head. He desperately craves his father's approval and admiration and is cut to the quick when the King sings the praises of Harry Percy, the gallant Hotspur:

> I will redeem all this on Percy's head,
> And in the closing of some glorious day
> Be bold to tell you that I am your son ...
> And that shall be the day, whene'er it lights,
> That this same child of honour and renown,
> This gallant Hotspur, this all-praised knight,
> And your unthought-of Harry chance to meet.

The Histories

It is easy for a young actor to identify with these aspects of Hal—the resentful teenager rebelling against an autocratic father yet desperately seeking his approval; what amounts to a sibling rivalry with the show pony Hotspur, and the desire to escape the close confines of stuffy respectability and sow a few wild oats. It seems to be the destined path for many a Prince of Wales.

There is a wit and ingenuity in Hal; there is a love of life and adventure and a good deal of generosity—when it suits him. He covers up for Falstaff in an embarrassing confrontation with the Sheriff and, despite the cruelty of his rejection of Falstaff, there is provision made for his future.

Hal has a sense of honour and is big enough to admire Hotspur's qualities, yet one cannot afford to sentimentalise him or apologise for his ruthlessness. He is above all a realist—not altogether admirable but nor is he devious like his younger brother. When Falstaff challenges him, 'Banish plump Jack, and banish all the world,' Hal warns him: 'I do. I will.'

For me the sustaining interest in *Henry IV* is the emotional triangle between Hal, his father and his surrogate father, Falstaff. The latter gives him the affection and companionship his real father denies him, but Hal is shrewd enough to recognise Falstaff's self-interest and ambition. In spite of Falstaff's enormous appeal he is a fraud, a liar and a user of people. He is quite brazen and unrepentant in his misuse of his office as a recruiting sergeant. He tries to enlist wealthy yeomen's sons who will pay a bribe to be excused. The recruits he is left with are feeble and useless to the army, but Falstaff callously dismisses them as 'food for powder; they'll fill a pit as well as better'.

Hal is one of Shakespeare's 'new men', whom he seems to regard with a mixture of fascination and distaste. They are creatures of the Renaissance, students of Machiavelli—shrewd, calculating and cold-hearted. At their best they are men like Hal and Falconbridge in *King John*. At their worst, Iago in *Othello* and *King Lear*'s Edmund. *Macbeth*'s Malcolm is one of them, Octavius in *Julius Caesar* another and so is

Hamlet's Young Fortinbras. They always come out on top but you wouldn't necessarily want to get too close to them.

Despite the inevitability of the new men and the triumph of Elizabethan 'policy', one feels that a lot of Shakespeare's sympathy and affection belongs to an older England, the carnival riot of Falstaff and chivalric flourishes of Hotspur. With the death of those two, the last vestiges of medieval England fade away.

Henry IV is an easily accessible play even though some of the prose vernacular is a little arcane. But it's wonderful stuff, recorded with such accuracy. One of my favourite passages is often cut in production, for various reasons: to save time; to reduce cast size; and because it seems irrelevant to the action. But it's a little window into London life as Shakespeare witnessed it. Two carriers are stabling their horses for the night and whingeing about the pub they are staying in:

[ACT II, Scene 1. Rochester. *An inn yard*]

Enter a Carrier with a lantern in his hand.

First Carrier:	Heigh-ho! An it be not four by the day, I'll be hanged. Charles' wain is over the new chimney, and yet our horse not packed. What, ostler!
Ostler:	[*Within*] Anon, anon.
First Carrier:	I prithee, Tom, beat Cut's saddle, put a few flocks in the point; the poor jade is wrung in the withers out of all cess.

Enter another Carrier.

Second Carrier:	Peas and beans are as dank here as a dog, and that is the next way to give poor jades the bots. This house is turned upside down since Robin Ostler died.
First Carrier:	Poor fellow never joyed since the price of oats rose; it was the death of him.

Second Carrier: I think this be the most villainous house in all London road for fleas: I am stung like a tench.

First Carrier: Like a tench? By the mass, there is ne'er a king christen could be better bit than I have been since the first cock.

Second Carrier: Why, they will allow us ne'er a jordan, and then we leak in your chimney, and your chamber-lye breeds fleas like a loach.

First Carrier: What, ostler! Come away and be hanged! Come away!

Second Carrier: I have a gammon of bacon and two razes of ginger, to be delivered as far as Charing Cross.

First Carrier: God's body! The turkeys in my pannier are quite starved. What, ostler! A plague on thee, hast thou never an eye in thy head? Canst not hear? And 'twere not as good deed as drink to break the pate on thee, I am a very villain. Come, and be hanged! Hast no faith in thee?

I directed *Henry IV* for Bell Shakespeare in 1998 and it was one of the most personally satisfying productions I have done. As with the Nimrod production of 1978 I conflated the two plays into one evening, sacrificing a large chunk of Part 2, which deals with a second rebellion being quelled by John of Lancaster. This was because I wanted to concentrate on that intimate three-way struggle between Hal, Falstaff and King Henry. It's nothing new: Orson Welles created a notable version along the same lines. He played Falstaff as well as directing, and after the successful stage version made the film *Chimes at Midnight*.

But whereas both Welles and Richard Wherrett in his Nimrod production had gone for a medieval look, I wanted to bring the plays sharply into focus as a comment on contemporary Britain and examine Australian attitudes to monarchy, war and family.

Justin Kurzel's set featured a steep cement ramp with piles of furniture strewn either side, as if a highway had been driven through a housing estate, sweeping aside the people. Industrial wire gates could seal off the ramp when necessary. Furniture was scavenged from the rubble when required but most of the props were mimed, and minimal. Clothes denoted both rank and location: the tavern habitués wore second-hand cast-offs, the court three-piece suits and the northern rebels fur-lined coats. Alan John's music score was heavy rock (four of the cast played electric guitar) which could accommodate war-like anthems. Hal and Hotspur were locked inside a wire cage for their knife fight while their supporters bashed on the wire and egged them on with football-hooligan chants. The battle scenes were ugly brawls stripped of any semblance of chivalry.

The ironic tone of the production is probably best illustrated by the treatment of King Henry's soliloquy in Act III, Scene 1. He bemoans the burden of kingship and envies the lot of the simple citizen. Instead of keeping Henry safely closeted in his royal apartments, I brought him out into the street. The stage was littered with bodies huddled under blankets or taking refuge in cardboard boxes, coughing, wheezing and moaning in their sleep, just as I've seen them under the bridges along South Bank in London. The King, warmly wrapped in his overcoat and muffler, wandered among them, commenting on their good fortune:

Then, happy low, lie down;
Uneasy lies the head that wears a crown.

I think the production said a lot about Australian attitudes not only to the monarchy and the English class system, but about war, violence, mateship, sexism and what constitutes 'honour'.

John Gaden's Falstaff could be sly and lewd yet move with ease up and down the social scale, while Joel Edgerton's Hal endowed the troubled teenager with a fundamental decency.

Henry V

This is probably the play that opened the Globe Theatre in 1599. Shakespeare finished it in a hurry amid rumours that the Master of the Revels would soon prohibit all re-enactments of English history on the stage. Where the preceding plays are a sprawling human epic, *Henry V* is more like a pageant and is somewhat harder to bring off today. But that's a recent phenomenon: the play was enormously popular throughout the nineteenth century (in England at least), representing the very essence of Empire and 'Rule Britannia'. The play's popularity peaked again during the outbursts of patriotic fervour that accompanied both World Wars.

But war has begun to look decidedly less glamorous in the wake of the Holocaust and subsequent conflicts, including Vietnam and Iraq, and other atrocities around the globe. We can no longer be fobbed off with patriotic headlines and spin in the daily newspapers but have immediate footage beamed into our living rooms.

Laurence Olivier was withdrawn from the British Royal Navy's Fleet Air Arm to make a propaganda movie in 1943. It was to be a patriotic morale booster for troops and civilians alike. Olivier chose *Henry V*. The story he told goes like this:

Henry V is a dashing young English king who is insulted by the French crown prince. Henry V responds by invading France to reclaim territories that are rightly his. After a series of quick victories he finds himself confronted by a huge French army with his own greatly outnumbered. Despite this, he rallies his troops and scores a stunning victory at Agincourt. He woos and marries the beautiful French princess and all ends in peace and happiness.

To ensure the film's wide appeal, Olivier made it extremely picturesque and escapist. The charming landscapes were based on the gorgeous medieval miniatures in *Les très riches heures du Duc de Berry*, a Book of Hours illustrated by Peter and Paul de Limbourg. To overcome the slight embarrassment that the enemy was not German but French (Britain's ally), the French king was made into a harmless old duffer and the Constable of France a warmly attractive 'good sport'. The Battle of Agincourt was a colourful and bloodless affair—a bit like a footy grand final—and to distance the play still further from uncomfortable reality, it was set within the framework of a performance at the Globe Theatre. These were just a bunch of actors 'putting on a play'. As a populist morale booster the film was a great success, but as a serious interpretation of Shakespeare's play there was a lot missing. Kenneth Branagh's film version filled in some of the gaps: his Battle of Agincourt was a grisly affair, as was his capture of Harfleur. He included some of Henry's ruthless acts (which Olivier chose to omit), such as the executions of his treacherous nobles and his old mate Bardolph. Both versions chose to overlook Henry's slaughter of his French prisoners in their desire to keep the eponymous hero as attractive as possible.

Now let's look at an alternative reading of the story as Shakespeare tells it:

A new young king inherits from his usurper father a kingdom that is factious and rebellious. His legitimacy as king is questionable. With his dying breath the father advises the son to 'giddy busy minds with foreign quarrels'; a patriotic war will deflect rebellion, unite the country and make the new king a national hero. English pride will be restored by the reclaiming of territories held by the French. The new King Henry bullies and blackmails the Church into sanctioning his cause. If the bishops refuse:

> We lose the better half of our possession;
> For all the temporal lands which men devout
> By testament have given to the Church
> Would they strip from us.

With the Church's blessing Henry undertakes a war of invasion, using as a pretext a minor insult from the French Dauphin. When Harfleur resists his attack he threatens them:

> ... why, in a moment look to see
> The blind and bloody soldier with foul hand
> Defile the locks of your shrill-shrieking daughters;
> Your fathers taken by the silver beards,
> And their most reverend heads dashed to the walls;
> Your naked infants spitted upon pikes,
> Whiles the mad mothers with their howls confused
> Do break the clouds, as did the wives of Jewry
> At Herod's bloody-hunting slaughtermen.
> What say you? Will you yield, and this avoid?
> Or, guilty in defence, be thus destroyed?

Olivier and Branagh chose to leave that out too. It is somewhat at odds with Henry's pious statement earlier on: 'We are no tyrant, but a Christian King.'

Shakespeare's Henry sets a trap for three of his nobles who are planning to assassinate him. He refuses to show them mercy, nor is he merciful to poor old Bardolph, who is hanged for robbing a church. But his most heinous act takes place during the Battle of Agincourt. Thousands of French nobles have surrendered and are rounded up as prisoners. The scattered French forces regroup and threaten to attack Henry's rear. He cannot fight this rearguard and risk the prisoners' escape, so he orders 'every soldier kill his prisoners!' Even by medieval standards this was a war crime against all rules of chivalry. It was also unpopular with the soldiers, who could expect a princely ransom for each prisoner—dead they were worth nothing. Tactically speaking maybe Henry was right, but it leaves an ugly stain on his reputation, which is why most productions skate over the moment or omit it altogether.

In my Bell Shakespeare production of 1999 I chose instead to highlight the incident. When Henry gave the order, his generals stood in shocked silence and would not move. Henry took out his revolver, pointed it at an officer's head and commanded, 'Give the word through.' The officer reluctantly obeyed.

Why did Shakespeare include the incident? Because he wanted to show us all sides of war. Henry's motivation in going to war is made very clear, as are the motives of the common soldiers and camp followers. Pistol sums it up best:

> ... I shall sutler [providore] be
> Unto the camp, and profits will accrue ...
> Let us to France, like horse-leeches, my boys,
> To suck, to suck, the very blood to suck!

The yeomen's, farmers' and peasants' sons drafted into the army have no illusions about the glamour of war as one of them says:

> But if the cause be not good, the King himself hath a heavy reckoning to make, when all those legs and arms and heads, chopped off in a battle, shall join together at the latter day and cry all, 'We died at such a place,' some swearing, some crying for a surgeon, some upon their wives left poor behind them, some upon the debts they owe, some upon their children rawly left. I am afeard there are few die well that die in a battle; for how can they charitably dispose of anything when blood is their argument? Now, if these men do not die well, it will be a black matter for the King that led them to it ...

This is a stinging rebuke to the King and the last thing he wants to hear the night before the battle. But Shakespeare places it very deliberately.

In case we haven't got the point about Henry's ruthlessness, Gower and Fluellen enter to debate the King's action, with Gower declaring:

> ... the King most worthily hath caused every soldier to cut his prisoner's throat. O, 'tis a gallant king!

As if that were not irony enough, Fluellen enthusiastically agrees, comparing Harry to Alexander the Great, but with a sting:

Fluellen: ... as Alexander killed his friend Cleitus, being in his ales and his cups, so also Harry Monmouth, being in his right wits and good judgements, turned away the fat knight with the great belly doublet—he was full of jests and gipes, and knaveries and mocks; I have forgot his name.
Gower: Sir John Falstaff.
Fluellen: That is he: I'll tell you there is good men porn at Monmouth.

It is an odd moment, at the height of Henry's glorious victory, for us to be reminded of his heartlessness in banishing Falstaff. The fat knight dies again before our eyes and the last glimmering rays of Old England die with him.

Just before Henry forces the French king to surrender his daughter in marriage, the Duke of Burgundy gives an eloquent and moving description of the devastated French landscape, bringing the horrors of war vividly into focus and, to drive a final nail into the coffin of chivalry, the epilogue reminds us that the whole campaign was fought in vain: following Henry's death a few years later, the French regained all their territories and England collapsed into the bloody epoch known as the Wars of the Roses ... *Curtain*.

How are we meant to react? Are we meant to cheer for Harry, England and Saint George? Are we meant to applaud the number of the slaughtered French? To be tickled by the forced marriage of the young princess? Many directors these days set out to present *Henry V* as an anti-war play. This takes considerable dexterity and demands as much fiddling with the text as it does to present it as a pro-war play. The text defeats you: there is too strong a presence of genuine heroics and celebration. The only realistic approach is to regard the play as neither anti- nor pro-war but *about* war in all its aspects; and, much as we may dislike it, there are aspects of war, while it is happening, that many people respond to with enthusiasm.

We must also take on board the fact that warfare is a different business today to what it was in Shakespeare's day. From the time of Homer up until the early twentieth century, poets have sung of 'the pride, pomp and circumstance of glorious war'—as well as its horrors and waste. World War I and poets like Wilfred Owen changed all that. But in 1600 the chivalric exploits of Sir Philip Sidney and the Earl of Essex still stirred men's hearts. Shakespeare was twenty-four at the time of the Armada—still young and excitable enough to get caught up in the national fever of celebration attending the Armada's defeat. Patriotic feelings were running high: the little island was asserting itself and beating off a huge invading force that meant to enslave it. In Elizabeth, England had a bold and charismatic leader with a great talent for rhetoric.

Ten years after the Armada's defeat, the Globe needed a celebratory pageant for its opening season. *Henry V* recalls the glory days of the Armada and Elizabeth's stirring address to her troops at Tilbury:

> I know I have the body of a weak and feeble woman, but I have the heart and stomach of a king, and of a king of England too ... Not doubting but by your concord in the camp and valour in the field and your obedience to myself and my general, we shall shortly have a famous victory over these enemies of my God and of my kingdom.

We can hear the echo of this in King Harry's:

> And Crispin Crispian shall ne'er go by
> From this day to the ending of the world
> But we in it shall be remembered,
> We few, we happy few, we band of brothers.

Warfare retained something of its glamour right through the nineteenth century with its drums, bugles, resplendent uniforms and cavalry charges. The carnage of battles like Waterloo was glorified in heroic canvases. But the development of modern weaponry has put the kybosh on 'glorious war', apart from individual acts of heroism and self-sacrifice. Perhaps the most pathetic image of this catastrophe is to be seen in photos of the Polish cavalry in World War I (decked out in armour with angels' wings) charging the German machine guns. In the wake of World War I, Hiroshima, Vietnam, the peace movement, Iraq, wide-scale civilian casualties and massacres, there's precious little positive spin even the most hawkish commentator can put on war. It's no longer a small-scale affair but involves weapons of mass destruction and fears of a nuclear holocaust.

So is it still possible to put on *Henry V*? It certainly is, but one needs a context. When I joined the RSC in 1965 I was given a couple of small roles (Gloucester, Governor of Harfleur, etc.) in the Barton–Hall *Henry V* with Ian Holm as Henry and Ian Richardson as Chorus. The compact Holm was like a plucky, shaggy Welsh pony and the French campaign recalled the Somme, with soldiers caked in mud dragging heavy wagons. The costumes had an earthy, homespun medieval reality and stood in sharp contrast to Chorus, who was a glamorous Elizabethan courier. This was a neat idea: the rhapsodic and unapologetic jingoism of Chorus was subverted by the ugly face of war itself.

When I came to direct *Henry V* for Bell Shakespeare in 1999 I was much perplexed as to context. The mood of the day was even more anti-war than it had been back at the RSC in 1965. The closest I could get the play to a contemporary setting was 1914. This seemed to me to be the last time the lads (whether British or Australian) sailed off voluntarily, innocent and enthusiastic, to fight on foreign soil. Prompted by the image of Kitchener and music-hall patriotic songs, they displayed a pathetic idealism and naivety. In newsreels of the day we watch them cheerily waving goodbye and we know the horrors awaiting them.

Our stage proscenium was decorated with patriotic bunting and a huge poster of Kitchener served as the backdrop. Music-hall songs were interspersed throughout the action, which was kept as grimly realistic as possible. Joel Edgerton's Henry was a decent and candid young soldier, no chauvinist bully. I found an Australian connection by making the three discontented soldiers (Bates, Court and Williams) Aussie diggers. These are the three who have no respect for rank or title; Bates says of the King:

> He may show what outward courage he will; but I believe, as cold a night as 'tis, he could wish himself in Thames up to the neck; and so I would he were, and I by him, at all adventures, so we were quit here.

Henry came across them sitting around their campfire, boiling the billy and mournfully playing 'Waltzing Matilda' on a mouth organ.

I'm sure many a digger on the Somme felt a similar disenchantment with 'God, King and Country'.

I was reasonably satisfied with the production and served by an excellent cast, but I still felt frustrated that it remained a 'period' piece. I would have loved to have found a way to bring it right into line with here and now. The play still has enough resonance to make that possible. And the King's great orations are masterpieces of spin. They are often played as if the second ('St Crispin's Day') is merely an echo of the first ('Once more unto the breach'), but in fact they are very different. 'Once more unto the breach' is full-on rhetoric and hyperbole and demands a bravura delivery. The heroics are shot through with xenophobia ('Be copy now to men of grosser blood/And teach them how to war!'), personal provocation ('Dishonour not your mothers; now attest that those whom you called fathers did beget you!') and appeals to national sentiment ('... And you, good Yeomen, whose limbs were made in England, show us here the mettle of your pasture'). The speech is rousing, confronting, virtually irresistible and has the desired effect on troops and audience alike. This is the speech that leads to victory at Harfleur.

When it comes time for the Crispin's Day speech, Henry is in a very different situation. The victory at Harfleur is a distant memory. The campaign has dragged on for months and the English army is now bogged down in the middle of France, dispirited, sick, weary and depleted in numbers. Henry has spent the night before the great battle walking about the camp, listening to the apprehensions of his troops and undergoing something of a dark night of the soul. Fears about the legitimacy of his crown come flooding back as well as a general disenchantment with the very notion of kingship:

> . . . O, be sick, great greatness,
> And bid thy ceremony give thee cure!
> Think'st thou the fiery fever will go out
> With titles blown from adulation?

Earlier on he has admitted to his troops,

> The King is but a man, as I am: the violet smells to him as it doth to me . . . His ceremonies laid by, in his nakedness he appears but a man.

In this one hears echoes of King Lear; for a 'patriotic' play, *Henry V* sometimes sails close to sedition. Shakespeare's great political cunning is in putting these sentiments in the mouth not of a malcontent, but of the King himself.

Next morning he faces his troops on the field of Agincourt. They are outnumbered five to one. Time for another rousing speech . . . But this time it's a different kind of rhetoric. Henry realises that barnstorming isn't going to work; he looks around for inspiration. Ian Holm found a nice bit of business for this moment: one of the soldiers was kneeling in prayer, reading from his missal. Henry glanced over his shoulder and noticed that the nominated Feast Day was that of Saint Crispin and Saint Crispian, martyrs. He took the missal, looked at it thoughtfully and murmured, 'This day is called the Feast of Crispian . . .' The speech was improvised from there. It's a quiet, homely speech—no grandiose words or sentiments. Henry calls all his comrades by name (including himself, 'Harry the King') and conjures images of rural England, of neighbours feasting, drinking, good men teaching their sons and comparing their battle scars. There's no jot of doubt that they are going to win and return home. This quiet assurance reaches its apogee with:

> We few, we happy few, we band of brothers;
> For he today that sheds his blood with me
> Shall be my brother; be he ne'er so vile,
> This day shall gentle his condition.

No one has ever stopped to ask whether, after the battle, this promise is kept. By contrasting those two speeches one gets a very clear picture of Henry's qualities as a leader. The art of diplomacy is largely knowing what to say and when.

So was Henry Shakespeare's ideal king? It's hard to say. Shakespeare seemed fascinated and repelled by him at the same time. He's undoubtedly effective, but too reminiscent of Shakespeare's other 'new men', cold-blooded pragmatists like Malcolm, Fortinbras and Octavius. His brutality is often veiled by the kind of piety we find in Richard III. But without that cold-blooded pragmatism how do you rule effectively? This is a question Shakespeare poses over and over. There is nothing inherently wrong with having power, but as Brutus notes:

> The abuse of greatness is when it disjoins Remorse from power . . .

Shakespeare might have admired King Henry, but he loved Falstaff.

By the time he wrote the two parts of *Henry IV*, Shakespeare had fully mastered the art of characterisation. Characters such as Nym, Bardolph, Pistol, Doll, Mistress Quickly and especially Falstaff are so original, so spontaneous and individual, that they seem to write their own scripts. The machinations of the author cannot be detected. As Hazlitt puts it: 'all the persons concerned must have been present in the Poet's imagination, as at a kind of rehearsal, so that whatever passed through their minds passed through his.'

In *Henry V* the robust heroic verse is interspersed with the most natural-sounding and easy-flowing prose, as if Shakespeare had simply lifted his characters off the street outside the Globe and deposited them on the stage. Those who suggest that *Henry V* is simply a pageant without much plot—an invasion, a battle and a love scene—miss the point that the real plot of *Henry V* is the ongoing debate about war. We hear it from a conglomeration of disparate voices: the crafty churchmen, the grotty camp followers, the decent common soldiers, the boy who grows increasingly cynical and disenchanted, and the King himself, who adopts various voices and modes of speech to suit the occasion.

King John

As I mentioned earlier, I have been involved with all of Shakespeare's history plays except two, *King John* and *Henry VIII*.

Why does no one put on *King John*? It really is a most interesting play with great scenes and great characters. If I put the question to myself as to why *I* have never put the play on, I guess it comes back to the boring old matter of box office. Would there be an audience for it? I hope I get the chance to find out one day. Admittedly, King John himself is not a charismatic drawcard; he is wily, cowardly and treacherous. And apart from defying the power of the Pope and making a stand for English

Protestantism, the play is not a great historical epic. (It doesn't even mention Magna Carta!)

The play is more concerned with personalities than historical chronicle. Constance may be the last of Shakespeare's wailing women but she is no mere choric figure like the queens in *Richard III*. Her grief is humanised and affecting:

> I am not mad: this hair I tear is mine;
> My name is Constance, I was Geoffrey's wife;
> Young Arthur is my son, and he is lost!
> I am not mad: I would to heaven I were,
> For then 'tis like I should forget myself!
> O, if I could, what grief should I forget!
> Preach some philosophy to make me mad,
> And thou shalt be canonized, Cardinal.

Falconbridge is by far the most interesting character in the play. The bastard son of Richard the Lionheart, he is the only 'good' bastard in Shakespeare. *Lear*'s Edmund and *Much Ado*'s Don John are embittered and malevolent social outcasts, but Falconbridge wears his bastardy as a badge of independence, of someone standing outside conventional pieties, relying on his own integrity and conscience—a good Protestant. He chooses a different path to that taken by Edmund, and is more akin to the gallant Hotspur in his disdain for self-interest, 'commodity':

> That smooth-faced gentleman, tickling commodity;
> Commodity, the bias of the world,
> The world, who of itself is peised well,
> Made to run even upon even ground,
> Till this advantage, this vile-drawing bias,
> This sway of motion, this commodity,
> Makes it take head from all indifferency,

From all direction, purpose, course, intent.
And this same bias, this commodity,
This bawd, this broker, this all-changing word,
Clapped on the outward eye of fickle France,
Hath drawn him from his own determined aid,
From a resolved and honourable war,
To a most base and vile-concluded peace.
And why rail I on this commodity?
But for because he hath not wooed me yet:
Not that I have the power to clutch my hand,
When his fair angels would salute my palm,
But for my hand, as unattempted yet,
Like a poor beggar, raileth on the rich.
Well, whiles I am a beggar, I will rail
And say there is no sin but to be rich;
And being rich, my virtue then shall be
To say there is no vice but beggary.
Since kings break faith upon commodity,
Gain, be my lord, for I will worship thee!

This easygoing cynicism smacks of Edmund or even Iago, but Falconbridge is unlike the other 'new men' in that he has a heart. Note his compassion as he watches Hubert pick up the body of young Prince Arthur, who has leapt off the castle walls to escape his murderous uncle, King John:

Go, bear him in thine arms.
I am amazed, methinks, and lose my way
Among the thorns and dangers of this world.
How easy dost thou take all England up!
From forth this morsel of dead royalty,
The life, the right and truth of all this realm
Is fled to heaven . . .

And following King John's ignominious death, poisoned by a monk, Falconbridge finishes the play with a stirring and patriotic call to arms:

> This England never did, nor never shall,
> Lie at the proud foot of a conqueror
> But when it first did help to wound itself.
> Now these her princes are come home again,
> Come the three corners of the world in arms,
> And we shall shock them! Naught shall make us rue
> If England to itself do rest but true!

With its strong Protestant bias, *King John* provides a few problems for those who would like to see Shakespeare as a devout Catholic.

Richard II

Richard II is a more accomplished and satisfying play and, again, performed too infrequently. Maybe the poetry seems too ornate and self-conscious for contemporary tastes, but it's very appropriate to the character of King Richard, a selfish peacock. He's not a particularly admirable character—but how many of Shakespeare's kings are? Those who see Shakespeare as a staunch monarchist are missing out on levels of irony and subversion.

The play was very popular throughout the nineteenth century and the first half of the twentieth, when public attitude to the monarchy was more romantic and nostalgic than it is today. John Gielgud's classic performance embodied all that was sonorous, effete and decorative in the role. But since the 1960s Shakespeare has been considerably butched up.

The mid-century revolution in theatre design and directorial aesthetics that occurred in Britain was fired by the new wave of dramatists like Osborne and Wesker, the realpolitik of Polish critic Jan Kott and the leftish putsch of Oxbridge graduates who were devotees of Brecht and the Theatre of the Absurd.

In such a climate you had to look at a play like *Richard II* critically and ironically. But then, so did Shakespeare. He exposed Richard's concept of Divine Right to be no more than a chimera. Richard fully expects angels to come and fight on his side but no angels front up. His faults are laid out before us; he is effeminate, treacherous (he is implicated in the death of Gloucester of Woodstock), cold and sarcastic when dealing with the dying John of Gaunt, unscrupulous in seizing the banished Bolingbroke's property and a weak, uninspiring military leader.

But unlike King John, Richard's faults are balanced by virtues and a humanity that eventually earn our empathy and turn him into a tragic hero. He has a great sensitivity that makes him the wrong man for the job when pitted against a pragmatist like Bolingbroke. He has intelligence, wit, a gift for poetry and rhetoric, affection for his friends and, most importantly, a growing self-awareness. He does learn something during his journey:

I wasted time, and now doth time waste me.

Richard, a delicate flower, is crushed by a brutal social environment that has no room for such an exotic. In this he reminds me of Oscar Wilde, who might serve as a role model.

While I was with the RSC I was 'loaned out' a few times to various regional companies, and I played Richard II at the Oldham Rep, outside Manchester. It was a very forgettable production but I was thrilled when the crates of hired costumes arrived from London. Mine was the costume Paul Scofield had worn when he played the role at Stratford. It was a great buzz for me to speak that wonderful verse and feel myself to be a part of that Gielgud/Scofield tradition.

Richard II came close to tipping Shakespeare into a catastrophe. The day before the Earl of Essex made his disastrous attempt to storm the court and wrest power from his enemies, his cronies commissioned a special performance of *Richard II* at the Globe on Saturday 7 February 1601. Apparently they hoped it would further their cause by demonstrating that the forced abdication of a monarch could be legitimised. The coup failed, Essex was executed and the players hauled before the authorities. Their spokesman, Augustine Phillips, was able to convince his interrogators that the actors were innocent of complicity in the plot. They had been unwilling to perform, protesting that the play was out of date and wouldn't pull an audience; but offered a forty-shilling bonus, they had agreed to play.

The players were released, but the Earl of Southampton, Shakespeare's patron, was condemned for high treason and thrown into the Tower. His death sentence was later commuted and, after Elizabeth's death, the new monarch released him. It's interesting to note that one of the interrogators in the case was Francis Bacon—one more nail in the coffin of the absurd assertion that he was the real author of Shakespeare's plays. It's also worth noting that Bacon despised the English language to the extent of writing or translating all his own works in Latin. He complained that 'these modern languages will at one time play the bankrupt with books'. Not something you'd expect from the author of the greatest plays and poems in the English language! The story of the Essex rebellion and Shakespeare's involvement in it is brilliantly recounted in Jonathan Bate's *Soul of the Age*.

Henry VI

Henry VI, among Shakespeare's earliest work, is comparatively primitive. Most of the nobles and aristocrats tend to be interchangeable. Nevertheless, looking over the vast expanse of all three *Henry VI* plays, we find a great gallery of characters: the saintly and mournful King himself, the magnificently feisty Queen Margaret, scheming Warwick, doughty York, brave Talbot, silky Somerset, the outrageous rebel Jack Cade and, coming

The Histories

up through the pack, a malevolent young hunchback named Richard, Duke of Gloucester.

To see all three plays on one day is an unforgettable theatrical experience. A great historical canvas is flung before us, its epic story crammed with plots and murders, battles and pageants, pathos and comedy. There are dozens of cameo roles that make the event an actors' feast. It is an extraordinary feat of sustained energy, storytelling, imagination and artistic control. As someone remarked, it's as if Shakespeare had launched his career by writing the *Ring Cycle*.

The big question is how a twenty-four-year-old actor and playwright came to undertake such a mighty project. He would not have ventured on it without assurance of its being produced, and it calls for a very large cast of actors with elaborate props and costumes. There are processions, coronations, battle scenes, all sorts of pomp and ceremony—making for a very lavish production, well beyond the means of most theatre companies. So someone must have commissioned it, but who? And why?

Let's take a look at Shakespeare's arrival in London . . . He probably left Stratford in 1587, aged twenty-three. That year had been a big year for theatre in Stratford. At least five major companies performed there in the Guild Hall, including Sussex's Men, Leicester's Men and the Queen's Men. The last of these was the most prestigious and had been set up in 1583 as a propaganda tool by Sir Francis Walsingham, Secretary of the Privy Council and the Queen's spymaster. Its leading actor was the great comedian Dick Tarlton. During the tour to Stratford a brawl broke out at the White Hound in the village of Thame. One of the Queen's Men, John Town, killed his fellow actor William Knell. This left the company short one actor. It's quite possible that this gave Shakespeare his break. Incidentally, Knell's sixteen-year-old widow Rebecca, nine months after her husband's death, married another actor from the troupe, John Heminges. Heminges was to become one of Shakespeare's closest friends and one of the producers of the *First Folio*.

The Queen's Men were given an agenda by Walsingham: they were primarily to spread Protestant and royalist propaganda throughout the country and their plays were to have English history themes. Their repertoire included *The Famous Victories of Henry V*, *The Troublesome Reign of King John* and *The True Tragedy of Richard III*. All the histories were labelled as 'true' but were in fact violently partisan. These were among the old plays that Shakespeare was later to revise and reimagine.

The Queen's Men toured extensively, as far as Scotland and Dublin. Among the great houses they visited was Knowsley Park, the seat of the Stanley family and its head, Ferdinando, Lord Strange.

In September 1588 the Queen's Men lost both their star player, Dick Tarlton, and their patron, Lord Dudley. A few months later Shakespeare joined a new company, Lord Strange's Men, and stayed with them for two years. The first play he wrote for them was *Titus Andronicus*, an enormous success that put its young author on the map.

Ferdinando, Lord Strange, was desperately seeking some good propaganda himself. He stood eighth in line to the throne—a bit too close for comfort, as one could always be suspected of involvement in plots and sedition. He was also the head of one of England's oldest and most staunch Catholic families and under surveillance for harbouring priests, as were other members of his family. His cousin, William Stanley, was responsible for a good deal of the regime's distrust of the family. In 1586 he served under Leicester in the Netherlands campaign, but behind his leader's back handed over Deventer to the Spanish. Three hundred of his troops who wished to remain loyal to the Queen were shipped out; the other six hundred crossed over, with Stanley, to Spain and the Catholics.

It was crucial for Ferdinando to make a public demonstration of his and his family's loyalty. What better way than by commissioning the hotshot young playwright of his own private theatre troupe to write a magnificent epic spectacular depicting the Stanleys in a good light? It would be seen on the public stage by thousands of people and would serve as a stunning piece of propaganda.

Shakespeare took to his task with enthusiasm and throughout the *Henry VI* trilogy the Stanleys feature prominently. The three plays were written and performed by Strange's Men in 1592 and were hugely popular. But Shakespeare saved his big finish for *Richard III* in 1593. Henry Tudor has arrived to liberate England from the tyrant. Shakespeare gives the Stanleys all the credit for saving the day, much exaggerating their contribution to the victory of Bosworth. In his most blatant rewriting of history, he ignores the chronicles' record that it was Richard Bray who found the dead tyrant's crown in a thornbush at the end of the battle. Shakespeare has Thomas Stanley himself pluck it 'from the dead temples of this bloody wretch' and place it on the head of Henry Tudor. What a magnificent bit of spin! According to this version it was the Stanleys who effected the end of the Plantagenets and empowered the Tudor dynasty. What more could Elizabeth ask for?

Unfortunately, the good lady seems to have been unimpressed. Suspicions against Lord Strange only increased and on 16 April 1594 he died suddenly, aged thirty-five, from a massive dose of arsenic.

Elizabeth, predictably, was distraught:

> with tears ... she professed she thought not that any man in the world loved her better than he did, that he was the most honourable, worthiest and absolutely honest man that she had in her life ever known ...

What a performer.

The first time I saw the *Henry VI* plays was a television recording of the RSC's *Wars of the Roses* produced in the mid-1960s by Peter Hall and John Barton. As I've described, for the time it was startlingly modern and topical. Costumes were still basically 'medieval' but not as glamorous and fussy as the previous generation of theatre design. The emphasis was on toughness and a simplicity of line. The sets were vast and brutal metallic walls. The acting was unaffected, anti-'poetical' and colloquial without losing its driving rhythms.

Stand-out performances included David Warner's soulful Henry VI, Brewster Mason's crafty Warwick and Peggy Ashcroft's Margaret, who grew miraculously over the course of the tetralogy from skittish schoolgirl to virago military leader to a crazed, haunted crone.

Henry VI and *Richard III* carry on the tradition of the Queen's Men history plays, but they are no longer mere propaganda pieces: they exhibit a great interest in character, aggression, the ethics of politics, the ambivalent nature of much human intercourse, role-playing and conscience.

Their popularity was vast. Henslowe's account book for the Rose Theatre in April, May and June 1592 show that *Henry VI: Part 1* was pulling an average audience of almost three thousand.

Its most popular scene depicted the death of Lord Talbot and his son at Bordeaux. The young Tom Nashe dashed off a 'Defence of plays', remarking how, despite the claims of 'some petitioners of the Council' that plays 'corrupt the youth of the city', there was a deal of patriotic fervour to be had from the theatre:

> How it would have joyed brave Talbot (the terror of the French) to think that after he had lain two hundred years in his tomb, he should triumph again on the stage, and have his bones now embalmed with the tears of ten thousand spectators at least (at several times) who, in the tragedian that represents his person, imagine they behold him fresh bleeding...

I made my own adaptation of *Henry VI* for Bell Shakespeare in 2005 under the title *Wars of the Roses*, and, for the sake of convenience, conflated the three parts into two, which I called *Henry VI* and *Edward IV*.

At first I wanted to stage *Henry VI* and *Edward IV* on alternate nights, but as budget blowouts loomed, management became increasingly nervous about attracting audiences to the theatre on successive nights. I was persuaded, with difficulty, to further conflate the plays into one evening. I kept hacking away at the script till I got it down to three hours plus interval, still a longish evening.

The play was set in a kind of gladiatorial gymnasium with galleries of metal seats where the actors sat and watched when not involved in the action. The costuming was as contemporary as possible: different sets of camouflage fatigues with the armour a conglomerate of police riot gear and the stuff you wear for protection in gridiron, ice hockey and other 'contact' sports—some of it quite bizarre.

My disappointment with the severe conflation was that there was no room for characters or relationships to develop; people were no sooner on than they were off again. When all is said and done, the main thing people want from a Shakespeare production is humanity and the interplay of characters.

Richard III

Richard III remains the most popular and frequently performed of all the Histories because it is the greatest star vehicle (although Falstaff is a greater role). It also withstands the vagaries of political change: there's no way it can be seen as a propaganda tool for the monarchy (although Olivier came surprisingly close to making it one; with a charismatic Stanley Baker as Richmond and a swelling musical score by William Walton with overtones of Elgar, he made Richard seem a mere aberration; the integrity of the crown itself remained intact).

Shakespeare's attitude is, as always, more ambivalent than that and his play has to be seen in context of the whole cycle of history plays. Jan Kott in his seminal study *Shakespeare Our Contemporary* comes closest to a modern view of the Histories, seeing them as a picture of a vast political machine somewhat akin to the Wheel of Fortune. As one protagonist sinks to the bottom, another rises to the top in an inexorable cycle. This was the image I took away from the superb Georgian production starring Ramaz Chkhikvadze which I first saw at London's Roundhouse and later at the Adelaide Festival. Richmond was a rather sinister figure: when his time came to take the crown he uttered the same manic rooster-crow that he had heard earlier from Richard.

I was lucky enough to meet Ramaz Chkhikvadze when he came to Australia. In fact he was gracious enough to come to our own version of *Richard III*, which was playing at the Theatre Royal in Sydney. He gripped my hand after the show and said, 'Very plastic! Very plastic!' I hope it was a compliment.

When I first saw Ramaz play Richard in London he had a distinctly Napoleonic look with a greatcoat, tricorn and kiss curl. (Fair enough— Napoleon was the despot who had dared invade Russia.) But when I saw the show again some years later in Adelaide, Napoleon had morphed into something resembling Stalin. When I quizzed Ramaz about this later, he gave me a wink and said, 'Ah well, times have changed . . . Richard III is always with us.' He also gave me an amusing illustration of how Soviet artists fooled bureaucratic spooks during the Iron Curtain era. When they mounted *Richard III* originally, they brought on an ailing Edward IV who was a dead ringer for Brezhnev. 'He had medals all down the front . . . even a few down the back,' chuckled Ramaz. The censors were checking out the dress rehearsal. '"Who's that supposed to be?" they snapped. "Why, it's Edward IV of England." "Are you sure?" "Of course . . ."' And the actors went on to give a very convincing pitch about Edward IV. Somehow they got away with it. 'Richard wasn't such a bad fellow,' mused Ramaz. 'He only killed fifteen people. Stalin killed twenty million.'

Unlike *Henry V*, *Richard III* is always with us. The point doesn't need hammering home as in the Ian McKellen film version which was based on the palpably false thesis that Oswald Mosley took over Britain in the 1940s.

My earliest incarnation as Richard was based on a similar thesis, only this time it was a parody. Bertolt Brecht's play *The Resistible Rise of Arturo Ui* is a blank-verse reworking of *Richard III* set in 1930s Chicago with Richard as a grotesque morphing of Al Capone and Adolf Hitler. Richard Wherrett's production of the play for Sydney's Old Tote Theatre was a great success which we subsequently revived for the Nimrod Theatre. All of Hitler's henchmen are portrayed as two-bit gangsters, idiotic and brutish. Playing a parody sometimes gets you close to the heart of the real thing: by going to the extremes of grotesque body language, emotional states and vocal gymnastics, you can release an energy and inventiveness you don't find through text study and psychoanalysis. Playfulness can get you there quicker. Brecht loved Shakespeare's theatre—its plain empty stage that can become anything you want; its rhetoric, its bawdiness, its violence and its political danger.

I've now played Richard III three times. The first was at Nimrod in a production by Richard Wherrett, designed by Kim Carpenter on a set by Larry Eastwood. We wanted something tough and menacing. Richard's vision was of an industrial site, a kind of underground boiler or furnace room with a big oven door (overtones of Auschwitz). Larry's set was entirely of the kind of metal plates you find in a factory environment and the clothes were based on uniforms of navvies and factory workers. I was also keen to toughen up the vocal delivery, to get away from polite middle- or upper-class delivery. So we invented a dialect which was a combination of Northern English (Yorkshire) and whatever research told us about Shakespeare's own Warwickshire accent. In retrospect I'm not sure how well it worked but it freed us up considerably; we were still experimenting with ways not to sound 'Shakespearean'. (We ran *Richard*

III in repertoire with my production of *Much Ado* which employed Italian greengrocer accents.)

In my determination to get away from the Olivier mould—the black-haired, saturnine reptile image—I went the other way and played Richard as a fallen angel with an innocent face and mop of blond hair. My friend Peter Kenna remarked that I 'looked like the idiot son who's been sent out to chop the wood and comes back with the axe'. I kept the disfigurement fairly subtle except for a nasty facial birthmark and a black contact lens designed to make one eye appear smaller than the other. But one night I accidentally melted it while cleaning it.

When I directed the play for Bell Shakespeare in 1992, I played Richard again and took the production in a very different direction. Our first two productions, *Hamlet* and *Merchant of Venice*, were deliberately as contemporary as possible, so I set out to confound expectations. I wanted to explore the surreal imagery and poetry of the play, its nightmare quality (dreams and nightmares feature heavily in the text). So my designer, Sue Field, and I explored Kabuki theatre, which appealed to me for its formalism and ritualistic quality; a lot of *Richard III* has echoes of the medieval Mystery Plays. My central image was that of feral animals trapped at the bottom of a well shaft, scrambling over each other in their attempt to get to the top. So in the rehearsals we did quite a lot of animal improvisations from which the designer took ideas to create costumes using fur, feathers and claws. James Wardlaw based his Buckingham on a combination of panther and snake. My own references were the fox and the wolf. My favourite was Marian Dvorokovsky's description of Lord Rivers as 'a rooster who thinks he's a peacock'. Where the production fell short was in that essential element of any Shakespeare production, humanity. The stylisation was all very well, but somehow the world you create on stage has to coincide at some point with a world the audience knows; the characters cannot become so stylised as to cease to be human. We have to share their dilemmas and their emotions.

I had my third crack at the role in 2002 when Michael Gow persuaded me we should do the play as a co-production between Bell and the Queensland Theatre Company. Michael's production concept was very different to my revious two experiences. He set the play in the late eighteenth century of Hogarth on a solidly realistic set. It looked like a combination of a Georgian house interior and the Tower of London, with a winding stone staircase and French windows with iron grilles. The set had a false perspective and slightly crazy rake that made it quite quirky. It looked fairly knocked around, as did the once-splendid costumes—now stained and tattered. The impression was one of post-war devastation, appropriate to the narrative of Richard III, who emerges at the end of the Wars of the Roses. This time I based Richard on a combination of boar and hedgehog. (That's the great thing about the role—he gets called a dog, a toad, a boar, a spider, a hedgehog—you've got a large menagerie from which to choose.)

I also determined to explore more scientifically the nature of his physical deformity and how that might impact on him psychologically. I sought the advice of a medical specialist who gave me a very precise analysis of Richard's challenges—the hunchback, the shortened leg, the withered arm—and how these would have come about. I could then talk to Robert Kemp, the costume designer, about how to build those elements into the costume so that I could really feel how Richard felt. After that, the psychology is easy and Shakespeare spells out all you need to know: Richard tells you exactly how he feels about his blighted physicality and how it poisons his outlook on the world. But I still immersed myself in literature regarding psychopaths and people devoid of empathy. As well as the obvious examples like Hitler, Stalin and Pol Pot, I tried to find people with absolutely no moral compass, no concept of the suffering of others.

The relative naturalism and historical specificity of Michael Gow's production meant I had to focus on Richard's interplay with the other characters rather than present images of moral deformity as I had tried to in my second Richard. I felt it essential that Richard exude as much charm as possible and be plausible to the people he's talking to. I saw Antony Sher in the role for the RSC, and though he was very nifty on his crutches, I found him such a snarling, sour and vitriolic character that I couldn't believe for a moment that anybody would trust or support him. Unless he convinces Lady Anne of his sincere contrition and his passion for her, she looks like a fool. So do Buckingham and Clarence unless Richard persuades them of his friendship and loyalty.

The only people who see Richard's real face are the audience; and the thrill of the performance is watching him adopt a series of masks and characteristics to suit his purpose. It's all set up in his Act III soliloquy in *Henry VI: Part 3*:

> Why, I can smile, and murder whiles I smile,
> And cry 'content' to that which grieves my heart,
> And wet my cheeks with artificial tears,
> And frame my face to all occasions.
> I'll drown more sailors than the mermaid shall;
> I'll play the orator as well as Nestor,
> Deceive more slyly than Ulysses could,
> And, like a Sinon, take another Troy.
> I can add colours to the chameleon,
> Change shapes with Proteus for advantages,
> And set the murderous Machiavel to school.
> Can I do this, and cannot get a crown?
> Tut, were it farther off, I'll pluck it down.

We feel the shiver of complicity as Richard confides in us, then sets about to ensnare his victims. Chkhikvadze took this deceitfulness to delightful extremes, dropping the limp when chatting to the audience and putting it on again when talking to the other characters. His Richard was a totally political animal, embodying the lies and violence of a hated Soviet regime. In a deeply ironic performance he created a comedic monster.

Richard has often been described as a sketch for Macbeth but *Richard III* is theatre in its own right, and its hero a marvellous creation. He has his basis in the Vice of the medieval Morality Plays, and rejoices in his pedigree; but he is one of the first of Shakespeare's true originals, a character with his own distinctive voice.

Towards the end of the play he suffers the nightmares and paranoia that Macbeth experiences on a more profound level, but otherwise the characters are remarkably dissimilar. Richard lusts after the crown from the very beginning. He hates and despises all mankind and is driven by the desire to be revenged on the world and humanity in general. He has not a jot of conscience in disposing of his brothers, his nephews, his wife or anyone who stands in his way. On the contrary, he delights in his machinations.

Macbeth, on the other hand, is a victim of conscience. He wants the crown but is 'too full of the milk of human kindness' to seize it. He has to be prompted by the witches and badgered by his wife. After he has killed Duncan he is plagued by guilt and terrible dreams. Realising there is no going back, he commissions the assassination of Banquo, which only results in a new torment, to the extent that he hallucinates. There is no character in Shakespeare with a more exquisite conscience than Macbeth.

But like Macbeth, Richard goes down fighting. Shakespeare gives both these monsters a magnificent exit, and one can't help feeling, when they're gone, that the world is a smaller place without them. You might not much like Macbeth, but the scale of his suffering is grand, as is his criminality.

King Henry VIII

Apart from *King John*, the only other Shakespeare history I haven't been involved in is *King Henry VIII*, or *All Is True*. This play was written in 1613, two years after *The Tempest*, in collaboration with John Fletcher. The play is relatively disappointing given such fantastic potential for drama—the charismatic heroic prince who grows into an obese ogre;

the saga of the six women unfortunate enough to become his wives; the birth of the English Reformation; the persecution of its Catholic martyrs... There's enough there for two or three plays, but what we get is a stately pageant with mostly choric figures. The reason is obvious: it was far too early to write a critical appraisal of that era; the dust of the Tudor dynasty had not yet settled. So the characterisation of Henry himself is necessarily bland. The play steers clear of religious controversy. But staged with full panoply the play can still work in terms of a pageant and it does boast a couple of notable characters, namely Katharine of Aragon and Cardinal Wolsey. The latter lacks personal greatness but his downfall elicits true pathos:

> ... O Cromwell, Cromwell,
> Had I but served my God with half the zeal
> I served my King, he would not in mine age
> Have left me naked to mine enemies...

Likewise, Queen Katharine in her trial scene shows courage, spirit and dignity and emerges as a true tragic heroine.

Today *Henry VIII* is best known for the fact that it was directly responsible for the destruction of the Globe Theatre. Sir Henry Wotton describes what happened at one of the first performances, on 29 June 1613:

> I will entertain you at the present with what has happened this week at the Bank's side. The King's players had a new play, called *All Is True,* representing some Principal Pieces of the Reign of Henry VIII, which was set forth with many extraordinary circumstances of pomp and majesty.
>
> Now, King Henry making a masque at the Cardinal Wolsey's house, and certain chambers being shot off at his entry, some of the paper, or other stuff, wherewith one of them was stopped, did light on the thatch, where being thought at first but an idle smoke, and

their eyes more attentive to the show, it kindled inwardly, and ran round like a train, consuming within less than an hour the whole house to the very grounds. This was the fatal period of that virtuous fabric, wherein yet nothing did perish but wood and straw, and a few forsaken cloaks; only one man had his breeches set on fire, that would perhaps have broiled him, if he had not by the benefit of a provident wit put it out with bottle ale.

With remarkable industry the King's Men set about rebuilding their theatre and within a year the new Globe arose from the ashes, bigger and better than before—and this time with a tiled roof!

•

All in all, the Histories amount to an extraordinary panorama of English history. With his *Henry VI* trilogy the twenty-something Shakespeare had achieved the greatest dramatic epic since the ancient Greeks (excluding some of the medieval Mystery cycles). From *King John* through to *Henry VIII* we get an almost unbroken chronicle of amazing personalities and events. Shakespeare exults in the fluidity of his open stage to create a saga that constantly shifts in mood and colour—from the exquisite lyricism of *Richard II* to the rowdy tavern japes of *Henry IV* to the sinister and grotesque in *Richard III*. How thrilling would be the opportunity to see all ten plays in the space of a week, all performed by the same company. What a reflection on humanity, kingship, power, politics, ambition, villainy, cruelty, honour, courage and the vagaries of fortune.

There is a curious little scene towards the beginning of *Henry V* at the siege of Harfleur. During a lull in the fighting an argument develops between four captains—an Englishman, a Scot, a Welshman and an Irishman. They are about to come to blows when the trumpet sounds, calling a parley, and they all exit together. Henry V is bringing together all the disparate elements in his territories to fight in a common cause, just as James I was doing his utmost to forge England and Scotland into a United Kingdom. What Shakespeare is dramatising is the creation of a nation, and in so doing he is largely responsible for creating that nation's soul.

Shakespeare is above all writers, at least above all modern writers, the poet of nature . . . Shakespeare's plays are not in the rigorous and critical sense either tragedies or comedies, but compositions of a distinct kind; exhibiting the real state of sublunary nature, which partakes of good and evil, joy and sorrow, mingled with endless variety of proportion and innumerable modes of combination; and expressing the course of the world, in which the loss of one is the gain of another; in which, at the same time, the reveller is hasting to his wine, and the mourner burying his friend; in which the malignity of one is sometimes defeated by the frolic of another; and many mischiefs and many benefits are done and hindered without design.

Dr Samuel Johnson, *Preface to Shakespeare*

10

The Tragedies

Do audiences today have a difficulty with Tragedy—or at least the idea of classical Tragedy?

The word has been somewhat generalised (some would say debased) and too thoughtlessly applied in ways that could be considered hyperbolic. For example, TWO DIE IN BOATING TRAGEDY, or even TRAGEDY STRIKES ESSENDON: MCCANN TWISTS ANKLE. In the former case, those two deaths may affect grieving families, but it's not tragedy in generally accepted dramatic terms. Why not? Because dramatic Tragedy involves something more significant than a boating accident. It is widely understood to depict the corruption and destruction of an individual or group of people through some inherent fault or act of malice. The individual or group of people involved are usually notable for their eminent social position or their integrity or self-awareness, thus making their suffering horrible and pitiable to behold. In watching their downfall we are forced to contemplate the fragile nature of human happiness and success, the frailties we have in common with the protagonist, the ways in which various characters cope with grief, treachery or the blows of fortune, and to reconcile

The Tragedies

ourselves to the fact that we may very possibly undergo similar trials and tribulations during our life's brief span. Just as Comedy celebrates the joys of youth, sex and good fortune, Tragedy alerts us to the darker side of life's possibilities.

In Greek tragedies, protagonists were often the victims of fate or a spiteful deity. Aphrodite might afflict you with unquenchable desire because you had failed to sacrifice to her. Or else some indifferent fate might permit you to kill your own father and marry your mother through ignorance and misunderstanding. To the Greeks, the gods who presided over their lives were capricious, indifferent, malicious or partial. If they took a set against you, you were doomed.

Shakespeare's tragic figures have little truck with gods or fate. They carry the seeds of their own destruction. In some cases (Macbeth, Othello) these flaws are played upon by malign external forces. In others (Lear, Coriolanus, Caesar) an inherent blind arrogance invites retribution. And others, like Richard II, Hamlet and Antony, possess personal traits that disable them when faced with particular scenarios.

Gods and fate may occasionally be invoked or blamed:

My fate cries out ...
... O, cursed spite
That ever I was born to set it right.

But Shakespeare's Tragedies take place in a godless universe. At best, if there are any gods, they are as indifferent or malicious as their Greek counterparts—'they kill us for their sport'.

Macbeth, *Othello*, *Hamlet* and *Romeo and Juliet* are all set in specifically Christian locations. Religious imagery, metaphor and allusion pervade all of them. Macbeth and Othello are fully cognisant of hellfire and damnation. Hamlet wrestles with the dichotomy between the old Catholic faith of Denmark and the Protestant doctrines of Wittenberg. Romeo and Juliet seek the solace and advice of their family confessor.

Yet despite the heavy Church presence, the protagonists display little regard for its dictates. Even the conventional boy next door Laertes can abuse a priest and yell, 'I dare damnation!' And despite his acute consciousness that Duncan's virtues

> Will plead like angels, trumpet-tongued against
> The deep damnation of his taking off,

Macbeth proceeds to murder him, then Banquo, and sets out to destroy the family of Macduff.

His dying act is not one of repentance but defiance:

> . . . Lay on, Macduff;
> And damn'd be he that first cries, 'Hold, enough!'

Othello, the Moor turned Christian convert, is fully aware that by lying to cover up for him, the dying Desdemona is 'like a liar gone to burning hell'. He then commits suicide, damning himself as well.

Hamlet, so steeped in moral philosophy and the religious debates of his time, so conscious of 'the dread of something after death', is quite prepared to murder his uncle once he has sufficient proof of his guilt. Meanwhile he passes the time in knocking off Polonius and Laertes as well as Rosencrantz and Guildenstern (but first making sure their souls will go straight to hell by having them executed with 'no shriving time allowed'). He contemplates a similar eternity of hell for Claudius by waiting for an opportunity to

> trip him, that his heels may kick at heaven,
> and that his soul may be as damn'd and black
> As hell whereto it goes.

The Tragedies

Having effected all this mayhem and slaughter, the 'sweet prince' is farewelled by the faithful Horatio with the directive: 'flights of angels sing thee to thy rest.' An unlikely outcome. Just as unlikely is the heavenly rest of the world's favourite young lovers, Romeo and Juliet. Having killed Tybalt and the hapless Paris, Romeo joins Juliet in a suicide pact. No salvation for them, according to Christian orthodoxy!

This deliberate paganism on Shakespeare's part is striking because in real life even the blackest villain was exhorted to make a repentant speech on the scaffold. And most of them did, thus turning a bloodthirsty public execution into an edifying as well as entertaining spectacle. No such edification in Shakespeare. His 'Christian' heroes, as well as his pagan ones (Brutus, Cassius, Antony, Cleopatra, Lear, Titus and Timon), all face death without a hint of repentance or thought of eternity.

This element of existential humanism may be one of the things that still connects us to Shakespeare's Tragedies. Those of a religious inclination can claim to find some element of 'redemption' in them, although I must say I cannot. To my mind the protagonists struggle, suffer and die in what is essentially an absurd and meaningless universe

> Of carnal, bloody and unnatural acts;
> Of accidental judgements, casual slaughters,
> Of deaths put on by cunning and forc'd cause;
> And, in this upshot, purposes mistook
> Fallen on the inventor's heads.

That sort of universe, described in *Hamlet*, makes sense to me; I can believe in it. As far as I am concerned, the only thing that gives our universe meaning is human endeavour—through art, science, philosophy, law, kindness, family and love.

We must do our best to do great and glorious things in the knowledge that one day we will melt into air, into thin air, and—in words from *The Tempest*—

> The cloud-capp'd towers, the gorgeous palaces,
> The solemn temples, the great globe itself,
> Yea, all which it inherit, shall dissolve,
> And... Leave not a rack behind.
> We are such stuff
> As dreams are made on; And our little life
> Is rounded with a sleep.

In watching a tragic hero's fall, Elizabethan and Jacobean audiences were watching something very close to everyday life. They had seen two wives of Henry VIII, Queens of England, go to the execution block, along with Lord Chancellor Thomas More and Lord Great Chamberlain Thomas Cromwell. They had witnessed the rash career and untimely downfall of Elizabeth's brilliant favourite, the Earl of Essex. They had seen the beheading of the great courtier, explorer and poet Sir Walter Raleigh and heard dozens of courtiers, statesmen and martyrs make stirring orations on the scaffold before laying their heads on the block or being disembowelled and chopped into pieces. Tragedy was a tangible and familiar spectacle.

A couple of hundred years later, the character of Tragedy had changed. The nineteenth century, with its Romantic movement, endorsed the idea of Tragedy being something grand and ennobling, its heroes and heroines larger than life. This was the great age of the individual—explorers, empire builders, generals and missionaries pitting themselves against formidable obstacles. This was the age of the Romantic hero in fact and fiction: Don Juan, Egmont, Manfred, and the recognition of literary giants like Goethe, Byron, Tolstoy, Hugo and Dostoyevsky. It was the age of grand operas with powerful, ear-splitting tenors and sopranos moving the multitudes through the emotive music and heart-rending travails of Tosca, Rigoletto, Tristan and Isolde, Violetta. It was the age of huge theatres, elaborate spectacles with enormous casts. This kind of theatre called for big acting,

The Tragedies

'the grand manner', actors who could hold their own and not be swamped by the scenery. At its best this kind of acting was hailed as sublime, at its worst it was bombastic, earning Tragedy a bad name.

There had been a big shift in public sentiment as well. Victorian sentiment began to demand that art should be edifying and should reflect (or at least not offend) the tastes and values of a Christian society. And since Shakespeare had become enshrined as 'a classic'—the cornerstone of British culture, the spokesman for all that was best about British values—the impolite, subversive or negative elements in his plays were ignored or edited out and his characters imbued with a 'nobility' that sometimes is at odds with the writing.

It's hard to imagine a Hamlet of the nineteenth or early twentieth centuries relishing smutty jokes with his mates and bawdy chat with Ophelia. There is a coarse grain in Shakespeare which makes his characters not just lifelike, but life-size, bringing them down off their lofty pedestals and placing them among us.

However, by the middle of the twentieth century both the grand manner of acting and the ennobling nature of Tragedy were being seriously challenged. For one thing, theatres became smaller and more intimate for live drama. Acting needed to be scaled down accordingly. The increased popularity of movies and television also radically changed the public perception as to what constituted good acting. Masters of modernity like Marlon Brando and Robert De Niro demonstrated the power of understatement and subtly disguised technique. Anything larger than life was dismissed as hammy, over the top, invalid.

The twentieth century also continued the push to democratise Tragedy. Whereas the Tragedies of the seventeenth and eighteenth centuries dealt almost exclusively with kings, queens, the nobility and military heroes, the nineteenth century made Tragedy mostly a middle-class affair—Hedda Gabler, John Gabriel Borkman, Helen Alving, Uncle Vanya and Konstantin Trepliov. In the hands of writers like Tennessee Williams and Arthur

Miller the downward social spiral continued until it could embrace everyman—and woman: Blanche DuBois, Stanley Kowalski and Willy Loman, people to whom 'attention must be paid'.

But the greatest blows to the Romantic concept of Tragedy were dealt by key historical events of the twentieth century—two World Wars, the Great Depression, the Communist revolution and the Holocaust. In the wake of these events it became impossible to regard Tragedy as a pious and edifying spectacle. Henceforth a degree of ironic detachment was called for. One playwright who heralded this new approach was Bertolt Brecht. His Mother Courage is a true tragic heroine but one without a trace of nobility—a tough and cynical survivor battling against the flood tide of historical disasters.

In the light of this new scrutiny, Romantic attitudes to Tragedy were stripped away, but the great dramatic Tragedies of the past shone with a new clarity and relevance. The expansive vision and fatalism of the Greeks, the brutality, passion and realpolitik of Shakespeare's world, took on new meaning for the twentieth and twenty-first centuries. The job of theatre-makers today is to continue that quest begun by Brecht and his contemporaries—to reassess the great Tragedies of the past in the light of our own recent experience, to reveal the truth and beauty they contain, to expand our theatrical language in order to accommodate them and enrich our lives, immeasurably, in the process.

It's not easy. We have to convince a public suspicious of lofty sentiment and big emotional statements, familiar as they are with television naturalism. Some of the best cinema succeeds with sparse, understated dialogue reinforced with subtle close-up shots that speak volumes of subtext.

Worse still, there is a widespread suspicion of the exalted nature of Tragedy. A modern phrase that seeks to undermine this status is 'the banality of evil'. The phrase is easy to comprehend when applied to mediocre men who happen to be mass murderers, like Adolf Hitler, and even more so to small-scale criminals and racketeers. Brecht warns us of the dangers of glorifying these people, of romanticising gangsters and hoodlums. He would apply the same strictures against Napoleon, Alexander the Great or Genghis Khan. The fact that they toppled empires and slaughtered hundreds of thousands of people should earn them eternal odium, not admiration.

But to apply the same reductionism to Macbeth or Shakespeare's other tragic villains is to miss the point. Shakespeare is not asking us to admire or excuse Macbeth, Edmund, Iago or Richard III. He is inviting us to be appalled by their actions and their self-destruction. Iago stands outside any moral universe. He is the embodiment of pitiless and pointless malice. Macbeth is a man of huge imagination trapped in a waking nightmare; there is no escape. If we reduce Macbeth, Iago, Richard or Shylock to the Brechtian level of common crook, we risk turning Tragedy to melodrama.

This is the challenge facing the contemporary director and Tragic actor: how to bring these great vehicles into focus, to somehow reflect a world we know and believe in with acting that is credible and lifelike, but still takes us beyond the banal, the everyday experience, and leaves us feeling awestruck by having witnessed a timeless universal vision of human folly and suffering.

> Shakespeare looked deeply into the seeds of things. He tried to understand life, to see whether it had a meaning or not, at the same time refusing the consolations afforded by traditional religion. His is the most articulate voice from a time when the deity of the western world was first unthroned, when the certainties of the godhead became the doubts of ordinary men and women.
> RENÉ WEIS, *SHAKESPEARE REVEALED—A BIOGRAPHY*

Hamlet

I first encountered Hamlet when I was eight, the year Olivier's film came out. My mother took me to see it at the now-demolished Lyric cinema in Newcastle. The event had such an impact on me that I can still remember the heat of the footpath outside the cinema, the feeling of going down the dark stairs, a general sense of the film's moodiness and haunting music, a thrilling sword fight and moments of such luminosity that I believed for years afterwards that the black and white screen had burst into colour. I was deeply moved by the vocal cadences of Olivier and the enigma of this strange, melancholic, ironic and somewhat androgynous hero/anti-hero.

So when the textbooks were handed around in the classroom some seven years later, I was ready for it. At the age of fifteen I felt I had got *Hamlet* in one, understood the whole thing, and on one level I had. What transported me then was the Gothic, primitive yet complex world of intrigue, and a visceral response to treachery and the supernatural. I found the play thrilling, disturbing and a huge release from the workaday drudgery of school and domesticity.

Olivier's screen performance no doubt had a lot to do with it; a combination of effete narcissism and violent derring-do, it was understandably appealing to an adolescent. There are other points of contact too: the violent mood swings, the desire to be alone and indulge in introspection, sexual possessiveness of the mother and jealousy of the parents' relationship, cheeking authority, contempt for one's elders (in this case Polonius), a fondness for philosophising on the Big Questions, an ineptness in handling one's first sexual relationship (Ophelia) and the need for a buddy (Horatio), sibling rivalry (Laertes) and a shallow cynicism about things outside one's experience. What does Hamlet know of the insolence of office or the law's delays?

In the fifty-odd years since that first experience, I have encountered many Hamlets, played him twice, directed the play three times (so far), and boned up on all the latest theory as it relentlessly churns off the presses. I feel that my first response to the play and its hero has in no way been diminished. My mind now contains a hefty portfolio of alternative actors and interpretations, but they are all fruit off the same tree.

By the time I had finished high school and studied *Hamlet* intensively for twelve months for my final exams, I not only knew the play by heart but it was part of me. At university I studied the play more fully and from a number of different angles prompted by the professors. So by the time I graduated at the age of twenty-two, my head was pumped full of so many conflicting schools of thought that I was as incapacitated as Hamlet himself when it came to deciding on a course of action. Picture then my dilemma and my heart-stopping excitement when I was offered the role only a few months later.

I graduated from university at a fortuitous moment. A new full-time professional theatre company had just been established and was about to launch its first season. This was the Old Tote, so called because of its headquarters in the old totalisator building of Randwick racecourse. The abandoned relic now stood within the grounds of the University of New South Wales, and was currently occupied by students of the National Institute of Dramatic Art. Across the cobbled courtyard under the shade of ancient Moreton Bay figs was a picturesque weatherboard two-storey house, formerly the jockeys' change room, now the offices of NIDA. And nearby stood the tin shed with a hundred seats and modest foyer that was to be our theatre (It's at present called the Fig Tree Theatre).

The company was headed by Professor Robert Quentin along with John Clark, Tom Brown and Joe McCallum, who were tutors at NIDA and on the university payroll.

I was offered juicy roles in the first two plays of the season—Trofimov in *The Cherry Orchard* and Eisenring in Max Frisch's *The Fire Raisers*. One day during *Cherry Orchard* rehearsals Tom Brown casually remarked, 'We've got *Hamlet* coming up. Are you any good at sword fighting?'

My heart skipped several beats and I thought in wild excitement, 'My God! They're going to offer me Laertes!' I confidently proclaimed my excellence in fencing (having taken two or three lessons in the university fencing club).

'Okay then,' he answered. 'How'd you like to play Hamlet?'

By the time I'd picked myself up off the ground he'd vanished.

I became Hamlet-obsessed, even to the point of neglecting to learn my lines for the next gig, *The Fire Raisers*, which I was playing at night while rehearsing *Hamlet* by day.

Tom Brown's production was very 'traditional', which suited me fine at the time. The set consisted of a couple of 'Gothic' columns and a black backdrop. The costumes were velvet and satin 'Elizabethan'. Claudius had a red cloak and a crown, Hamlet was dressed in black with a white Peter Pan collar, and the Ghost, in armour, had a greenish spotlight. Just as you'd expect.

It was only a hundred-seat theatre but I acted like I was playing the Colosseum. In the cramped dressing room I sat next to my Horatio, Neil Fitzpatrick. He watched me etching my face with wrinkles. 'How old are you trying to look?' he queried. 'Thirty!' I replied, desperately applying the makeup pencil. I was a very angst-ridden Hamlet (as you'd expect at twenty-two), shitty with my mother, shitty with my lover, shitty with the world. The only time I lightened up was with Horatio, the players and the gravedigger.

In other words, Hamlet was the perfect vehicle for getting your rocks off and tilting at all your favourite windmills. I think the role retains something of that no matter what age you are when you play it, but as you get older other things intrude and the circle of concentration widens to take in more than just your own ego.

I played Hamlet again nine years later at the Nimrod. This was another small venue of just over a hundred seats but in a more intimate wrap-around configuration. The stage space was tiny, but along with my co-director, Richard Wherrett, we made the space seem bigger by surrounding it with panels of mirrors that reflected the audience as well as the actors. My Hamlet was pretty intense this time too, but I hope a little more outward-looking and compassionate. I think you ought to play Hamlet every ten years as a barometer of where you're at in your personal life and relationships.

The role has been successfully played by young actors (some freakishly young, like the child prodigy Master Betty), who make Hamlet's tender years the rationale for his erratic behaviour, cruelty and self-obsession. Youth gives the role credibility but can deprive it of gravitas. I remember a patron at my initial Bell Shakespeare production of *Hamlet* in 1991 saying of John Polson's grotty adolescent prince, 'I just wanted to give him a good spanking!' But of course younger audiences loved it.

For most of the nineteenth and early twentieth centuries Hamlet was played by classical actors in their maturity—that is, in their late thirties to mid-forties. Johnston Forbes-Robertson played it when he was sixty. Age certainly adds weight to the philosophical speculation of the soliloquies: here's a man who does know something about the law's delays, the insolence of office and the pangs of despised love—not just from speculation but from bitter experience. When he ponders, 'What a piece of work is man,' or marvels at armies dying for a useless plot of ground, you're inclined to give more credence to his ideas than those of a university dropout.

On the other hand, you can get very cross with a mature-age Hamlet abusing his mother, sneering at his uncle, trashing his girlfriend and tying himself into knots of inactivity; the excuse of youth is gone. You feel inclined to yell, 'Grow up!'

So what age should Hamlet be? The role was written for a young man. Richard Burbage was about thirty when he first played it. He was renowned for the truthfulness of his acting, his dexterity of mind and robust physicality—on stage and off. We have to imagine a very mercurial performance, confronting the audience with those astonishingly candid, revealing soliloquies as he strode about the Globe stage talking to them face to face—passionately, urgently. A far cry from the Victorian Hamlet in his vast Gothic set, brooding in a follow-spot and talking not to the audience but to himself, or to the ether.

We know that Shakespeare's generation grew up faster than their modern counterparts and assumed responsibilities earlier, but at the beginning of the play a lot of emphasis is placed on Hamlet's youth. He is referred to as 'young Hamlet' by Horatio in the first scene and by the gravedigger almost at the end. But in the interim Hamlet has grown up: 'How long has thou been a grave-maker?' he asks the gravedigger.

'I have been sexton here, man and boy, thirty years,' comes the reply. 'It was that very day that young Hamlet was born'.

So Hamlet is thirty. Exactly thirty. At the end of the play . . . But is he thirty at the beginning? Surely not—maybe eighteen or twenty at most. So have ten years passed since Act I, Scene 1? Not at all. If you calculate the action of the play day by day, hour by hour, it's a couple of months at most.

It's Shakespeare up to one of his favourite tricks—a double time scheme that keeps the action moving at breakneck pace, yet gives the impression of time passing and characters evolving. In the space of four days Romeo and Juliet grow from innocent teenagers to adults of remarkable resolution and profound feelings.

In *Julius Caesar*, the month between the Lupercalia and the Ides of March is squeezed into one stormy night. The real Macbeth reigned for about eleven years; in Shakespeare's version his reign is a couple of weeks, but in that time he changes from a mature warrior to a shrunken middle-aged has-been whose life has grown into 'the sear, the yellow leaf'.

Something similar happens to Hamlet. In the space of three and a bit hours of theatre time he experiences more (and expresses more) than most of us do in a lifetime. The actor playing the role must chart that progress and factor in the body blows that forge Hamlet's transformation, particularly after his return from the aborted voyage to England. Shakespeare thoughtfully gives the actor a bit of a break before bringing him back for the great denouement. The audience starts to miss him, and when he does return he is a wiser and older Hamlet than the one who killed Polonius. He seems fatalistic and death-fixated—hence his dallying in the graveyard to interrogate the gravedigger about the finer points of decomposition. Death is no longer something abstract but a physical reality—the skulls, the bones, the dust that might be that of Caesar or Alexander, now used to plug a beer barrel or patch a hole in the wall. He finds some comfort in meditating on this ultimate reality. That comfort is cruelly shattered by the sudden appearance of Ophelia's coffin. But this final outrage of fortune only hardens his resolve to embrace his fate whatever the outcome.

The biggest challenge facing the actor who would be Hamlet is to make the part your own. It's good to have a knowledge and respect of tradition and to study the great actors of the past. It will remind you of what a great privilege it is to play a role like Hamlet and humble you to think of how many fine actors have excelled in it and thrilled audiences for the last four hundred years. But you must not get cowed by tradition or hung up on it. When your turn comes you have to put all that to one side and look at the role as if it's never been played before and you have no idea of how it's going to come out. You start with a clean slate and begin to identify with the role. But that doesn't mean limiting it to your own personality and frame of reference. You can't scale it down to fit your own comfort zone. Rather, you have to go out to it, stretch yourself wide, open yourself to all possibilities by applying the old *what if* exercise: *What if* I met my father's ghost? What if I found out he'd been murdered? How would I feel if my mother hurriedly married my uncle, a man I despised? What would I do if I found out he'd murdered my father? How would I feel if my girlfriend, my lover, committed suicide? They are all very big *what if*s and demand a huge stretch of your imagination and emotional response. You'll find discrepancies between your own reaction and what Hamlet does. Your feelings about revenge, about the afterlife, about honour, may not accord with his. That's where the acting comes in: to step into Hamlet's shoes, see the world through his eyes, make his *what if*s your own.

Most Hamlets don't go far enough. I haven't seen many who convinced me they'd seen a ghost. I haven't seen many who convinced me they loved Ophelia. A lot of Hamlets flatten the role out, try to create a consistent 'character'. But there is no 'character', just a series of situations, reactions, decisions, impulses that, when added up, give us a Hamlet. Forget about 'consistency', which is such an abstract notion. Play each scene, each situation for what it gives you. In this scene he's loving, in this scene bloody-minded; in this one suicidal, in this one jokey and light-hearted. In this scene he is cruel, in this one kind. In this one sluggish, in the next hyperactive. Just as we are in life—inconsistent. In Hamlet's case the inconsistencies are heightened by his superior brain and the extreme situations he finds himself in.

Harold Bloom argues that Shakespeare invented the idea of 'personality'. Before Shakespeare, playwrights presented us with 'types' governed by one particular characteristic or 'humour', as Ben Jonson would have it. They were consistent and predictable.

In Hamlet we have the opposite—someone more resembling ourselves: inconsistent, unpredictable, changing, evolving. As much as we think we know ourselves, we can't say for sure how we would react in certain situations, how true we'd be to our principles, how courageous, truthful or loyal. We can easily give a quick character sketch of someone we know, but it can never be the whole truth—there are corners we cannot see into.

Every notable Hamlet has tapped into his zeitgeist. While Burbage had the dash and flamboyance of a Jacobean courtier, the nineteenth century churned out a succession of Romantic Hamlets, some with a demonic and

Byronic gloom, some with the gentle melancholy of a Keats or Shelley. This tradition persisted well into the twentieth century. Olivier had the melancholy in spades, along with a splash of Burbage reinvented as a Hollywood matinee idol.

Since the 1950s, we have had Hamlets responding to the theatrical revolution spearheaded by John Osborne's Jimmy Porter, the original Angry Young Man in *Look Back in Anger*. Peter O'Toole, Nicol Williamson and David Warner were among the first of the post-Romantic Hamlets, and since then Hamlet has been banished from his princely pedestal. He has become the universal dropout, the anti-establishment everyman, the rebel with a cause, a rallying point for dissent.

During the Cold War era, when new drama was seriously curtailed in the Soviet Bloc and the classics were carefully scrutinised by censors for hidden subversive messages, audiences would watch intently to see what Hamlet was reading when he entered with his book, hoping for codified reassurance that the hero was on their side.

So if you're playing Hamlet, it's important to look not so much to the past as to the world around you. What's your specific reference when you talk about the corruption of the state, the pointlessness of a war where men die for a patch of useless territory, the law's delays, the insolence of office? Who are you speaking for and what response do you want from us?

The post-Romantic wave has given us a lot of Hamlets who are grotty and snotty: teenage rebels and political radicals or anarchists. We have seen boorish ranters and sneering cynics. Words like 'noble' or 'regal' are not to be countenanced. I have seen so many Hamlets content with being cool, tight-lipped and superior. And yet, to be a successful Hamlet, I think you have to touch the heart and elicit some empathy from your audience, otherwise they are going to ask themselves why they should bother spending three and a bit hours in your company or care what happens to you.

Like Lear, like Othello, Hamlet gives a lot of love and expects a lot in return. This is one of the things that make him both vulnerable and sympathetic. He loves his father in a painful, idealising and doting way. You could say much the same of the way he loves his mother, except this love is poisoned by the presence of sexual jealousy and possessiveness. His love for Ophelia is of the awkward, fragile adolescent kind, but it has to be intense and present, otherwise the agonising 'nunnery' scene is just a misogynist rant. His love for Horatio is almost taken for granted (by Hamlet) because it is so comfortable and familiar.

He is wryly amused by the fustiness of Polonius and is genuinely delighted by his conversations with the players and the gravedigger. He is more at home with common soldiers than with peacock courtiers like Osric, whom he treats with ironic contempt. It is this democratic and egalitarian streak in Hamlet that is part of his appeal. Lear has to learn it the painful way. Macbeth never has it. But it comes naturally to Hamlet. I suspect there is something of Shakespeare in this. He too seems to have been more at home with actors and writers than with courtiers.

So you tot up all Hamlet's good qualities and his less endearing ones. You lay them out side by side and you don't deny any of them. Then you play them as they come up, one by one, identifying each one as closely as possible with yourself, your own imagination, your own experiences, your own covert wishes and desires. You give us all of yourself, you tell the truth, you hold back nothing. Then an audience might say, 'Yes, I know how you feel. I know why you're doing this . . . I know you.' And you've got your Hamlet.

Why was Shakespeare so interested in the Hamlet story and why does his treatment of it still grab us all these years later? The original is a pretty hoary and barbaric old yarn, well known in folklore and obviously dramatised at least once before the Shakespeare version we now have. As for why he kept reworking and revising it, well obviously it had great box-office potential, always a prime consideration with our playwright.

The Tragedies

Revenge plays had the sort of popular appeal Western movies once enjoyed and which cop/hospital/domestic sitcoms currently have on TV. We tend to think of Elizabethan or Jacobean theatre as a blanket term, forgetting that theatre was just as modish then as it is now, with certain genres coming in and out of fashion. One year historical chronicles would be all the rage, next year pastoral comedies or revenge tragedies or whatever. Shakespeare was adroit at tacking about and writing to satisfy each fad.

Some biographers have become very fanciful, linking the writing of *Hamlet* to the recent loss of his father and death of his son Hamnet. They point out, a little ghoulishly, that Shakespeare himself played the Ghost in the original performance, so here he was in the guise of the dead father communing with his dead son.

Even if that were the case, there is more to it than that. Shakespeare found in the person of this troubled procrastinator who feigns madness as a refuge from the world an emblem of the times: a protagonist who could hold the mirror up to Nature and show Virtue her own feature, Scorn her own image and the very age and body of the time its form and pressure.

I guess all of us come to feel at certain points in our lives that we are straddling the worlds of past and present; sometimes we feel stuck at an impasse. I work with young people today, eighteen- or twenty-year-olds, and remark to myself that I was born seventy years ago in a world so different to theirs! How to begin to explain the changes, the difference in aspirations and expectations?

Leaving superficial coincidences aside, I think *Hamlet* contains a certain amount of autobiographical content at quite a profound level. Shakespeare himself was a man suspended between two universes. On the one hand was Old England with its Old Faith—medieval Catholicism. This was the religion of his forebears and not-so-distant relatives. Warwickshire was regarded as a hotbed of Catholic fealty. Shakespeare's father was very possibly a closet Catholic and the Ardens, on Shakespeare's mother's side, were under suspicion. Whatever his later agnosticism or even atheism,

Shakespeare seems never to have lost a certain affection for the old ways, quaint rituals and homely pieties, just as he retained an affection for rustic pastimes and folklore—fairies, goblins and the like. No doubt he shared this nostalgic sentiment with many of his contemporaries, especially in the countryside where the Reformation was a lot slower to take root. You can't eradicate centuries of practices and deeply held beliefs overnight or by a simple edict. He very likely deplored the destruction of ancient statuary, frescoes, missals and beautiful stained-glass windows that adorned the Guild Chapel and parish churches. A nostalgia for medieval England, its romance and chivalry, shines through his plays about Henry IV and Henry V.

But in the city and in the court where he spent his professional life he encountered a very different set of values. Here the Reformation was firmly entrenched and jealously prosecuted. At its extreme edge, Puritan preachers denounced all display and frivolity, including the theatre. Catholic practices were reviled as superstition and papists regarded with hostility and occasional persecution. Whatever his private opinions, the prudent Shakespeare would have paid lip service to the prevailing Protestant orthodoxy.

Hamlet encapsulates some of this double-think. He is a university student at Wittenberg, Luther's university and the home of Protestantism. As a good student of philosophy there he has learned that purgatory is nonexistent, a Catholic superstition. He arrives home to be confronted by his father's Ghost, who actually *lives* in purgatory:

> And for the day confined to fast in fires
> Till the foul crimes done in my days of nature
> Are burnt and purged away.

This supernatural visitation is enough to throw Hamlet's whole belief system into chaos and impel him to inform his fellow student:

> There are more things in heaven and earth, Horatio,
> Than are dreamt of in your philosophy.

So what and who can he believe? Who is to be trusted? The world is corrupt, treacherous, a garden gone to seed.

He can no longer have faith in womankind. His mother, far from displaying grief over his father's sudden (and suspicious) death has remarried 'within a month'. Not only that, she has married a man Hamlet despises—'a satyr', 'a mildewed ear', a 'bloat king' who later turns out to be 'a murderer and a villain'. Hamlet heaves with disgust at his mother's presumed carnal appetite, 'honeying and making love over the nasty sty'.

Add to this his confusion and rage when his beloved Ophelia returns his love tokens and letters and is set up to spy on him. Well might he exclaim, 'Frailty, thy name is woman.'

He can no longer have faith in friendship except for the constant Horatio. His 'excellent good friends', Rosencrantz and Guildenstern, he soon realises, have been sent to spy on him and report back to the King. Before long they have become Claudius's creatures, capturing Hamlet and escorting him (though possibly unwittingly) to his death. Hamlet has no compunction in disposing of them.

One thing he retains faith in is theatre. Because it is transparently artificial, you can believe it: because the actors are so upfront about feigning emotions, you can trust them. They are not duplicitous like Ophelia, Claudius or his 'friends'.

In Hamlet's metaphysical quandaries, in his speculations about mortality, fame, honour, friendship and responsibility, maybe we come close to hearing the authentic voice of Shakespeare. But that is always a dangerous speculation.

The best Hamlets encompass an enigma, they don't try to explain it. No matter how well you know someone you're aware of private corners; not necessarily dark, just private. Even your wife and children have a right to areas you don't pry into. Hamlet has lots of dark corners. He is a mass of contradictions. Any actor who tries to iron out those contradictions will produce a bland Hamlet. He must remain unpredictable. Neither he nor the audience must know how a scene is going to end. He sets up the play in order to observe Claudius's reaction but then can't help commenting, provoking and nudging Claudius, thereby blowing his cover. He resolves to confront his mother and to speak daggers but use none. Five minutes later, he's killed Polonius in a fit of rashness. His leaping into Ophelia's grave, his killing of Laertes and Claudius are all done on impulse, totally unpremeditated. This rashness is interspersed with episodes of intense and paralysing introspection and self-flagellation over his inertia.

So, as I said earlier, my advice to Hamlets is simply to play the moments—one moment you're cruel, next minute you're kind; now tender, now tough; now hyperactive, now sluggish. Play the moments, let the audience join the dots. Don't try to explain Hamlet, just experience him. Keep the audience intrigued. And the performance can vary every night—not the essentials, but certainly in the details. You don't play the role, you live it. You use it to tell the audience all about yourself—well, not all; you keep a few dark corners, just to keep them guessing.

Incidentally, I've always felt that 'To be or not to be' doesn't belong in the play—at least not where it occurs. That's an odd thing to say, because in one sense 'To be or not to be' encapsulates all of *Hamlet* and is as much a signifier of the play as Yorick's skull. Its philosophical tone is very much in the spirit of the play overall and sounds like the sort of thing Hamlet would have said at Wittenberg, in a seminar maybe, before he came home. It has a Protestant emphasis on 'conscience' and negates purgatory, 'from whose bourn no traveller returns' (a rather difficult thing to say *after* he's seen the Ghost). But it comes at a very odd place in the play. Last time we saw Hamlet he was all fired up with excitement about his plans to stage the play and 'catch the conscience of the King'. Why this sudden and irrelevant relapse?

It's also a difficult piece to stage. Polonius and Claudius withdraw, having planted Ophelia to ambush Hamlet. He walks on and soliloquises for some time before noticing her. Either she takes refuge somewhere and reappears at the end of the soliloquy or else she hovers around, pulling focus, while he utters it. And poor old Polonius and Claudius are stuck behind the arras wishing he'd get on with it.

It proves far more dynamic if you take the soliloquy out and bring Hamlet straight into confrontation with Ophelia as is set up to happen. No time out for a soliloquy. But of course simply cutting it is hardly an option. Audiences would demand their money back. But when I've directed the play I have found it very useful to put 'To be or not to be' earlier in the piece, in the middle of Act II, Scene 2. Polonius has just told Claudius and Gertrude that Hamlet is mad and spends hours walking in the lobby. Then they spot him approaching, book in hand, and withdraw so that Polonius may interrogate him. This seems to me the perfect place to pop in 'To be or not to be', as if Hamlet is chewing over a thesis in the book he has been reading. It is not a passionate, urgent speech but academically discursive. It leads very well into the dialogue with the nosey Polonius: 'What do you read, my Lord?' Hamlet: 'Words, words, words...'

But I can never get over the feeling that it was a speech Shakespeare pulled out of a bottom drawer and snuck into *Hamlet*.

Macbeth

> Life's but a walking shadow, a poor player
> That struts and frets his hour upon the stage,
> And then is heard no more. It is a tale
> Told by an idiot, full of sound and fury,
> Signifying nothing.

I can't think of any more nihilistic statement in all of literature. As with Shakespeare's other Tragedies, there is no sense of redemption for the protagonists. Life goes on without them but it somehow seems reduced. Fortinbras is no substitute for Hamlet, nor the devious, scrupulous Malcolm a replacement for the force of nature that is Macbeth. There is something sublime and magnificent about him as he faces eternal damnation and flings himself recklessly against his last impregnable and fatal enemy, Macduff.

The most compelling feature of Macbeth is the scope of his imagination. He is so overwrought as he approaches Duncan's bedchamber, knife in hand, that he starts to hallucinate. He sees a dagger in the air, pointing the way, and watches as it congeals with blood. His mind is flooded with a vision of universal wickedness:

> ... Now o'er the one half-world
> Nature seems dead, and wicked dreams abuse
> The curtained sleep. Witchcraft celebrates
> Pale Hecate's offerings, and withered murder,
> Alarum'd by his sentinel the wolf,
> Whose howl's his watch, thus with his stealthy pace,
> With Tarquin's ravishing strides, towards his design
> Moves like a ghost.

After Duncan's murder he feels no joy or exultation, but sinks into sleeplessness and nightmares, a murky twilight existence:

> ... Light thickens, and the crow
> Makes wing to the rooky wood.
> Good things of day begin to droop and drowse,
> Whiles night's black agents to their preys do rouse.

His ultimate downfall is presaged by a public display of guilt and terror as he conjures up the ghost of Banquo at his coronation banquet.

The Tragedies

Macbeth is one of the most readable of Shakespeare's plays. The story is simple, linear and moves at a cracking pace. The verse is urgent and muscular and the imagery both concrete and sensuous. As a schoolboy I thrilled to the sinister atmosphere of Macbeth's castle, the witches' cavern, the blasted Scottish heath, the gloomy forest that witnesses the murder of Banquo. The male/female struggle for supremacy between Macbeth and his dynamic wife is at once domestic and epic. And the play comes to a grand finale with the powers of good rallying to overthrow the tyrant:

> ... Macbeth
> is ripe for shaking, and the powers above
> Put on their instruments.

For a play so compact and thrilling to read, it is usually disappointing in performance. I have directed it twice and twice played Macbeth, and feel a kinship with Ingmar Bergman, who said after directing it eight times that next time he hoped to get it right ...

I studied the play in high school and loved it to the point of learning it off by heart and making my own production of it. My first professional encounter with it was in 1967 when I played Lennox in Peter Hall's RSC production starring Paul Scofield and Harold Pinter's then wife, Vivien Merchant, in Stratford. John Bury's set consisted of a huge cave made of red fur which covered the walls and floor. There were giant rips in it for entrances. It was like the inside of some enormous beast or else a vision of hell itself. Hall had decided that there were only two real 'characters' in the play, the Macbeths; the rest of us were choric figures grouped like chess pieces to comment on the action. This seriously undersold the other protagonists like Banquo and Macduff, besides stripping the play of its humanity. It became a sort of spoken oratorio.

Too late in the day Hall realised his mistake and urged us each to scramble around and invent 'a character', but as we were dressed more or less identically, this wasn't so easy. It was yet another example of the design getting in the way of the play; some people thought a quick look at the set said it all—there was nowhere left to go. Although we all scoffed at the old theatre superstition that equates *Macbeth* with bad luck, we were touched by the famous curse: Peter Hall contracted a severe attack of shingles and the production had to be postponed for six weeks.

Reviews in England were mixed but we took the production to Moscow and Leningrad as part of the USSR's fiftieth-anniversary celebrations and it met with great acclaim. Whether this was for the show's inherent virtues or because it was an exercise in international diplomacy was hard to gauge. We felt the Russians were just glad to see some foreign faces after so many years of Cold War.

Although Paul Scofield was one of the actors I most admired in the world, he did not seem able to encompass the evil nature of Macbeth. There was something too fundamentally sweet-natured, almost saintly, about him. And although Vivien Merchant projected the image of a glittering serpent, she seemed too small, both physically and vocally, on that mammoth set, especially next to the rugged and sonorous Scofield.

In the early days of the Nimrod Theatre (now the Stables Theatre, Kings Cross) I produced *Macbeth* as a sort of black mass with a cast of seven. It was well suited to that tiny intimate venue and was heavily ritualistic: Macbeth was vanquished and the theatre cleansed with a version of the Dies Irae. The production was heavily influenced by the murder of Sharon Tate by Charles Manson and his weird cult members. Gillian Jones as Lady M gave a compelling and febrile performance of someone with a moral vacuum addicted to substance abuse. That's one of the fascinating aspects of Lady Macbeth: she has far less imagination than her husband and is oblivious to the consequences of her actions:

Macbeth: If we should fail?
Lady Macbeth: We fail!

Yet she's the one who really cracks up. She is confident and commanding following the murder of Duncan: she mops up her husband and covers for him brilliantly. But as he steps deeper and deeper into crime he leaves her behind, confused and lonely. Macbeth hardens in resolve, becoming increasingly brutal, whereas Lady Macbeth begins to lose it and is finally reduced to a demented wraith, reliving the horrors of the past in her nightly sleepwalks.

When I directed the play for Bell Shakespeare in 2007, I went for a more contemporary approach and set the play on a blasted heath—a landscape devastated by years of warfare. Images of the US invasion of Iraq dominated the design. The actors were dressed in battle fatigues and the stage was littered with the detritus of war. It was a natural habitat for the witches—feral survivors and camp followers.

The two productions in which I played Macbeth were far more lavish affairs and I think were somewhat swamped by the design. Richard Wherrett directed Robyn Nevin and myself for the Sydney Theatre Company in the Opera House's Drama Theatre in 1982. Richard saw the Macbeths as a glamorous couple, revelling in celebrity and power—a sinister version of the Kennedys and their 'Camelot'. The set was spacious and entirely abstract. But I think the play works best in a small space with a sense of claustrophobia. 'I am cabin'd, cribb'd, confin'd,' growls Macbeth, and you need to feel the walls closing in.

David Fenton directed the play for Bell Shakespeare in 1998. Design dominated here, too. David depicted the witches as aliens in spacesuits, dabbling in genetic engineering. Their cave was a well-equipped laboratory and their incantations were like scientific formulae. The spectacular banquet scene featured a crucified white horse with its entrails spilling out—Banquo's ghost appeared amid the offal.

This time my wife Anna played Lady Macbeth and we spent a gruelling research period reading up on monsters like Brady and Hindley, the child murderers. One of the problems the Macbeths have is that they cannot live in the moment: 'tomorrow' is the most oft-repeated word in their lexicon. They are always projecting themselves into the future, perhaps because, as Jan Kott suggests, 'they have suffered some great erotic defeat'. Devoid of children himself, Macbeth seems determined to wipe out everyone else's progeny. Fleance must perish along with his father and Macduff's entire family is wiped out. Anna and I worked hard on the psychology and inner life of the Macbeths—but it was the witches and disembowelled horse that got all the attention.

Of all the productions I've seen, the most successful is probably Trevor Nunn's RSC production at The Other Place in Stratford with Judi Dench and Ian McKellen. You can still see it on DVD and a lot of the acting now looks arch and affected, but Judi Dench is compelling and truthful as always. A shiver of terror runs through her as she invokes her demons:

> . . . Come you spirits
> That tend on mortal thoughts, unsex me here,
> And fill me from the crown until the toe top-full
> Of direst cruelty.

Many actresses play Lady Macbeth like an evil bitch from the beginning. Dench shows us the terrible effort it takes for this woman to overcome and suppress her natural femininity. If she's evil already, she has no need to invoke the powers of darkness.

Orson Welles' film version is full of great images (even if they are all too clearly indebted to Sergei Eisenstein) but suffers from some bizarre casting choices. Polanski's is the more popular film and he handles the witches very credibly. But the film is weakened by the decision to internalise all the soliloquies. It gets very boring looking at an actor's static face while a voiceover murmurs the text reflectively. It's no substitute for a live actor on stage eyeballing you and spitting out those speeches with white-hot passion. Macbeth's soliloquies are not reflective—they are full of action, anguish and torment. Most soliloquies are: it's the chance for a character to rip off his mask and tear open his bosom, letting the audience in on his most intimate thoughts and emotions. Soliloquies are never time out for reflection; they are the highlights, the linchpin of the drama, and should feel shockingly candid and intimate.

The main reason the Trevor Nunn production worked so well was this very intimacy. Productions of *Macbeth* tend to go off the rails when they get too grand, too epic and too busy. The Other Place provided a very confined space and close actor/audience relationship. A small cast sat in a circle, stepping in and out of the space to play their scenes. It must have been reasonably similar to the atmosphere of the Blackfriars Theatre where *Macbeth* was performed at night, indoors, by torch and candlelight. Very spooky... But such is the play's power over the imagination that it succeeded with the big popular Globe audience in broad daylight as well.

In directing *Macbeth* you face a number of challenges. How do you convincingly embody and convey a sense of evil, and how do you maintain the tension and the horror without tipping into bathos or melodrama? Extreme images and situations must be handled boldly: the witches' cauldron scene, the appearance of Banquo's ghost, the chaos following Duncan's murder. If you play safe and pull back on those moments they can be easily dismissed or become laughable. As with the playing of the Macbeths, you need courage and a wide-ranging imagination. You need great emotional commitment.

Macbeth in particular is in danger of dwindling as the play progresses. Striving for power is exciting but having it can be boring.

I know it is said of him:

... Now does he feel his title
Hang loose about him, like a giant's robe
Upon a dwarfish thief.

But Macbeth cannot afford to see himself that way. On the contrary, he sees himself as a brave bear surrounded by yapping dogs:

> They have tied me to a stake. I cannot fly,
> But bear-like I must fight the course...

Treacherous, murderous and bloody as he is, there is something awesome about his final confrontation with Macduff, so you can't fire all your big guns in the banquet scene. Save a bit of puff for the end.

Some directors are uneasy, too, with what little humour there is in the play. The witches seem to possess magical qualities as well as being vile, vindictive crones. Shakespeare's audience would have had no problem with that, nor with finding them simultaneously funny and horrific. Too often directors tie themselves into knots trying to rationalise or intellectualise the witches.

At school we were taught that the porter is there for 'comic relief'. That's only partly true. He is also there to screw the tension to breaking point. We have just seen the guilty Macbeths with blood on their hands startled by a knocking at the gate—like the sound of doom. They hurry off to wash their hands and put on fresh clothes. Meanwhile the knocking continues. We want to know who's there—will they come in and discover the murderers? But the entry of Macduff and Lennox is delayed by a drunken porter slowly coming to his senses and playing knock-knock jokes as he dresses himself.

To Shakespeare's audience (the older ones at least) he would have been a familiar figure. In the old Mystery Plays such as Shakespeare saw in Coventry when he was a boy, the porter of hell's gate was a comic knockabout figure who tormented the souls of the condemned sinners. It was a comic interlude with sinister connotations. In *Macbeth* the porter has something of the same function; but more importantly he identifies Inverness with hell and Macbeth with Satan himself. The play is elevated to a metaphysical level appropriate to the worst of all crimes, regicide:

> Most sacrilegious murder hath broke ope
> The Lord's anointed temple...

The visceral impact of *Macbeth* on its audience was guaranteed by the fact that treason, powder and plot were very much in the forefront of everybody's mind. Only months before, Guy Fawkes and his fellow conspirators had attempted to blow up Parliament. Had they succeeded they would have wiped out not only the King but a goodly number of the royal family, the nobility, judiciary and military. The subsequent round of executions was savage, as was the crackdown on Catholics, especially in Warwickshire, the home of one of the leading conspirators, Robert Catesby. (Ben Jonson seems to have been involved in fingering him.) The trial and execution of the equivocator, Father Henry Garnet, gets a guernsey in the porter's monologue. The already paranoid King James took to wearing armour under his doublet and shunning public appearances. He was also greatly fascinated by witchcraft, sat in on witch trials and wrote an authoritative book on the subject.

As a new King's Man, Shakespeare was writing a piece calculated to please his royal master. To cap it off, he takes the minor and rather dubious historical figure of Banquo (James's ancestor) and gives him heroic status. And as one final little flourish of flattery he makes mention of a saintly English king who can cure disease by merely touching the afflicted. James was conceited enough to believe he possessed this power himself.

For an actor and director, Shakespeare's Tragedies are the peaks of challenge and achievement. They are the most engrossing, exciting, fulfilling and finally frustrating of all theatrical endeavours—frustrating because you always fall short of expectations.

You can read glowing accounts of the great nineteenth-century tragedians, but in my lifetime's experience there have not been many productions or performances of Lear, Macbeth or Othello that have won universal praise. People seem to have in their minds some ideal performance of those roles that few modern actors can satisfy. Maybe Kean, Kemble, Siddons and Macready playing 'in the grand manner' in those large auditoria satisfied the nineteenth-century taste for the epic and the grandiose, something modern audiences find hammy. The twenty-first-century actor is still caught between the conventions of cinematic naturalism and the demands of heightened seventeenth-century verse. Where to turn? Do you try to reduce the scale of the work to contemporary realism, and mumble and stumble your way through the text in an attempt to make it as 'natural' as possible? Or do you eschew all those naturalistic signals and invent a whole new theatrical language, something that can embrace the epic and metaphysical? This is the path chosen by contemporary German theatre, one which is impacting on a new generation of actors and directors in Australia.

The extremes of passion and suffering experienced by Lear, Macbeth and Othello defeat most actors—you can never really win. Hamlet is the exception—with him you can never really fail. Whereas the three former protagonists are locked in a blind obsession that intensifies as the play progresses, Hamlet remains open to suggestion, ready for change, flexible and playful to the end. With the first three we stand back in horror while we witness their pain and disintegration. We cannot imagine ourselves in their shoes, or see ourselves behaving the way they do. But Hamlet is more like us, or we like him. His doubts, his hurts and mistakes are all familiar—we've all more or less been there.

It's harder to imagine oneself travelling the same road with Macbeth.

Othello

Othello is one of the few Shakespeare plays I haven't been in or directed. But it has a special place in my memory and in my heart because it was the first time I saw Laurence Olivier act on stage. And I still regard it as the greatest live performance I've ever seen.

The Tragedies

Olivier was my acting idol since the age of fifteen and the biggest single influence on my love of Shakespeare and my decision to be an actor. And then there I was at the age of twenty-three, flying into London to take up my scholarship at the Bristol Old Vic Theatre School. As the plane flew low over the little red roofs my dominant thought was, 'Laurence Olivier lives here!'

My friend Neil Fitzpatrick had joined the National a couple of years previously and was playing the herald in *Othello*. He couldn't get me a ticket but said if I was prepared to sleep on the pavement outside the Old Vic I might get a ticket next morning because they always held a few in reserve for sale on the day. I saw *Othello* four times, mostly by sleeping on the pavement. The seat was always the same one in the back row of the gods, but it was worth it. Olivier seemed to fill the entire theatre with an easy unforced power and feline grace. Some critics complained that his Othello was like a West Indian bus driver, but Olivier always had that populist knack of relating his characters to someone familiar to us. Nowadays his performance would be seen as grossly insensitive and 'politically incorrect', but putting that to one side, his impersonation of a coloured man was impeccable and brilliantly observed. Unfortunately he committed his performance to film, where it looks grotesque and overblown. You can't just stick a movie camera in the theatre and call it a true record of the experience.

Olivier was one of the last white actors to take on the role. At present it is out of bounds, which I think is a pity. I fully understand cultural sensitivities and the peril of racial stereotypes, but how far are we prepared to go? Should only a Jewish actor be allowed to play Shylock? Should only a Russian play Uncle Vanya? I guess fashion will change again, the dust will settle and we'll find a new way to address the issue. And it's a good temporary corrective to some of the mindless casting in Hollywood in the forties and fifties. Did you ever see John Wayne as Genghis Khan? Or Robert Morley as the Emperor of China? Slightly better (but just as 'incorrect') were Alec Guinness's Arab chieftain in *Lawrence of Arabia*, Olivier's Mahdi in *Khartoum* and Marlon Brando's Japanese houseboy in *Teahouse of the August Moon*. As for Anthony Quinn, well, he played every nationality under the sun . . .

One of the points Olivier's performance made was that Othello's great weakness is not jealousy but pride: he cannot bear the thought of being cuckolded. If anyone's jealous, it's Iago. He hates everyone who has the qualities he himself lacks. He says Cassio must die, for example, because

> He hath a daily beauty in his life
> That makes me ugly.

In his essay 'Of Envy', Francis Bacon says:

> A man that hath no virtue in himself ever envieth virtue in others. For men's minds will either feed upon their own good or upon other's evil; and who wanteth the one will prey upon the other; and whoso is out of the hope to attain to another's virtue will seek to come at even hand by depressing another's fortune.

Coleridge summed up Iago as the embodiment of 'motiveless malignity', but that's a hard thing for an actor to play. Iago does have a motive: to destroy the love, virtue or beauty of others so that he does not have to withstand comparison with them. His hatred of others is surpassed only by his hatred of himself.

William Hazlitt, that great Shakespearean critic, sums it up thus:

> Iago in fact belongs to a class of character, common to Shakespeare and at the same time peculiar to him; whose heads are as acute and active as their hearts are hard and callous.

Iago's jealousy has not specific cause but is a permanent disposition. When Emilia speaks of jealousy she is speaking not about Othello but Iago:

> But jealous souls will not be answered so.
> They are not ever jealous for the cause,
> But jealous for they're jealous. It's a monster
> Begot upon itself, born of itself.

Orson Welles is a great speaker of verse, with a voice that is both ringing and mellifluous. It is a joy to listen to his Othello in his film version. The movie suffers from a queeny and one-dimensional Iago, Michael MacLiammoir, but the visual aspects, the camera work and editing are stunning, as always with Welles. His earlier stage performance was not to everyone's taste. A precocious schoolboy named Kenneth Tynan reviewed it for his school magazine under the headline CITIZEN COON.

My other favourite Othello is Plácido Domingo in Zeffirelli's film version of Verdi's opera. Domingo has the size, passion and emotional commitment to carry it off, his task made easier by Verdi's sympathetic score. One of the hardest things for the actor playing Othello, according to Olivier and others, is to maintain the required level of impassioned rage. Here the music helps.

In Othello, Shakespeare created the first 'noble' black man in Western literature. Hitherto blackness was associated with evil, as with Marlowe's Ithamor in *The Jew of Malta* or Shakespeare's own Aaron the Moor in *Titus Andronicus*. His sympathetic portrayal of a black man may have been typical of his cussedness in running against the tide of popular opinion. At the time he wrote *Othello*, London was experiencing a tide of Moorish refugees fleeing persecution in Spain. And, as always, the arrival of refugees created racial tensions in the city. Secretary Cecil complained about blackamoors 'infiltrating' English society and Queen Elizabeth issued an edict against 'the great number of negars and blackamoors which are crept into the realm'.

Apart from the shock of seeing a 'noble' black man on the stage, Shakespeare's audience would have found the play excitingly modern and topical. Anti-Spanish feeling was running high and it had been reported that the Spanish King Philip II was an insanely jealous man who had murdered his wife. He became suspicious when she inadvertently dropped her handkerchief and he ended up strangling her in her bed. The villain of the piece is given a Spanish name, Iago, after St Iago of Compostela, nicknamed Metamoros—the Moor killer.

As always Shakespeare researched his subject well and seems to have drawn heavily on Pliny's *Natural History*. Pliny talks of 'medicinal gums of the Arabian trees, mines of sulphur, a state made of chrycolite, mandragora and coloquintida, the Pontic sea and the Anthropophagi', all familiar to us from *Othello*.

If you were directing *Othello* you could set it in a remote army base today in the country of your choice (Australia, Britain, the USA) where a company of white soldiers is commanded by a black general. The word 'race' need never be mentioned—it would be implicit. And an army base has that same insular, confined hothouse atmosphere Shakespeare conjures up in his Cyprus: a remote island, full of soldiers, bored and idle, prone to drinking and quarrelling, open to intrigue, sexual frustration, whoring and wife-swapping. The play needs an air of claustrophobia, of the walls gradually closing in; we start out in the Doge's Palace in Venice, but end up in a bedroom on the island of Cyprus.

This tension was missing from the film version with Laurence Fishburne and Kenneth Branagh—although Branagh is among the best Iagos I have seen, along with Marcus Graham for Bell Shakespeare in 2007. Iago must be intelligent, jovial and credible. If he is at all transparent it makes Othello look like a fool. Everyone trusts Iago: Desdemona, Cassio, Roderigo. Only Emilia has her doubts and only the audience knows the truth. It should be agonising for an audience watching Iago spin his evil web, and seeing his victims becoming increasingly enmeshed. It certainly seems to have worked when Macready played Othello: at the moment he seized Iago by the throat, a gentleman in the audience, overcome with rage and frustration, yelled, 'Choke the devil! Choke him!'

When Bell Shakespeare produced *Othello* in 2007 it was gratifying to see a fine Indigenous actor, Wayne Blair, in the role and to realise that no other country in the world could have produced that particular *Othello*. It was our own.

King Lear

> To watch *King Lear* is to approach the recognition that there is indeed no meaning to life and that there are limits to human understanding. So we lay down a heavy burden and are made humble. That is what Shakespearean tragedy accomplishes for us.
>
> PETER ACKROYD, SHAKESPEARE: *THE BIOGRAPHY*

I have had the great privilege of playing King Lear twice in my career and, as I write this, am limbering up (literally) for a third attempt.

My first effort was in the Nimrod production of 1984 directed by Aubrey Mellor with a strong cast: Judy Davis doubled as the Fool and Cordelia, Colin Friels played Edmund and Robert Menzies was Edgar, John Ewing was Gloucester, John Howard played Kent and Michael Gow was Oswald. Goneril and Regan were played by Gillian Jones and Kris McQuade. After a try-out schools season in the unlikely setting of the Penrith Panthers Club, we played the York Theatre in the Seymour Centre. The set consisted of a huge pile of rubble, as of some bombed European city at the end of World War II, and the costumes were the rag-tag clothes of guerrilla fighters. This certainly gave the second half of the play a suitably blighted landscape but was not helpful for the beginning, when Lear is carving up his kingdom and doling out 'shadowy forests and with champains riched/With plenteous rivers and wide-skirted meads'.

Barrie Kosky's 1998 production for Bell Shakespeare was more successful in this regard. The curtain rose on a scene of fairytale splendour with Lear on his throne in front of a gold curtain, his court garbed in a dazzling array of colourful furs and jewels. Something of this fairytale approach seems appropriate. 'There once was an old king with three daughters. To whoever loved him most he would give the richest part of his kingdom . . .' This simple set-up suggests the parable-like nature of the story, the folly of the king's plan, and sounds a warning note of impending hypocrisy and treachery.

Kosky's production was a far cry from the determined realism of Aubrey Mellor's. From start to finish it was intensely theatrical. Kosky sat on stage throughout, pounding on an upright piano. Beside him stood two ageing trumpeters who were more at home on the club circuit than in the 'legit' theatre. All three were dressed in black tie, dinner jackets and red fez hats. Instead of his accompanying knights, Lear had four 'dogs' on leashes. These were four young men stripped to the waist sporting plastic shower caps and white clown makeup. They wore baggy pants from which protruded outsized genitalia. Louise Fox's Fool was a Shirley Temple look-alike who led the tapdancing dogs in a rendition of 'My Heart Belongs to Daddy'. These were some of the *least* controversial aspects of the production.

More provocative were Goneril and Regan sucking out Gloucester's eyes and swallowing them; or Matt Whittet's Poor Tom: he disguised himself by stripping down to his jocks from which he scraped handfuls of shit, daubing himself with it and eating a bit on the way. The hovel was a big gold box with holes in it. We mad folk crammed inside it, stuck our arms and legs out of the holes and jabbered insanely. Probably the most memorable scene was that set in Dover, which was reminiscent of one of those ghastly bus terminals with rows of plastic chairs and flickering neon lights. People wandered about wearing huge grotesque puppet masks while I chatted away to Gloucester, dressed in Cordelia's discarded pink fur coat, handing out rubber dildos to passers-by ... Barrie never did explain the rubber dildos.

It was a bit of a wild ride, that *Lear*. A lot of people walked out, we got bags of hate mail and sometimes the audience would yell things like 'Rubbish!' during the curtain call ... but people still talk about it. I found the production freed me up a lot, removing the constraints of naturalism, of trying to reconcile heightened verse with everyday behaviour as well as act both old age and insanity. There was certainly no need to act the insanity—the production did that for me; the imagery of the hovel and Dover scenes suggested the inside of Lear's head.

My next attempt at the role will perforce be very different—another director, another vision. I look forward to coming back to the psychology of the role, the interplay of characters and Shakespeare's dissection of monarchy, of patriarchy and of family.

Kosky dismissed Goneril and Regan as 'monsters'. I don't see that at all. I am interested in the relationship between Lear and his daughters that has made them the way they are. He makes no secret of the fact that he loves and prefers Cordelia and wants to give her the biggest slice of his kingdom. Enough to embitter her siblings, I should think. Even so, they begin quite reasonably in their treatment of their father until his demands and his behaviour get too much for them. What a lousy deal: 'I'm going to give each of you half my kingdom to administer but I'll hang on to the title and all the perks of a king and have a happy old retirement. I'll come and stay with you in turn, month and month about, and I'll be bringing with me a hundred knights, my hunting buddies, to be housed at your expense.'

Bad enough, especially when the hundred knights turn out to be a drunken rabble and that bloody Fool never stops insulting you with his wisecracks. Incensed by their father's capriciousness, and driven increasingly apart from one another by their fear and ambition, the two sisters find themselves stuck in a quagmire of resentment no family counsellor could resolve. And what of Cordelia? Is she Lear's favourite because she is so docile? I suspect rather the reverse—she's a chip off the old block, as stubborn as he is. Her refusal to play in the flattering love contest is a show of wilful independence, a public humiliation of her father.

Lear's folly is evident from the very start: the idea of breaking up a prosperous and successful business just so that one can enjoy a comfortable retirement is as indolent as it is short-sighted. Surely Lear should see that all he is doing is brewing rivalry and conflict. Worse, the game is rigged. He knows in advance he is going to give 'a third more opulent' to Cordelia. What kind of equal third is that? He means he is going to give her the choice bit and spend his retirement with her. Worse still, he is not just selling off the farm—he's giving it away. He intends to marry off Cordelia to either the Duke of Burgundy or the King of France, and one of *them* will inherit the choicest slice of Britain. No wonder Kent labels it 'hideous rashness'.

Once I crack that opening scene the rest is pretty plain sailing. But that first scene is tricky. Some commentators suggest Lear is mad at the beginning and the rest of the play is about him coming to his senses. I don't think so. That first scene isn't about madness—it's about the pitfalls of power. It's what happens when a man has got used to having absolute power and is convinced he has a divine right to it. It's important that Lear is old. He's been in the job too long. He's bored and wants out of responsibility. Because he demands and basks in flattery he is out of touch with the business and with the people around him, and most of all with his subjects—the homeless, poor and hungry whom he has never encountered. His grand plan has been tossed off without a thought to its ramifications and consequences. He is indeed 'King' Lear and the rest of the play is about learning what it is to lose that title, that authority, and to realise that he is only a 'poor, bare, forked animal' like other men.

In that opening scene we see Lear at his worst: vain, shallow, stupid, short-sighted, bullying and childish ... Yet we're told that people *love* him! Cordelia, Kent, Gloucester and the Fool are all ready to lay down their lives for him. I can't recall seeing a Lear who deserved that sort of devotion. One has to invent some sort of back-story to say that he has had a long and successful reign and the kingdom is in great shape. He has earned the love of at least some of his subjects, those named above. They remain loyal and loving, despite the fact that he is hardening into a cranky old tyrant. So I have to find something in the first scene that suggests that back-story. A celebratory atmosphere might help, with Lear getting a bit pissed and irresponsible? We'll see . . .

After that things get easier. Lear is certainly ugly in his confrontations with Goneril and Regan, but by now we start to feel some compassion for him given their rough treatment of him. Some humanity starts to bleed through the carapace of his folly. His pain finds relief in the violence of the storm—he exults in it and starts to come to his senses. He suddenly realises that the hungry and homeless are constantly exposed to these forces of nature: 'O, I have taken too little care of this.'

The sight of mad Poor Tom tips his senses into a new kind of consciousness which I would hesitate to call madness because it is so piercingly clear-sighted. Lear now realises his common humanity. He sees through the privileges of wealth and power that stand in the way of justice. One is awed by Lear's devastating critique of human institutions and hierarchy. His humility and patience when he is awakened from his torment cannot fail to attract a sympathy that turns to admiration when he defies his captors and accompanies Cordelia to prison.

Not that the play is about 'feeling sorry' for King Lear. The last thing you could accuse the play of is sentimentality . . . We should not feel a cheap thrill of satisfaction at the downfall of Goneril, Regan and Edmund. Rather, we are asked to reflect on the tearing apart of family, of community, of country, due to arrogance, moral blindness, emotional deadness and the abuse of authority.

Lear's 'madness' is liberating. He has always denied the female (flexible and forgiving) part of himself. He refuses to weep, suppressing his natural instincts. This repression turns into a vehement disgust of all things feminine. He has renounced his warmth and a unifying principle of human existence, and he gives away his kingdom not because he loves his daughters but because he wants to own them. He mistakes this impulse for paternal affection, but he has to undergo a painful journey to learn what real love is.

I'm always amazed to reflect that *King Lear* was first performed for James I as a Christmas entertainment! It's hard to imagine the present royal family sitting through *King Lear* at the best of times, let alone after the Christmas pud. Anyway, it was performed for the King at Whitehall on Boxing Day 1606. What was Shakespeare thinking? King James seems to have been no great lover of plays (especially long ones) despite his generous patronage of the King's Men. As I've mentioned he was a great believer in the divine right of kings and their spiritual power to cure the King's Evil (scrofula) by touch. So for a Christmas show Shakespeare puts on this play about a mad king who comes to realise that he is no better than other men, throws away his clothes and trappings of majesty and delivers a furious tirade against hierarchy, the hypocrisy of the court, the abuses of the judiciary and the speciousness of all human institutions. What on earth was King James meant to make of it? Perhaps history has underestimated him and he really was 'the wisest fool in Christendom'. It's hard to imagine the diplomatic and socially aspirational Shakespeare taking such a risk otherwise.

One thing that would have appealed to the King is the folly of carving up the kingdom. He was at the time trying hard to unite the kingdoms of England and Scotland but meeting with stiff opposition.

For all its bleakness and horrors, *King Lear* seemed to strike a chord with its Jacobean audience and was performed at the Globe as well as at court. Jacobean drama had, overall, a love of horror and cruelty that surpasses that of the previous Elizabethan age—think of plays like *The Duchess of Malfi* and *The White Devil*; *King Lear* is a fit, but much greater, companion piece. With the reopening of the theatres during the Restoration came a change in taste. *Lear* was now regarded as too horrifying, too barbaric. So in 1681 Nahum Tate undertook to rewrite it and make it fit for public consumption. He cut the Fool, nobody dies, Lear gives his kingdom to the young lovers Edgar and Cordelia, and goes off to live 'in some cool cell' with Kent and Gloucester. This was the version to be performed for the next hundred and seventy years. Not until the 1850s was a more or less restored version of Shakespeare's *Lear* performed in public.

The last fifty years or so have seen a division between those who want to see *Lear* as a 'redemptive' piece and those who see it more as an existentialist, nihilistic statement. The latter interpretation was given a fillip by Jan Kott in his influential work *Shakespeare Our Contemporary*. His essay *'King Lear, or Endgame'* yoked *Lear* to Beckett's *Endgame* as a vision of an absurd and godless universe, an expression of twentieth-century disillusionment. Kott's work had a big impact on directors like Peter Brook, whose landmark production of *Lear* in 1962 at Stratford starred Paul Scofield. The performance annoyed Laurence Olivier, who dubbed it *'Mister Lear'*. Brook had stripped away all the grandeur and panoply of the setting as well as guiding Scofield to play a down-to-earth, life-size monarch instead of the Job-like figure of biblical grandeur that had been the norm from Macready to Wolfit to Olivier himself.

I must say I find it hard to find any 'redemptive' message in *Lear*. All is 'cheerless, dark and deadly'. If there *are* any gods (which is doubtful), they toy with us as boys do with flies and 'kill us for their sport'. Our only weapon against this bleakness is stoic patience:

... men must endure
Their going hence even as their coming hither.

Where would I set the play? Which historical period of the past? Or would I set it in the present? Neither. I'd be inclined to set it in the future. It's about the end of the world:

Kent: Is this the promised end?
Edgar: Or image of that horror?
Albany: Fall and cease.

King Lear hovers on the brink of nihilism but something holds it back. There are acts of extraordinary love, courage and loyalty from Kent, Cordelia and Edgar.

It is a miracle that these green shoots can survive in such a blasted landscape.

And it is a miracle that someone could write it all down.

Postscript

Since writing this section I have now played Lear for the third time, in a Bell Shakespeare production directed by Marion Potts to mark the company's twentieth anniversary. It was a pretty gruelling tour of five months (including rehearsals) with seasons in Sydney, Canberra, Brisbane, Melbourne and Perth. We played to large audiences, breaking previous box-office records in most places, but the critics were negative almost to a man or woman.

I have never worked so hard on a role in terms of research and meditation (even though I'd played it twice before), physical and vocal preparation, and total commitment to every single performance—I gave it everything I had and came off stage wrung out after every show.

And yet I regard it as possibly the greatest failure of my career.

Why? I still can't figure it out . . . Maybe the setting was too abstract and sterile; maybe we did not create a convincing world for the characters to inhabit; maybe the scale of the acting was inappropriate or misjudged—I don't know. But I would have had a miserable time had not the audience response been so positive. Shakespearean Tragedy is a dangerous ocean. You might be lucky enough to catch the crest of a wave, but more often than not you'll be dashed to pieces on the rocks.

Each play has a continuous stream of images or metaphors that are intrinsic to that play. They convey a unity of feeling rather than one of meaning, rather in the way that film-music works in the cinema. There is a cohesiveness, an internal harmony, within each play; it touches even the most minor character, and places all of the protagonists together in the same circle of enchantment. In *A Midsummer Night's Dream* the rude mechanicals are quite unlike the fairies, but they partake of the same reality. They have been touched by the same lightning.

Peter Ackroyd

11

The Comedies

If we put aside the so-called 'Romances', we can call twelve of Shakespeare's plays 'Comedies', though their humour varies greatly, often diverging from what we might regard as funny. In fact there are no two alike and their stylistic differences are remarkable, ranging from bawdy slapstick to lyrical romance to rancid satire.

They are concerned mainly with love and sex—which do not always go hand in hand. The sex is frequently predatory and opportunistic (Touchstone and Audrey in *As You Like It*, Lucio in *Measure for Measure*), while love is anatomised from many angles—homoerotic (*Twelfth Night*, *As You Like It*), starry-eyed (*As You Like It*'s Orlando, or Helena in *All's Well*), repressed desire (Angelo in *Measure for Measure*), courtly affectation as opposed to rustic wholesomeness (*Love's Labour's Lost*). Shakespeare's survey of love encompasses teenage angst and fickleness (the young lovers in *A Midsummer Night's Dream*), and, most entertainingly, the age-old 'battle of the sexes' where a well-matched couple of egos ply their wits in the war for supremacy, to sort out who will 'wear the pants'. Into this category fall Beatrice and Benedick in *Much Ado*, Katharina and Petruchio in *Shrew*, Rosaline and Berowne in *Love's Labour's Lost*. As the Comedies mature, the women's roles become more assured and dominant, with the dazzling personalities of Portia, Rosalind, Beatrice and Viola determining the outcome. This would seem to reflect the development of Shakespeare's own sexual and intellectual maturity as well as being an indicator of the growing expertise of his boy actors and the delight audiences took in seeing them excel in female roles.

Peggy Ashcroft, one of the greatest twentieth-century Shakespearean actors, remarked:

> I think Shakespeare must have loved women very much . . . he felt that even when women were capable of acts of cruelty or violence, there was a compulsion of emotion or frustration which forced them on.

The earliest comedies appear around 1590, when Shakespeare was in his mid-twenties. *The Two Gentlemen of Verona* and *The Taming of the Shrew* are both Italianate in their settings but full of English characters. Bell Shakespeare produced *The Two Gentlemen* in 2005. Directed by Peter Evans, the play was performed in some thirty-six venues in all parts of Australia. Its main interest is in the promise of things to come in the later and greater works: the girl who disguises herself as a pageboy so that she can be near her lover (*Twelfth Night*), the planned elopement using a cord ladder (*Romeo and Juliet*). A highlight of the play is Launce's double act with his dog, Crab. It's still a crowd pleaser and precursor to a tradition of vaudeville schtick using animals.

The play has a fairly unsatisfying resolution—at least for a modern audience: mateship triumphs over heterosexual love. It's possible that Shakespeare was being ironic; but if this ending is contentious there is a lot worse to come in another Comedy of around the same time, *The Taming of the Shrew*.

The Taming of the Shrew

For all its perceived sexism and misogyny, *Shrew* has always been a great hit with audiences. I guess our great-grandparents would have found nothing to quibble with in its sexual politics and affirmation of male supremacy, and well into the twentieth century the play was still taken at face value. The Zeffirelli film with Richard Burton and Elizabeth Taylor was big box office and there were successful spin-offs like the Broadway musical *Kiss Me, Kate*, which upheld the play's perceived traditional values.

With the rise of the feminist movement in the seventies, *Shrew*, among other classics, came in for particular disapproval, though oddly enough one of feminism's high priestesses, Germaine Greer, staunchly defends the play. Audiences delight in seeing the eternal 'battle of the sexes' played out on stage, even when, as has generally been the case, the dice is loaded in favour of the men. And like it or not, Kate and Petruchio are a couple of attractive feisty roles that frequently appeal to celebrity actors. They have a zest for life, a passionate commitment to their individual agendas and a quick wit which sets them apart from the dullards around them. Putting its contentious sexual politics to one side, the play is a brilliantly constructed comedy full of well-defined and colourful characters. The subplot with its rival lovers, tricks, disguises, cunning servants and double crosses is marvellously realised, a feast for a company of character-comedians.

I have played Petruchio twice—once for the Old Tote in 1972, in a production by Robin Lovejoy with a cast that included Ron Haddrick, John Gaden and Drew Forsythe, and later in a production by Aarne Neeme in Perth's reconstructed Fortune Theatre, an approximation of an Elizabethan playhouse. This time Anna Volska played Katharina.

I directed the play for Bell Shakespeare in 1994 with Chris Stollery as Petruchio, Essie Davis as Kate and Darren Gilshenan as Grumio. Marion

Potts directed the play again for Bell Shakespeare's regional tour in 2009 with an all-female cast.

In approaching the play as director you have a number of options. First, you can present it as a period piece with what we assume is an accurate reflection of Elizabethan values and sentiments. Jonathan Miller came close to this with his TV production for the BBC starring John Cleese as Petruchio. For once Cleese wasn't playing for laughs. His Petruchio was a tough-minded Protestant Englishman determined to uphold a Puritan's view of divine order. Having brought Kate into line he led the company in singing a psalm as the end credits rolled. Miller is a director who believes the key to a play is keeping it in its 'period'.

The more widely accepted tradition of staging the play is to see it as a good-natured rough-and-tumble romp. In this version Kate and Petruchio really fancy each other from the start, but since they are both stubborn, wilful and domineering, they have some heavy negotiating to do, just as in any marriage. A variant of this interpretation is to see them as a pair of mavericks who are absolutely made for each other; nobody else could bear to live with either of them, but once they've arrived at a contract they are fair set for a blissful marriage. Yet another approach is to see Petruchio as the shrew; he has to learn as much as Kate does, and change his life accordingly. Chris Stollery, by contrast, saw Petruchio as a kind of Zen master who, through rigorous treatment, brings Kate to a stage of self-realisation: her unfocused rage was strangling her and obscuring her true virtues.

As for the famous or infamous final speech of Kate, that is the clincher. There's no doubt that it's a masterful piece of writing, and if you buy into its sentiments, a beautiful and moving one. It would seem a surprising number of women still heartily agree with everything Kate says... But if you don't, what are your options? A common recourse is to play it ironically, as did Peggy Ashcroft, paying lip service but underneath still deeply defiant. Then again, you could remind yourself that this is a comedy and that one of comedy's staple tricks is to have a character who has sworn all night that black is white suddenly do a complete about face and swear the opposite: confirmed bachelors like Benedick and Berowne eventually become marriage's greatest advocates. But a simple comic turnaround does not do justice to Kate's speech; there's a lot more to it.

Charles Marowitz's cut-and-paste version of the play turned it into a vehicle for the Theatre of Cruelty, and perhaps taking this as his cue, Michael Bogdanov in his RSC production showed Kate as both brainwashed and broken in spirit. As she mechanically parroted her final speech the other characters looked away in embarrassment.

A more cynical but comical viewpoint might see Kate and Petruchio in cahoots by the end. They have already reached an agreement and in this last scene she is aware that he was wagered a great deal of money on her playing ball. Aware of this, she delivers her speech with great panache then helps her husband scoop up the winnings. This would be in line with the play's insistence on the mercenary nature of marriage contracts and Petruchio's self-proclaimed status as a fortune hunter:

> I come to wive it wealthily in Padua;
> If wealthily, then happily in Padua.

In all of Shakespeare, romantic love is constantly underscored by mercenary considerations. As Juliet's nurse says:

> He that lays hold of her shall have the chinks.

Rather than avoiding the gender politics, Marion Potts' BSC production sought to comment on them by using an all-female cast. Actresses were allowed to depict male 'bad behaviours' so that we were simultaneously distanced from it and confronted by it.

When I played Petruchio I tried to find everything that was appealing about him—especially his candour. He is absolutely straight with the other characters and with the audience as to what he wants and how he's going to get it. Initially all he's seeking from a marriage is wealth and security. When he learns about the lively Katharina he's intrigued, and when he sees her he realises that here is a person of real worth, undervalued by those around her and getting in her own way through her rages and sullenness. He decides to train and tame her just as a falconer trains a wild bird in order to realise its full potential. Admittedly this is a very male and presumptuous attitude, but that's the world of the play, where women are simply commodities to be auctioned off to the highest bidder. (It should be noted that Petruchio never strikes Kate, though in *Kiss Me, Kate* he spanks her and stamps around with a whip in his hand—a very American way of taming a wife.) Physical abuse is minimal—he deprives her of food and sleep for a little until she learns to say 'thank you'. The abuse is mainly psychological—a determination to break her wilfulness. How far this goes, how seriously to take it, is a choice for each production.

When I directed the play in 1994 I tried to shift the emphasis away from Kate's bad temper to an examination of what lay behind it. I gave the play a deliberately Australian setting—an RSL club in somewhere resembling Surfers Paradise, where the emphasis was on rampant materialism: financial wheeling and dealing, gambling, bling and big boys' toys. Instead of the induction we had a chook raffle and talent quest in which members of the audience were invited to participate. So when the play began the ambience of an RSL club was firmly established. Kate's rebellion against this world and its marriage market set her apart and one could see her point of view.

In this production Petruchio was a footloose Vietnam vet who lived with a pretty rough crew of his mates in a junky old car yard in Nimbin. He too had no taste for the glitzy world of Baptista and co. and was determined to get Kate out of it. Her capitulation was based on gratitude for this as well as a temperamental kinship. In the end Kate and Petruchio are the lucky ones; they've sorted out their differences and seem destined to become one of the few happy couples in all of Shakespeare. The marriages of Lucentio and Bianca, Hortensio and his widow, seem far less assured of success. The play probably caused as much debate in 1590 as it does today. The recipe for a happy marriage and the negotiations necessary to achieve it will always be as fascinating as they are contentious.

The Comedy of Errors

There is a fair deal of farce and horseplay in *Shrew* and this is carried a lot further in *The Comedy of Errors*. Like *Shrew* it owes a lot to the commedia dell'arte shows Shakespeare and Ben Jonson saw performed by the Italian troupes in London, but its prime source is an old comedy by Plautus. Whereas Plautus has a set of twins searching for each other, Shakespeare doubles the fun by supplying each of them with a servant, who are *also* identical twins. *Comedy* is a cleverly contrived piece and the dialogue rattles along with a couple of cross-talk routines that would be quite at home on the modern vaudeville stage. It's curious to see in this very early play some of the themes that preoccupied Shakespeare throughout his career. We have a shipwreck, a family split asunder, twins searching for each other and being reunited, husband and wife finding each other after years of separation. Some of these ingredients recur in *Twelfth Night*, some in *The Tempest* and others in *Pericles*. In fact *Comedy* and *Pericles* are connected by the action taking place in Ephesus, a city condemned by Saint Paul as a centre of witchcraft and debauchery. Shakespeare's Ephesus is in *Comedy* a hospitable, friendly town, although strangers, like Antipholus of Syracuse and his servant Dromio, persist in their superstitious prejudice:

> They say this town is full of cozenage;
> As, nimble jugglers that deceive the eye,
> Dark-working sorcerers that change the mind,

Soul-killing witches that deform the body,
Disguised cheaters, prating mountebanks,
And many such-like liberties of sin ...

The Comedy of Errors was a palpable hit for Bell Shakespeare in 2002. We revived it two years later and in 2006 took it to the Bath Shakespeare Festival. Although we had toured parts of Asia (our education teams to Malaysia and Singapore, *Dance of Death* to Tokyo and Nagoya), this was our first venture to the UK, which we undertook with some trepidation, bearing in mind the old adage about taking coal to Newcastle.

We need not have worried. The audiences in Bath and Blackpool were warm and appreciative, the Blackpool newspaper critic lamenting that the Aussies had not only won the Ashes, they were trouncing the Brits at Shakespeare too. That was pushing it a bit far, but I did agree with him that the show was a ray of sunshine in a bleak English winter. And Blackpool in winter is as bleak as it gets. We were only there because an old mate from my Nimrod days, Paul Iles, was running the lovely old theatre, and hearing we were going to be in Bath, extended our tour by a couple of weeks.

Although it has its fair share of slapstick, gutter humour and broad characterisation, the play is indeed a comedy—not a farce. To me comedy has a certain humanity which farce dispenses with. In farce the characters are stock types, not people. We are never meant to identify with the characters, empathise with them or take them seriously. They are simply part of a mechanism—they are there to get into a pickle and gag their way out of it. We laugh *at* them, never *with* them. Comedy is more warm-hearted. Although we know it's all a set-up and that things are going to work out for the best, we do feel for the characters' dilemmas and anxieties. They have experiences close enough to our own; we share their joys and sorrows and enjoy the anticipation of a happy ending. They can move us to tears. Comedy has the potential for tragedy if things don't turn out right.

Playing farce is a very mechanical operation—it's all about timing the jokes and opening the doors on cue. It's essential that the characters are bold, one-dimensional and predictable. In comedy there is room for ambiguity and multi-layered characterisations. People can behave atypically, they can change. So in rehearsing comedy it's a fatal mistake to think about being funny. Avoid 'funny' costumes and props, 'funny' voices and walks. To work well comedy has to be grounded in reality. In rehearsing *The Comedy of Errors* we began by imagining how disconcerting, how frightening it would be to arrive in a foreign city where you are greeted by total strangers who know you by name. They claim you owe them money—one even claims to be married to you! This is the crisis faced by Antipholus and Dromio of Syracuse. Once you have established their bewilderment and confusion, the comedy can start to roll. The audience, one step ahead, knows that there are two sets of twins, laughs at their dilemma.

In rehearsing a tragedy I try to keep the atmosphere buoyant and relaxed so that we don't get bogged down in solemnity. But there comes a point in rehearsing comedy when it's deadly serious and has to be got just right; anything loose or sloppy will kill it. I recall the last words of the great David Garrick: 'Dying is easy—comedy is hard.'

As with tragedy it's essential that all the hard work must be left in the rehearsal room and what appears on stage is light, deft and effortless. In the last days of rehearsal it's good to do a 'speed run' to see how much time can be knocked off the show by cutting unnecessary pauses and laborious overexplaining.

Directing Shakespeare Comedies has been one of the greatest joys of my life. You have to keep reminding the actors, 'Don't expect any laughs in the first couple of acts—in fact, do your best to kill them; you don't want to wear the audience out. The first couple of acts are all set-up: the audience has to take in a lot of information. Keep it light, keep it truthful and keep it moving and you get all the pay-offs in the last scene.' The last scene of any Shakespeare Comedy is a delight, once you've sorted out the traffic, because for the first time you have all the characters on stage together. All the chickens come home to roost, all the pay-offs occur and you are swamped by gales of laughter and euphoria that engulfs both stage and auditorium. I recall the last night of my Nimrod *Much Ado* in Adelaide when the audience stood and walked down the aisles and onto the acting space to embrace the actors.

Love's Labour's Lost

While I was studying for my arts degree at Sydney University in the late 1950s, I lived a fairly impecunious existence. But when I saw a copy of *Euphues* published in 1623 in a bookshop near Circular Quay, I knew I had to have it. The *First Folio* was published in 1623 and this little copy of *Euphues* hit the bookstalls at the same time. I even fantasised that Shakespeare might have handled this very volume, because *Euphues* was the target of his satire in *Love's Labour's Lost*. The book cost me ten pounds, and the bookseller agreed to my paying it off at a pound per week, which was quite a struggle.

John Lyly's *Euphues* was enormously popular in its day and created a vogue for flowery poetry full of conceits and cleverness. Shakespeare himself was not averse to this and is occasionally overindulgent by our standards. But he was still able to laugh at the excesses of euphuism, as it came to be known. The four young courtiers in *Love's Labour's Lost* are prone to euphuism, none more so than the play's hero, Berowne. Like so many of the other characters in the play he is obsessed with language and word games. With his three companions Berowne has sworn to live a monastic life—to fast, study and abjure the company of women. But when the Princess of France and her three comely companions appear on the scene, the young men's oaths fly out the window and they fling themselves into an orgy of sonneteering and lovemaking. The fantastical Spanish knight Don Armado follows suit, penning poems to the country wench Jaquenetta, while the schoolmaster and parson entertain each other with Latin tags and quibbles.

All this preoccupation with language, says Shakespeare, gets in the way of true feelings and simple honest expression. He demands that affectation be stripped away in favour of sincerity and plainness. Reproved by his mistress, Rosaline, for his verbal excesses, Berowne promises:

> Taffeta phrases, silken terms precise
> Three-pil'd hyperboles, spruce affectation,
> Figures pedantical—these summer flies
> Have blown me full of maggot ostentation.
> I do forswear them . . .
> Henceforth my wooing mind shall be express'd
> In russet yeas and honest kersey noes.

The play's merriment reaches its climax in a performance of *The Nine Worthies* by the village folk for the entertainment of the court. The festivities are interrupted by the appearance of a French messenger:

> *Marcade*: God save you, Madam!
> *Princess*: Welcome, Marcade;
> But that thou interrupts't our merriment.
> *Marcade*: I am sorry, Madam, for the news I bring is heavy in my tongue. The King, your Father . . .
> *Princess*: Dead, for my life!
> *Marcade*: Even so; my tale is told.
> *Berowne*: Worthies, away; the scene begins to cloud.

With this masterful stroke, a cloud does indeed descend over the end of the play, which achieves an instant gravitas. The four ladies make their lovers promise to study and meditate for a year as a sign of their seriousness and then return to proffer their love. The hardest task is reserved for Berowne, who is enjoined by Rosaline to exercise his wit by giving solace to the sick and dying in hospitals. Berowne remarks:

>Our wooing doth not end like an old play;
>Jack hath not Jill. These ladies' courtesy
>Might well have made our sport a comedy.

King: Come sir, it wants a twelvemonth and a day, and then 'twill end.

Berowne: That's too long for a play.

I've seen a few productions of *Love's Labour's Lost*. One of the most memorable was John Barton's in Stratford in 1965 when I joined the RSC. It was staged in Elizabethan costume in a big empty space indicative of a forest glade. On the opening night it seemed tedious and overwrought, but as the season wore on it ripened, all of Barton's scholarship and attention to the language taking effect. By the end of the season it had become one of the most satisfying and moving, multi-layered readings of a comedy I had seen. A play like that is hard to bring off with five weeks' rehearsal, even for an experienced ensemble. You need time for things to sink in, relax and breathe, for the juices to flow.

Before I returned to Australia in 1970 I spent six months back at my old drama school in Bristol and undertook as my first essay in directing *Love's Labour's Lost* with second-year students. It was a frustrating exercise, trying to impart, in such a limited time and with such inexperienced actors, the complexities of the language, the sophisticated humour, and the underlying humanity and seriousness. A tough first lesson in directing.

My next encounter with the play was a production for Sydney's Old Tote at the Sydney Opera House in 1973. It was directed by Bill Gaskill, whose work at the National (including *The Recruiting Officer* with Olivier,

The Comedies

Robert Stephens and Maggie Smith) I had much admired. It had a strong cast, including my wife Anna, Jacki Weaver, Drew Forsythe and Alexander Hay. I found the production a bit stodgy. It was set in a sort of rural Oxbridge in Edwardian costume—all tweeds and pipes and button-up boots. That is somehow antithetical to the spirit of Shakespeare, especially his Comedies. A play about vibrant youthful sexuality is not helped by shutting it within the confines of Edwardian respectability.

But during the rehearsals Gaskill did two very good things. He could be a real martinet and insisted on absolute clarity. The language of *Love's Labour's Lost* can be knotty and intricate. We were rehearsing in a vast concrete warehouse and Gaskill made each of us in turn stand at one end of the room and deliver a complex speech to the rest of the group at the other end. This demanded not only the highest level of voice projection, breath control and diction, but precision of thought, meaning and intention. Gaskill's only response, time and again, would be, 'I can't understand you. Do it again.'

It was a frustrating exercise but focused the mind wonderfully and was a very good piece of direction. After an exhausting afternoon with the four young men, I heard Gaskill mutter to the stage manager, 'That went well . . . Tomorrow I'll give the ladies a bit of stick.'

His other good move was to help us appreciate the art of the sonnet. Each of us was supposed to compose a sonnet to his mistress in the play, so Gaskill had us each compose a sonnet to the actress playing opposite us. This made us really look at and think about the qualities of our 'lovers', which was a nice bonding exercise. It also made us realise what a difficult thing it is to compose a sonnet, so that when we came to recite them in the play we did so with a lot more understanding and respect.

Berowne was a very enjoyable role to play: he is smart, witty, passionate and sceptical. He enjoys life, he enjoys love and he enjoys a joke. If you are looking for a self-portrait of the young Shakespeare, I suggest you look no further than Berowne. He is deprecating about sonneteering and flowery love-talk in the same way that Shakespeare is. Rather than being resentful at being shown up by Rosaline and the other ladies, he graciously accepts defeat and ruefully confesses his shortcomings.

Anyone wanting to charge Shakespeare with misogyny had better reread *Love's Labour's Lost*. The young men of the play are portrayed as naive, affected and as shallow as youth dictates. The young women, on the other hand, are a lot smarter as well as being more mature. At the end of the play they bring their lovers to heel and impose on them penances for their folly and presumption. These penances are designed to bring the boys to a realisation of the true nature of love and its place in the world. It's the same lesson that the other Rosalind teaches her Orlando: love isn't about writing fluffy poetry and playing at dress-ups.

Love's Labour's Lost is seen infrequently, which is a pity. It needs a large cast—at least eighteen—and people are probably frightened off by the deliberate preciousness of the language. Kenneth Branagh, a renowned populariser of Shakespeare, made a valiant attempt to film the play, but made the disastrous choice to fill it with pop songs to make it more palatable.

A Midsummer Night's Dream

A play that is perhaps presented a little too often is *A Midsummer Night's Dream*, surely the most popular of all the Comedies. I'm not gainsaying its greatness but cannot help suppressing a groan when I look at the theatre program for the year ahead and note that there are at least half a dozen productions of the *Dream* about to descend on us: on the beach, by the pool, in the park; Indian versions, hip-hop, circus, high school, pro-am, along with opera, ballet and concert versions. In spite of all this the play survives and is assuredly one of the finest works of art ever created.

It is entirely original. Shakespeare usually resorted to old plays, historical chronicles or novellas for inspiration, but the *Dream* is all his own. And despite the fact that it deals with three utterly different worlds and genres—the mischievous and lyrical land of faerie, the earthy prosaic endeavours of the artisans and the bickering entanglements of the young lovers—the play has a wonderful homogeneity, all its elements caught in the web of an enchanted moonlit forest. The stories of the fairies and the lovers certainly overlap, as do those of the fairies and the artisans, but then all three stories meet in the grand conclusion where the love-suicide of Pyramus and Thisbe shows up the fickle behaviour of the lovers who are watching the play. Like *The Magic Flute*, Shakespeare's *Dream* is a perfect gem and you can't cut a note or a line without damaging the fabric.

As with others of the Comedies, English names and characters infiltrate an ostensibly foreign setting. We are told we're in Athens, ruled by Duke Theseus. He is attended by convincingly Greek counterparts—Egeon, Hermia, Helena and Demetrius. But in this same Athens we find a bunch of artisans with very un-Greek names: Peter Quince, Nick Bottom, Francis Flute, Snug, Snout and Starveling.

Like the artisans, the fairies belong not in classical Athens but in the world of English folklore and so does the forest:

The fold stands empty in the drowned field,
And crows are fatted with the murrion flock,
The nine men's morris is fill'd up with mud . . .

Puck is also known as Robin Goodfellow and Hobgoblin, and is renowned for tormenting milkmaids and farmers' wives, for playing tricks on gossips and solemn aunts as they sit by the fireside.

Again, this odd amalgamation of classical Greece and Elizabethan Warwickshire is entirely acceptable in the theatre. Peter Hall achieved a magical production in Stratford in the fifties by setting the whole piece in a sort of Elizabethan great hall, with even the fairies in Elizabethan costume—but with bare feet. He also had a stellar cast, including Charles

Laughton, Ian Holm, Robert Hardy and a very young Albert Finney and Vanessa Redgrave. The production was recorded for television and still stands up very well, as does Elijah Moshinksy's more recent production for BBC TV. But the production that became a touchstone for the play and for Shakespeare productions generally was Peter Brook's remarkable rethink at Stratford in 1970.

By placing the action in a stark white box, Brook maintained that real theatrical magic could be created by words and by actors rather than by scenic artists and lighting effects. Brook not only rejected any vestige of literalism, he demonstrated that speaking verse can be a sexual act and that the essence of theatre is playfulness. But his production possessed gravitas and challenged preconceptions. His forest could be a cruel and exposing place, one of traps and obstacles. And by playing *Pyramus and Thisbe* with heartfelt sincerity, the artisans revealed the true wonder of theatre:

> For never anything can be amiss
> When simpleness and duty tender it.

For all its clumsiness their performances had integrity, making the lovers' posturing seem shallow and fickle, their wisecracks all the more heartless.

It's a pity that so many productions of the *Dream* miss out on its delicacy, its lyricism and poignancy, settling instead for noisy horseplay and wild caricature. I've had only one go at directing the play and that was back in 1970 at NIDA, where I spent a year as head of acting. It was my second production and I still had a lot to learn, but even then I was deeply conscious of trying to find an 'Australian' way of performing Shakespeare, of wrenching ourselves away from aping what we thought was the 'right' way, the 'English' way, of doing the plays. I had been back in Australia only a few months after nearly five years with the RSC, but I made the decision that I would not try to transplant that experience. Rather, I would try to start from scratch and involve myself in developing a kind of theatre that was appropriate and necessary in Australia then and there. I felt a bit dashed at the time that all I had seen and learned in England was of no use here. But of course that was far from true. I had seen great performances and worked with great actors and directors who had made their mark on me and taught me invaluable lessons on which I would draw for the rest of my life.

The Merchant of Venice

In 1595, the year after *A Midsummer Night's Dream*, Shakespeare staged *The Merchant of Venice*, which has remained an equally popular but more controversial comedy. Shakespeare was now thirty-one years old and riding high. Besides the comedies so far listed, he had scored with his *Henry VI* trilogy, *Richard III*, *King John*, *Richard II*, *Titus Andronicus* and *Romeo and Juliet*.

He was still locked in competition with Christopher Marlowe, who had recently had a great success with a grotesque comi-tragedy, *The Jew of Malta*. Like Shakespeare, Marlowe was an opportunist with a keen nose for popular subject matter. A recent court scandal gave him what he was looking for. Roderigo Lopez was a Portuguese Jew and the Queen's personal physician. Caught up in factional intrigues at court, Lopez was found guilty of attempting to poison the Queen. The charge was most likely quite unfounded, but the unfortunate Lopez was hanged, drawn and quartered.

Riding the wave of anti-Semitic hysteria that attended the Lopez case, Marlowe dashed off *The Jew of Malta*, whose hero-villain Barabas, attended by his evil black sidekick Ithamore, poisons a whole conventful of nuns.

Barabas is a fantastical and nightmarish Jewish monster, the kind of caricature you see in Nazi propaganda movies and posters. Anti-Semitism was hardly an issue in Elizabethan England, mainly because there were so few Jews around. The majority had been banished by King Edward I in

1290. By the sixteenth century a small Jewish population was tolerated in London and being Jewish was no bar to Dr Lopez becoming the Queen's physician. But prejudice was always there, ready to be tapped, just as prejudice against Dutch and Moorish refugees would occasionally flare up in ugly riots.

Noting the success of *The Jew of Malta*, Shakespeare responded with his own Jewish villain, Shylock; but as always with Shakespeare, there was a surprise in store. He seems to have delighted in turning audience expectations on their heads, subverting established models. No doubt the audience flocked eagerly to the Globe to see another amusing and damning Jewish caricature, and that's the way Shylock seems to be set up. But then we see him being kicked, spurned and spat on by the pious Christians, one of whom not only elopes with Shylock's daughter but persuades her to steal her father's money and convert to Christianity!

By the time we get to the trial scene in Act IV, it's hard not to feel some sympathy for Shylock, despite his murderous intentions. Earlier, at the top of Act III, he is given the floor to air his grievances in one of the most affecting speeches in all of Shakespeare:

> He hath disgraced me and hindered me half a million; laughed at my losses, mocked at my gains, scorned my nation, thwarted my bargains, cooled my friends, heated mine enemies. And what's his reason? I am a Jew. Hath not a Jew eyes? Hath not a Jew hands, organs, dimensions, senses, affections, passions, fed with the same food, hurt with the same weapons, subject to the same diseases, healed by the same means, warmed and cooled by the same winter and summer, as a Christian is? If you prick us, do we not bleed? If you tickle us, do we not laugh? If you poison us, do we not die? And if you wrong us, shall we not revenge? If we are like you in the rest, we will resemble you in that. If a Jew wrong a Christian, what is his humility? Revenge. If a Christian wrong a Jew, what should his sufferance be by Christian

example? Why, revenge. The villainy you teach me I will execute; and it shall go hard but I will better the instruction.

It must have shocked an Elizabethan audience to the core to hear from a Jew such an eloquent rebuttal of Christian bigotry, especially in a theatre where there was so much direct address to the audience. Shylock is damning not just Antonio and all the other Christians on stage, but those looking on from the pit and the galleries as well.

Bell Shakespeare has produced *Merchant* three times so far. It was one of the productions of our opening season in 1991, in repertoire with *Hamlet*. Carol Woodrow directed the production, in which I played Shylock. We brought the production back for the following two seasons. We staged a new production in 1999, this time directed by Richard Wherrett with the late Percy Sieff playing Shylock, and in 2006 Anna Volska directed the play for our thirty-six-venue regional tour, with Robert Alexander playing Shylock.

Merchant is always a hit with audiences despite the contentious subject matter. Perceived anti-Semitism is not the only thing to leave a slightly nasty taste in the mouth. The bigotry and racial prejudice expressed by some of the characters extends beyond reviling the Jews. The second scene of the play opens with the glamorous and virtuous heroine Portia launching into a catalogue of bitchy remarks about the Neapolitans, the French, the English, the Scots and the Germans. A few scenes later she dismisses the black Prince of Morocco with:

A gentle riddance. Draw the curtains, go.
Let all of his complexion choose me so.

Bassanio's friends Solanio, Salerio and Gratiano are all Jew-baiters, Gratiano being the nastiest of the bunch, for all his merriment. The clown Launcelot Gobbo embodies simple-minded medieval superstition, equating the Jew with the devil.

All of this is unpleasant enough, but then add the play's fixation with materialism. It's supposed to be a romantic comedy, but Bassanio makes it very clear from the start that his wooing of Portia is as much a mercantile gamble as are Antonio's argosies. He has thrown away his inheritance and wasted the money he borrowed from Antonio. Now he wants to borrow more so that he can woo a rich heiress.

The rivalry between Antonio and Shylock is business-based, even though it is poisoned by Antonio's virulent, almost hysterical anti-Semitism. Lorenzo's wooing of Jessica might seem a romantic escapade (all that Venetian carnival atmosphere, masks, moonlight and disguise) but the fun is undercut by the fact that she robs her father in the process, renouncing both him and her religion. Launcelot is a treacherous little sod who happily quits his master when made a better offer. Despite Antonio's generosity and his being placed in mortal peril, it's hard to feel warmly towards such a racist bigot and even the warm and sunny Portia can chill one with her xenophobic one-liners.

So, given all this nastiness, where lies the play's charm and enduring popularity? To begin with, the play is fantastically well structured, with all the best elements of courtroom drama, romantic comedy and melodramatic cliffhanger.

At its centre is a fascinating love triangle between Antonio, Bassanio and Portia. Bassanio undoubtedly trades on his youthful charm and the fact that Antonio is smitten with him. Although Antonio can never possess Bassanio, he will sacrifice his fortune and even his life for him. He seems almost to welcome the opportunity to prove his devotion by submitting himself to Shylock's knife:

Commend me to your honourable wife;
Tell her the process of Antonio's end;
Say how I loved you; speak me fair in death;

> And, when the tale is told, bid her be judge
> Whether Bassanio had not once a love.

At the beginning of the play we are presented with the enigma of Antonio's habitual and deep-seated melancholy. What is it but 'the love that dare not speak its name'? And why else should Antonio regard himself as 'a tainted wether of the flock, Meetest for death'?

By sacrificing his life for Bassanio he will have a hold on him from beyond the grave, a nexus that Portia will never be able to break. Realising this, Portia is determined to thwart Antonio's death wish by saving his life. She tests Bassanio's constancy by giving him a ring and bidding him never to part with it. Then, in the character of the lawyer Balthazar, Antonio's saviour, she demands the ring as a reward, a demand backed by Antonio. In the final scene she reveals the ruse but imposes another binding ring on Bassanio and this time makes Antonio the go-between, dissolving whatever bond remains between the two men. The 'ring scene' at the end of the play is by no means a frivolous anticlimax but the resolution of the love triangle and a proclamation of Portia's victory. As the three newlywed couples stroll off into the moonlight, Antonio is left alone on stage, much like the other lovelorn homosexual, Antonio in *Twelfth Night*—another outsider excluded from the all-white, all-Christian, all-heterosexual club.

Without its cruelty, its racial and religious tensions, its running commentary on a materialistic and exclusive society, *Merchant* could be a cheesy romantic comedy. As it is, it remains a troubling, ambivalent and exciting work, both a challenge and delight for actors and directors.

Part of its enduring charm is the play's lyricism, irony and forceful rhetoric. The play bestrides two worlds, the tough, pragmatic, mercenary and legalistic Venice and the almost fairytale floating world of Belmont, where dwells the exotic Portia:

> ... the four winds blow in from every coast
> Renowned suitors, and her sunny locks
> Hang on her temples like a golden fleece,
> Which makes her seat of Belmont Colchos' strand
> And many Jasons come in quest of her.

Belmont is a site for romantic wooers, mysterious caskets governed by a dead father's love test—all legendary stuff. It is a world of feasting, marriage, music and moonlight expressed in exquisite lyrical poetry. The juxtaposition of Venice and Belmont is a remarkable achievement. Without the softening effect of Belmont, *Merchant* would be a cruel play indeed.

To our post-Holocaust sensibilities, Shylock will always be a problem to be got around. Interestingly, Jewish actors are not self-conscious about the role and take to it with relish. In recent years Antony Sher, David Suchet and Henry Goodman have all had great success in the role, and Goodman's performance in the televised version of Trevor Nunn's production for the National is the best Shylock I have seen. American actors who have played Shylock recently include Al Pacino and Dustin Hoffman. Orson Welles played the role in his unfinished film version.

Throughout the eighteenth and nineteenth centuries, when anti-Semitism was rife throughout Europe, audiences had no problem laughing at Shylock, but even then actors like Kean and Irving invested the character with pathos, dignity and some heroic stature. Don't forget that around the same time as Irving Charles Dickens, that compassionate champion of the underdog, was creating Fagin, a far less sympathetic character than Shylock.

When I came to play Shylock in 1991, I was very aware of the controversy surrounding the play and the character, and I was determined to see things from Shylock's point of view. I studied Jewish history and culture, got myself invited to synagogue and Friday night Shabbat gatherings. I had already attended weddings and funerals of various Jewish friends and I now spent time in Bondi coffee shops observing Jewish businessmen, listening to conversations and observing behaviour. One ultra-Orthodox couple I interviewed advised me, 'Watch *Fiddler on the Roof*—that's pretty accurate.' I was so determined to make Shylock sympathetic I may have pushed it too far out of whack. Some Jewish friends who came backstage after the first night said, 'I think you were a bit tough on the Christians.'

And I guess there's the essence of it: Shakespeare shows us people with both their faults and virtues, always the product of a particular environment. He is non-judgmental and so should we be. We have to accept the ambivalences, the inconsistencies, show all facets of a character or situation and let the audience draw their own conclusions.

One of the most remarkable Shylocks I have seen was that of Gert Voss with the Berliner Ensemble. He looked and behaved like all the other German businessmen on stage. He wore the same clothes, read the same newspaper; until he was pointed out you didn't know which one was the Jew. It reminded the audience how integrated the Jews were into pre-war Germany; how much they regarded themselves as Germans and could not comprehend why they were suddenly being rounded up.

The Merry Wives of Windsor

In 1599, Shakespeare delivered *The Merry Wives of Windsor* in response, legend has it, to a demand by Queen Elizabeth, who had so enjoyed Falstaff in *Henry IV* that she wanted to see the fat knight in love. Apparently Shakespeare knocked off the play in a fortnight so that it might be ready in time for the Garter ceremony at Windsor Castle. The piece is a pleasant prosaic comedy, chiefly notable for its depiction of small-town life with, as I've mentioned, particular insights into the classroom that only a grammar school boy would have had. Falstaff is only a shadow of his former self, but the other characters are presented with verve. The only stage performance I have seen was one by the RSC in 1965.

Ian Richardson was born to play the explosive and obsessively jealous Master Ford, but the whole show fell victim to the tyranny of the design concept. It was a prime example of how not to approach a comedy. The director and designer obviously thought it would be terribly funny to have everyone dress in very exaggerated versions of Elizabethan hats and pantaloons which the actors then tried to inhabit with funny walks and funny voices . . . No truth. No reality. No funny.

Much Ado About Nothing

Fifteen ninety-nine also saw Shakespeare produce what is to my mind his sunniest comedy, *Much Ado About Nothing*. There is a touch of darkness in the malignant character of Don John and a cloud settles over the action when Claudio rejects Hero at the altar. Friendships look like cracking and a duel is impending. But thanks to the timely intervention of Constable Dogberry and his bumbling Watchmen, the situation is saved and the way clear for a canter to a happy ending. It's basically a good-natured play, which is something you can't say of *Measure for Measure*, *Timon of Athens* or *Troilus and Cressida*.

The tone of the play and its main attraction is to be found in its leading couple, Beatrice and Benedick. As Leonard Digges remarked in 1640:

> . . . let but Beatrice and Benedick be seen, lo in a trice
> The Cockpit, Galleries, Boxes all are full.

Both characters are witty, egotistical and fiercely independent. Each decries the opposite sex and mocks the idea of marriage: obviously they are made for each other. Tricked into declaring their true feelings, their love is sorely tested when Beatrice demands that Benedick challenge his bosom buddy Claudio for slighting Beatrice's cousin Hero. To the very end they battle for supremacy but there can be no doubt they can look forward to a future of high-spirited marital bliss. The same can be said of Kate and Petruchio, Berowne and Rosaline. They are usually cast as young and feisty but a lot of fun can be had when both Benedick and Beatrice are a touch older, set in their ways, in danger of being left on the shelf. This gives their friends' matchmaking a touch of urgency.

Like several of the other Comedies the play is set in Italy. (Apart from *Merry Wives* none of Shakespeare's Comedies is set in England, although an Englishness pervades them.) The Italian (Sicilian) setting is important to remember because it helps to explain (if not excuse) a lot of what happens. Claudio's rejection of Hero on such flimsy evidence is reprehensible, especially if played with a cold British priggishness. But if Claudio is a hot-headed young Italian, impulsive and passionate, his actions are more easy to forgive. So are Beatrice's vengeful rage and the macho posturing of the young soldiers. We accept, in the theatre at least, that this Sicily is fiercely proud of its codes of honour, of vendetta, of female chastity and family names. They go with the territory and are attended by a degree of romance and the sort of fascination with which we watch movies like *The Godfather*.

I highlighted the Italian setting very deliberately when I directed the play for Nimrod in 1975. It was my first attempt to bust open the way of performing Shakespeare and take it away from the 'proper' English way of speaking the text. This was not because I am averse to good diction and affecting cadences but because I had found that in trying to sound 'proper', actors often adopted a self-conscious pose accompanied by stiff, conventional and meaningless gestures. It was a third-hand attempt at what they thought was a 'classical style'. I had been guilty of it myself and knew how this preoccupation killed truth and spontaneity.

So first I tried to free up the actors by freeing up the space. I put some acting areas in the auditorium and some of the seats on stage. Actors were encouraged to enter through the audience, sit and hide among them, crawl over the top of them and involve them as much as possible in the action—without harassing or embarrassing them. I removed any sense of 'naturalism' by setting the play in a circus tent with the costumes influenced by those of circus performers. I brought in actors from the Theatre for the Deaf to teach us a whole new repertoire of sign language and physicality to counter any temptation to fall back on 'Shakespearean' gestures. And, most radically, I had the actors rehearse the whole play in broad 'greengrocer' mock Italian accents. This was designed purely as a rehearsal technique to have fun with the language, free it up and steer clear of pomposity.

As opening night drew near, I said, 'Okay, it's time to drop the Italian accents,' but I was met with looks of horror. 'We can't drop them now! They're in our bodies, they're part of our characters.' I realised that the actors were right; so the accents stayed—to overall general audience acceptance except, of course, for a few who strongly disapproved. But that freeing up of voice and body, that sense of fun and irreverence, that deliberate cocking a snook at tradition, these became an important part of my work from then on.

Peter Brook's influence was still very much with me, as was his endorsement of 'rough theatre'. It accorded well with my own earliest and happiest theatre experiences: the circus, the pantomime and travelling tent shows. I had a good company of actors who revelled in the homely informality of it all and Anna Volska's Beatrice was a creation of heartbreaking warmth and beauty. Her combination of tenderness, vulnerability and feisty passion set the tone of the production.

As You Like It

I first directed *As You Like It* (with Anna, who also played Rosalind) at Nimrod, then directed it again for Bell Shakespeare thirty years later. It's a tricky piece in that it ceases to be plot-driven after the first couple of acts. The play begins with a wrestling match, a conflict between brothers, some dastardly plotting and characters fleeing from danger. Then after all this excitement it settles down into meandering pastoral idyll where people 'fleet the time carelessly as they did in the Golden world'. They fall in love, they write bad poetry, they feast, sing, dance and philosophise and seem in no hurry to move things along. If you get it wrong it all seems rather pointless, but if you can get it right it has all the joy of a long, lazy picnic in the summer sun. The play seems carelessly flung together, but is in fact beautifully paced and structured.

The greatest strength of the play is the character of Rosalind and the most charming scenes are her love games with Orlando. Like Juliet, and like her namesake in *Love's Labour's Lost*, Rosalind's job is to teach her callow suitor the real meaning of love. In Orlando's case love isn't about writing corny poems and pinning them up on the trees—it's about being punctual, practical and realistic:

> Men have died from time to time, and
> Worms have eaten them, but not for love.

Her magic is contagious and enlightening. She educates not only Orlando, but also the flirtatious Phebe and moony Silvius, who come to realise that love is

> All made of passion, and all made of wishes,
> All adoration, duty and observance,
> All humbleness, all patience and impatience,
> All purity, all trial; all obedience...

Rosalind has wisdom beyond her years and is an amazing amalgam of spontaneity, intelligence, wit, tenderness, passion and vulnerability—perhaps the most convincingly feminine of all Shakespeare's creations apart from Cleopatra. And all this to be portrayed by an adolescent male actor!

The second most interesting character in the play is Jaques, who can be played in many different ways. The actor and director have to decide how seriously we are meant to take Jaques and how much he is meant to be a figure of fun. It seems Shakespeare is making light of that stock character, the Melancholy Man, of whom Hamlet is the serious version. Every generation has its affectations, its poseurs. Jaques takes his melancholy terribly seriously:

> I have neither the scholar's melancholy, which is emulation; nor the musician's, which is fantastical; nor the courtier's, which is proud; nor the soldier's, which is ambitious; nor the lawyer's, which is politic; nor the lady's, which is nice; nor the lover's, which is all these; but it is a melancholy of mine own, compounded of many simples, extracted from many objects, and indeed the sundry contemplation of my travels, in which my often rumination wraps me in a most humorous sadness.

He is, to some extent, affected and self-deceived. He is also a self-appointed critic and scourge of social evils, but here his authority is undercut by the fact that he is a reformed libertine. There is no one more self-righteous than an ex-smoker or reformed alcoholic. It is possible to see in Jaques a satirical sketch of Ben Jonson, a 'humorous' man and avowed social reformer.

Jaques undoubtedly sees himself as being on a spiritual quest and at the end of the play, when the assembled company line up for a wedding dance, Jaques absents himself. He is off to find the penitent Duke Frederick and pick his brains. The other characters treat him with a mix of amusement and bewilderment, and maybe that's our cue too. His famous 'seven ages of Man' speech may be no more than a catalogue of commonplaces but it is wonderfully written. It can be delivered with acid sarcasm, wry amusement or a worldly-wise sadness. But it's entertaining however you do it. Duke

Senior treats Jaques as a sort of court jester and delights in baiting him; he's a sour version of Touchstone, with whom he feels a certain kinship. He adds a necessary touch of vinegar to the overall high spirits of this good-natured play. Shakespeare is very far from being a Jaques himself and enjoys taking the mickey out of this self-obsessed courtly poseur; even his name is a pun on 'Jakes', the Elizabethan slang for a dunny.

Of all Shakespeare's clowns, Touchstone runs the greatest risk of being terminally unfunny. We have to bear in mind that all of Shakespeare's clown roles were written for particular comedians who had their personal repertoire of facial expressions, physical and vocal mannerisms, and familiar schtick. Kemp was renowned for his dancing, tumbling and bawdry; Armin for his dry wit and musicality. So I have no problem with cutting, translating or even rewriting gags that have ceased to mean anything to a modern audience. The important thing is for the clown to be both funny and comfortable with his material.

There's not much that endears us to Touchstone. He has quick wit, but is always whingeing about how tough his lot is. He has a courtier's contempt for rustics or anyone lower than himself on the social ladder, failing to appreciate the homespun wisdom of Corin. He is a sexual predator who is willing to go through a shonky marriage with the goatherd Audrey, and employs a hedge priest for the purpose:

> I were better to be married of him than of another; for he is not like to marry me well; and not being well married, it will be a good excuse for me hereafter to leave my wife.

Jaques is amused by Touchstone but shocked by his gutter morality.

The original story of 'Rosalynde' by Thomas Lodge was set in France, in the forest of the Ardennes. (*As You Like It* is set in Arden, the forest playground of Shakespeare's childhood.) Shakespeare happily throws together French names such as Le Beau and Amiens with a clutch of

English ones—William, Audrey, Sir Oliver Martext. He throws some classical pastoral names into the mix as well (Corin, Phebe, Silvius) and a few from medieval Romance—Orlando, Rosalind, Celia and Oliver). He embraces the popular escapism of the pastoral, interpolating songs, dances and a masque of Hymen, but undercuts audience expectations of pastoral bliss by stressing the hardships of winter and rough weather, the dispossession of the shepherds and the slaughter of wild animals, the 'native burghers' of the forest. The pastoral idyll is shown to be no more than a courtly confection; after their brief sojourn in the forest, most of the characters return happily to 'civilisation', refreshed and rejuvenated by their holiday and having learned a few things along the way. As always with Shakespeare's comedies there are a few deliberate loose ends. The newly smitten Oliver decides to remain in the forest and turn shepherd, while Jaques settles for a hermit's cave. Four weddings are celebrated but only three, according to Jaques, are going to last: a final squeeze of lemon to forestall a cloying sweetness.

During the tour of my Bell Shakespeare production I was called upon at short notice to go on for Jaques, as Damien Ryan was suffering from food poisoning in Moonee Ponds. It was a rather terrifying experience. I had a pretty good handle on Jaques, but I was also doubling as Monsieur Le Beau, about whom I had no idea, even though I had directed the piece. I was grateful to the other actors for shunting me around the stage. A few weeks later I had to go on as Duke Senior because Julian Garner had taken ill. (With only eleven in the cast it was impossible to understudy all the roles from within the company on its lengthy regional tour.)

The only more terrifying experience was having to go on for Rhys McConnochie in my production of *Henry V*. Rhys was playing the King of France plus Sir Thomas Erpingham (a spit and a cough) and also the Archbishop of Canterbury, who opens the play with that hair-raising speech about the genealogy of French kings—so many Pepins, Clothairs, Childerics, Ermengards and Blithilds! Again, even though I had directed the show, I had no idea of Rhys's moves and the other actors kindly shepherded me around with mingled expressions of pity, apprehension and suppressed hysteria.

Twelfth Night

The first performance of *Twelfth Night* was in 1600. Shakespeare was nearing the end of his comic vein. Two years later came *Hamlet* and the melancholy shades of one tend to bleed into the other, along with some cruel comedy and strains of madness. Of all Shakespeare's comedies I find *Twelfth Night* the most irresistible in its heart-stopping mix of lyrical pathos, melancholy and outrageous foolery. It carries echoes of Chekhov's great comedies and the exquisite sadness of Mozart's *Marriage of Figaro* and *Cosi Fan Tutti*.

In too many productions the subtle shades can be obliterated by boisterous horseplay. While I was at Stratford I played Valentine—or Curio, I forget which—in a pretty disastrous production by Clifford Williams. It had a good cast, including Diana Rigg as Viola, Ian Holm as Malvolio and David Warner as Aguecheek. But it was dressed in bright primary colours on a starkly lit stage that we shared with a brass band. It was all gags and slapstick upon which no moment of pathos intruded. Clifford reasoned that the play embodied a night of chaos and misrule—but it's about other things too. The play is a whirling carousel of mismatched love affairs: Viola is in love with Orsino, who thinks he's in love with Olivia. She is being pursued by Sir Andrew and Malvolio. Maria loves Sir Toby and Antonio loves Sebastian, who is finally possessed by Olivia, while Orsino finds his real love in Viola. All these threads are marvellously pulled together and interwoven—yet some critics have complained that Shakespeare was weak on structure! In fact, Shakespeare's sense of structure is remarkably sound—nowhere more so than in *Twelfth Night*, *Merchant of Venice* and *Midsummer Night's Dream*, all of them perfect models.

I played Malvolio with the Sydney University Players in 1960 in a production directed by Ken Horler with whom, ten years later, I would set up the Nimrod Theatre. John Gaden played a very funny but rather thin Sir Toby while Bob Ellis provided a somewhat rumpled Regency courtier. I'm sure my Malvolio was all flap and dash—histrionic gestures and outlandish affectations—but, as students, we had the kind of fun you can have only with Shakespeare.

I played the role again in 1994, this time with Bell Shakespeare. The great delight of this production was having my daughter Lucy play Viola—the one time we've worked together, and that for only one brief scene. This time I sketched Malvolio as a stitched-up Tory with repressed sexual desires and lubricious fantasies. The press had recently carried a story about an English Tory MP who had been found hanged with an orange in his mouth and a plastic bag over his head. He was also wearing ladies' knickers and seems to have been dabbling in a bit of masturbatory fantasy. Shakespeare had no love of the Puritans, who were always trying to put him out of business. He hated their hypocrisy as much as their wowserism and got his revenge with Malvolio, whose name roughly translates as 'evil thoughts'. For all his assumed moral rectitude, Malvolio's daydreams are centred around screwing his mistress and lording it over her household. I adopted an Enoch Powell persona—brushed-back hair and clipped military moustache—then slipped into a suspender belt with yellow stockings and high heels for his attempt at seduction. The cruelty of the play was well brought out in this production by David Fenton. When Malvolio is shut up in 'a dark room', I was tipped, with the household rubbish, into a metal garbage dumpster. Darren Gilshenan as Feste clambered over it and banged on the lid with a baseball bat.

I directed the play for Nimrod back in 1976 in a glamorous production designed by Kim Carpenter, who drew inspiration from Visconti's film of *Death in Venice*. It tried to evoke that air of nostalgia and otherworldliness which Venice inevitably conjures up, and the motif of wistful homoeroticism was enhanced by having a male Viola (Russell Kiefel) who wore a sailor suit identical to that of Sebastian (Tony Sheldon).

For those who are puzzled over the meaning of the title, it should be recalled that the play was written to be performed on the twelfth night of Christmas, the last night of the courtly Christmas revels. (Shakespeare carelessly threw in an alternative title: *What You Will.*) Twelfth Night was traditionally a night of misrule, when all normal protocols were turned topsy-turvy and masters and servants swapped roles. All sorts of practical jokes could be played without fear of retribution. (There were inevitably a lot of sore heads next morning; the closest we come to it—and it's pretty close—is New Year's Eve.) This is how Toby, Andrew and Feste come to play such a cruel trick on Malvolio; this is how Malvolio dares to daydream about marrying his mistress and being transformed from a mere steward to being Count Malvolio; this is why Toby and Andrew are so furious with Malvolio for banning their carousing.

Because the original performance was aimed at a specific audience it is full of private jokes whose references are now lost. Malvolio was almost certainly a caricature of the prominent courtier Sir William Knollys, and the reference to 'Mistress Mall' must have raised a few titters since Mary (Mall) Fitton was the object of his lust. We know that the Queen disliked the colour yellow, but there are dozens of other in-jokes which go on providing fertile ground for academic research and conjecture.

There are a number of exquisite songs in *Twelfth Night* and their original settings have never been bettered. They seem to have been well suited to the talents of the original Feste, Robert Armin, a sharp-witted and dwarfish figure, noted for his excellent singing voice as well as his dry, acerbic wit.

There are many different voices in *Twelfth Night*—the languorous affectation of Orsino, the sly bawdry of Sir Toby, the giggling inanities of Sir Andrew, the trenchant sarcasm of Feste, the inflated pomposity of Malvolio and the rapturous, heartbreaking sincerity of Viola:

Viola: Ay, but I know—
Duke: What dost thou know?
Viola: Too well what love women to men may owe:
           In faith, they are as true of heart as we.
           My father had a daughter lov'd a man,
           As it might be perhaps, were I a woman,
           I should your lordship.
Duke: And what's her history?
Viola: A blank, my lord: she never told her love,
           But let concealment like a worm i' th' bud
           Feed on her damask cheek: she pin'd in thought,
           And with a green and yellow melancholy
           She sat like Patience on a monument,
           Smiling at grief. Was not this love indeed?
           We men may say more, swear more, but indeed
           Our shows are more than will: for still we prove
           Much in our vows, but little in our love.
Duke: But died thy sister of her love, my boy?
Viola: I am all the daughters of my father's house,
           And all the brothers too: and yet I know not.
           Sir, shall I to this lady?

All these voices meld effortlessly in this sweet symphony of a play. But there are very few productions which manage to extract and balance them all, to capture that particular Elizabethan mix of lyricism, bawdry, sadness, cruelty and reckless high spirits. The two I have seen come nearest I have referred to earlier in this book: John Barton's RSC production with Judi Dench and Donald Sinden, and Declan Donnellan's all-male, all-Russian company of wonderful actors.

    Maybe the note of wistful sadness that pervades the play stems from the fact that Shakespeare's younger daughter, Judith, was now sixteen.

Her dead twin, Hamnet, would have been the same age. Is Shakespeare bringing the drowned twin back from the dead and uniting brother and sister in an heroic act of wish fulfilment?

Lee Lewis's 2010 production of *Twelfth Night* for Bell Shakespeare was based on this possibility. The production was designed to do a long national tour, including those parts of regional Victoria which had recently been devastated by bushfires. So the actors were dressed as refugees from a natural disaster drifting into a community hall piled high with old clothes. Here they acted out *Twelfth Night* as a healing exercise, an attempt at bonding and dealing with their grief and loss. At the end there was a hint that the actress playing Viola's brother had survived the catastrophe and she rushed off joyfully to embrace him. The production had the desired impact on the community it was designed for, but even audiences in metropolitan centres appreciated this show that revelled in robust horseplay while maintaining a peculiar poignancy.

Measure for Measure

The years between 1602 and 1604 produced the last of Shakespeare's Comedies and they share some of the darkness of his other plays around that time. Before *Measure for Measure* (1604) Shakespeare wrote that most bitter, bleak and nasty deconstruction of the Trojan War, *Troilus and Cressida* (1602); then we get *All's Well That Ends Well* (1602) followed by *Othello* (1604).

Measure for Measure has never been a box-office favourite. Its leading characters are resistible in various ways, its subject matter distasteful to squeamish stomachs, its resolution and moral standpoint ambiguous and its locations (the cold prison, judicial headquarters and seedy brothels) not necessarily places you want to spend time in. Nor can you take much refuge in lyrical or uplifting language—it tends to be dry and legalistic or shrill with anguish verging on hysteria or else downright filthy.

Yet the play has many admirers and I count myself among them, having had the pleasure of directing it twice, for the Nimrod and for Bell Shakespeare. *Measure* is one of those Shakespeare plays we readily identify as Jacobean rather than Elizabethan. Gone are the last vestiges of linguistic ornament and carefree ostentation. We are now in a gloomier world of dungeons, spies, the rack, disguise and eavesdropping. There is a stench of moral corruption that hangs over Jacobean drama, and it's hard to know if that was merely literary fashion or a true reflection of the mood of the times.

The Duke in *Measure* has some similarities to King James himself. They both abhor crowds and popular demonstrations. Both are obsessed with seeking out and exposing evildoers. Both are secretive and both believe in administering tough justice with the occasional magnanimous display of mercy. James must have seen his likeness in the Duke and one has to conclude that he approved of it. But the role remains one of the most difficult in all of Shakespeare and very few actors succeed in bringing it off to universal satisfaction. In playing the role you have to take a strong line and make firm decisions upfront. Why does he pretend to leave his city in the care of Angelo, a man he suspects of being corrupt? Why does he come back, in disguise, to spy on him? Is he (as in Tyrone Guthrie's very Catholic reading) an avenging angel, a Christ-like figure of divine justice? Or is he a moral coward who wants to pass the buck for his own incompetence? Is he driven by prurience to eavesdrop on the privacy of Claudio, Isabella and Juliet?

How outrageous is his behaviour in hearing confessions while disguised as a monk! How cruel is his deceit of Isabella (telling her that her brother is dead, just so he can miraculously 'resurrect' him), and how appalling his presumption in demanding her hand in marriage! Of course if you take the Guthrie line that this is the course of divine justice, all the above can be swallowed (just), but I suspect Shakespeare's intention is more darkly comic than that.

On a human, rather than divine, level, this Duke is fallible, paranoid, spiteful, sexually inhibited, punitive, opportunistic and manipulative. Of course, he would be the last person to recognise or acknowledge any of this, but it makes him human and far more interesting to play than trying to impersonate a symbol of divine justice. Sean O'Shea, in my Bell Shakespeare production of 2005, captured many of these jarring inconsistencies, as did Garry McDonald in my 1973 Nimrod production; in fact Garry played him as not merely eccentric but mildly crazy.

Angelo, his opposite number, is not easy to warm to either. So self-righteous, so sexually repressed, so lacking in empathy, he is a mere legalistic machine until a sudden onrush of sexual desire brings him face to face with his real self. If he acknowledged this it could be the start of a transformation, but he is so hamstrung by pride, fear and a desire to maintain his public image that he decides to use his newfound authority like a tyrant, first of all forcing Isabella to sleep with him to save her brother's life and then, worse, by double-crossing her. His contrition at the end seems sincere, but his forced marriage to the jilted Mariana doesn't bode well for either of them.

It was customary during the nineteenth and early twentieth centuries to play Isabella as a saint, an unassailable icon of chastity, the perfect Victorian or Edwardian heroine. Modern actors and directors (and audiences too, I imagine) find this too pallid and simplistic a rendering. Fair enough that she repudiates Angelo's advances and revolting proposition—every feminist in the house should be cheering for her. But we feel a chill run through us when she calmly announces, 'More than our brother is our chastity.' We understand her dilemma and are forced to ask ourselves how much of our own integrity or sense of personal honour would we be prepared to sacrifice to save the life of a loved one. (And Shakespeare does raise the stakes by making her a novice nun!)

But our sympathy for Isabella is tested when poor callow Claudio begs her to do the deed of darkness to save his life. She rounds on him with a fury bordering on hysteria:

> . . . O, you beast! O faithless coward, O dishonest wretch . . .
> Die, Perish! Might but my bending down
> Reprieve thee from thy fate, it should proceed.
> I'll pray a thousand prayers for thy death,
> No word to save thee.

This has led most modern actors and directors to see Isabella warped by the same kind of sexual repression that torments Angelo and, to some extent, the Duke, who is most insistent about his sexual probity. Maybe it's this fear of sex rather than a spiritual quest that has led her to the convent. For all her virginal posturing she is more than willing to play the 'bed-trick' on Angelo, sending Mariana in her place—apparently Mariana's virginity is of no great account. To see Isabella in these terms—as a repressed, awkward and stubborn woman, fallible and inconsistent, is far more interesting than the version which presents her as a put-upon plaster saint. It places her in the same world as the other characters, where straitlaced priggishness is assailed by callous licentiousness.

At first glance the low-life world of Pompey Bum, Lucio and Mistress Overdone looks more attractive than the stitched-up court. But this world of pimps and brothels is raddled with disease and selfishness—it's not as much fun as you'd expect. Shakespeare seems to have been no stranger to London's brothels. Both here and in *Pericles* he shows great familiarity with the habitués and their language. Incidentally, his co-author of *Pericles* was George Wilkins, his next-door neighbour in Silver Street, who was himself a brothel-keeper as well as literary hack. Whatever the apparent fun and camaraderie of the brothel and the tavern, their ethos is summed up in Lucio, who openly brags about getting Kate Keepdown pregnant then dumping her. At least 'the better sort' wrestle with their consciences and agonise over moral dilemmas, even if they do the wrong thing.

We can be amused by Pompey and spare some tender feelings for Claudio and Juliet, but overall *Measure* is easier to admire than to love. Like all of Shakespeare's plays—Comedies, Tragedies, whatever—*Measure* is full of matter to ponder, with many contrary viewpoints to consider and ambiguities that are left unresolved. Performed unsentimentally, with the right mix of dry observation and sympathy for every character, *Measure* can hit you like a refreshing dash of cold water in the face.

All's Well That Ends Well

All's Well That Ends Well is performed even less frequently than *Measure for Measure*. It is not a 'feel-good' comedy like *As You Like It* and *Much Ado*, nor does it have the magic of *Twelfth Night* or the drama of *Merchant of Venice*. It has a sobering commentary on the relationship between integrity and courtly 'honour', it has a very affecting heroine in Helena and in the Countess a role that George Bernard Shaw regarded as the loveliest in the canon for an older actress. It also has a great clown's role in the cowardly rogue Parolles. Plot-wise we return to the 'bed-trick', which is by now wearing out its welcome, and in the role of Bertram a character who can expect to win very little audience sympathy. He comes across as a particularly cold and selfish individual, try as we might to excuse his behaviour because of his strict upbringing, the unreasonable expectations of his elders and their stifling social mores. He's still a cad.

It's the one Shakespeare Comedy with which I have had almost no personal connection, apart from the fact that my wife Anna was in John Barton's RSC production which toured with Peter Hall's *Macbeth* to Russia in 1967. The two shows played in repertoire in Moscow and Leningrad (as it was then) and *All's Well* dropped in to Paris on the way home. I was playing Lennox in *Macbeth* in which Anna was a very pretty third apparition, popping out of the witches' cauldron.

It was fascinating to get a look behind the Iron Curtain on its fiftieth anniversary but it was a very showcase kind of tour. We were carefully shepherded from place to place and had little opportunity to meet or relate to people in the street. After performances we were given prolonged standing ovations, but were not convinced this was altogether to do with the quality of the shows. It may have been mere political protocol or maybe a sign of genuine gratitude that we had made the effort to visit this still relatively closed country—hands-across-the-sea stuff.

One thing in Anna's and my favour was that we had a baby with us. Hilary was eighteen months old and we had little choice but to take her with us into the depths of a Russian winter. The few exchanges we had with the citizenry were when we were stopped in the street by clucking old ladies who wrapped her bonnet even more firmly about her little ears. The food in the hotels was very plain and pretty dire, but when we had Hilary with us an egg might magically appear or even a piece of fruit—much to the envy of the rest of the company.

•

The relative popularity of Shakespeare's plays tends to be subject to fashion. At certain times the Histories seem most resonant, depending on the state of global politics. Individual Tragedies will be rediscovered as the result of some astonishing star performance or directorial vision. The great Romances, always in danger of being dismissed as too fantastical, will suddenly strike a chord with a generation and manifest their spiritual nourishment. And at certain times in our lives, or due to the vagaries of fashionable taste, it is the Comedies that speak to us most directly and feelingly. They are a monument to half of Shakespeare's soul, and actors and directors are obliged to take them seriously. They should eschew the funny hats, funny voices, general campery and effete buffoonery that calls itself 'style'. They should chuck out all the tired old gags and clichés and go to the heart of the matter. For no two of Shakespeare's Comedies are alike. Each has an individual voice, and if we listen carefully we can hear the subtlest tones of the human heart making its grave demand for love.

The first page of his that I read made me his for life; and when I had finished a single play, I stood like one born blind, on whom a miraculous hand bestows sight in a moment. I saw, I felt, in the most vivid manner, that my existence was infinitely expanded . . . I did not hesitate for a moment about renouncing the classical drama. The unity of place seemed to me irksome as a prison, the unities of action and of time burthensome fetters to our imagination; I sprang into the open air, and felt for the first time that I had hands and feet.

                        Goethe

12

Shakespeare's books

A chat with Richard Field

> The first taste or feeling I had of bookes, was of
> the pleasure I tooke in reading the fables of Ovid's
> *Metamorphosies*; for being but seven or eight years old,
> I would steale and sequester my selfe from all other
> delights, only to reade them.
> MONTAIGNE

A lot of people wonder how much of a scholar Shakespeare was, what books he read and collected, and what became of them when he died. So I have come to Blackfriar's—to the shop of the publisher and printer Richard Field. It is 1619, three years after Shakespeare's death, and Richard Field is now Master of the Stationers' Company.

It is a fair-sized and tidy shopfront and Master Field is a brisk and tidy gentleman, a bit on the smallish side, with alert dark eyes and an engaging smile—the sort of chap who could make a success of anything, you imagine. He sits me down by a corner window so he can keep an eye out for customers. Behind a heavy curtain at the end of the room I can hear evidence of the printing press at work. The shop itself is light and airy, the walls lined with handsome walnut bookcases with glass doors. Small occasional tables display open copies of the most prized editions as well as stacks of pamphlets.

JB: 'They tell me you were Will Shakespeare's oldest and closest friend.'

RF: 'Well, I don't know about closest—Dick Burbage might make a claim in that direction—but oldest friend, certainly: we went to school together. My father was a tanner and Will's old man, John, was a master glover. He dealt in skins and hides as well as wool, so they had a few business interests in common. I lived round in Bridge Street, so most mornings Will and I would meet at the Market Cross and walk to school together. I was actually two and a half years older than Will but we shared a passion for the classics.'

JB: 'How did you get into the publishing business?'

RF: 'I always loved books and I didn't fancy following my old man into the tanning trade, so I made my way to London and was lucky enough to find work with a man named Thomas Vautrollier, a top publisher. When the boss died I married his widow Jacqueline and inherited the business.'

JB: 'Did you see a lot of young Shakespeare when he first came to London?'

RF: 'My word yes. The Vautrolliers, who were French Huguenot refugees, had some Huguenot friends called the Mountjoys who lived in Silver Street—they used to make fancy hats for the ladies at court. When Will came to London he took lodgings with them. He was struggling to make a bob or two—acting small parts, patching up old plays and collaborating on new ones. The money all had to go back to Stratford to feed the wife and kids. But the Burbages over in Shoreditch looked after him and it didn't take him long to make his mark. He was ambitious, competitive and a hard worker, not a tearaway like a lot of the other actors and writers I met. He spent a lot of time with us and the Mountjoys, so he picked up a fair bit of French—he had a good ear for languages.'

JB: 'When was the first time you actually worked together?'
RF: 'Well, it must have been back in 1593. It was a particularly bad plague year and all the theatres were closed down for twelve months or more. Will spent some time in Stratford but then he went to Titchfield, the home of his patron, the young Earl of Southampton. While he was there he wrote *Venus and Adonis* and dedicated it to Southampton. That was a smart move. It was a fantastic success—I reprinted it nine times in Will's lifetime and six more since he died . . . Unheard of! They reckon every student in Cambridge had a copy of Venus and Adonis under his pillow. Southampton was, of course, terribly chuffed, so Will dedicated his next poem, *The Rape of Lucrece*, to him too. That had eight reprints.'

JB: 'It looks as if Shakespeare was thinking of giving up theatre and becoming a gentleman poet?'
RF: 'He may have been tempted for a moment or two, but the theatre was where his heart was. He'd rather be with a bunch of actors than be the pet monkey to a lot

of courtiers. In fact he came back from Titchfield a new man, quite recharged.'

JB: 'What was the reason for that?'

RF: 'There was this character called John Florio who'd been hired to teach the Earl Italian. He taught Will a bit on the side and let him use his library. He had a vast collection of Italian novellas, poems and plays and probably took Will to task over his poor knowledge of Italian geography. Anyway, Will's Italian plays got a lot better after meeting John Florio. But it seems that not all of Will's time was spent in the study: Florio had a very pretty wife, a clever lass from Somerset. Some people reckon she is the so-called Dark Lady of the Sonnets and that Will was bonking her while borrowing her husband's books. Who knows? I wouldn't put it past him.'

JB: 'So when Shakespeare settled again in London was he a regular book buyer?'

RF: 'Certainly not from me. I'd never call Will a tight-fisted man, but he was frugal; I guess as a jobbing actor you learn to be. And, let's face it, books are expensive. Not many people build up a library. Anyway, Will had nowhere to keep them—always moving, sometimes to avoid the tax man, back and forth between London and Stratford...'

JB: 'But surely *some* people must buy books; you seem to have a thriving business here....?'

RF: 'Oh yes, there are a few great collectors, thank God. Now take Ben Jonson, for instance... Ben feels cheated that he never got to university—he'd been apprenticed to a bricklayer. So he set out to become more erudite than the best of them and built up a personal library. He collected over two hundred books and on each one he'd write 'Sui Ben: Jonson liber'—Ben Jonson, his book. He'd read them slowly and carefully, underlining and making notes. He was devastated when he lost the lot in a fire, but he straightaway started rebuilding it—buying new books and buying back old ones he'd sold when he was short of cash. But a library of that size is quite rare.'

JB: 'So would you say that Jonson was a greater scholar than Shakespeare?'

RF: 'Oh certainly—but Will never aspired to that sort of erudition. He didn't need to. We all had our Horace and Virgil, our Plutarch and Seneca soundly beaten into us in grammar school. Any other information he needed as a playwright he could pick up on the run. Will wasn't a bookish man; he used books but he didn't hoard them. Once he'd got what he wanted out of a book he'd sell it or give it away. Besides, he had free access to Southampton's library and later my Lord Pembroke's, when he became the patron of Will's company. He was a generous man, Pembroke: I know for a fact that he used to give Ben Jonson twenty pounds every New Year's Day to buy books—that's a lot of money.'

JB: 'Did Shakespeare borrow books from you as well?'
RF: 'He did indeed. I never begrudged him; he didn't keep them long and always returned them in good nick.'

JB: 'What are some of the books you loaned him?'
RF: 'Well . . . let's have a look on the shelves here . . . Now here's one: Arthur Brooke's *Tragical History of Romeo and Juliet*. It's a dry-as-dust old morality tale—you know, wicked children crossing their parents' wishes and so

on... But it gave Will the plot for his play. Here's an interesting one: *Palace of Pleasure* by William Painter. It's got a hundred stories from the Greek, Italian and French, including twelve of Boccaccio's *Decameron* yarns. Everyone says this book was ransacked to furnish the playhouses of London. They all pinched their plots from it. Will pinched the plot of *All's Well*.'

JB: 'Audiences didn't mind that they weren't being given original stories?'

RF: 'On the contrary: they liked the old stories best. With at least one new play coming out every week you wouldn't want to buy a pig in a poke!'

JB: 'But Shakespeare did make up some new stories...'

RF: 'Not that many. *A Midsummer Night's Dream*, that's all his. So is *The Tempest* and *Merry Wives of Windsor*. The rest he picked up and adapted. On this shelf we have more Italian works—Bandello: (*Twelfth Night* owes a bit to him); Fiorentino (*The Merchant of Venice*); Cinthion's *Hundred Stories*—look here: 'There was a Moor of Venice'... Ah, excuse me, there's a customer...'

Master Field steps outside his front door to converse with a prosperous-looking gent in a short cloak and black velvet cap—a courtier, perhaps. As they seem quite engrossed, I take a stroll to the back of the shop and take a peek behind the heavy arras curtain that divides the shop from the publishing house. It's a hive of industry back there.

The compositor is busy digging around for the leaden pieces of type and arranging them, letter by letter, in trays which he then sets in rows and places in frames. The pointer inks them over and an apprentice turns the heavy screws that press the inked frames down onto large sheets of paper.

The printing press casts off the sheets which are collected by another apprentice and folded to make the pages. He hands them one by one to a proofreader who scans them for typos and misspellings and returns them to the compositor to make corrections before they are handed over for stitching and binding. It all looks very calm, focused and well organised.

I turn to find Master Field looking over my shoulder and observing his printing house with satisfaction. We resume our conversation:

RF: 'Will developed a very particular pattern of movement on the days he went to perform at the Globe,' he informs me as we sit down again. 'He had to get there before two o'clock, so you'd catch him leaving his lodgings round about nine, after breakfast. He was staying with the Mountjoys, as I mentioned, corner of Muggle and Silver streets. He'd set off down Aldergate to St Paul's with all its bookstalls and that's where he'd spend the next two or three hours before walking along Cheapside, down Lombard Street, then down Gracious Street and across London Bridge to the Globe. Some days he'd catch a wherry from Puddle Dock or Dowgate . . . You'd see him standing there in St Paul's churchyard, browsing, moving from stall to stall, picking up book after book and skimming them, the eyes moving quickly up and down the pages, the hands mechanically turning them.

'Occasionally he'd take out his tables and make a note, but mostly he could absorb and remember whatever he needed. He had a prodigious memory; well, we all did to some extent. We'd been taught to recite whole books by rote at school, and Will was an actor who had to carry up to twenty different roles in his head at any given time. Plays were revived at short notice without much rehearsal time, so you couldn't afford to forget any of your major parts.'

JB: 'How many books had he when he died, and what happened to them?'

RF: 'Hard to say—maybe thirty or forty. The rest he'd sold or given away or returned to their rightful owners ... He hung on to his Ovid of course—that was the favourite of all his books; and he had some Plautus and Seneca in Latin. He was fond of Chaucer and had a copy of his *Troilus and Criseyde* as well as John Gower's *Confessio Amantis*, which gave him the story of Pericles. By the by, Gower's buried over there in Southwark Cathedral, along with Will's brother Edmund; lovely old monument—have you seen it?'

JB: 'Indeed I have—any more books you can remember?'

RF: 'He held on to his old Geneva Bible but probably more for reference than out of piety. And Florio gave him a copy of his translation of Montaigne's essays, which Will devoured. He was very attached to Marlowe's *Hero and Leander* too, and Sidney's *Arcadia*, where he got his Gloucester plot in *King Lear*.'

JB: 'How about *Hamlet*? Where did he come across that one?'

RF: 'I know he read Belleforest's *Histoire Tragiques*—I've got a copy here. But whether he used that or an older version of the play itself is hard to say.'

JB: 'Were there any authors who had a particularly strong influence on him, apart from Marlowe?'

RF: 'Well of course when he was younger he was smitten with John Lyly's *Euphues*—everyone was. Really fancy, clever writing, full of decorations and conceits. Everybody imitated it. Lyly was the man of the hour. But the fashion wore off; people got tired of it and Will sent it up rotten in *Love's Labour's Lost*—people tying themselves in knots with fancy language.

'Now look at this battered old playscript—it's *Pandosto* by Robert Greene. He was the one who attacked Will as an "upstart crow" when he first came to London. But Will used *Pandosto* as a source for his *Winter's Tale*—so either he'd forgotten the insult, or didn't give a toss, or else he may have been exacting sweet revenge—who knows?

'And look at this—it's a first edition in English of *Don Quixote*—Will was much taken with it and used a chapter of it for his play *Cardenio*. Did you know that he and Cervantes died the same day? How about that? The two greatest writers of their day . . . you wouldn't read about it.

'One unusual book he kept was this one by Sam Harsnett: A *Declaration of Popish Impostures*. I guess part of its fascination may have been its denunciation of Father Robert Debdale, whom Will knew from his school days. He was a Stratford man, a neighbour of the Hathaways, went to Douai to be trained for the Catholic priesthood and was hanged, drawn and quartered at Tyburn. It lists papist superstitions and the names of demons such as Hoppedance, Flibberdigibbet, Modo and Mahu pop up in *King Lear*.

'And when he died? Well, as I said, there weren't that many books to leave . . . I kept one myself, this little one here—it's pretty worn and well-thumbed as you can see. It's his Ovid:

"Thou know'st that we two went to school together;
Even for that, our love of old . . ."

I don't think he'd have minded.'

13

The Romans

What pageantry, what feats, what shows . . .
PERICLES, ACT V, SCENE 2

Shakespeare was born at a good time in history. He lived during a good time and he died at the right time. Some forty years after his death most of what he had built would be destroyed, or at least driven underground for a considerable time. With the execution of Charles I and the ascendancy of Cromwell, a puritanical tyranny settled over England; the theatres were torn down and artistic exuberance drastically curtailed. The great era of Elizabethan and Jacobean drama was over and English theatre would never quite recover from the devastation.

The execution of the King could have led to the establishment of a republic, but it was too soon for that. Most of Europe would have to wait for more than a hundred years until the political philosophers had laid a gunpowder trail all the way to the Bastille. But republican ideas were in the air and being openly flirted with. Venice, with its elected Doge and senators, had proved what a vibrant republic could achieve. The Renaissance love affair with democratic Athens and republican Rome threw up plenty of heroic role models, and somewhat idealised images of those ancient civilisations were posited as utopian alternatives to absolute monarchy.

What did Shakespeare think of all this? Was he a dyed-in-the-wool monarchist, a closet republican, an anarchist? Or a detached observer, a political agnostic? Although he is sometimes accused of sucking up to his royal patrons, he was censured for not contributing to the ostentations of public mourning following the death of Queen Elizabeth. And although he engaged the interest of King James with his portrayal of Macbeth, treason and witchcraft, he was playing a dangerous game. A play about a paranoid Scottish tyrant might be taken the wrong way, as might his portrayal of the snooping, manipulative ruler in *Measure for Measure*, not to mention *King Lear*, where a king has to go mad before realising that he has no divine status, but is only a poor, bare, forked animal like other men.

All of Shakespeare's monarchs (even the mighty Henry V) are fallible, insecure human beings. Some are downright wicked; others, like Bolingbroke, are opportunistic usurpers; some weak and unworthy; all painfully aware that the hollow crown that rounds the mortal temples of a king is no shield against treachery and death. Henry V is sometimes exhibited as Shakespeare's 'ideal' of what a king ought to be, but as I suggested in my earlier chapter on the Histories, there is enough in Shakespeare's text, let alone history, to see Henry as a pious hypocrite and unscrupulous war criminal. All in all, it's very difficult to accept Shakespeare as an apologist for the monarchy. Over and over he stresses the idea that 'the king is but a man as I am'. Kings may claim a semi-divine status and authority but it is a chimera. Death will eventually bore through their castle wall 'and farewell, King'.

This stance of Shakespeare is all the more remarkable in that he was, actually, a servant of the King, one of the King's Men players and a Groom of the Chamber, a part-time courtier and hired hand. One might have expected his flattery of the crown to be both fulsome and servile.

It is neither. But that doesn't necessarily mean he was an enthusiastic republican.

In *The Tempest*, Shakespeare mocks the likeable but slightly dotty Gonzalo's vision of a utopian republic. It's a kind of Garden of Eden, innocent, pure, free of all traffic and commerce—an idyllic commonwealth. The only catch is that Gonzalo sees himself as the king of it. Debating the merits of republicanism in Elizabethan England was simply out of the question. Despite the Queen's charisma, she was aware that her grip on power was tenuous and that there were frequent plots against her. She had been denounced as a bastard and her cousin, Mary Queen of Scots, had schemed to take her place, backed by Catholic noblemen and French sympathisers. Spain too was her deadly enemy and the Pope condoned her assassination. Childless, with no named successor, she held on to power by sheer strength of character. King James was a devout exponent of the divine right of kings but crept about, fearful of treason, with armour under his doublet.

The only safe place to sing the virtues of republicanism was ancient Rome, which became a haven for Elizabethan dramatists. Shakespeare wrote four Roman plays: *Titus Andronicus, Coriolanus, Julius Caesar* and *Antony and Cleopatra*. In the last three particularly he pits the man against the system, examining the role of the individual personality in shaping history, just as he had done in his English history plays.

Titus Andronicus stands apart from the other three. Its aim is not to dissect a political situation but to cash in on the public taste for blood-soaked melodrama. It's a deliberate challenge to established playwrights like Thomas Kyd, Robert Greene and Christopher Marlowe. Like every grammar-school boy, Shakespeare had studied Seneca and must have been thrilled by his gory, extravagant tragedies. Seneca was private tutor to the young emperor Nero, who later had him murdered. He must have witnessed his fair share of horrors and was playing up to the decadent taste of a public who got off on the wholesale slaughter of wild beasts, prisoners of war and gladiators in the arena.

This relish of bloody spectacle was not far removed from that of Shakespeare's audience, who flocked to public executions to see victims hanged, drawn and quartered, or else to the animal shows to watch bears, bulls, horses and apes torn apart by English mastiffs. Up to a hundred and twenty of these huge dogs were kept in kennels next to the cages for the bears, bulls and other animals in an area now occupied by the Tate Modern. Foreign visitors were dismayed by the stench of the area, but that did not deter Philip Henslowe, father-in-law of the actor Edward Alleyn. He set up home here in Pike Garden, and from here he ran his empire of taverns, theatres and brothels. His Rose Theatre stood a mere eighty yards away from Shakespeare's Globe.

Titus Andronicus

I began writing this book while sitting backstage in Brisbane during a performance of *Anatomy Titus Fall of Rome: A Shakespeare Commentary* by Heiner Müller, which really set out to test an audience's staying power and caused a considerable number of walk-outs every night. But that's nothing new with *Titus*. When Peter Brook did the play at Stratford with Olivier and Vivien Leigh in 1955, audience members fainted every night and extra St John Ambulance officers were put on duty.

Many academics over the years have dismissed *Titus* as a vulgar horror show and have been loath to associate it with Shakespeare's name, but in performance the play has enjoyed considerable success. (In Shakespeare's day it was calculated that half the population of London went to see *Titus*.) In Eastern Europe since World War II the play has enjoyed wide popularity, its horrors being commensurate with those suffered by its audiences. The mutilations, brutality and casual violence were a true reflection of their everyday experience. More recent events in Srebrenica,

Rwanda, Iraq, Pakistan and Afghanistan have reinforced the play's vision of a world careering into madness. And when put next to the mindless violence and destructiveness of so many Hollywood blockbusters, *Titus* looks like a model of dramatic decorum and restraint.

People rarely complain or walk out of such movies, but with an on-stage *Titus* it's a different matter—they are disgusted, shocked and outraged. Why? Is it because it's live? Is it because the play is supposed to be a classic and therefore chaste and respectable—something you'd take your mother to? (Incidentally, when we played Kosky's *King Lear* in Canberra, some woman made the mistake of bringing her mother as a treat on her eighty-third birthday. The poor old dear was sick for a week afterwards and the outraged daughter demanded her money back! Of course we agreed—on compassionate grounds.)

Those who can stomach the violence in *Titus* relish the play's irony, its dark humour, its grotesquery and Shakespeare's provocative image of an absurd and godless universe—a precursor to *King Lear* and *Waiting for Godot*.

The world conjured up by Shakespeare obviously appealed to Heiner Müller, who had first-hand experience of life under the Nazis, the devastation of Germany in World War II and the subsequent grim reign of terror in the German Democratic Republic. He adapted the play, cutting some of the more arcane or verbose passages, substituting his own running commentary which brought Titus's Rome and the GDR into a synthesis:

> THE CORRUGATED IRON IN THE OUTSKIRTS
> ALREADY TREMBLES FROM THE MARCHING FEET
> THE LOOKOUTS IN THEIR TOWERS CAN SEE THE DUST
> COLUMN FROM THE ADVANCING ARMY ROME WAITS FOR
> THE SPOILS SLAVES FOR WORK MEAT FOR BROTHELS
> GOLD FOR THE BANKS WEAPONS FOR THE ARMOURY
> THE PEOPLE AT THE BEER TENT AND HOT DOG STANDS

AND IN THE EMPTY FOOTBALL STADIUMS WAIT FOR HEROES DEAD AND LIVING...

When Michael Gow, artistic director of the Queensland Theatre Company, suggested we collaborate on Heiner Müller's *Titus* I was attracted to the idea for several reasons: it meant we could share the risks of a notoriously difficult box office, while engaging with a major contemporary European playwright and collaborating with another major theatre company from interstate. The production costs would be split, Michael would direct and Robert Kemp would design the show. I would play Titus and the rest of the all-male cast would consist of actors from both Sydney and Brisbane.

The decision to use an all-male cast turned out to be a felicitous one. Audience members remarked that to see a female actor as Lavinia being abused and humiliated in the way it was done would have been too much to take. The fact that it was a male actor—making no attempt to play feminine—gave the horror the necessary degree of alienation and distance to make it more or less bearable.

The all-male presence had a whiff of the locker room about it and the violence was pretty full-on. Not that it was simulated naturalism: a large bucket of blood stood in the middle of the empty stage and was freely splattered around until most of us were drenched in it. (It was a good recipe, imported from Wales—it looked real, didn't harm the skin and washed out of clothes easily.)

A high wooden wall was lined with Penguin copies of Shakespeare and these were trashed, dunked in blood and flung about as weapons; the play was about the destruction of literature and culture as much as it was about the destruction of bodies. Given this degree of stylisation, I am surprised some audiences were so distressed. I guess it demonstrates the power of metaphor and suggestion as well as the potency of live performance.

The stylisation made it quite difficult for me to find my feet in the first part of the play—was I being a 'character' or a choric figure? It's not until about halfway through that Heiner Müller pulls back and gives Shakespeare free rein, at which point I was able to engage with Titus on an emotional as well as purely cerebral level. Titus is the epitome of the military man. As far back as we can trace military history, whether we're talking about Leonidas and his Spartans, the Imperial Japanese forces, the SS or the United States Marines, the army has found it necessary to drum into soldiers that their enemies are not people but subhuman objects. Titus, after his many campaigns and the loss of many sons, can feel no empathy for the grief-stricken Tamora, whose sons must be butchered as a Roman sacrifice.

It is only when his daughter is raped and mutilated, his younger sons unjustly executed, that Titus's humanity is rekindled, his heart torn by a father's grief. He is apparently driven crazy by his despair and engages in bizarre rituals. But I chose to keep him sane, coldly calculating and bent on revenge in much the same way that Hamlet dons the disguise of madness to throw his enemies off the scent.

Of course in this play all talk of madness is relative, and you may well judge Titus to be insane in plotting to kill Tamora's remaining sons (the ones who ravished his daughter) and serve them up to her baked in a pie; but that is the world of *Titus Andronicus*, a world gone mad with blood lust, conquest, vengefulness and cruelty. It was also close enough to the experience of Elizabethan Englishmen to cause them to flock to the theatre in multitudes to witness this exercise in Senecan tragedy.

Looking over the body of his work, one has the impression that Shakespeare felt a certain attraction to 'the pride, pomp and circumstance of glorious war', but was also fully alert to its horrors and futility. The seductive glamour of military might persists today, with so many countries ploughing their treasure into an endless arms race while their citizens die of hunger and disease. So it's refreshing to meet the occasional enlightened military man like the Commandant of the Royal Military College, Duntroon, who contacted my wife and me some twenty years ago. He invited us to Duntroon, just outside Canberra's CBD, for the day, and asked us to perform some Shakespeare for his junior officers. Over lunch in the mess I asked him the purpose of the exercise, and he said, 'Well, in the future soldiers will have to know how to do a lot more than just arrive in a war zone and start shooting people. They'll be flung into emergency situations in foreign countries and will have to make instant assessments of the problems, the people, the culture . . . In other words, they'll have to empathise—and what better way to approach empathy than by studying scenes from Shakespeare?'

Julius Caesar

Up until the age of fifteen I had my heart set on going to art school and being a painter. Then I discovered Shakespeare and all my energy and passion switched to theatre. But from a very early age I was obsessed with drawing and would spend hours crouched by the radio with my paints, crayons or coloured pencils and piles of scrap paper. I loved making storybooks and comic books for my three younger sisters, but it was really for my pleasure rather than theirs. I guess there were also early intimations of my future as a performer and theatrical producer: I made a series of toy theatres featuring homemade puppets and, later, 'movies', which consisted of long scrolls of adding-machine paper (like toilet rolls, only better quality) with up to a couple of hundred coloured drawings—like comic strips without the speech bubbles. These would be scrolled, spool to spool, through a small proscenium opening while I sat behind doing all the voices and sound effects. At first they were versions of Disney movies, but then I graduated to Shakespeare and Orwell. I made full-length versions of *Animal Farm* and *Macbeth*. For the latter I created a tape-recorded soundtrack complete with music and atmospherics, but I still did all the voices.

Anyway, it was one evening when I was sitting by the radio beavering away with my coloured pencils that I experienced my first real shock of Shakespeare. The ABC was broadcasting *Julius Caesar* and I was mildly interested in hearing the story; all I knew was that it had something to do with Roman soldiers and murders and battles.

I'm pretty sure Ron Haddrick was playing Brutus and it was early on in the play. Brutus was agonising over whether or not he should join the conspiracy to assassinate Caesar. He acknowledges Caesar's friendship and sterling qualities but is fearful that public acclaim may stir Caesar's latent ambition and make him a threat to the Republic. He says:

> It is the bright day that brings forth the adder,
> And that craves wary walking . . .

I felt a cold shiver run down my spine and the hairs on my neck stand on end. Suddenly I knew what poetry meant. Rather than stating a blunt prosaic fact, you employ metaphor, allusion, metre and sound so that the idea resonates and stays with you. It's a creepy and sinister image: Caesar's ambition is like a deadly snake that slithers from hiding in response to the sunshine. It's an unsettling image and it stays in your mind, especially when reinforced by the steady, deliberate rhythm of that first line: every word is monosyllabic except the last, 'adder', which thereby gains in strength despite its feminine ending. The next line, in contrast, has long, slow vowels—'craves wary walking', a deliberately ironic understatement.

Shortly after this my father took me to see the Mankiewicz movie. I responded to the film very emotionally, finding it both exciting and deeply disturbing. I couldn't figure out why it was called *Julius Caesar* when the hero dies so early on. Was it really about Julius Caesar, or something else? And, in movie terms, he was an unlikely hero. I'd been expecting someone more like Alexander the Great, an exercise in hagiography, yet Shakespeare seemed intent on making him somewhat decrepit and fallible. And as for the others, who were we supposed to side with? Was Brutus the real hero or was it Mark Antony? It was a puzzle . . .

Julius Caesar was one of the plays in the first season of the new Globe Theatre in 1599. London's grandest playhouse was a great drawcard, especially with plays like *Julius Caesar* and *Henry V* in its repertoire. Perhaps stung by Ben Jonson's criticism of his verbosity, Shakespeare set out to write a play in simple, classic, unadorned language. He was also competing with Jonson on his own turf. Jonson regarded himself as the great classicist and delivered a couple of epics set in ancient Rome: *Sejanus* (1602) and *Catiline* (1611). Shakespeare himself acted in *Sejanus*. Jonson's plays were big on erudition but made for stodgy theatre. As Leonard Digges wrote in 1640:

> So have I seen, when Caesar would appear,
> And on the stage at half-sword parley were
> Brutus and Cassius; O, how the audience
> Were ravished, with what wonder they went thence,
> When some new day they would not brook a line
> Of tedious though well-laboured *Catiline*.

As opposed to Jonson's cardboard ancients, Shakespeare's Romans are human, fallible, wrong-headed. They were not Romans at all, of course, but Elizabethan Englishmen. It was always Shakespeare's natural bent to reflect his own life, times and fellow citizens, but in this instance he was dealing with explosive material—regicide and republicanism—and that indeed craved wary walking. If he had called the play *The Tragedy of Marcus Brutus*, that would have signalled that he approved of Brutus's part in the assassination. By titling the play after the relatively minor character of Caesar, who is a victim rather than a protagonist, Shakespeare deflected this criticism. Besides, the play is about more than regicide. It is about the chaos that follows and the collapse into civil war. This was a theme that preoccupied Shakespeare in his earliest work, his *Henry VI* trilogy. No matter how ambivalent he felt about the crown, his plays demonstrate a horror of anarchy, mob rule and civil war.

In some ways Brutus seems like a sketch for Hamlet—an intellectual almost paralysed by introspection, caught on the horns of a moral dilemma. Caesar is his friend and patron (perhaps, historical sources hinted, even his natural father). Caesar has iconic status as a war hero and is a natural leader of men. Yet there are hints that his ambition is urging him to overthrow the Republic, restore the monarchy and install himself as king. It would seem that others, such as Mark Antony, support this move. It would also seem that the only way to avert it is to kill Caesar—no other options are canvassed.

The hard part for Brutus is that Caesar's plans are only guessed at—there is no hard evidence; then again, if Brutus waits for the hard evidence to emerge, it may be too late to avoid disaster:

And therefore think him as a serpent's egg,
Which, hatch'd, would as his kind, grow mischievous,
And kill him in the shell.

Brutus is acknowledged, even by Mark Antony, as 'the noblest Roman of them all'. He is renowned for his integrity and sensitivity. That's why the other conspirators need him as their frontman. It's interesting that Shakespeare takes this angle on Brutus, who in earlier times had been reviled for regicide; Dante consigns him to hell for his crime. The Globe audience would have been surprised, even disconcerted, to see him receive such a sympathetic hearing. While Brutus and Cassius are, technically speaking, the villains of the play, Shakespeare gives them an heroic status at least equal to that of Caesar himself. But nothing is clear cut. Like all the people in this play, Brutus has his faults as well as his virtues. He has an air of moral superiority that comes dangerously close to smugness, and he is a harsh judge of others' failings. When threatened by Cassius in the heat of their great quarrel he responds:

> There is no terror, Cassius, in your threats;
> For I am arm'd so strong in honesty that they pass by me as the idle wind,
> Which I respect not.

Convinced that he is always in the right, he can be stubborn and inflexible and so make catastrophic mistakes. Maybe his first mistake is joining the conspiracy; but putting that aside, he should have listened to Cassius's advice that Mark Antony and Caesar should die together. Antony turns out to be a wily and deadly enemy, the nemesis of all the conspirators. But Brutus's high-mindedness, combined with a contempt for Antony, means he can't see it coming. His next mistake is overruling the others' advice and allowing Antony to speak at Caesar's funeral. Again he vastly underestimates Antony's abilities, trusting that his own oratorical skills will carry the day. Finally he quashes Cassius's battle plan for Philippi, even though Cassius is the more experienced soldier. In each of these key moments, Brutus makes the wrong call.

And at each of them, Cassius gives way. While Brutus may have a superiority complex, Cassius has too little sense of self-worth. Of all the conspirators, Cassius is the most passionate and committed. But his motives are mixed and his republican ideology swamped by envy and bitterness. He sneers at Caesar's physical infirmities and cannot bear the thought that his old comrade in arms

> Is now become a god; and Cassius is
> A wretched creature, and must bend his body
> If Caesar carelessly but nod on him . . .

> ... Ye gods! It doth amaze me
> A man of such a feeble temper should
> So get the start of the majestic world,
> And bear the palm alone.

That 'alone' is a giveaway of all the resentment Cassius feels at having been sidelined after years of service. Cassius is clear-eyed enough to admit this weakness in himself and to see that he needs Brutus as an ally, someone who will give the cause a respectable image. But he can't help resenting Brutus's sense of moral superiority and, in a Machiavellian way, relishes the thought of corrupting him:

> Well, Brutus, thou art noble, yet, I see,
> Thy honourable metal may be wrought
> From that it is dispos'd. Therefore it is meet
> That noble minds keep ever with their likes;
> For who so firm that cannot be seduc'd?
> Caesar doth bear me hard; but he loves Brutus.

His bitterness makes it hard for us to warm to Cassius, yet he is intensely human; perhaps nowhere more so than in his dependence on Brutus and desire to be loved by him. He idolises Brutus and by constantly yielding to Brutus's stubbornness brings about his own downfall and the failure of the coup.

If Brutus and Cassius have their failings, so does the eponymous hero of the play. Throughout medieval times and the Renaissance, Julius Caesar was revered as one of the Nine Worthies, the heroes of antiquity. Shakespeare paints a very different picture and cuts this epic hero down to size. His Caesar is a man in decline: deaf in one ear, prey to epilepsy, superstitious, vain, arrogant and easily swayed. Yet there is something expansive about him that sets him apart from the more mean-minded of the conspirators—he is generous, brave and trusting. He reposes too much trust in Brutus, but can be a shrewd judge of character:

> Yond Cassius has a lean and hungry look,
> He thinks too much. Such men are dangerous . . .
> . . . He reads much,
> He is a great observer, and he looks
> Quite through the deeds of men . . .
> Such men as he be never at heart's ease
> Whiles they behold a greater than themselves,
> And therefore are they very dangerous.

Caesar's protégé Antony is an indolent playboy who gets a lucky break and runs with it. He proves himself to be a master of improvisation as well as a master opportunist. His funeral oration, besides being a model of rhetoric, is a model of spin. He plays his audience like a fiddle, and stages a couple of theatrical coups: the first is displaying Caesar's torn garment while recalling his past glories. (At this point in my 2001 Bell Shakespeare production I had Antony signal the sound operator to bring up the schmaltzy background music.) His second is flourishing Caesar's will and reading out his legacies to the populace. (Here I had Antony kiss a baby and sign a few autographs.)

The speech is a masterpiece of crowd manipulation. John Weever saw the play in 1599 during its first season at the Globe, and wrote:

> The many-headed multitude were drawn
> By Brutus' speech that Caesar was ambitious.
> When eloquent Mark Antony had shown
> His virtues, who but Brutus then was vicious?

After the mob had rushed off stage to lynch the conspirators, I had Antony show the will to the audience: it was a blank piece of paper. I did this for two reasons: first to show that Antony had invented the whole thing in order to fire up the mob, and second because it is borne out by the text. In the scene following the funeral, Antony, Octavius and Lepidus are at Antony's house devising death warrants for their opponents. Antony says to Lepidus:

> But Lepidus, go you to Caesar's house;
> Fetch the will hither, and we shall determine
> How to cut off some charge in legacies.

If Lepidus is now being despatched to Caesar's house to fetch the will, what was the piece of paper Antony read to the mob? It follows Plutarch's assertion that Antony manipulated Caesar's will to serve his own ends. My staging of the scene was deliberately ironic, playing up Antony's insincerity, because too often it is taken at face value as an exhibition of raw emotion and misses Shakespeare's point about political wheeling and dealing. Antony certainly has a lot of charisma but that should not blind us to other characteristics: he can be selfish, treacherous, punitive, brutal and cynical. In the scene I have just mentioned (Act IV, Scene 1), the triumvirs are preparing their proscription list and doing deals over who is for the chop. Antony sends Lepidus off to fetch the will then immediately suggests to Octavius that Lepidus should be dumped:

> This is a slight unmeritable man,
> Meet to be sent on errands. Is it fit,
> The threefold world divided, he should stand
> One of the three to share it?

Antony's brutality here recalls Plutarch's story regarding his hatred of Cicero, who had denounced him in the Senate house. Antony hunted Cicero down, murdered him and had his hands and tongue nailed to the door of the Senate. Yet for all his brilliance, Antony turns out to be no match for the cold-eyed young Octavius, whom he totally underestimates.

In this very male world of politics and the military, women have a subservient role, but both Portia and Calpurnia are strong-willed and persuasive. Brutus's wife Portia fights desperately to change her husband's course, wounding herself in the thigh as a mark of her constancy. Calpurnia for a time actually changes Caesar's mind, persuading him not to go to the Capitol. Her recounting of her nightmare visions is sometimes played as if she were an hysteric, but this is not the case. She herself is not frightened but she knows her husband is superstitious and these visions will impact on him. Unfortunately her good work is undone by the wily Decius who plays on Caesar's vanity and ambition to lure him to the Capitol, thus making him change his mind again.

In the long run it's a man's world; women are disempowered and the only way they can register their despair is by swallowing fire, as Portia does.

Given the complexity of the characters, their inconsistencies and ambivalences, it is a grave mistake to be judgmental when acting in or directing the play. Brutus can come across as too ingenuous, too sonorous or too priggish; Cassius too sinister and manipulative, etc. You must never take sides but give each character his or her due, playing them with empathy from their points of view, and let the audience decide. In fact the audience should be something like the mob on stage—now siding with this person, now that—unsure who to believe. If you load the dice, what you get is political commentary or satire. If you want to show the face of tragedy then you must play each role with all its facets. Just as in life, each character has strengths and weaknesses, attributes that are admirable and some that are less so. That's true of the mob as well, who are often portrayed as ragged blockheads from central casting.

Shakespeare is sometimes accused of snobbery, flattering the aristocrats and putting down the lower classes. As I've demonstrated many times elsewhere in this book, the obverse is true. It is aristocrats who are the most common butts of his satire and the common folk who earn his approbation. Nevertheless he does have a recurring fear of mob rule, or mob mentality, which is not the same thing as class snobbery. He could see in the theatre as well as in other public places how a crowd could be manipulated by clever oratory. I think we've all seen enough of mass hysteria and violence to share his apprehension. TV footage of race-hate riots or football hooligans on the rampage remind us how easily the wild beast can be unleashed. In the 1590s London had seen a string of serious riots (largely against foreign refugees) resulting in mass executions.

The mobs in *Julius Caesar, Coriolanus, King John, Richard III*, and *Henry VI* with its rebel leader, Jack Cade, are all examples of crowds being swayed and persuaded by crafty orators. But how can we exclude ourselves from this? How can we kid ourselves that a lot of the ideas and opinions we espouse are not the scraps we pick up from the media, the shock-jocks, the advertisers, the opinion pages? Of course they are. We are a lot less original than we like to think.

That's why the mob in my *Julius Caesar* was not a crowd of ragged blockheads. They were a mix of lawyers, doctors, teachers, students and housewives. They were us. And they were not stupid—just persuadable, like us. If you play the mob as a lot of dolts, they're a pushover. There's no tension. The more intelligent and aware you make the citizens, the higher the stakes and the more frightening the reality.

Inspiration for a production can come from various sources. Sometimes a particular painter will provide an image that gets the imagination going. When I directed *The Comedy of Errors* Matisse provided the colour palette and nonchalant joyfulness that play seemed to demand. When I was seeking an Australian reference for *As You Like It*, Fred Williams had a spaciousness and lightness that underpinned the design. With *Julius Caesar* I turned to de Chirico, who has always intrigued me with his vast, haunted public spaces, deserted and ominous. They are full of extreme perspectives and sick, heavy colours. There are long shadows, sometimes without explanation. The light is always harsh but overcast, not cheerful, and you feel that hidden eyes are watching you, that at any moment danger could spring out of one of those long and meaningless colonnades.

I scattered my sparse mob throughout the auditorium so that the audience itself became the mob and Brutus and Antony could address us directly. And they were dressed in such a way that you could not distinguish who were the actors and who were not—except at school matinees, where it became a bit obvious.

What do we take away from *Julius Caesar*? We have seen, on the one hand, misguided idealism, self-deception and mixed motives. On the other, opportunism, insincerity, casual brutality and an exercise in smoke and mirrors.

We have seen the world of politics: as it was, as it is, and, no doubt, as it shall always be.

Antony and Cleopatra

You'd expect *Antony and Cleopatra* to be a natural follow-on to *Julius Caesar* but it didn't appear till eight years later (1607) and the plays could hardly be more different. The language of *Julius Caesar* is spare, straightforward and unadorned, whereas the poetry of *Antony and Cleopatra* is lush and extravagant, studded with fanciful metaphor, sensuality and playfulness. *Julius Caesar* has a tight structure and obeys pretty closely the classical unities of time and place so beloved of Ben Jonson. But *Antony and Cleopatra* ranges across half the world, hopping from one location to another with an almost bewildering rapidity.

It's as if Shakespeare deliberately set out, in *Julius Caesar*, to show Jonson that he could beat him at his own game. He experienced as a performer the constraints of the classical model and saw how readily a slavish obedience to the rules could produce barren entertainment. But in *Julius Caesar* he demonstrated that he could be as good a classicist as the best of them and still produce a political thriller that was both human and modern. Now, in *Antony and Cleopatra*, he threw the classical rules to the winds and unleashed his vast imagination and passion for theatricality.

The play is yet one more example of Shakespeare's fascination with how individual people shape the course of history. In *Julius Caesar* we saw men trying to save the Roman Republic, only to end up tearing it apart by civil war. Now we are presented with irreconcilable factions burying the Republic altogether and on its grave establishing the foundations of Imperial Rome and its first emperor, Augustus. Shakespeare gives us two mutually exclusive worlds, Rome and Egypt. Where Egypt is female, Rome is rigidly male. Egypt is flexible, Rome is not. Egypt is sensual whereas Rome is cold-blooded and politic. Egypt is playfully irresponsible, Rome sternly businesslike. While Egypt is fantastical, Rome is practical and pragmatic.

Again Shakespeare allows himself to wander through a pagan classical landscape free of Judeo-Christian inhibitions. Sexuality and adultery are openly enjoyed—Cleopatra herself is 'with Phoebus' amorous pinches black'.

The play's triumph is in so successfully melding the global and the domestic. We feel the size of empire with messengers scuttling to and fro, with sea battles and armies on the march. Shakespeare gives himself an enormous canvas on which to splash his extravagant colours. The Antony of this play is a far cry from the ruthlessly ambitious and energised young politician of *Julius Caesar*. He is now a ruin of his former self, an overindulged raging bull, losing control of his destiny. It would have been both inspiring and depressing to see Marlon Brando attack this role in his later years. He gave us a superlative Mark Antony in *Julius Caesar*—to see him play the older Antony would have shown us a marker of both his and the character's sad decline. Brando was one of the greatest actors of his generation and I feel cheated that he never gave us a Hamlet or a Lear. Like Antony he threw away an empire.

Cleopatra is undoubtedly one of Shakespeare's most magnificent creations and probably the greatest female role ever written. She is fantastically intelligent, sensual and self-regarding; comfortable with her body and her passions but painfully aware of encroaching age. One of the funniest scenes in the play shows Cleopatra receiving news from Rome that Antony has made a political marriage with Octavia. Having physically attacked and abused the unfortunate messenger, Cleopatra calms down sufficiently to recall him and question him about her rival.

The terrified messenger answers all her questions as diplomatically as he can and we see how ready Cleopatra is to deceive herself by believing him:

Cleopatra: Come thou near.
Messenger: Most gracious majesty!
Cleopatra: Didst thou behold Octavia?
Messenger: Ay, dread Queen.
Cleopatra: Where?
Messenger: Madam, in Rome. I looked her in the face and saw her led between her brother and Mark Antony.
Cleopatra: Is she as tall as me?
Messenger: She is not, madam.
Cleopatra: Didst hear her speak? Is she shrill-tongued or low?
Messenger: Madam, I heard her speak. She is low-voiced.
Cleopatra: That is not so good. He cannot like her long.
Charmian: Like her? O Isis, 'tis impossible!
Cleopatra: I think so, Charmian. Dull of tongue and dwarfish. What majesty is in her gait? Remember, if e'er though looked'st on majesty.
Messenger: She creeps. Her motion and her station are as one. She shows a body rather than a life, a statue than a breather.

Cleopatra: Is this certain?

Messenger: Or I have no observance.

Charmian: Three in Egypt cannot make better note.

Cleopatra: He's very knowing, I do perceive't. There's nothing in her yet. The fellow has good judgement.

Charmian: Excellent.

Cleopatra: Guess at her years, I prithee.

Messenger: Madam, she was a widow—

Cleopatra: Widow! Charmian, hark.

Messenger: And I do think she's thirty.

Cleopatra: Bear'st thou her face in mind? Is't long or round?

Messenger: Round, even to faultiness.

Cleopatra: For the most part, too, they are foolish that are so. Her hair—what colour?

Messenger: Brown, madam; and her forehead as low as she would wish it.

Cleopatra [*giving money*]: There's gold for thee.

Probably the only sour note is struck by the messenger's 'And I do think she's thirty'. He is no doubt exaggerating Octavia's age, but it doesn't do much good: Cleopatra herself saw thirty some time ago. It's a wonderfully comic scene for the two actors (assisted by the faithful Charmian) and gives us yet another colour in the portrait of this charming, domineering, selfish, generous, formidable yet vulnerable woman.

Like Antony, Cleopatra is wildly extravagant and admires that quality in others. Of Antony she says:

For his bounty,
There was no winter in't: an autumn 'twas
That grew the more by reaping: his delights
Were dolphin-like, they showed his back above
The element they lived in: in his livery

Walked crowns and crownets: realms and islands were
As plates dropped from his pocket.

She can be selfish, treacherous and sarcastic but her enormous charm, wit and sexual allure are matched by a girlish vivacity, as Enobarbus describes her:

I saw her once,
Hop forty paces through the public street;
And having lost her breath, she spoke, and panted,
That she did make defect perfection
And, breathless, power breathe forth.

Put this against the eloquent profundity of her grief as Antony lies dying:

O, see, my women,
The crown of the earth doth melt. My lord!
O, withered is the garland of the war,
The soldier's pole is fallen: young boys and girls
Are level now with men. The odds is gone,
And there is nothing left remarkable
Beneath the visiting moon.

Enobarbus supplies her only possible epitaph:

Age cannot wither her, nor custom stale
Her infinite variety: other women cloy
The appetites they feed, but she makes hungry
Where most she satisfies. For vilest things
Become themselves in her, that the holy Priests
Bless her when she is riggish.

She is indeed a lass unparalleled. When stood alongside Antony and Cleopatra, Octavius must needs appear cold-blooded and humourless, but it reduces the play's impact to present these facets only. The actor playing the role has to find the qualities in Octavius that make his victory inevitable, not simply won by default. Seen from his point of view, Antony's sloth and abdication of responsibility spell disaster for the triumvirate. This may suit Octavius's long-term ambitions, but meantime there is an empire to run. Octavius is not simply a prude: to his stoic Roman upbringing the wantonness and extravagance of 'the Orient' are distasteful if not downright disgusting. It is both possible and necessary in the playing of Octavius to demonstrate a genuine love for his sister, a frustrated admiration for Antony and a degree of compassion for Cleopatra. Without these the play lacks a certain tragic strain. While he is undoubtedly one of the 'new men' whom Shakespeare regarded with suspicion and distaste—pragmatic opportunists like Malcolm, Fortinbras and John of Lancaster—Octavius needs to be played with a sympathy and understanding that make him a substantial protagonist. After all, this was the man destined to become Augustus.

In an exceptionally large cast of characters, Enobarbus stands out as a true original, Shakespeare's own creation. His betrayal of Antony is one of the play's most tragic episodes and Antony's subsequent forgiveness an overwhelming display of magnanimity. It says a lot for the highly charged emotional world of *Antony and Cleopatra* that the worldly, witty, sceptical Enobarbus can die of a broken heart.

One of the few productions of the play I have seen was directed by Peter Brook for the RSC, starring Alan Howard and Glenda Jackson. It was curious casting: in place of a pair of fleshy voluptuaries we had two dry, reedy intellectuals, skinny and ironical. This gave a squeeze of lemon to the verbal contests but there was little evidence of sensuality in their relationship or in the production overall. There was more sex and passion in a TV production I saw (black and white) in the early sixties.

Keith Michell and Mary Morris had the bigness of passion and fire in the belly the roles demand—the relationship is not a cerebral one.

When I directed the play for Bell Shakespeare in 2001, I wanted to avoid togas and loincloths; that sort of production can easily end up looking like *Carry On, Cleo*. I wanted to create a space where fortunes are easily won, lost and frittered away, a place of materialistic irresponsibility like Cleopatra's court. So I finished up with something reminiscent of a casino: the text is full of references to cards, dice, chance and fortune. I must admit those places both intrigue and horrify me. They are often fitted out with fake palm trees, waterfalls and grottoes like something out of the *Arabian Nights*. You lose all track of time and cannot tell whether it's day or night because the romantic lighting is as constant as the muzak and free drinks. Sometimes people dress up and pretend they're in Las Vegas, but even if they don't there is an air of fantasy and escapism like you used to get in the old picture palaces during the Depression.

This sense of unreality, of being perpetually on holiday—'Let's to supper, come, And down consideration'—seemed appropriate to Antony and Cleopatra's view of the world.

I could not have wished for a more emotionally free and committed pair of lovers than Paula Arundell and Bill Zappa, and for the most part the casino environment worked well with the Romans in black tie and the Egyptian court dressed in flowing *haute couture* silks. The battle scenes posed something of a problem—a shoot-out in the casino is not quite the Battle of Actium. Battle scenes work better the more metaphorical and suggestive they are, and I trimmed and elided some of the battles just as I had done in *Julius Caesar*. They do get very confusing if you don't know your ancient history and, by today's standards, Shakespeare was perhaps being a little too faithful to his sources. But then, if he had not been he would no doubt have had angry audiences accusing him of getting his history wrong: every schoolboy knew his Plutarch.

It's likely that Shakespeare's audience saw in Cleopatra—imperious, intelligent, witty and charismatic—a shadow of the late Queen Elizabeth and in the crumbling of her empire the passing of a Golden Age.

Antony and Cleopatra succeed in convincing us that it's a world well lost, and, as with others of Shakespeare's mighty protagonists—Hamlet, Othello, Macbeth—their passing seems to leave the world a shrunken and less interesting place.

Coriolanus

> So our virtues
> Lie in the interpretation of the time.

My first day at Sydney University in 1959 was a fateful one. An eager freshman, I strolled through the gates of the Gothic pile and down Manning Road past the Union. The roadway was crowded with the booths of the various student societies spruiking their wares and drumming up recruits. The first one I came to was that of the Sydney University Players, manned by the stocky and persuasive Ken Horler. Ten years later he and I would go on to found the Nimrod Theatre: for now he was president of the Players. After the briefest of introductions I signed up and continued on my way with the feeling that I now had a passport, a stake in the place. A few yards further on I came across the booth of the older and more established Sydney University Dramatic Society; but it was too late—I had thrown in my lot with the opposition. The two groups enjoyed a friendly rivalry and people occasionally slipped from one to the other as well as seeking a billet with the Revue, the Gilbert and Sullivan productions, and whatever else came along. We enjoyed a substantial audience from 'downtown', as we called it, because whatever the productions' shortcomings, there was nowhere else in Sydney where you could see Brecht, Sartre, Aristophanes, e.e. cummings, Goldoni, Anouilh, or even Shakespeare.

The politics of the Players were not very complicated and anybody could make a pitch. So having scored a couple of successes, including Malvolio in Ken's *Twelfth Night*, I proposed we put on *Coriolanus* with Ken directing and myself playing the title role as well as designing the set and costumes. My designs were not inspiring, but we were able to hire, at a very reasonable rate, some bits and pieces from the Elizabethan Theatre Trust's recent production of *Julius Caesar*. We were fortunate to have in the cast John Gaden playing Menenius (John excelled at aged character roles even then) and Arthur Dignam as Titus Lartius. The reason I proposed *Coriolanus* was, of course, because it was another of Olivier's great roles and I was still very much under his spell, seeking to imbibe, through imitation, some of his qualities.

As undergrads we responded enthusiastically to what we saw as the cynicism of the play's attitude to politics and militarism. The plebeians are a shallow, cowardly lot, their Tribunes devious and manipulative. But the patricians are just as bad—arrogant, contemptuous and presumptuous; real old-style Tories. This view of the political spectrum fitted neatly with our admiration of Brecht, the mentor of much student theatre and politics.

In 1966, the year after I joined the RSC, the company mounted *Coriolanus* with Ian Richardson in the title role. John Barton directed the production which was tough and austere. I had the very minor role of Nicanor, a Roman spy, and hammed it up appallingly, being as sinister as possible, lurking all over the set. (The most important part of being in the RSC was getting *noticed*.) To augment still further my sinister mien I suggested to Barton, 'Perhaps I could play it with an eye patch?' He dismissed me curtly with, 'You're playing it with *two* eye patches already!'

I remained intrigued by both the role of Coriolanus and the play itself, and when I heard that Steven Berkoff had done a production of it, I invited him to come and replicate the show for Bell Shakespeare in 1996.

Replication is the right word for it because Berkoff directed like a choreographer. There was little room for input from the cast because Berkoff had predetermined the staging, the tempi, almost every gesture and how it should be executed. His way of directing was by demonstration—'Do it like me'—and much of the declamation was accompanied by precise percussion and underscoring. While this method has its limitations (mainly in denying the actors any individual contribution), I had to admire the painstaking attention to detail. There were no props in the show—everything was mimed, including the weapons. This meant that the fight scenes could be as graphic and violent as you wanted without the risk of anyone getting hurt. But you had to act the exact weight and deadliness of the weapons, otherwise it would have looked paltry.

Where Berkoff got it wrong, to my mind, was the politics. Given his London East End and Russian-Jewish background, Berkoff saw Coriolanus simply as a fascist—black shirt, jackboots and all. But that is both inaccurate and simplistic—the character is prejudged as soon as he walks on. (Ian McKellen and his director made the same mistake with the film of *Richard III*. That play is not about fascism either. Apart from lacking credibility—we *know* the Nazis didn't take over England in the 1940s—it skews the entire social apparatus of the play. It's true that members of the British royal family may have had fascist sympathies, but that is a red herring and makes Richard's aberration less remarkable. Richard is not driven by political ideology but by a selfish and psychopathic desire to be top dog. His victims have no political ideology either apart from clannish self-interest.) The politics of *Coriolanus* are far more complex and fascinating than simply sticking labels on people.

Shakespeare wrote the play in 1608. It's a late play, coming between *Pericles* and *The Winter's Tale*. It was partly inspired by the dramatic events of the year before—the Midland Rising which saw savage riots directed against landowners. The violence was particularly acute in the Forest of Arden: there were food shortages and landowners had enclosed the common land hitherto used for pasture. Much of the forest also disappeared to feed the ironworks in Birmingham and elsewhere.

The rising began on May Day and quickly spread throughout the Midlands. The military killed scores of rioters and many of those captured were hanged, drawn and quartered. This took place, almost literally, on Shakespeare's doorstep in Stratford, and he must indeed have had ambivalent feelings about the events, himself being a substantial landowner and under suspicion of hoarding malt in his barns in order to force up the price.

The play begins with the Roman citizens rioting because of food shortages and blaming the patricians, especially Coriolanus, for hoarding grain for themselves. The silver-tongued patrician Menenius almost succeeds in talking the mob down when Coriolanus enters and treats them with the utmost derision and contempt. The stand-off is resolved by the urgent news that the Volsces are about to attack Rome and the so-called rabble are instantly conscripted into the army. In the ensuing campaign Coriolanus again proves himself an outstanding military leader, but then comes the peace. He proves to be an impossible candidate for political office because of his entrenched patrician views and values, a man incapable of compromise or respect for any class other than his own.

Wyndham Lewis remarked that snobs like Coriolanus must have 'pullulated' in the courts of Elizabeth and James—overgrown schoolboys with 'crazed' notions of privilege and a 'demented' ideal of authority. Plutarch provided a Coriolanus who was merely 'churlish and uncivil, and altogether unfit for any man's conversation'. But Shakespeare makes him much more complex—a potentially great man of stern integrity who is undone by his absence of fellow feeling and a pride that bars him from playing politics. He is not a character who inspires affection in an audience the way a Hamlet or Rosalind does, but some actors have made the role a formidable vehicle for their talents. Olivier had great success with it (largely by finding the comedy in the character) and Richard Burton endowed it with a fierce glamour. Shakespeare makes no excuses for him. On his first entrance Coriolanus drips with venomous contempt for the plebs. He is a killing machine as well as a stiff-necked patrician. He believes the lower orders should have no voice in government and despises their cowardice as well as their ingratitude for his military service.

The plebs are an unappealing lot. They are led by the nose by their Tribunes—canny, opportunistic shop stewards who seek out Coriolanus's weak spots in order to destroy him. The patricians find their true epitome in Volumnia—the ultimate matriarch wedded to the myth of military glory. You can see where Coriolanus gets it from, which goes some way to mitigating our harsh assessment of him. What chance had he with Volumnia for a mother? She is the only one with any real influence over Coriolanus and, in the scene where she dissuades him from sacking Rome, proves herself to be a powerful orator, moving, manipulative and relentless.

The most agreeable of the patricians is Menenius, a bon vivant and wheeler-dealer; a power broker, a numbers man and kingmaker—a figure not unfamiliar in Australian politics.

One may detect an inkling of Shakespeare's political views in his depiction of the citizens and their Tribunes. He undoubtedly has an empathy with the common man, but also a dread of the unruly mob. They are as much in need of political education as are their aristocratic overlords. Hazlitt said that reading *Coriolanus* saves one the trouble of reading Burke attacking the French Revolution and of Paine defending it, because Shakespeare gave both sides of the argument. There is no doubt that *Coriolanus* is a marvellous commentary on politics, but can it be a great tragedy when it elicits so little sympathy for its protagonists? Many critics have thought it can and that Shakespeare proves himself yet again capable of arguing an empirical case in terms of the most profound humanity. T.S. Eliot called *Coriolanus* Shakespeare's 'finest artistic achievement in tragedy'. George Bernard Shaw was making much the same point, in a typically perverse paradox, by calling it the best of his Comedies.

Which side does Shakespeare himself take in the political debate? Typically, neither. As Peter Ackroyd says: 'There is no need to take sides when the characters are doing it for you.' That's the key to directing *Coriolanus*—to fully expose the faults of all parties but also to seek out their virtues; be reasonable to all sides—they each have a case to make. If you dress them as fascists or French revolutionaries (that's been done too) you are telling the audience what to think rather than making them puzzle it out for themselves. If you can achieve that balance then the production may go beyond commentary or satire and achieve tragic status. Tragedy is experienced when you, the audience, can see a way out of a dilemma but the characters can't.

As an actor you cannot play a type, you can't play an attitude, you can't play a message and you can't play a concept. You have to play a person. I guess the frustration I felt playing in Berkoff's *Coriolanus* (despite admiring features of the production) stemmed from the fact that I was trying to play Steven's concept. There was no room for flexibility, for ambiguity, spontaneity, or those fascinating psychological contradictions at the heart of Shakespeare's characters. I was just being a big, bad fascist.

Coriolanus's tragedy is that what virtues he has (and they are considerable) are inappropriate to the circumstances. Both his greatness and his folly lie in the fact that he cannot adapt to an unfamiliar situation. Bred as a war machine, he (like George Patton among many others) is redundant in peacetime, leaving room for the lesser men, the bureaucrats, time servers and men of no conviction to scuttle in and claim their place in the sun.

. . . the biggest disservice anyone can do to Shakespeare is to be so dazzled by his works as to argue that they could not have been written by anyone so ordinary as a Stratford-upon-Avon-born actor. The very essence of Shakespeare was his humanity: that he was neither a blue-blooded nobleman nor a university-trained academic, but a humbly born player who wanted to give his calling the sort of material that could really make it soar, to reach every level of society. Where he was different from his contemporaries is that he felt with and for others in all their faults and frailties. In *Julius Caesar* Shakespeare has Julius say of Cassius, 'He is a great observer, and he looks quite through the deeds of men,' and he could hardly have coined a more appropriate description of himself.

Ian Wilson, *Shakespeare: The Evidence*

14

A fireside chat with John and Harry

> Never did a man of genius penetrate more deeply into the abysses of the human heart nor cause 'passion to speak the language of nature with greater truth'.
> PIERRE LE TOURNEUR

Two of the people I am most keen to talk to are John Heminges and Henry Condell, Shakespeare's fellow actors and business associates—the two men responsible for publishing the *First Folio* of his collected plays seven years after his death. Without their endeavours it is unlikely that his plays would have survived.

I have been invited to Condell's house in the rural village of Fulham. It is a moonless winter evening and a light snow has just begun to fall. The door is opened by a girl who takes my coat, shakes off the powdery snow and shows me into the parlour where the two old luvvies are seated on a settee by a sea-coal fire. The best armchair is occupied by a fat black cat who meets my look with a scornful glare so I make do with a joint-stool on the other side of the fire.

The sideboard bears a promising display of small cakes, crab-apples, nuts and comfits which I am duly offered.

'Here, this'll warm you up,' says Heminges, handing me a pewter pot of malmsey. Taking the poker from the fire he thrusts it into the wine to make it sizzle then sprinkles it with a generous pinch of nutmeg. Mmm, delicious . . . a couple of these could see me to bed quite early.

'Now,' says Henry, his little black eyes gleaming with enthusiasm, 'you wanted to talk to us about our dear friend, Will Shakespeare . . .'

'Well, first of all, I want to thank you for the absolutely amazing job you did collecting, editing and publishing his plays. It's a horrifying thought that without you they may have been lost forever.'

'It was a labour of love,' says Heminges. 'A hard slog, but it had to be done—took us six years in all; about three years to collect and edit all the scripts and then the publishing was delayed for a time. But the year Will died, Ben Jonson published his own plays and called them his "works", and everyone scoffed at him. He was putting his plays up there alongside the classics. In those days nobody collected play scripts—they were just words for actors to play with, not to be taken seriously like poetry, essays, sermons and so on. But we thought, "If Ben Jonson's done it, we've got to do the same for Will."'

'Scripts did exist, of course,' says Condell. 'After we'd got full use out of them, we'd publish them in quarto size and sell them in St Paul's, or the White Hart in Fleet Street, or Carter Lane or wherever the printer's shop happened to be. But while we were still performing them they were kept under lock and key. That didn't stop piracy, though. Actors were always running off to printers with bits of scripts they'd stolen or cobbled together from memory. They were absolutely shocking, weren't they, Jack?'

Heminges nods sadly.

'So when we published the *Folio* we were right upfront,' continues Condell. 'We said it was to keep the memory of so worthy a friend and fellow as was our Shakespeare. We wished he had been alive to oversee the publishing himself; but since it had been ordained otherwise, whereas before readers had been abused with stolen, surreptitious copies, maimed and deformed by the frauds and stealths of injurious impostors, we now offered his plays cured and perfect in their limbs.'

'You see, up till then,' says Heminges, 'printers were publishing all sorts of rubbishy collections of plays and poems and sticking "by W. Shakespeare" on the front to ensure good sales. It was scandalous, but there's no law against it. In fact, Will was one of the first to have his name on the front of a published play script. Before him no one much cared who wrote it; the plays were anonymous, which makes it a bit hard sometimes, looking back on it, to remember who wrote what.'

'I remember Ben Jonson getting very shirty when Sir Thomas Bodley opened his great new library in Oxford,' chuckles Condell, 'to house all the world's greatest books. But he didn't want any play scripts—Shakespeare or Jonson or anyone. They were just rubbish, he said. I think that's what spurred Ben on to publish his "works" and claim the high ground for drama . . . But eventually old Bodley bought our *First Folio*. It sold well—a thousand copies at a pound a pop.'

'Given the size of the task,' I say, 'you did a great job—so few mistakes.'

'Well, we have to thank Ted Knight for a lot of that—he was the bookkeeper for the King's Men and had a great eye for detail. We had good compositors too, but there are a few obscure passages here and there, and no doubt some mistakes when we had no access to the originals but were going by the quartos. Where we did have Will's originals it was no problem because his mind and hand went together, and what he thought he uttered with that easiness that we have scarce received from him a blot in his papers.'

'You both first met Shakespeare in the theatre, I presume?'

'That's right,' says Heminges. 'I was a member of Lord Strange's Men when young Will joined the troupe. We were touring a lot with Kit Marlowe's plays—Ned Alleyn was playing most of the leads. It was a tough time for me because Rebecca and I had four kids by then (we had twelve eventually—well, twelve who survived, anyway). Then when the Lord Chamberlain's troupe was formed we both joined that, and that's when I met Harry here.'

'That's correct,' rejoins Condell, 'and I first acted with Will in Ben's *Every Man in His Humour*—a big hit.'

'You have children too?' I ask.

'Yes, nine surviving,' says Condell.

'So what plays did Shakespeare write for Lord Strange's company?'

'Oh, some beauties!' exclaims Condell. 'He gave us his *Two Gentlemen of Verona*, his *Taming of the Shrew*, his *Henry VI* plays and *Richard III* (we had Dickie Burbage with us by then because Ned Alleyn had joined the Admiral's Men at the Rose). And then he finished off *Titus Andronicus*, which George Peele had started but was a bit of a mess. And that turned out to be the hit of the season! It's on record that half the population of London came to see *Titus*.'

'So by 1594 you were all members of the Lord Chamberlain's Men?'

'My word yes!' enthuses Heminges. 'Nine great years; and then of course we became the King's Men in 1603 when King James took us over.'

'And what would you say was your favourite role in all that time?' I ask him.

'Well, it'd be hard to go past Falstaff. I was the original Falstaff but later Will Kemp took it over and I must say he made it his own. He was amazing, wasn't he, Harry?'

'Unforgettable,' agrees Condell. 'The greatest clown since Dickie Tarlton. His Dogberry was an absolute classic. And of course he was famous for the jigs he devised for the end of each show.'

'The jig was a kind of dance?'

'Yes, but it was more than that. Kemp was a great dancer of course, and at first the jig was just a solo sort of song-and-dance act. But Tarlton and Will Kemp developed it into a kind of little comic opera for a number of characters with bawdy words sung to popular ballad tunes. They were very funny and pretty dirty. All over London you could hear whores and soldiers singing the filthy words of Kemp's jigs.'

'And were all jigs like that?'

'No, not necessarily. Sometimes, after a tragedy like *Julius Caesar*, the jig would be more solemn and stately—but the audience always expected a dance of some sort.'

'Did Kemp stay with you all the way through?'

'No. He joined the Chamberlain's same time as we did and when we opened the Globe in 1599 he bought shares in it. But he wasn't what you'd call a great company man, was he, Jack? A bit of an individualist—so he sold his shares and took a bet that he could do a morris dance all the way from London to Norwich. And he did! Took him nine days, but he made it.'

'He came back to the Chamberlain's for a while later on,' says Heminges, 'but Will's comedy had changed by then. He wasn't writing those broad clown roles anymore because after Kemp left, Bob Armin took his place. He was only thirty but he was a much more subtle sort of comic—sharp and witty, a bit melancholy. Will wrote Feste in *Twelfth Night* for him (he was a lovely singer) as well as Touchstone and the Fool in *King Lear*, which was the greatest of all his roles, eh, Harry?'

'Yes, indeed,' sighs Condell. 'Oh, we had a great bunch of actors. Here, Jack, pile some more coals on the fire and give the gentleman some more of that mulled wine.'

'Tell me about some of the other actors in the company . . .'

'Oh, there were so many—Will Slye (a great Osric), Dick Cowley (Verges to Kemp's Dogberry), Gus Phillips (lovely fellow and a great musician), Jack Lowin who played Harry the Eighth, that little William Ostler who married your daughter, Jack.'

'Yes, Thomasina made a bad match there! He died stony broke and she and I had a nasty court case wrangling over his shares in the Globe.'

'And of course dear old Sinklo,' laughs Condell. 'His name was John Sincler but we all called him Sinklo. You look at some of the scripts and Will has written "Sinklo" instead of the character's name, just as he sometimes wrote "Kemp" or "Nick" because he was always thinking of the actor rather than the character. Ah, that Sinklo was a funny bugger—you only had to look at him, it'd make you laugh. He was as thin as a rake so Will wrote all the skinny parts for him: Doctor Pinch, Shadow, Slender, Starveling, Feeble, Andrew Aguecheek—dear old Sinklo. Where is he now, I wonder?'

'Oh, dead, Harry... these seven years or more.'

'No, don't tell me! Sinklo dead? It can't be...'

'Well, he was getting on, Harry.'

'Oh, of course, he was old; he couldn't choose but be old... Well, poor old Sinklo, dead! What do you know?'

'You talk of all those wonderful actors at the Globe, but before that you were all at the theatre in Shoreditch, weren't you?'

'Yes, that was the home of the Lord Chamberlain's Men. But we lost it in 1598.'

'What happened?'

'Well,' explains Heminges. 'You see we only had a lease until 1597. Then Jim and Dickie Burbage tried to renew it, but Giles Allen, the bastard, refused. First of all he wanted to double the rent (stuff that!) and then he wanted to pull down the theatre and repossess the land. And of course the authorities were in his pocket.

'We were in a right fix. Without a theatre we'd be well and truly buggered. Then one of the Burbage boys—I think it was Cuthbert—hit on a smart idea. Giles Allen might have owned the land but he didn't own the theatre. So we decided to pull it down and take it elsewhere!' Here Jack slaps his knee and bursts into gusts of wheezy laughter.

Harry cackles along with him and wipes away tears of mirth. 'Oh Jesu, Jesu, the mad days that we have seen! How did we get away with

A fireside chat with John and Harry

it?' Wheezing and chuckling, they take the opportunity to top up the pewter mugs.

'So,' resumes Heminges, 'just before Christmas 1598, we all met secretly one night at the theatre: ourselves, the Burbage boys and a dozen workmen. We'd brought along Peter Street, the original architect of the theatre, and he supervised us as we dismantled it and started transporting it across the river. It all took a couple of weeks of course and Giles Allen turned up spitting and fuming. But he couldn't do a thing about it; we were covered by the fine print in the contract. Christ, he was ropable!' Here they both cackle again and take a few more pulls at the pewter mugs.

'And then Peter Street helped us assemble the new theatre on the South Bank, in the Liberty of the Clink outside the city's jurisdiction,' concludes Harry.

'We called the new theatre the Globe,' says Jack triumphantly, 'because our motto was "All the World's a Stage"! And we formed a syndicate of sharers who put the money up for expenses and split the profits. Will was a sharer, of course, as were we and the Burbage boys, Will Kemp and four others of the original Chamberlain's Men. We played all the main roles, employed the hired men for the smaller roles and apprenticed the boy actors.'

'And how about these boy actors—where did they come from?'

'Well, most of them were apprenticed to actor-sharers in the companies for two to three years,' says Condell. 'During that time their master had to fully maintain them and teach them; acting, dancing, swordplay and so on. Other boys came to us from the various children's companies—the Chapel Royal, Paul's Children, the Children of the Queen's Revels and others.'

'The children's companies were very fashionable on and off,' says Heminges. 'At times they posed a serious threat to us. You see, up until the 1580s when the University Wits started making their mark, the adult companies were a pretty crude, rough-and-tumble lot. All right for inn yards and the provinces, but you couldn't take them to court. The Queen would much rather watch refined performances by well-trained boys from the schools of Westminster and Eton, or else the choirboys of Paul's, Windsor and the Chapel Royal.

'But after Jim Burbage (Dick's father) built the theatre and companies started to grow—first Leicester's, then the Admiral's and the Queen's Men—the competition from the children's companies started to fade away. But fifteen years later it all blew up again and the kids were performing not only at court but at the Blackfriars as well, mocking and abusing the adult players. It didn't affect either of us or Will Shakespeare directly, but Will does have a go at the boys' companies in *Hamlet*. He points out that it's pretty short-sighted of them to abuse the professional players, because as soon as their voices break, they'll be looking for jobs themselves.'

'He was right, you know,' says Heminges. 'Most of the kids had to give it up, but a few joined our company.'

'Some of them were wonderful,' Harry enthuses. 'Who were those two marvellous boys Will always used as a double act, Jack? You know, one was tall and fair and the other short and dark, kind of swarthy . . . Come on, you remember . . .'

'Certainly I do,' says Heminges. 'The tall fair one was my apprentice, Alexander Cook, we used to call him Sander. And the little one was Nick Tooley, Dick Burbage's apprentice. Normally the boys' names weren't written down. Backstage, you see, we had these plots pasted up to tell you what scene came next and who was in it. We wrote the men's names in full, but for the bit parts and the boys we just used nicknames or initials. But Sander and Nick, I'll never forget those two . . .'

'They were very funny in the *Dream*,' says Harry. 'Sander was Helena ("you painted maypole") and Nick was Hermia ("you dwarf! You nutmeg!"). Then they played Rosalind and Celia ("The woman low and browner than her brother") . . . Oh, and what else? Olivia and Maria, Desdemona and Emilia, Portia and Nerissa ("A little scrubby boy") and then, of course,

Nick went on to play Cleopatra. Now there's a role for you! Ah, those two boys were simply the best...'

'What clever actors they were...' says Jack. 'Naturally if they hadn't been that good, Will wouldn't have bothered writing such great roles for them; he couldn't have! He stretched them, all right, play by play, but my golly they rose to the occasion.'

'Did Will Shakespeare have an apprentice too?' I ask.

'Indeed he did,' sighs Heminges. 'His own younger brother, poor Edmund.'

'Why *poor* Edmund?'

'He died of the plague,' says Harry. 'He lodged with Will but stayed behind in London one time that Will went back to Stratford to escape the pestilence. Wasn't a great success as an actor, Ed; and he had a bastard child who died the year before he did.'

'Will was very cut up about it,' rejoins Heminges. 'Ordered a grand funeral in Southwark, just a short walk from the Globe. Pulled some strings to have him buried inside the church, which was usually not allowed for actors.'

'I remember that funeral well,' says Condell. 'Bloody freezing day—thirty-first of December 1607. Of course the whole company went and Will paid extra for the tolling of the great bell. Cost him twenty shillings.'

'So what was a normal day's work for an actor? Did you work hard?'

'Worked our socks off,' says Jack. 'Rehearse for four hours every morning (except Sunday of course), perform every afternoon from three till five or six, grab some supper, then home to learn lines for tomorrow because sometimes we'd be doing three different plays in the same week. There wasn't much time for mucking about. Discipline was strict: you'd be fined for being late for rehearsal, for being hung-over or for ducking across the road to the pub in your costume. And we had to keep up constant practice in dancing, tumbling and sword fighting. The audience was very discriminating and a sword fight had to be the real thing, naturally—so we lost a couple of people along the way.'

'Ah, but we were close, you know,' chimes in Harry. 'We looked after each other's families and we took good care of our apprentices. We were a very happy bunch—"We few, we happy few, we band of brothers." That's what Will was talking about; not soldiers, but a band of actors putting on a play! And it was all so exciting: the competition between the actors and the writers—Ned Alleyn slugging it out with Dick Burbage, Marlowe and Jonson going head to head with Shakespeare... All these great plays and great characters being performed for the first time, audiences not knowing what was coming next, all the sly hints and hidden messages about the court, the government and so on, seeing what you could get away with. It's no wonder the playhouses were always packed. It was a glorious time to be an actor.'

'And what was it like performing at court? Was that a thrill too?'

'Oh my word, yes,' says Jack. 'We'd pack all our props and costumes into barges, then up the river to Greenwich. If our costumes looked too tatty for the court, the Lord Chamberlain would dig us out some better ones from the Royal Wardrobe. Same with armour or weapons. Things you'd get away with at the Globe might get sneered at in court. They'd go to a lot of trouble to decorate the chamber and the Queen sat at one end on a dais with the court all around her. At the other end of the hall our musicians were above us in the musicians' gallery. The Queen had a very sharp wit and enjoyed wordplay. She loved gossip too, so Will filled the plays with topical jokes and skits on particular courtiers, especially in *Twelfth Night*. She enjoyed his little flatteries too: in *A Midsummer Night's Dream* he recalls her visit to Kenilworth. Will was only a lad, but he was there with his father who was Mayor of Stratford at the time. Lord Leicester had turned on a spectacular welcome for her: a mermaid on a dolphin's back rose out of the lake and Cupid fired a love arrow at the Queen. Will remembered that and has Oberon say to Puck: "I heard a mermaid on a dolphin's back . . . I might see young Cupid's fiery shaft/ Quench'd in the chaste beams of the watery moon/And the imperial votaress passed on/In maiden meditation, fancy free . . ."'

'He used it again in *Twelfth Night*,' Harry butts in: '"Arion on the dolphin's back . . ." It must have made quite an impression.'

'The old Queen loved flattery but she loved bawdy humour too,' Jack resumes. '. . . I remember one time she had to ask Dickie Tarlton to leave the stage because she was laughing too much . . .'

'Of course we really came into our own after she died and King Jamie took us over as the King's Men. We performed for Eliza about three times a year but for Jamie we performed at least fourteen times a year. Compared to the tight-fisted Old Lady, King Jamie was extravagantly generous; I remember the first time we performed for him—it was at the Pembrokes' place in Wiltshire—he gave the company thirty pounds! An absolute fortune!'

'Maybe,' says Heminges gravely. 'But even though he had us perform more frequently, I'm not sure how much of a theatre-lover he was. It was his wife, Queen Anne, who was the real enthusiast. Jamie had a short attention span and probably preferred the masques that Ben Jonson and Inigo Jones put together for him: they were shorter and less intellectually challenging. He was a bit of a buffoon, wasn't he, Harry? His tongue seemed too big for his mouth and he lolled about, scratching his balls and looking distracted—funny bugger.'

'So what with performing at court and playing the Globe, you were pretty flat out?'

'Not just that,' says Jack. 'Whenever the court went on progress through the countryside or to escape the plague, we could be sent for at any time to get our arses up there quick-smart—His or Her Majesty fancied a play.'

'Speaking of the plague, what happened to the company when the theatres were closed down, as they so frequently were?'

'Oh it was a nightmare,' says Harry. 'Pack up everything into carts and off into the provinces, trying to set up dates and persuade the city fathers to let us perform. Those of us who had horses were the lucky ones; for most of the company it was foot-slogging all day and helping to push the carts. Hearing we were from London, some towns would try to keep us out in case we were carrying the plague. And we were always worried about those we left behind in town. Poor Rob Browne left his wife and kids in Shoreditch. They were touched by the plague and were boarded up inside the house and they all died. People had no idea how to cope. They killed the cats and dogs thinking maybe they were the plague carriers, but of course the real carriers were the rats, and they simply flourished with all the cats and dogs out of the way! Oh God, they were miserable times.'

'Will took the smart way out,' observes Heminges. 'That time the plague hit us back in 1593, Will opted out of London altogether and settled himself in the country for a while and wrote *Venus and Adonis*. It was such a huge success that Will was tempted for a while to chuck the theatre and devote himself to being a gentleman poet. But he decided eventually that it wasn't the life for him—hobnobbing with courtiers, fawning on patrons, acting as their secretaries like John Donne and Ed Spenser did.

'Will preferred the comradeship of the theatre. The audience—they were his *real* patrons. He wanted his independence and to make his own way. He liked living in the rough part of town (Southwark had the biggest number of prisons, pubs, theatres and brothels in London, you know)—it was colourful, lively, full of weird odds and sods . . . Much more fun than hanging around some nobleman's establishment as a servant. He loved actors. People sometimes think we're a shallow lot—up ourselves, showy or precious. But somehow being part of a theatre company, you learn how to rub along, you learn how to tolerate people's weaknesses, you have to depend on each other and really strong bonds are formed—wouldn't you say, Harry?'

A fireside chat with John and Harry

'Yes, I reckon so,' responds Condell. 'And working together on really great material—well, it sort of ups your faith in human nature.'

'If there was such a camaraderie at the Globe, it must have been pretty traumatic when it burned down.'

'Oh God, it was terrible!' laments Jack. 'No one got hurt but we did lose a few props and costumes. Luckily we saved all our scripts—they were our prize possessions. Within two hours the whole theatre was ashes. Biggest fire since St Paul's. The whole of London turned out to watch and the next day the town was full of ballads, one of them mocking "poor old stuttering Heminges"! Well, wouldn't you be crying and stuttering watching your theatre burn down?'

'There, let it go, Jack,' says Harry, patting his shoulder. 'Stuff 'em. It was all a long time ago, and we did rebuild the Globe in just twelve months, even bigger and better than before—cost us a tidy fourteen hundred pounds, too.'

'But Will took no real interest,' says Jack. 'He was moving on by then, spending more time back in Stratford. I think he'd pretty well written all he had to say. He kept his hand in, of course. Collaborated on a few pieces like *Two Noble Kinsmen* and *Cardenio* with Jack Fletcher. He seemed to be devoting more time to his domestic affairs and property business, tying up loose ends. Maybe he felt the light thickening towards the close of day.'

'How would you sum him up as a person?'

Jack scratches his head and stares into the fire. 'Well, it's hard, you know, to sum up *anyone* . . . . Harry and I knew Will for nigh on thirty years, acted with him, travelled with him, worked with him day and night. He wasn't a tearaway like Kit Marlowe or a raconteur like Ben Jonson. I suppose you could say he was mild-mannered, diplomatic, watchful; pleasant but not boisterous company. Not exactly close-fisted but prudent with his money—very *clever* with money . . . There was something enigmatic about him. I think he lived through his characters. He entered right into them, because above all he was an actor.'

'What kind of roles did he play?'

'Mostly the kings and dukes, nobility.'

'He was very graceful and light on his feet. Well-modulated voice. John Davies remarked that if he hadn't been an actor he could have passed himself off for a king in real life! But he was good at character parts too—old men like Adam in *As You Like It*.'

I say, 'Some people claim the plays must have been written by a nobleman—someone like the Earl of Oxford—with a good education and a knowledge of life at court.'

Harry almost chokes on his mulled wine and Heminges scoffs in derision. 'Oxford! That useless fop! He was the one who went into voluntary exile after farting as he bowed to the Queen, remember, Harry?'

'Indeed I do,' laughs Harry. 'He stayed away seven years and when he came back the Queen greeted him with, "Welcome my lord; we have forgot the fart."'

They both collapse in mirth for a bit and then Harry splutters, 'These bloody aristocrats . . . They write the odd little poem or playlet and waft it nonchalantly in front of you with, "I say, Condell, old chap, cast your professional eye over this and see what you think of it . . ." Of course you tell them it's bloody marvellous and they put it on in one of their private chambers, acting the parts themselves, but it's stuff that wouldn't last a minute on the stage of the Globe.'

'As to good education,' says Heminges, 'I doubt any aristocrat got as good a classical education as we grammar-school boys! We got it flogged into us eleven hours a day, six days a week. We needed it more than they did, because we had to have a profession.'

'And when it comes to life at court,' chimes in Harry, 'we had a good dose of that, let me tell you. Always at the Queen's or King's beck and call, performing days at a time wherever they wanted us to be; and when we were made Grooms of the Chamber we had to hang about at a loose end hour after hour to be part of some boring ceremony. But it gave us a good chance to observe courtiers and their behaviour. Will couldn't stomach them—characters like Osric and Monsieur Le Beau; he sticks it right up them...'

'Besides,' says Heminges, 'Will's pictures of court life are not much different to anyone else's. Pretty standard stuff—stereotypical. It's his rustics and pub characters, his artisans, common soldiers and petty crooks who are really authentic—and no aristocrat could have written *them*!'

'Certainly not Oxford!' sneers Harry. 'He was dead by 1604 before the last dozen or so plays were written.'

'How about Francis Bacon—could *he* have written the plays?'

'Bacon? A dry old stick,' scoffs Heminges. 'A moralist, an essayist. He never liked the theatre. In fact he was one of our interrogators when we got in the soup for staging *Richard II* just before Essex's attempted coup! He never even liked the English language, for Christ's sake! Wrote all his stuff in Latin or else wrote it in English first and then *translated* it into Latin. He reckoned that English would be the death of literature. Now tell me,' he says solemnly, laying a hand on my knee, 'does that sound like Shakespeare?' Again the two old actors enjoy a fit of wheezing merriment and a resort to the pint-pot.

'No,' says Harry, recovering and wiping the tears from his eyes. 'What people have to realise is that playwriting is a *profession*... A play's not something some amateur tosses off in his spare time. You practise it daily, working with actors on the floor, you collaborate, you develop your craft. Will was a good listener. He took note of audience reaction and was always cutting and revising. He knew us, the actors, intimately and wrote roles according to our individual capacities. Ben Jonson remarked what a worker he was and noted that a good playwright is not just born, but made. Will kept raising the bar, pushing himself and us. His plays get tougher, more demanding, more experimental—there aren't two alike.

He was intensely competitive both artistically and commercially. He was determined to rule the roost.'

'That's right,' affirms Jack. 'Theatre has no room for aristocratic amateurs—except as audience members. And don't forget that Will's poems are all dedicated to aristocratic patrons. What nobleman would have needed a patron? Such nonsense, really. People don't use their heads . . .'

It's getting late and my eyelids are feeling heavy. We all gaze into the dying embers of the fire and the only sound is the heavy snoring of the fat black cat on the best armchair.

At length Harry murmurs, 'And is poor Sinklo dead?'

'Dead . . . dead . . .'

I open my eyes to find that the two old ghosts have faded or wafted like wisps of smoke up the chimney . . .

Harry Condell died in 1627 and John Heminges three years later.

Harry left his shares in the Globe to his widow. Jack acquired 'greate lyveing, wealth and power', owning a quarter of the shares in both the Globe and Blackfriars theatres.

Harry and Jack were buried side by side in the lovely old church of St Mary Aldonbury, but it was destroyed by the Great Fire of London in 1666. Rebuilt by Sir Christopher Wren, it was obliterated by German bombs in 1942.

In 1946 Winston Churchill made a gift of the church to the USA and it was transported stone by stone to Fulton, Missouri, where it now stands in the grounds of Westminster College.

As to the dust of Jack and Harry—where that rests is anybody's guess.

A man's life of any worth is a continual allegory—and very few eyes can see the mystery of his life—a life like the scriptures, figurative . . . Shakespeare led a life of Allegory; his works are the comments on it.

John Keats

15

The sonnets

The sonnets are either the most amazing work of imaginative fiction, or else the most breathtaking and intimate confessions penned by any writer, including St Augustine. And if they are the latter, would a man as sensitive to his honour and respectability as Shakespeare publish them for all the world to read?

Of all Shakespeare's work, I find the sonnets the most baffling. Not the poems themselves, for each one is a gem, a miniature play, exquisitely wrought, full of life and passion. No, the baffling bit is the simple question: 'Is the story they tell a fiction or are the poems autobiographical?' Scholars have debated the question back and forth for the last hundred years.

First, the story they tell: the poet seems to have been commissioned to write a series of sonnets to a young man, urging him to marry. The poet does so, but falls in love with the young man's beauty and personal attributes. The ensuing sequence enables him to express the full gamut of a lover's emotions: ecstasy, longing, jealousy, anger, despair, forgiveness. Then the poet feels threatened by the arrival on the scene of a rival poet seeking the young man's attention—but this threat is short-lived.

Next, the poet becomes sexually involved with a mistress—the so-called Dark Lady—with whom he has a stormy relationship, particularly when she becomes entangled with the young man. This sequence allows the poet to castigate the woman and eventually forgive the boy.

Interspersed in this fractured narrative are reflections on time, the corrosive force of lust and the beauty of marriage. The tone swings from lyrical to bawdy, from irony to revulsion to resignation.

Read as a sequence, the sonnets seem overwhelmingly personal and revelatory—a lover's diary. And there's the rub: are they any such thing, or are they purely a literary exercise, a fictitious drama in sonnet form, or, a third possibility, are they a fictitious drama, but informed (as so much great drama is) by personal experience?

Let's first examine the theory that the poems are addressed to and about real people. Who are they?

The main contenders for the 'lovely boy' are Henry Wroithsley, Earl of Southampton, and William Herbert, Earl of Pembroke, depending on how you date the composition of the sonnets. Southampton has long been the favourite, as he was Shakespeare's first patron and dedicatee of two narrative poems, *Venus and Adonis* and *The Rape of Lucrece*. He was renowned for his almost feminine physical beauty, and a miniature painted by Nicholas Hilliard when the boy was twenty years old shows him with long auburn tresses draped over one shoulder. Scion of a great Catholic family, he was a ward of Lord Burghley, Elizabeth's treasurer and the most powerful man in England. Burghley had the authority to negotiate his ward's marriage and took the unscrupulous step of engaging the boy to his granddaughter on forfeit of a staggering five thousand pounds. Wroithsley resisted the marriage and it's here that Shakespeare's services were allegedly pressed into service. Obviously the sonnets failed to do the trick and Wroithsley paid the fine instead of marrying the girl.

Despite financial setbacks, Southampton was a generous patron of the arts and an avid theatregoer. He loved hunting and earned sufficient distinction as a soldier for Essex to appoint him General of the Horse in the ill-fated Irish campaign. His effeminate appearance must be weighed against his heterosexual adventurism, which earned him the disfavour of the Queen when he became involved with one of her ladies in waiting.

A second candidate for the 'lovely boy' is William Herbert, Earl of Pembroke, to whom Heminges and Condell dedicated the *First Folio*. He too had a strong aversion to marriage but not to women. Having worried his father sick by turning down four suitable matches, he had an affair with another of Elizabeth's maids of honour, Mary Fitton, and was thrown into prison (briefly) for getting her pregnant. Like his uncle, Sir Philip Sidney, he was a generous supporter of the arts and had a close association with the theatre. When Richard Burbage (Shakespeare's leading actor) died, Herbert was overcome with grief for well over two months. Being invited by the Duke of Lennox to 'a great supper' to farewell the French ambassador, he replied:

> Even now all the company are at play, which I being tender hearted could not endure to see so soone after the loss of my old acquaintance Burbage.

After Elizabeth's death, Pembroke became a favourite of King James and played along with the overtly homoerotic atmosphere of the new court. At the King's coronation, where the other lords kneeled to profess their fealty, Pembroke strode boldly up to the King and kissed him full on the lips, at which James laughed and playfully slapped his cheek.

When the sonnets were published, they were dedicated to 'Mr W.H.' ... Who is he? They are unlikely to refer to a nobleman like the Earl of Pembroke, and would be a major typographical error if applied to Henry Wroithsley, with the initials reversed.

A popular candidate is Sir William Harvey, Southampton's stepfather. According to this theory, Southampton had the original manuscript of the sonnets and left it in his mother's keeping. On her death, her husband, seeing the financial potential, passed the manuscript on to Thomas Thorpe, who dedicated the publication to 'Mr W.H.... the only begetter of these ensuing sonnets...' The initials 'W.H.' could therefore apply to Sir William Harvey, but according to this scenario, the sonnets were published without Shakespeare's permission. Yet Thorpe was a respected and conscientious publisher, not a pirate. Moreover, the poet Thomas Heywood asserts that Shakespeare was miffed by William Jaggard's publishing, in 1599, a pirated collection called *The Passionate Pilgrime by W. Shakespeare*, containing various poems and sonnets, only some of which were by Shakespeare. So in 1609, says Heywood, Shakespeare, 'to do himself right, hath since published them in his own name'. However, the jury is still out as to whether the sonnets were published with Shakespeare's consent.

Next puzzle: who is the 'rival poet' who threatens to come between the author and his patron, stealing both affection and patronage?

Probably because he is the most obvious and dramatic candidate, Christopher Marlowe is most people's choice. There is something very Marlovian in the opening lines of Sonnet 86:

Was it the proud full sail of his great verse,
Bound for the prize of all-too-precious you?

And there may be a glance at Marlowe's *Dr Faustus* and the conjuring of spirits a little later in the same sonnet:

Was it his spirit, taught by spirits to write
Above a mortal pitch that struck me dead?
No, neither he nor his compeers by night,
Giving him aid, my verse astonished.

Then again, Thomas Fuller had compared Ben Jonson to a 'Spanish great Galleon' and Shakespeare to a light and lively 'English Man Of War', so is Jonson the rival poet? Or could it be George Chapman, who spoke of Homer's spirit guiding him as his muse? There could be a reference to Marlowe's murder in the line:

> Above a mortal pitch *that struck me dead* ...

That may be just a coincidence, although it does find an echo in Touchstone's speech, in *As You Like It*, referring to the same incident:

> When a man's verses cannot be understood ... *it strikes a man more dead* than a great reckoning in a little room.

Samuel Daniel, John Davies and Francis Davison have also been advanced as possible contenders. It's unlikely we will ever know for sure.

Then what of the 'Dark Lady'—who is she?

Here again there are several contenders, including a prostitute known as Black Luce or Lucy Negro, the Prioress of Clerkenwell. But the most popular choice is Emilia Lanier, who was certainly known to Shakespeare. The illegitimate daughter of Baptista Bassano, part of a family of Venetian Jews who became court musicians, she was popular in Elizabeth's court and soon caught the eye of the former patron of the Chamberlain's Men, Lord Hunsdon, fifty years her senior. When she became pregnant to him he concealed the affair by marrying her to a musician named Alphonse Lanier. Being a Venetian Jewess she was probably no English rose, but dark-haired and of a 'swarthy' complexion. She was a talented musician and published poetry in her own right. Much of our information concerning her comes from the diary of the quack Simon Forman, whom she consulted about her husband's horoscope. She was one of the many whom Forman notched up as sexual conquests.

So much for the protagonists; what of the content?

The sonnets

The first seventeen sonnets are devoted to urging a young man to marry. The poet's main tactic is flattery, playing on the youth's narcissism, assuring him of immortality in that his beauty will be perpetuated in his offspring. But towards the end of this sequence the poet gains confidence and assures the boy of immortality a second way—through the sonnets themselves.

> And all in war with time for love of you
> As he takes from you, I engraft you new.

And:

> But were some child of yours alive that time,
> You should live twice: in it, and in my rhyme.

The bulk of the collection, from sonnets 18 to 126, is assumed to be addressed to this same young man and examines every imaginable aspect of being a lover. There is the rhapsodic praise of the love object's beauty and rueful acceptance that this beauty must wither. A fair bit of special pleading comes in here as the poet assures the youth, again and again, that he will live forever, not anymore by having offspring, but by being loyal to his chronicler:

> So long as men can breathe or eyes can see,
> So long lives this, and this gives life to thee.

> Not marble, nor the gilded monuments
> Of princes, shall outlive this powerful rhyme;
> ...
> You live in this, and dwell in lovers' eyes.

Some of the loveliest of the poems deal with separation, longing and pining for the beloved. Others portray quarrels, fallings-out, mutual betrayals, forgiveness and reconciliation. Some portray jealousy when rivals, including the rival poet, seek the boy's attentions. Some describe the poet's anxiety about his failing powers and sense of getting old.

The love expressed for the youth, although highly romantic, remains platonic. It is clear that the relationship is never consummated. This is made most explicit in Sonnet 20:

> And for a woman wert thou first created,
> Till Nature as she wrought thee fell a-doting
> And by addition me of thee defeated,
> By adding one thing to my purpose nothing.
> But since she pricked thee out for women's pleasure,
> Mine be thy love and thy love's use their treasure.

In other words, Nature got carried away when creating the love object and added a penis, thus making a physical relationship out of the question. But the poet is quite content for the boy to go and screw around with women as long as he can have the boy's affection. This kind of 'Grecian' model was widely accepted during the Renaissance and part of the identity of a courtier. It was not a substitute for genuine male friendship, but a 'noble refinement', sometimes affected by those who didn't actually experience it but did not want to seem to be lacking in sensitivity.

Sonnets 127 to 152 are preoccupied with the 'Dark Lady' and describe a very different kind of passion. This is an intensely physical relationship and one which the poet sometimes revels in, sometimes observes with wry amusement, and sometimes recoils from in self-disgust. He becomes enraged when the lady seduces his male friend, and although hurt by the friend's betrayal, lays the blame at the feet of the seductress. But sexually addicted as he is to the lady, there is no way out of his pain:

> My love is as a fever, longing still
> For that which longer nurseth the disease,

The sonnets

Feeding on that which doth preserve the ill,
Th' uncertain sickly appetite to please:
. . .
Past cure I am, now reason is past care,
And frantic mad with ever more unrest.

The sonnet sequence ends abruptly with no resolution. The last two poems, numbers 153 and 154, are conventional love poems that have no bearing on the preceding narrative.

Early in the relationship with the lady, the emphasis is on the playful, the bawdy, and even the downright filthy—the ecstasies of sexual excess. Given that the word 'will' meant sexual appetite as well as being a slang word for both male and female genitalia, and was also the poet's first name, consider the following verbal gymnastics in Sonnet 135:

Whoever hath her wish, thou hast thy Will,
And Will to boot, and Will in overplus;
More than enough am I, that vex thee still,
To thy sweet will making addition thus.
Wilt thou, whose will is large and spacious,
Not once vouchsafe to hide my will in thine?
Shall will in others seem right gracious,
And in my will no fair acceptance shine?
The sea, all water, yet receives rain still,
And in abundance addeth to his store;
So thou, being rich in Will, add to thy Will
One will of mine, to make thy large Will more;
Let no unkind, no fair beseechers kill;
Think all but one, and me in that one Will.

It may not be the most gracious of Shakespeare's sonnets, but it's one of the funniest. Throughout his career he seems to have delighted in punning on his own name. Sonnet 136, following the one just quoted, concludes with the couplet:

> Make but my name thy love, and love that still;
> And then thou lov'st me, for my name is Will.

(One in the eye for those foolish enough to claim that the works of Shakespeare were written by somebody else.)

So what *is* it about the sonnets that makes them so intriguing? It's the fact that Shakespeare took such a straitjacket of a form, so confining and demanding, and breathed such life into it. Just look at the rules a moment: the Petrarchan form (named after its inventor, Francesco Petrarca) had to consist of fourteen lines of iambic pentameter with the following rhyme scheme: ab, ab, cd, cd, ef, ef, gg. The first eight lines establish a thesis, the next four counter with an antithesis and the couplet provides a resolution. Given these constraints, no wonder sonnets can be so stiff and stodgy. If you want to find out how hard it is, try writing one yourself.

Shakespeare took this difficult form and filled it with such passion, such warmth, humour, pain, vulnerability, anguish, tenderness, sadness and spontaneity that we are convinced, *while we are reading them*, that they must be the sincere outpourings of emotion from one human being to another. We think, 'This cannot be a fiction; it is too genuine; it feels so true.'

But now let's apply a bit of logic and test that reaction. To start with the dedication: 'To the only begetter of these ensuing sonnets, Mr W.H. . . .' If Sir William Harvey was indeed the person who gave the sonnets to Thomas Thorpe, is it likely that they revealed a real relationship between his stepson, Henry Wroithsley, Earl of Southampton, and a common player? Wroithsley was well ensconced at court again in 1609, a favourite of King James. Is it likely his stepfather would expose him to shame and ridicule as someone caught up in a steamy sexual triangle? Is it likely

The sonnets

that Southampton himself would have welcomed their publication? On the contrary, he would have been furious with Shakespeare and cut off all contact. But instead the publication of the sonnets caused no ruckus at all, and there is every indication that Shakespeare's relationships with both Southampton and Pembroke continued amiably, as the dedication of the *First Folio* to Pembroke in 1623 would show.

Has anyone stopped to wonder how likely it is that a mere poet, a common player, would form an intimate relationship with a young aristocrat and address him with such familiarity? Anyone with the slightest experience of the English class system knows how exclusive and snobbish it still is. Multiply that about four hundred times for Elizabethan England and you'll see it's absurd to suggest that Shakespeare could have dared presume to woo, blame, criticise or advise one of the highest ranking noblemen of the age. Sure, aristocrats liked to go slumming occasionally and may have formed the odd casual liaison with an actor, especially a boy actor, but nothing as sustained, intimate or intense as the narrative of the sonnets implies.

It's a pretty fantasy to imagine the parents or guardians of a wayward young aristocrat hiring a poet to compose sonnets urging him to marry. But do we imagine a headstrong, wilful young man like a Southampton or a Pembroke so easily coming to heel? He would more likely tell said parents or guardian to jump in the lake and take their sonnets with them.

The true relationship of Shakespeare to an aristocratic patron is reflected in his dedication of *Venus and Adonis* to Southampton:

> Right Honourable, I know not how I shall offend in dedicating my unpolished lines to your Lordship, nor how the world will censure me for choosing so strong a prop to support so weak a burthen. Only if your Honour seem but pleased, I account myself highly praised, and vow to take advantage of all idle hours, till I have honoured you with some graver labour.

Your Honour's in all duty,
William Shakespeare.

This is the tone of the modest and humble supplicant to the wealthy and influential patron, without whom the poet has no chance of survival. And it's another smack in the eye for those who claim Shakespeare's works were written by the Earl of Oxford, or Rutland or Sir Francis Bacon. Why would any of them need a patron and have to debase themselves thus? If Christopher Marlowe wrote the poem in 1593, why would he sign himself 'William Shakespeare'? The claims of the 'anti-Stratfordians' become more laughable the more you look at them.

Although the tone of the sonnets addressed to the youth is platonic, there is enough of a gay frisson to raise eyebrows in a society where sodomy was still a capital offence. Of course it all went on behind closed doors, especially in James's court circle, but no one would publish poems like these if any real-life model was suspected. Some critics have argued that because the sonnets had only one print run, they may have been suppressed by Southampton; but as I said earlier, that is unlikely, given his continued friendship and support of Shakespeare. It is more likely that the sonnets just didn't catch on, either because they were out of vogue and seemed a little old-fashioned, or because they were too unconventional and personal to be properly understood.

But most importantly, would Shakespeare himself have wanted them published if he thought there would be a scandal attached? Throughout his life he demonstrated a most urgent desire for respectability and status. He worked hard at securing the coat of arms with its motto 'Not Without Right'. He steered clear of debauchery and trouble, determined to establish himself as a gentleman in both London and Stratford, where he was revered as a leading citizen worthy of a tomb within the chancel of Holy Trinity. It is simply absurd to think he would pass his sonnets around among his friends, let alone publish them, if they were to proclaim him a homosexual and serial adulterer. Yet the sonnets caused no ripple of gossip in either London or at home with his wife and family. In other words, no one assumed for a moment that the sonnets were autobiographical. It was rightly assumed that they encapsulated a fiction, a play, and one that was toying with the conventions of the sonnet sequence as a form.

As for the 'Dark Lady', be it Emilia Lanier or anyone else, does an outraged lover really sit down to compose sonnets as a way of letting off steam? Does he then send them to her, expecting some response? He might well let fly a filthy letter, but not one of the exquisite gems of this sonnet sequence.

A further problem with trying to construct a meaningful narrative of the sequence is that we can't be really sure of what order the poems should be in, or the gender of the person addressed in every case. By rearranging the sequence you get many different meanings and the gender of the addressee in many cases becomes a matter of conjecture.

It is entirely possible that the poems urging marriage were written with one young man in mind while the others were written to or about a different young man (or men) altogether. There is nothing to identify any of the subjects, male or female. The only person we know for sure is Will, the author.

So if all those sonnets promising eternity to the subject were for real, they have entirely misfired, because we are never given his, or her, name. If you really want to immortalise someone and guarantee that his

> ... beauty shall in these black lines be seen

or

> 'Gainst death, and all oblivious enmity,
> Shall you pace forth; your praise shall still find room
> Even in the eyes of all posterity
> That wear this world out to the ending doom,

then you'd better let us know who you're talking about.

The fact that Shakespeare never told us and nobody thought to ask should reassure us that it is meaningless to look for real-life subjects in the sonnets. Rather, they should be understood as universal love poems, reflecting all the vagaries, the triumphs and despairs of love written over the space of a decade. If we want to find the real subject we should look in the mirror. This is Shakespeare the actor/dramatist playing a series of roles, just as he does in his plays.

Shakespeare's attitude towards sonneteering had always been a bit ambivalent. The models provided by Petrarch to his Laura and Sidney to his Stella had become debased by being so widely imitated. Every courtier or scholar was supposed to be able to reel off sonnets as a proof of his breeding, and all too many of them did. These are the young men Shakespeare is mocking in *Love's Labour's Lost* and Jaques' 'lover, sighing like furnace, with a woeful ballad made to his mistress' eyebrow'. Don Adriano de Armado, smitten by love, implores:

Assist me, some extemporal god of rhyme,
For I am sure I shall turn sonneteer.

Sometimes Shakespeare takes the sonnet seriously. The first meeting of Romeo and Juliet is remarkable in that they jointly improvise a sonnet to illustrate their 'marriage of true minds'.

But one suspects that in his great sonnet collection as published in 1609, Shakespeare is doing his best to subvert earlier models and blow them wide open. Where Petrarch is obsessed with a noble chaste lady who cannot be seduced, Shakespeare addresses a lady who is decidedly worldly, sexual and unconventional. He declares 'my mistress's eyes are nothing like the sun' and then proceeds to demolish the established catalogue of graces with which sonneteers were supposed to endow their subjects. The very act of addressing a male love object instead of a female one is a deliberate reversal of convention, one meant to shock or at least destabilise expectations.

So who is Shakespeare being in this drama? He is being 'the poet', the hired hack who knows how to flatter and write to order; the lover rhapsodising, agonising, castigating, forgiving. He talks about writer's block, the artist's insecurity, the slog of being an actor on tour, the older man routinely betrayed by younger lovers. Is any of Shakespeare in this? Of course. Whatever life experience he had he brought to bear in all his work. Did he ever fall in love with a younger man? It's entirely possible, but he didn't need to in order to write the sonnets, any more than he needed to murder a man to write *Macbeth* or to go mad in order to write *King Lear*. By observation, intuition and imagination he could put himself in *anyone's* shoes. Part of his great genius was his openness. His 'feminine' side was easily available to him and he seems to have loved women wholeheartedly. Yes, he is 'the poet' of the sonnets, just as he is Rosalind, Hamlet, Falstaff and Cleopatra. He is all of them and they are all aspects of him.

The sonnet collection is an exquisite work of art and among Shakespeare's greatest achievements. If he had written nothing else, it would still mark him out as pre-eminent among English poets. The more you read them the more you grow to love them. They are best read quietly aloud so that you can mull over the wit, the cadences, the long melancholy vowels and sprightly skipping rhythms. The heartfelt passion, joy, anguish, delight and bawdy fun are all immediately accessible. Each needs to be read over and over because each is a toy, a complex little puzzle, and it's handy to have a good edition, like the Arden, with copious notes and commentary to help with the obscurities. Once that hurdle is over, it's a joy to return again and again to a particular sonnet, relishing its compact cleverness and digging a little deeper each time.

I'd find it hard to choose my personal favourites—there are too many, and the more you read them, they increasingly become part of a mosaic, difficult to prise from the whole. So let me just pick three at random, each different in tone from its fellows. First, number 73:

> That time of year thou mayst in me behold,
> When yellow leaves, or none, or few do hang
> Upon those boughs which shake against the cold,
> Bare ruined choirs where late the sweet birds sang.
> In me thou seest the twilight of such day
> As after sunset fadeth in the west,
> Which by and by black night doth take away,
> Death's second self that seals up all in rest;
> In me thou seest the glowing of such fire
> That on the ashes of his youth doth lie,
> As on the deathbed, whereon it must expire;
> Consumed with that which it was nourished by;
> This thou perceiv'st, which makes thy love more strong,
> To love that well, which thou must leave ere long.

After the joy and exuberance of so many of the earlier sonnets this one has a wintry melancholy reinforced by the funeral bell reiteration of 'in me . . .' The tempo is sad, slow and deliberate.

The poem reminds us how often Shakespeare reverts to nature for his metaphors, here comparing himself to the lapse of autumn into winter, the setting sun and the embers of a dying fire. The second line has a very effective anti-diminuendo going from 'yellow leaves, or none, or few . . .' making the sequence less predictable and making us focus more clearly on the image of autumn leaves dropping.

The 'bare ruined choirs', it has often been remarked, conjure up the image of leafless trees bereft of birds but also the monasteries and convents stripped and destroyed by Henry VIII, now bereft of the monks and nuns who once sang there. It is one of the few hints we find in Shakespeare of a sympathy and nostalgia for the old religion.

'Death's second self' here means night-time but reminds us of Macbeth's description of sleep, 'The death of each day's life', and the phrase 'That seals up all in rest' also calls to mind Macbeth's calling on darkness to 'scarf up the tender eye of pitiful day'. It is a reference to the abhorrent custom of sealing or sewing up the eyes of falcons to keep them tame. But in this sonnet it also suggests the sealing up of a tomb, especially following on 'Death's second self'.

The final strong image of youth lying in its own ashes harks back to the relentless character of Time, who simultaneously nourishes the body by bringing it to maturity while hastening it towards death.

The final couplet smacks of emotional blackmail and could be paraphrased as: 'Note all this and make sure you appreciate me because you won't have me for long.' A more generous reading might be: 'I know that you are aware of this and that is why you love me so much.' Given the overall tone of the narrative and the relationship, I incline towards the first option.

Now let's look at number 147, which I mentioned earlier:

My love is as a fever, longing still
For that which longer nurseth the disease,
Feeding on that which doth preserve the ill,
Th' uncertain sickly appetite to please:
My reason, the physician to my love,
Angry that his prescriptions are not kept,
Hath left me, and I, desperate, now approve
Desire is death, which physic did except.
Past cure I am, now reason is past care,
And frantic mad with ever more unrest,
My thoughts and my discourse as madmen's are,
At random from the truth vainly expressed:

> For I have sworn thee fair, and thought thee bright,
> Who art as black as hell, as dark as night.

This is the nadir of the poet's frustration and rage concerning the Dark Lady. It is a wild, despairing and lethal outpouring and breaks the conventional sonnet structure by having one thesis only and driving it through to the end, building in emotional pitch and frenzy to the hammer-blow monosyllables of the final couplet, so full of hatred and contempt. It's amazing how flexible Shakespeare can make the constricting sonnet form by writing in such varied tempi and emotional states. It is a sick mind speaking, one addicted to sex, full of self-disgust and flailing about trying to find the exit. It reminds me of the sexual revulsion of the mad Lear, which again expresses itself in gross and obscene language:

> Down from the waist they are centaurs,
> Though women all above:
> But to girdle do the gods inherit,
> Beneath is all the fiend's:
> There's hell, there's darkness, there is the sulphurous pit,
> Burning, scalding, stench, consumption . . .

For a complete change of pace, consider Sonnet 138:

> When my love swears that she is made of truth,
> I do believe her, though I know she lies,
> That she might think me some untutored youth
> Unlearned in the world's false subtleties.
> Thus vainly thinking that she thinks me young,
> Although she knows my days are past the best,
> Simply I credit her false-speaking tongue:
> On both sides thus is simple truth suppressed.
> But wherefore says she not she is unjust?

> And wherefore say not I that I am old?
> O Love's best habit is in seeming trust,
> And age in love loves not t' have years told.
> Therefore I lie with her, and she with me,
> And in our faults by lies we flattered be.

How different in tone to the last sonnet! This one is easygoing, world-weary and worldly-wise, the poet laughing wryly at his own vanity and his mistress's infidelities, cynically accepting that cohabitation can only work if based on deceit and wilful ignorance.

I particularly like the playful use of 'simply I credit her false-speaking tongue' (i.e. I play the simpleton), butting against 'thus is simple truth suppressed' (i.e. the plain, obvious truth). The spontaneity of the questions in lines eight and nine is very natural, followed by a sighing 'O' that leads to the cynical assurance that, to avoid trouble, it is best to pretend to believe whatever your lover tells you.

The final couplet expresses a lazy contentment with the charade as long as you're getting enough sex (playing on the double meaning of I lying with her and she lying with me).

These are just three random examples of the wit and wisdom contained in the sonnets. Every reader must perforce arrive at an original and individual response to them. Even more than in the plays we have to confront ourselves. There are no trappings or distractions—just us and the text. And we're all in there somewhere.

16

Romeo and Juliet

> A poet is the most unpoetical of anything in existence, because he has no identity—he is continually informing and filling some other Body.
> JOHN KEATS

When my wife Anna and I decided in 1968 to return from England to Australia we'd each had a good four years with the Royal Shakespeare Company in both London and Stratford-upon-Avon. We'd bought a little house in Stratford, not far from the Holy Trinity Church where Shakespeare was baptised and buried. Both our daughters had been born in Stratford, we'd made good friends there and acted in some inspiring productions (and some not so inspiring). But we had a hankering to come home. We were a bit sick of tramping between London and Stratford each season with the kids, the dog and the cat. And we wanted the girls to grow up with sunshine, the bush and the beach. London's leaden skies became more oppressive with each succeeding winter.

I was also becoming a little jaded with the uncertainties of a freelance actor's prospects and had aspirations to direct. I was now an Associate Artist of the RSC and was aware I could probably count on becoming a cog in the vast English theatre machine; or I could take my chances in Australia and perhaps do something more useful. I wrote to John Clark, the director of NIDA, who offered me the job of head of acting from the beginning of 1970. So before I returned to Sydney I spent six months teaching acting at my alma mater, the Bristol Old Vic Theatre School, and some months with Lincoln's Theatre Royal, which was being run by my old Sydney Uni friends Philip Hedley and Richard Wherrett.

One of the first roles I played for them was Romeo, a part I delighted in for its rapturous language, action and untrammelled emotionalism—a great role for a young actor but a difficult one. It's easy for Romeo to come across as passive and wussy, pushed around by Mercutio, Juliet, the Nurse and the Friar. You have to bring a positive energy to the part, even when you're moping over Rosaline (that name again!), taking directives from Juliet or thrashing about in self-pity in the Friar's cell. The role demands a youthful exuberance, naivety, openness and innocence. Yet by the last act Romeo has grown into a mature tragic figure, solemn and purposeful. Juliet undergoes a similar transformation. We first see her as a thirteen-year-old girl, lively and witty but still innocent of the world. By the end of the balcony scene she is decisive and pragmatic, and her development as a tragic heroine is clearly charted from one scene to the next. The greatest challenge for the director of the play lies in the casting of those two roles: to find actors who, first of all, have the right 'chemistry' to move and convince an audience and make that relationship incandescent, and second, come across as convincingly adolescent (she is thirteen, he is sixteen), yet can handle the high tragedy and demanding rhetoric of the second half of the play. This is particularly true for Juliet, with big set pieces like 'Gallop apace, you fiery-footed steeds', then the scene in which she confronts the Friar, and, toughest of all, the scene where she swallows the potion. The two boys for whom Shakespeare wrote the roles must have been formidable actors.

I have now directed the play three times, and never to my satisfaction, despite enthusiastic audience responses. It may well be one of Shakespeare's most popular plays, but I'm convinced it's also one of the hardest to direct—that and *Macbeth*. The first difficulty, as I said, is in the casting of the two lead roles. If you don't get that right, you're sunk. The first time I directed it, for Nimrod, I had Mel Gibson and Angela Punch McGregor in the leads. The next time, for Bell Shakespeare in 1993, I had Daniel Lapaine and Essie Davis, and my most recent production, again for Bell Shakespeare, featured Julian Garner and Chloe Armstrong. Essie and Daniel were the best matched in terms of that essential chemistry.

Another challenge for the director is finding the right balance between the romantic comedy and hi-jinks of the first half of the play and the crushing tragedy of the second half, following Tybalt's death. This was Shakespeare's first attempt at tragedy and he was still feeling his way. There is a great danger that the lively spirits of Mercutio will so endear him to the audience that they will be unwilling to let him go, which is why Shakespeare had to kill him off. But that's putting it too crudely; when Mercutio dies there is indeed a gap in nature and tragedy rushes in to fill the gulf. A cloud seems to pass over the sun and this is Romeo's cue to take the quantum leap from callow youth to doomed man of action. The director has to get the tone just right in both halves of the play, because without the joy, lyricism, bawdy fun and youthful exuberance, there will be no tragic pay-off.

Maintaining the tension of the balcony scene is another challenge. It's one of the most beautiful scenes in all of Shakespeare—rhapsodic, funny, touching and so natural in its expression of teenage love. The challenge in staging it is that she is up on a balcony for the whole scene and he is down below—they never touch! Some productions duck the issue by having Romeo climb up to the balcony, but then all the tension is gone.

The whole point of the scene is that they cannot touch and therefore have to express themselves through words only... If they could be together they'd use different words or, more likely, stop talking altogether.

This physical separation has a strong thematic base; Romeo and Juliet are always being torn apart and separated and this only intensifies their longing for what is an idealised relationship. Romantic love like that of Romeo and Juliet or Tristan and Isolde is based on the concept of forbidden fruit—wanting the one you can never have. Once you have him or her, the romance is gone; so the only logical consummation is in death—being together for all eternity. It is instructive that Romeo and Juliet, the most famous lovers in history, spend so little time together. They fall in love at first sight, and after only fourteen lines of poetry Juliet is snatched away by her nurse. The next time we see them is the balcony scene, where they are separated by distance and have no physical contact. They meet briefly the following day, but before they have time to embrace, the Friar hurries them off to the chapel.

They are totally separated by Romeo's banishment following the death of Tybalt, but Shakespeare allows them one precious night together (which we do not see, for obvious reasons) and a brief, painful leave-taking the morning after. And that's it... the next time they see each other Juliet is supposedly dead in her tomb. Romeo takes his farewell of her and swallows poison. She awakes from her drug-induced slumber and is allowed only a moment to mourn for him before she stabs herself. So the world's favourite love story is built around one night of marital bliss—the rest is all pining and fantasising.

That's a pretty good account of the nature of romantic love, but it has its practical side too. The roles were written for teenage boys, one of them dressed as a girl. There was doubtless a homoerotic frisson for some of the audience watching pretty boys play love scenes together; at least the Puritan preachers thought so and thundered in the pulpit against this 'lewdness'. So the theatre could only go so far. This is partly why Shakespeare keeps his lovers apart so much of the time. But they kiss when they first meet, they kiss again when parting after their night of love, and they kiss and embrace each other's dead bodies: enough to get the preachers steamed up!

The logic of the story doesn't bear too much scrutiny: the love at first sight, next day's marriage, the efficacy of the Friar's potion, his letter failing to reach Romeo—you have to take all of these with a rather large pinch of salt. So what makes it work so well? For a start, the irresistible poetry—language so energetic, imaginative and emotionally charged that it sweeps all before it and defies scepticism. And its lyrical extravagance is cunningly balanced by an earthy, bawdy prosaic presence in the characters of Mercutio, Peter and the Nurse, so that the play keeps its feet on the ground while its fancy roves among the stars. Mercutio's scepticism and carnality combined with the Nurse's earthiness stave off any danger of the play becoming effete. Through the power of poetry Shakespeare created on an empty stage and in broad daylight the hot streets of Verona, a lavish masquerade with its music, busy servants and call for lights, a magical moonlit garden, the spooky backstreets of Mantua (note the careful scene painting of the sinister apothecary's shop), and the cavernous sepulchre of the Capulets. The specificity of the locations help to give the play a strong sense of realism. This is reinforced by Shakespeare being very specific about time as well as place. The action takes place over four days, commencing just after nine o'clock in the morning ('but new struck nine') in mid-July ('How long is it now to Lammas-tide [1 August]?' 'A fortnight and odd days') 1596 (''Tis since the earthquake [of 1585] now eleven years'). The Prince commands Capulet and Montague to visit him that afternoon and the same night Romeo gatecrashes the Capulet ball, woos Juliet on her balcony and agrees to marry her at nine o'clock next morning. The sun is still rising when Romeo ambushes Friar Lawrence and cajoles him into performing the marriage ceremony that afternoon.

It is midday ('The bawdy hand of the dial is now upon the prick of noon') when the Nurse finds Romeo to confirm the arrangements.

In the next scene Juliet complains that she sent the Nurse to find Romeo at nine o'clock and that she's been gone over three hours. Then the Nurse returns. So it is still day two when Romeo and Juliet meet at the Friar's cell and are married. On his way home from the ceremony (we are told it's a hot afternoon) Romeo runs into Tybalt and his gang. Mercutio and Tybalt are both killed, Romeo hides in the Friar's cell and is banished by the Prince. Meanwhile Juliet is praying for evening to hurry on so that she and Romeo may meet, when the Nurse enters to tell her of Romeo's fate. At night Romeo is smuggled into her chamber and they spend their one and only night together... On day three Romeo flees to Mantua and Juliet is told she must marry Count Paris. She runs to the Friar, who gives her the sleeping potion. Her father has brought the wedding forward to the next day so she drinks the potion that night. On the morning of day four the 'dead' Juliet is discovered and conveyed to the Capulets' tomb. Romeo's servant Balthazar witnesses the funeral and hurries to Mantua to give Romeo the bad news. Meanwhile Friar Lawrence's letter goes astray. Romeo hastens back to Verona, breaks into the tomb, slays Paris and kills himself. Juliet wakes, refuses to leave Romeo and stabs herself just as dawn is breaking on day five. ('A glooming peace this morning with it brings.')

If you try to pace the action hour by hour, time hurtles by at an almost impossible pace. But a theatre audience doesn't make that sort of calculation. By pushing the action forward at such a rate and constantly reminding us of the time, Shakespeare ratchets up the tension and stresses the impetuosity of all the protagonists. If only Friar Lawrence had had time to play the peacemaker and negotiate a marriage, if only Capulet had not rushed the wedding to Paris—if only *anybody* had stopped to think, then tragedy might have been averted. But as we are reminded over and over, this is a rash, hot-blooded society where people fall in love and fight to the death on impulse. This is a play about youthful passion:

> It is too rash, too unadvis'd, too sudden,
> Too like the lightning which doth cease to be,
> Ere one can say, it lightens.

Another thing that makes the play work is its universality. Audiences have always embraced young lovers, whether tragic or comic. We warm to their idealism and innocence, their prospects for the future. And in this case we have the pathos of young love thwarted by senseless violence. The children pay the price of their parents' stupidity and stubbornness. You can locate the play wherever there is prejudice, bigotry, religious or ethnic conflict: on New York's West Side, in Belfast, in Gaza or Bosnia—the model is always contemporary and relevant. And young audiences have always responded to Shakespeare's depiction of the generation gap—teenagers misunderstood and driven to suicide by bullying parents who have forgotten what love is.

Shakespeare was twenty-nine when he wrote *Romeo and Juliet*, basing his play on a long narrative poem by Arthur Brooke, who found his source in Bandello, who in turn based his novella on still earlier Italian versions of the story. Brooke's narrative takes nine months to unfold as opposed to Shakespeare's four days. It is couched as a moral tale condemning youthful lust and disobedience—the lovers pay the ultimate price for their sins. The characters of Mercutio and the Nurse are Shakespeare's invention as is the remarkable psychological study of the Capulet family. Romeo and Juliet flout all the conventions of society and religion, yet we sympathise with their reckless suicides.

Gary O'Connor comments that the young lovers never get to know one another. They are in love with the idea of love, with passion, with

Eros, but not with reality: 'Their love is based on a false reciprocity, which conceals a twin narcissism. They love within one another the reflection of themselves.'

All very possibly true, but theatre audiences don't see it that way—we are too swept away by the spectacle of youth, beauty and innocence being needlessly wasted; of hopes for the future being dashed. The reconciliation of the families at the end of the play is a necessary and satisfying coda which gives the story both meaning and gravitas.

In Stratford in 1968 I played Paris in a production by the Greek director Karolos Koun, who was in England having fallen foul of the military junta in Athens. His production was quite dark and austere. The set consisted of two huge walls which, when moving, threatened to crush the characters (and, sometimes, unintentionally, the performers). We were all dressed in heavy woollen garments, and when somebody tentatively suggested that Verona was supposed to have a hot climate, Karolos responded, 'No, it's north.' He was speaking from an Athenian perspective. It was interesting to note that to the Englishman, Shakespeare's Verona was a hot place. To a Greek it was cold. It made a difference in the storytelling. Ian Holm was a doomed but plucky Romeo—his death wish seemed apparent from the start. Estelle Kohler played Juliet and Norman Rodway Mercutio. In her performance as the Nurse, Elizabeth Spriggs reminded me what a quintessentially English character she is in the midst of this supposedly Italian play. She is a marvellous creation, a perfect depiction of a Stratford gossip—vulgar, warm-hearted, foolish and devoted to Juliet, too easily caught up in her rash schemes. Her treachery in suggesting Juliet forget Romeo and marry Paris is as shocking as it is realistic. She is lacking not empathy but imagination, and is a simple workaday soul caught up in events too big for her capacities. Her vanity and vulgarity are beautifully captured when, at the ball, Romeo enquires as to the identity of Juliet. The Nurse proudly replies:

> Marry, bachelor,
> Her mother is the lady of the house,
> And a good lady, and a wise and virtuous,
> I nurs'd her daughter that you talk'd withal;
> I tell you, he that can lay hold of her
> Shall have the chinks.

The Friar, too, gets caught up in the youngsters' heady affair. One can argue that he should have followed a more prudent course, but how do you stand up against the force of young love? There is something of the white magician about Friar Lawrence, reminiscent of Prospero or *Pericles*' Cerimon. He is a naturalist and herbalist, but he knows his poisons. In his benevolent figure we see shadows of the old anti-Catholic propaganda which depicted monks and friars as meddling sinister characters, adept in poisons and treachery.

The spin-offs and transformations of *Romeo and Juliet* are too many to calculate—in movies, pop songs, opera, ballet and musicals. *West Side Story* is probably the most significant of the modern makeovers and is a considerable work in its own right—just one more example of Shakespeare's ever-expanding universe.

17

Troilus and Cressida

For some years I had been trying to lure Michael Bogdanov to come from England and work for Bell Shakespeare. I had been impressed by his English Shakespeare Company's *Wars of the Roses* and knocked out by his *Taming of the Shrew* in Stratford. We had corresponded and met a couple of times at conferences but I had the impression that, like most Britishers, he didn't have a high opinion of, or much interest in, the Australian theatre scene—and it was a long way to come for a busy man.

Leo Schofield was director of the Sydney Olympics Festival for the year 2000 and said he was open to suggestions if I could find an interesting product and artist of international standing. *Troilus and Cressida* was a play I had wanted to do for some time, but I knew it could be death at the box office. Still, I thought it could attract a festival audience and might appeal to Bogdanov. He leapt at the chance of being here for the Olympics and seeing something of the country as well. But he didn't come cheap: he would bring his partner (who was also his costume designer), two children, their 'nanny', his own fight director and weapons. We would also have to provide him with a house and a car. None of this would be possible without the festival's involvement. Happily, Leo responded positively and the deal was struck.

Even so, Michael's original ideas were challenging. He wanted to enlarge the stage of the Sydney Opera House Playhouse, take out all the seats and cover the stage in mud six inches deep. An armed personnel carrier or jeep must also be got on stage. Well, little by little these ideas were compromised. There was no way the Opera House would let us rebuild the stage, dump six inches of mud on it or take out the seats. But Michael Scott-Mitchell's imaginative design did succeed in making the space a lot bigger, and enough mud was employed to convey the desired effect. We had a large cast (twenty) with quite a few grizzled veterans, including myself as Ulysses, because Michael's idea was that the Greeks had been sitting out the siege of Troy in their makeshift camp for eleven years. They were no longer the heroic warriors of *The Odyssey* but had grown decrepit and gone to seed through lack of action. Achilles was flabby and overweight, and Patroclus, his catamite, was a daffy old queen with lots of makeup and a cardigan. The Trojans, meanwhile, sat all day in their spa pool, or else lolled around in towels, discussing strategy. The show was held together by Pandarus, transformed by Bille Brown into 'Uncle Pandy', a talk-show host in toupee and cravat who roamed about the stage and through the audience with a hand mic, accompanied by live video cameras, relaying onto large screens both the stage action and audience response. There was a good deal of nudity in the show (which undoubtedly boosted ticket sales) and a scene of two scantily clad girls mud-wrestling for the amusement of the Greek soldiers.

I was impressed with the pains Bogdanov took over the authenticity of the props and achieving desired effects. Even though we were running well behind schedule in production week, he spent hours rehearsing the killing of Hector, who had to be bound, hoisted up by the feet and have his throat cut in such a way that the blood spurted right across the stage.

Troilus and Cressida

I admired Michael's concern with detail and specifics, the time he took with pulleys and blood bags.

Written around 1602, *Troilus and Cressida* sits alongside other dark and troubling plays like *Measure for Measure* and *Timon of Athens* but is nastier than either of them. Shakespeare sets out to utterly subvert the myth of the Trojan War, so idealised by the Elizabethans as an tribute to heroic deeds and the glory of war. In his version the noble Hector is most vilely betrayed by Achilles, stabbed in the back by his Myrmidons. This is no heroic tale, but as the spiteful Thersites puts it:

> All the argument is a whore and a cuckold—a good quarrel to draw
>   emulous factions and bleed to death upon.
> Now the dry Serpigo on the subject, and war and lechery confound all!

Bogdanov was right to stress the squalor and ugliness of the campaign and show war as inglorious and wasteful. This message is at the heart of the play, which suggests there can never be any such thing as a moral absolute: the only values are those responsive to time and fashion. Whatever drove Shakespeare to write the piece, it appeals very much to modern sensibilities. We can accept its cynicism, its lack of optimism, its bitterness and sense of dislocation.

To mitigate the bleakness we have, as always, Shakespeare's sense of humour. Pandarus, vain, fluttering and epicene, is a hugely amusing character; and the vitriolic Thersites is devastatingly funny in his critique of heroic posturing. The epilogue, which generally serves to flatter the audience and thank them for their attention, is here delivered by the disillusioned and rejected Pandarus. He addresses us as if we are all, like him, pimps and bawds:

> Brothers and sisters of the hold-door trade,
> Some two months hence my will shall here be made

> Till then I'll sweat and seek about for eases,
> And at that time bequeath you my diseases.

But Shakespeare could never leave us with something that was merely bleak and cynical. There is always a dimension of humanity and tragedy; in this case it lies in the sincerity and trusting nature of Troilus, so desperate to believe in the fickle Cressida's fidelity:

> We two, that with so many thousand sighs
> Did buy each other, must poorly sell ourselves
> With the rude brevity and discharge of one.
> Injurious time now with a robber's haste
> Crams his rich thievery up, he knows not how.
> As many farewells as there be stars in heaven,
> With distinct breath and consign'd kisses to them,
> He fumbles up into a loose adieu,
> And scants us with a single famish'd kiss,
> Distasted with the salt of broken tears.

Such heartbreakingly beautiful poetry throws into sharp relief the cynicism and ugliness of the world around it.

I enjoyed working with Bogdanov. He was demanding, uncompromising, opinionated and very much the provocateur. His productions of *Shrew* and *Romeo and Juliet* at Stratford had caused great controversy as had his production of Howard Brenton's *The Romans in Britain* at the National: one scene depicts a couple of Roman soldiers sodomising a young Celt—a fitting metaphor for imperialism. The prudish moral watchdog Mary Whitehouse brought a charge of obscenity against Bogdanov and he was threatened with prison. Peter Hall (director of the National) tactfully suggested, 'Couldn't you do it up the back in half-light?' 'No,' Bogdanov insisted, 'it's got to be in full light down-stage centre.' To his credit, Hall backed Bogdanov when the case came to trial at the Old Bailey in March 1982. Three days later the prosecution backed down and dropped the case.

Playing Ulysses in *Troilus and Cressida* was an enjoyable exercise. We weren't being classical Greeks draped in sheets but a bunch of grotty old mercenaries in battered guerrilla uniforms squatting around our campfire. Ulysses has a couple of great set pieces, the first a hymn to the divine order of nature:

> Take but degree away, untune that string,
> And hark what discord follows! Each thing melts
> In mere oppugnancy: the bounded waters
> Should lift their bosoms higher than the shores,
> And make a sop of all this solid globe:
> Strength should be lord of imbecility;
> And the rude son should strike his father dead;
> Force should be right; or, rather, right and wrong.
> Between whose endless jar justice resides—
> Should lose their names, and so should justice too.

But this is not a case of Shakespeare defending the Jacobean establishment, as is often supposed. It's not Shakespeare but Ulysses talking, and his purpose is to ginger up the lethargic Greeks and make them see that Achilles, by defying the authority of Agamemnon, is sowing the seeds of mutiny among the ranks:

> ... The general's disdain'd
> By him one step below, he by the next,
> The next by him beneath; so every step,
> Exampl'd by the first pace that is sick
> Of his superior, grows to an envious fever
> Of pale and bloodless emulation.

Ulysses retains some of the qualities endowed on him by Homer: he is still the crafty, smooth-talking and hard-headed realist. He knows the Greeks can never win the war unless Achilles can be spurred on to face the Trojan hero Hector in single combat. To this end he beards Achilles in his den and suggests that the Greek commanders now idolise the blockhead Ajax because he is prominent in the field, whereas Achilles' past triumphs are forgotten. His speech is a marvellous and very Shakespearean meditation on the ingratitude of Time, the transience of all worldly achievement and the fickleness of fashion. I will quote the speech in full because it is one of my top favourites and is well worth mulling over.

Where one might expect Ulysses to employ logic, reason or patriotism to appeal to Achilles, he resorts to a series of images—all concrete and emotive: the monster ingratitude stuffing good deeds into his backpack, the coat of mail rusting on the wall, the thousand sons of emulation pushing and shoving, then metamorphosing into a tidal wave, and so on. What could have been a dry rhetorical argument becomes instead a brilliant piece of devious emotional blackmail. Particularly affecting is the image of the gallant warhorse leading the charge, stumbling and being trampled by the poltroons who follow. Then the tone switches to humorous satire in the description of the fashionable host lightly dismissing his departing guest and, 'with his arms outstretched as he would fly', welcoming a new arrival. The array of disparate images is dazzling, entertaining and avoids any risk of portentousness:

> Time hath, my lord,
> A wallet at his back, wherein he puts
> Alms for oblivion, a great-sized monster
> Of ingratitudes. Those scraps are good deeds past,
> Which are devoured as fast as they are made,
> Forgot as soon as done. Perseverance, dear my lord,
> Keeps honour bright. To have done is to hang

Quite out of fashion, like a rusty mail
In monumental mock'ry. Take the instant way,
For honour travels in a strait so narrow,
Where one but goes abreast. Keep then the path,
For emulation hath a thousand sons
That one by one pursue: if you give way,
Or hedge aside from the direct forthright,
Like to an entered tide they all rush by
And leave you hindmost;
Or, like a gallant horse fall'n in first rank,
Lie there for pavement to the abject rear,
O'errun and trampled on. Then what they do in present,
Though less than yours in past, must o'ertop yours.
For Time is like a fashionable host,
That slightly shakes his parting guest by th' hand
And, with his arms outstretched as he would fly,
Grasps in the comer. Welcome ever smiles,
And Farewell goes out sighing. O let not virtue seek
Remuneration for the thing it was;
For beauty, wit,
High birth, vigour of bone, desert in service,
Love, friendship, charity, are subjects all
To envious and calumniating Time.
One touch of nature makes the whole world kin,
That all with one consent praise new-born gauds,
Though they are made and moulded of things past,
And give to dust that is a little gilt
More laud than gilt o'er-dusted.
The present eye praises the present object.
Then marvel not, thou great and complete man,
That all the Greeks begin to worship Ajax,
Since things in motion sooner catch the eye

Than what not stirs. The cry went once on thee,
And still it might, and yet it may again,
If thou wouldst not entomb thyself alive
And case thy reputation in thy tent,
Whose glorious deeds but in these fields of late
Made emulous missions 'mongst the gods themselves,
And drove great Mars to faction.

18

Timon of Athens

> There is another aspect of his dramaturgy that generally goes unremarked. In modern drama the accepted context is one of naturalism which certain playwrights then work up into formality or ritual. In the early seventeenth century the essential context is one of ritualism and formality to which Shakespeare might then add touches of realism and naturalism. We must reverse all modern expectations...
> PETER ACKROYD, *SHAKESPEARE: THE BIOGRAPHY*

When Anna and I joined the Royal Shakespeare Company in Stratford, the first show I was in was *Timon of Athens,* directed by John Schlesinger and starring Paul Scofield. Although we were only supernumeraries this was a heady beginning. Scofield was an actor I had admired tremendously for many years and that admiration kept growing during the time I worked with him. I stood in the wings every moment I was off stage and watched his performance as Timon. He had a natural grace and beauty on stage as well as the most remarkable and idiosyncratic voice. It would range up and down the scale like a bird trying to find foothold on a cliff-face, and sometimes produce the most unexpected intonations. He was like that in rehearsal too—constantly testing inflexions, repeating phrases over and over to achieve the most expressive cadence. He never produced sound 'trippingly on the tongue' like an Ian Richardson. Rather, the voice was dredged up torturously from some deep inner well of turbulence and uncertainty. He could project a warmth and generosity of spirit like no actor I've ever seen and could also retreat into a reptilian stillness and watchfulness or explode unexpectedly like a summer's storm:

> ... His voice was propertied as all the tunéd spheres, and that to friends; But when he meant to quail and shake the orb, he was as rattling thunder.

He had a quiet dignity and easygoing authority and brought a sweetness of temperament into the rehearsal room that made him one of the most popular among his fellows that I've encountered. If you want to get a feeling of his personality, I can vouch that his performance in *A Man for All Seasons* is as close as you could get to the man himself, which is no doubt why it was such a classic performance.

I felt a sense of loss with the deaths of Olivier, Gielgud and Richardson, all of whom I admired greatly over many years, but it was the death of Paul Scofield that affected me the most deeply and gave rise to an anguished, 'Oh, no!'

Timon is one of the least performed of Shakespeare's plays. It is even more bleak and cynical than *Troilus and Cressida*. It was probably co-written with the young Thomas Middleton around 1608. Shakespeare was a professional playwright, not an aristocratic dilettante. At various times in his career (while jealous of his intellectual property) he was not averse to collaborating, providing fodder for the hungry theatre machine. Henslowe's diary records that of eighty-nine plays at the Swan, thirty-four were by a single author. The other fifty-five were collaborations.

This was the period of Jonson's *Volpone* and *The Alchemist*, both savage satires on greed and hypocrisy. Shakespeare was cashing in on their popularity with his *Timon*, a simple parable about a rich playboy who flings around his money. While he does so, friends and sycophants flock to his table. But when the money runs out, they all desert him and Timon, in misanthropic rage, retreats to a cave in the forest where he rails against man's ingratitude:

> The learnéd pate
> Ducks to the golden fool. All's oblique:
> There's nothing level in our curséd natures
> But direct villainy. Therefore be abhorr'd
> All feasts, societies, and throngs of men!
> His semblable, yea, himself, Timon disdains,
> Destruction fang mankind!

Ironically, as he scrabbles in the earth looking for roots to eat, Timon discovers a hoard of gold. Word of this gets out and various fair-weather friends come scurrying back for a handout. Timon pelts them with money and drives them off with curses. He dies a miserable and lonely death, hardened in his misanthropy. The one person whose company he tolerates for a while is the cynic Apemantus. In the old days Timon used to laugh at Apemantus's bitter diatribes; now he can out-rail him.

In Schlesinger's production Paul Rogers played Apemantus, and the chief delight of the evening was in watching him and Scofield playing off each other, especially in their final confrontation in the forest:

> *Timon*: What wouldst thou do with the world, Apemantus, if it lay in thy power?
> *Apemantus*: Give it the beasts, to be rid of the men.
> *Timon*: Wouldst thou have thyself fall in the confusion of men, and remain a beast with the beasts?

Apemantus:	Ay, Timon.
Timon:	A beastly ambition, which the gods grant thee t'attain to. If thou wert the lion, the fox would beguile thee. If thou wert the lamb, the fox would eat thee. If thou wert the fox, the lion would suspect thee when, peradventure, thou wert accused by the ass. If thou wert the ass, thy dullness would torment thee, and still thou lived'st but as a breakfast to the wolf. If thou wert the wolf, thy greediness would afflict thee, and oft thou shouldst hazard thy life for thy dinner. Wert thou the unicorn, pride and wrath would confound thee, and make thine own self the conquest of thy fury. Wert thou a bear, thou wouldst be killed by the horse. Wert thou a horse, thou wouldst be seized by the leopard. Wert thou a leopard, thou wert german to the lion, and the spots of thy kindred were jurors on thy life; all thy safety were remotion, and thy defence absence. What beast couldst thou be that were not subject to a beast? And what a beast art thou already, that seest not thy loss in transformation!

For all its grim satire, *Timon* seems to me to be a very modern play and one right for our times. Following the so-called Global Financial Crisis of 2008 there was a lot of breast-beating, soul-searching and finger-pointing about unbridled greed and a paucity of ethics in the banking sector. Some voices on the left gleefully pronounced the death of capitalism. There was much hue and cry about capping executive salaries. The crisis more or less passed for most people, at least in Australia. Consumer confidence picked up again, and criticism of executive salaries and golden handshakes became more subdued as we all went back to our old ways.

Australia, for all its much-vaunted egalitarianism, maintains a superstitious reverence for those who make the Rich List, and plutocrats like the late Richard Pratt and the late Kerry Packer achieve a state of beatification despite well-aired reservations about their characters and financial dealings. As Lear so neatly puts it:

> Plate sin with gold,
> And the strong lance of justice hurtles breaks;
> Arm it in rags, a pigmy's straw doth pierce it.

Timon of Athens should be seen more often.

No other writer, and with the exception of Mozart, no other artist, has brought us so close to the heart of the ultimate mystery of the universe and of man's place in it; no other has felt and presented the numinous with such certainty and power, no other penetrated so deeply into the source from which he derived his genius and from which we all, including him, derive our humanity. The ultimate wonder of Shakespeare is the deep, sustaining realisation that his work, in addition to all its other qualities—poetical, dramatic, philosophical, psychological—is above all *true*. It is hardly surprising that he, alone among mortals, has conquered mortality, and still speaks directly to us from lips that have been dust for hundreds of years, and a heart that stopped beating to mortal rhythms on St George's Day 1616. He alone has defeated the last enemy, that pitiless foe which he called 'cormorant devouring time,' no wonder that he knew it, and thought it no shame—'Not marble, nor the gilded monuments of princes shall outlive this powerful rhyme'—to proclaim it.

Bernard Levin, *Enthusiasms*

19

The Romances

> In Shakespeare one sentence begets the next naturally; the meaning is all interwoven. He goes on kindling like a meteor through the dark atmosphere
> S.T. COLERIDGE, *SPECIMENS OF THE TABLE TALK*

In his mid-forties Shakespeare did a remarkable thing. Between 1600 and 1606 he had written, as well as other plays, the four greatest Tragedies in the English language. These plays are full of violence, blackness and cries of despair. To my mind they are not only pagan and existentialist, but at times come close to utter nihilism.

Then, only a few years later, he writes what are essentially his last plays—four 'Romances'; plays that begin with some great crime or act of evil, but halfway through they turn around, thanks to some act of mercy, forgiveness or reconciliation, and become about hope, optimism and regeneration.

Pericles, *The Winter's Tale*, *Cymbeline* and *The Tempest* are full of music, magic and theatricality, yet they remain among Shakespeare's least appreciated works... Why?

For a start, their form and context are unfamiliar to us. They freely mix drama, comedy, philosophy, morality, song, dance and outrageous coincidence. How seriously are we meant to take them? How do we, as an audience, reconcile farce and spirituality?

We have to realise that they represent something of a vogue or shift in popular taste in the early seventeenth century and that this in turn was influenced by theatre moving indoors—away from the rough and tumble of the Globe to the more refined atmosphere of the Blackfriars, where the price of admission could be twelve times as much. The plays could be performed by candlelight and the theatre was able to accommodate quite elaborate stage effects, such as '*Jove descends in thunder and lightning, sitting upon an eagle. He throws a thunderbolt. The ghosts fall on their knees*', in Act V, Scene 5 of *Cymbeline*. Dumb shows accompanied by music were popular and much employed in *Pericles*, while in *The Tempest* an elaborate banquet is brought on by magical spirits but disappears in a crash of thunder when Ariel, dressed as a harpy, claps his wings. The use of spectacle, masque and music seems to have appealed to King James and his courtiers, who often played roles in the elaborate court masques concocted by Ben Jonson and Inigo Jones.

The Romances range freely over so many of the themes that occupy Shakespeare throughout his career: shipwrecks, pirates, families torn apart and reunited. We find these in one of his earliest plays, *The Comedy of Errors*, and again in *Twelfth Night*. They are given a proper workout in the four Romances along with the father/daughter conflicts and reconciliations we find throughout his work, culminating in *King Lear*. Either all these themes have a personal significance for him or he simply found them fertile ground for creating drama.

But given the above elements (adventure, music, song, dance, magic, comedy and the supernatural), you'd expect these plays to have a very wide appeal today, especially for younger audiences besotted with Tolkien, C.S. Lewis, Harry Potter, sci-fi and teenage love sagas. Why aren't they on the school syllabus? They might provide an easier entry point to Shakespeare than *Othello*, *Antony and Cleopatra* or *King Lear*.

The answer may be that the Romances are not seen often enough in the theatre. But when they are staged, they usually prove very popular with audiences. Both times I staged *Pericles* the audience response was tremendous. Academics and teachers need to see the plays afresh; and maybe they need to be shown the way by theatre practitioners reimagining the plays in productions that reveal their beauty and entertainment value.

Perhaps some theatre companies neglect the Romances because they don't seem 'relevant'. I get fed up when people start arguing about Shakespeare's 'relevance', with the implied suggestion that things are of interest only if they are about *us*. Is Mozart 'relevant'? Is a sunrise? Maybe instead of continually trying to claw everything back to our own tiny circle we should take a look outside it and reach out to the unfamiliar, the unknown, the exotic; try to experience the universe through the eyes of people in other times, in other places.

Directors have worked overtime on the Histories and Tragedies to show how 'relevant' they are—dressing everybody as Nazis, the KGB, the Taliban or whatever. This is not relevance, it's just topicality and it can prove very reductive. True and lasting relevance runs deeper. Looking at the Romances, what could be more relevant than mercy, love, forgiveness and reconciliation of family conflicts? The Romances offer positive messages to audiences of all ages: messages of hope, of optimism, of wisdom gained through experience and strength of character in the face of suffering. A white magic is at work in these plays that makes them uplifting in quite a profound way.

As for their theatricality, they are a gift for directors, designers, musicians and choreographers. But not many actors have made their names playing Pericles, Giacomo, Imogen or even Prospero. They are all good roles but are subservient to the overall story. They are not roles as seductive as Hamlet, Lear, Macbeth, Othello, Falstaff, Cleopatra or Rosalind—all recognised as vehicles for the star performer.

But vogues are just that—they come and go according to the zeitgeist. Sometimes the age craves to experience the Tragedies, sometimes the Histories seem to talk to us more urgently and sometimes the Comedies creep under our skin with their bittersweet concept of life. Shakespeare was well aware of the vagaries of fashion and wrote accordingly. No doubt the great Romances will have their day again.

Pericles

I have a great affection for *Pericles* and have directed it twice for the Bell Shakespeare Company (1994 and 2009). In most cases, directing a play, living with it for the best part of a year, does breed an affection—it becomes like an adopted child and, like a proud parent, you are determined to bring out the best in it and show it off to an admiring audience.

The thing that clinches *Pericles* for me is the penultimate scene, the recognition by Pericles of his long-lost daughter Marina, whom he had presumed dead. To me this is one of the finest scenes Shakespeare ever wrote. It is masterful in its tension and excruciating delay of the eventual recognition. It can be absolutely heartbreaking when well played. But in directing it, I discovered something rare for me in Shakespeare. Usually the tempo and pitch of playing is firmly determined by the structure of the verse (the closet scene in *Hamlet*, say, or the banquet scene in *Macbeth*), but in the final two scenes of *Pericles*, maximum effect is gained by unspoken subtext à la Chekhov or long pregnant pauses worthy of Pinter. If you simply play the text through glibly you will earn unwanted laughs because the coincidences, discoveries and accidents border on the outrageous. We discovered early on in the season of *Pericles* (as in the statue scene of *The Winter's Tale*) that the final scenes demand complete emotional commitment and hair-trigger timing on the part of the entire cast. I don't see this as a weakness in the writing, just an affirmation of Shakespeare's skill as a dramatist. He knew the power of the unspoken word, the long silence, the facial and physical reactions to circumstances that are the proper domain of the theatre. Shostakovich said that to understand movement you have to understand stillness; to understand music you have to understand silence. And that is the key to playing much of Shakespeare.

When Heminges and Condell published the *First Folio* in 1623 they didn't include *Pericles*. This was perhaps because it was not entirely Shakespeare's work; or, more likely, because another company had procured the rights to it. It is generally accepted that *Pericles* was written in 1608 and it is usually lumped in with the other three Romances because of stylistic and thematic similarities. But it could have been a much earlier play which Shakespeare reworked, or maybe someone else wrote part of it. The most widely accepted contender is a minor scribbler named George Wilkins who wrote to supplement his earnings as a brothel-keeper. He was a neighbour in Cripplegate when Shakespeare lodged in Silver Street in the large house owned by the Mountjoys, so it's entirely possible that over breakfast, or over a pint, Wilkins and Shakespeare discussed the idea of *Pericles*. Wilkins may even have written the first two acts, then given up, either because he ran out of puff or else went to prison—he was frequently in trouble for beating up the young prostitutes in his employ.

Shakespeare was no stranger to collaboration. We tend to forget what a play-factory the Elizabethan theatre was. Audiences demanded at least one new play a week, and just as today most TV 'soaps' and sitcoms are written by a committee, so in seventeenth-century London bits of plays were farmed out to different writers. Some excelled in comic scenes, some in high-flown rhetoric, and some in lyrics for songs. Such collaborations are the stuff of modern Broadway.

Shakespeare began his career as an apprentice actor and patcher-up of old plays, but once he had established a reputation he jealously guarded the bulk of his plays that were all his own work, as did all his fellow playwrights and competitors. (In his last years, when he had made his pile and lived in semi-retirement, he was not averse to pitching in and collaborating with John Fletcher on *The Two Noble Kinsmen* and the play of *Sir Thomas More*, which contains the only extant page of his handwriting.)

So why would he bother collaborating on *Pericles*, especially with such a desperado as George Wilkins? Probably because he saw a quid in it (it went on to be one of the most popular plays of its day). And there's no denying the presence of themes that seemed to preoccupy him: families divided by disaster, by shipwreck, but in the end reunited; the maiden daughter redeeming her father, forgiving his tyranny or neglect and thus rescuing him from despair; the jealous father relinquishing his daughter to a young lover, thus ensuring happiness and regeneration. These themes recur throughout the four Romances but they have echoes in one of Shakespeare's earliest plays, *The Comedy of Errors*. In that play we have the tragi-farcical situation of parents with two sets of identical twins being split apart in a shipwreck. Each parent with one of each set of twins is washed in a different direction. The twins with the mother, Emilia, are seized by pirates, so she takes refuge in a convent in Ephesus. The twins who are saved with their father, Aegeon, eventually travel to seek out their kin. In the last scene the whole family meets up in Ephesus—father, mother and both sets of twins. Emilia had become the Abbess of the convent, but now rejoins her husband.

Compare this plot with the story of Pericles, who loses his wife Thaisa at sea just after she has given birth to a daughter, Marina. When she grows to adolescence, Marina is kidnapped by pirates who sell her into a brothel. After months of mourning, Pericles is reunited with both wife and daughter in Ephesus, where Thaisa has become a priestess of Diana.

The choice of Ephesus as the location for both denouements is an interesting one. Ephesus was one of the great cult centres of the ancient world and the temple of Diana one of its holiest places. When Saint Paul arrived there he was determined to root out all memories of this great pagan cult and substitute a Christian icon, namely Mary, the other virgin goddess. Angels picked up Mary's house in Nazareth and carried it through the skies to Ephesus, where it stands today. (An order of nuns looks after it and will happily show you around and sell you a set of rosary beads.) So in *The Comedy of Errors*, Ephesus is regarded with fear and suspicion by the new arrivals, in an echo of Saint Paul's paranoia. In *Pericles*, on the other hand, Shakespeare pays homage to the pagan status of Ephesus. Diana is a benign protectress and the city's leading citizen is Cerimon, a wise healer, a white magician. Pagan Ephesus is a holy place.

Even if Shakespeare did take over *Pericles* only for the last three acts, he must surely have done some revision of the first two. The language and character of Gower, the chorus, is consistent from the beginning and the play does hang together coherently despite its picaresque nature. The dramatic shift is in the quality of the verse. When Pericles steps onto the deck of the storm-tossed ship at the top of Act III and declaims:

Thou God of this great vast, rebuke these surges,
Which wash both heaven and hell; and thou that hast
Upon the winds command, bind them in brass,
Having called them from the deep! O, still
Thy deaf'ning dreadful thunders; gently quench
Thy nimble sulph'rous flashes!

you know Shakespeare has arrived.

Although my two productions of *Pericles* were fifteen years apart, they were not fundamentally different. Both times I attempted an epic, poetic presentation eschewing any attempt at naturalism, except in the brothel scenes which are very different in style to the rest of the play. In my first version, the costume designer, Edie Kurzer, and I drew our inspiration from the *Arabian Nights*. This is, after all, a fairytale, a romance, and it takes in epic voyages like those of Sinbad. Andrew Raymond's set consisted of ropes and cloths which could be manipulated to suggest sails, pavilions or the interior of the brothel. The basic concept was that of a ship at sea and the sailors' costumes were adapted to suggest each different port of call. This effect was enhanced by devising a different body language and gestural repertoire for each location. The music, performed live by David King and Jonathon Maher, further contrasted the different cultures: Tyre, Antioch, Pentapolis, Tarsus, Ephesus and Mytelene. Physicality expressed in mime, dance and martial arts underpinned the production.

The same principles held true for my 2009 production, but this time the design aesthetic was governed by our association with the percussion group TaikOz. I had been looking for some time to collaborate with another performing company such as a dance or music group in order to revitalise our company and widen our potential audience. TaikOz and *Pericles* looked like a very good fit: this group was young, vigorous and attractive. Their Japanese drumming was thrilling and they could sing, dance and display martial arts skills as well. Their aesthetic was firmly Japanese and not just cosmetic. They study in Japan, tour there and have developed their appreciation of Japanese music and culture over a long period. I reckoned it would be no use referencing a Middle Eastern or Mediterranean visual imagery given TaikOz's involvement—we had to go along with their established image and disciplines—and I thought it would be a great chance for our actors to make an acquaintance with a whole new physical repertoire in dance, combat and mime.

Julie Lynch's set and costume designs were both exquisite and exotic, befitting the largest-scale show Bell Shakespeare had yet attempted. Her brief, as well as mine to the company, was to reference Japanese costume, dance, movement, etc., without in any way trying to *play* Japanese: we were not doing *The Mikado*. We had to evolve our own performance language and physical world which was specific to *Pericles* and take the audience, along with the hero, on a voyage of spiritual trial and fulfilment. The experiment was a very satisfying one and the collaboration with TaikOz both joyous and instructive. It paid off by attracting record audience numbers, especially in Melbourne, which has sometimes proved a difficult market for us to crack.

The role of Pericles is a challenging one as he is essentially reactive rather than proactive. Things happen to Pericles, but he does little to initiate action. He also has to age considerably, progressing from a naive and heroic young prince to a shrunken middle-aged man rendered comatose by grief.

It is essential that the production retains the simplicity of a biblical parable or folktale. There is psychological truth in the characters but they don't need to be probed too deeply: most of them are types rather than complex individuals. Played honestly and without pretension, *Pericles* can be a deeply satisfying piece of theatre:

> To glad your ears and please your eyes . . .
> And lords and ladies in their lives
> Have read it for restoratives.

Cymbeline

Of the four Romances, the one with which I am least familiar is *Cymbeline*. I have seen one student production and one as part of a BBC TV series. *Cymbeline* was one of their better efforts. The play has some tricky things to bring off: Imogen's lament over the headless body of her supposed husband is a challenge to any actress. On the other hand, there are scenes and speeches any actor would regard as a gift. Consider the following—Posthumus's rage at his wife's supposed adultery. Try spitting it out and note how it erupts like white-hot lava, the thoughts almost tumbling over each other. To feel its full effect, hit the nouns and verbs hard and submit to the hammer blows of the rhythm:

> . . . could I find out
> The woman's part in me! For there's no motion
> That tends to vice in man but I affirm
> It is the woman's part. Be it lying, note it,
> The woman's; flattering, hers; deceiving, hers;
> Lust and rank thoughts, hers, hers: revenges, hers;
> Ambitions, covetings, change of prides, disdain,
> Nice longing, slanders, mutability,
> All faults that man may name, nay, that hell knows
> Why, hers, in part or all, but rather all—
> For even to vice
> They are not constant, but are changing still
> One vice of but a minute old for one
> Not half so old as that. I'll write against them,
> Detest them, curse them. Yet 'tis greater skill
> In a true hate to pray they have their will:
> The very devils cannot plague them better.

Cymbeline also contains one of Shakespeare's loveliest songs, 'Fear no more the heat of the sun', and the sinister scene in which the wily Giacomo betrays the fair Imogen. He has wagered with her husband Posthumus that he can bed her. (When will these husbands learn to stop betting on their wives?)

Concealed in a trunk he is smuggled into her bedroom and when she is asleep he sidles out and takes note of all the salient details of the room (including the mole on her breast). Like some ghastly incubus he pollutes the chamber and, after stealing the bracelet from her arm as proof of his 'conquest', he creeps back into the trunk with the comment, 'Though this is a heavenly angel, hell is here.'

Even in the broad daylight of a rehearsal room the scene is unutterably creepy.

The Winter's Tale

It is required you do awake your faith.

To my mind *The Winter's Tale* is the most beautiful of the Romances—the most moving, uplifting and enlightened. Maybe *The Tempest* packs a bigger punch with an audience; it has the great Prospero arias, it's got Caliban, Ariel and a magical desert isle. And maybe audiences find the first half of *The Winter's Tale* too gruelling, what with Leontes' insane jealous rants, the torment of Hermione and the death of little Mamillius. It's pretty heavy going and then suddenly, bingo! We're into the song and dance of happy Bohemia with its lovers and clowns. The contrast could not be more stark. Some audiences might find this confusing or even unsatisfying: just what sort of play are they supposed to be watching?

Well, actually, they are watching a 'tale', a winter's story told around the fire, full of drama, excitement, pathos, fun, jokes and a miraculously happy ending. The audience is invited to shuffle off the cares and world-weariness of adulthood and slip back into childhood, to surrender to the magic of make-believe, to commit to that marvellous act of suspending disbelief and let the story take them where it will.

One of the great joys of parenthood is reading or telling stories to infants, to watch their eyes grow round with the wonder of it and let their understandings expand to admit the unknown. There is a similar thrill in directing and performing a play like *The Winter's Tale*. You as the director or actor submit to it totally, you believe it, and through that act you hope to transport the audience through the sheer power of storytelling. The four most powerful words in the English language are 'Once upon a time...'

The Romances

As Pericles says to Marina:

... I will believe thee
And make my senses credit thy relation
To points that seem impossible.

I have seen a couple of fine performances of *The Winter's Tale* and a few not so fine where the first half tipped into melodrama and the bucolic second half was overworked and coarsened by ribaldry. I directed the play with NIDA students in the mid 1970s and played Leontes when Adam Cook directed the play for Bell Shakespeare in 1997. Leontes is a monster of a role. In the very first scene of the play he launches into a crazy monologue, convincing himself that his wife, Hermione, is having an affair with his best friend, Polixenes. They are as innocent as Leontes is obviously psychotic. He works himself into a state of murderous paranoia, snatching his son Mamillius from his mother's grasp and throwing her (pregnant as she is) into prison. He sends an assassin to kill Polixenes, but the plot fails. When Hermione gives birth to a daughter, Leontes condemns it to be abandoned in the wilderness. Leontes is devastated when Apollo's oracle reveals that his wife and Polixenes are innocent. He is told that his wife is dead, his daughter lost and his son dead of grief. Thus begins Leontes' long penance and healing process.

I gave a copy of *The Winter's Tale* to Dr Tom Stanley, a Macquarie Street psychiatrist, who found it very intriguing. 'Leontes is certainly paranoid,' he told me. 'Shakespeare got it just right, especially when he speaks of tremor cordis, an attack of acute anxiety that heralds paranoid delusion. He's probably schizophrenic as well. He has an unshakeable delusion. He sighs, he is brooding, obsessed, always pacing. He's always watching, vigilant, listening. Always questioning. He is always cross-examining people.' And all this is in the text. You don't have to invent it. Amazing that through sheer observation, Shakespeare conveyed it so well.

Armed with this information I sought out back-up from other sources. Dr Francis Macnab of the Cairnmillar Institute concluded that Leontes is a classic paranoid schizophrenic. He suffers irrational rage and subsides within seconds to a subdued submission. He speaks gibberish and is offended or aghast when not understood. A TV documentary called *Spinning Out* defined paranoia as thinking everything is bugged, that food is poisoned and that people are talking about you. And in the tragic story of her son Jonathan, *Tell Me I'm Here*, Anne Deveson describes his physical activities, like rocking back and forth, hugging himself and keening, sudden violent mood changes, physical violence and loss of a sense of distance, shouting in people's faces, talking and giggling to himself, dropping the head to the left as if unbalanced. Many of these observations I was able to incorporate into my performance as Leontes, confident that I was not simply winging it or generalising, and that Shakespeare's text is very much in accordance with scientific evidence.

First performed at the Globe in 1610, *The Winter's Tale* was probably performed indoors at the Blackfriars as well, although much of its humour is tailored for the Bankside audience. A prime example is the famous stage direction '*Exit, pursued by a bear*'. Since the Bear Garden was within a stone's throw of the Globe, the appearance of a bear on stage would have caused much hilarity; maybe people even thought for a moment that a bear had escaped. It is hard for us nowadays to stomach the intolerable cruelty of bear-baiting. The screams of tortured animals were clearly audible to the Globe audience. It's that mix of ugliness and beauty, cruelty and refinement that makes the Elizabethans simultaneously fascinating and repellent. It underscores a lot of Shakespeare's writing and we do ourselves a disservice to play it down. The sight of ancient Antignous chased off stage by a bear is simultaneously horrible and comic. It provides a neat tipping point for the play from grim tragedy to pastoral comedy.

The Winter's Tale has a lot of crowd-pleasing elements. It is closer to a musical comedy than any other Shakespeare play: Autolycus has six songs (one of them a trio); there is a dance and spectacle as well as much buffoonery involving Autolycus and the two shepherds. The songs are an obvious showcase for the talent of Robert Armin, who became Shakespeare's chief clown after the departure of Will Kemp. The role of Autolycus tells us a lot about Armin's clowning skills. As well as the catchy musical routines he demonstrates his cunning in pickpocketing and cony-catching, routines much appreciated by a Bankside audience. Then he gets to impersonate an outrageously foppish courtier who runs rings around the two simple shepherds. Finally, he gets his comeuppance in an hilarious denouement. It's a great vehicle for a comedian; but that's just what it is—a vehicle, not a character.

We have a lot of trouble today with Shakespeare clowns; too often they're just not funny. This is partly because humour dates faster than other kinds of writing: topical references are lost, language, puns and witticisms change their meaning. But the problem goes deeper. Shakespeare wrote his Comedy for particular comedians, playing to their strengths and idiosyncrasies. Take a comedy script today from one comedian and give it to another and watch it fall flat on its face. So much of the comedy comes not from the material but what the comic does with it, through tone of voice, innuendo, facial expression, the lift of an eyebrow. Every good comedian is unique. So my advice to a Shakespeare clown of today is 'make it your own . . .' If something's not working, feel free to cut, translate or put in your own material and topical gags. Don't take it so far as to dominate the scene or pervert the overall meaning, but always 'better a wise fool than a foolish wit'.

Armin's versatility is demonstrated by the fact that he played that wonderfully acidic and melancholic clown Feste in *Twelfth Night*, Iago in *Othello*, the gravedigger in *Hamlet*, Caliban in *The Tempest*, the foul-mouthed Thersites in *Troilus and Cressida* and the greatest clown of them all—Lear's Fool. He combined wit and proverb, satire and philosophy, and studied each role with care. Small and wiry, he was also quite a successful playwright.

The longest role Shakespeare wrote for him was Touchstone in *As You Like It*, a notoriously difficult role for modern comedians. The 'Seven Degrees of the Lie' routine in Act V was written very much with Armin's talents in mind and has confounded many a clown since.

Critics have tied themselves into knots to elucidate the significance of the name 'Touchstone'. There is a simple explanation: before becoming an actor, Armin had been apprenticed to a goldsmith. The touchstone was their logo. Most actors and writers had served a trade apprenticeship. Shakespeare may have briefly served an apprenticeship as a glover, following his father's footsteps (there are a number of very specialised references to gloves and glove-making tools in his plays); Ben Jonson was apprenticed to a bricklayer and John Heminges to a grocer. No doubt parents back then weren't that different to our own: 'Alright, you can go off and be an actor, but only after you've got a trade first.'

The Tempest

There is a great deal of popular mythology clinging to *The Tempest*, the two most persistent assertions being that this was Shakespeare's last play and that it is heavily autobiographical: Prospero, the great magician, is Shakespeare himself, retiring from his magic island (the theatre), breaking his magic staff (his pen), drowning his book (his plays), and bidding farewell to his creative spirit, Ariel. Such a notion is imbued with an attractive sentimentality—but it ain't necessarily so.

For a start, Shakespeare didn't entirely give up on theatre after writing *The Tempest* in 1611. In the following few years he collaborated with John Fletcher on *The Two Noble Kinsmen* and *Henry VIII* (or *All Is True*). He contributed some scenes to *Sir Thomas More* and worked (again with Fletcher) on the recently rediscovered play *Cardenio*, based on an episode in *Don Quixote*. Although he stopped performing and writing for the Globe, he kept up his business interest in the enterprise and kept collecting royalties.

As for the self-portraiture, that's always a dubious claim to make with Shakespeare. It's true that great masterpieces, and even lesser works, reveal something about their authors even when they try to bury the evidence. But no one was more successful at concealing himself than Shakespeare. At grammar school he had been well trained in the art of rhetoric and arguing both sides of any question. For every assertion or sentiment voiced by one character, another will provide the antithesis. Which one did Shakespeare believe? One? Both? Neither? It doesn't matter: he was a playwright, not a pamphleteer, and the ideas expressed had to spring from the characters, not the author. (If only Shaw and Brecht had followed his example!)

It is tempting to draw analogies between Shakespeare and Prospero. For a start there is the father/daughter relationship which so haunts his later plays, nowhere more forcibly than in *King Lear*, where the spurned virtuous daughter forgives and redeems her father but then is cruelly taken from him. Leontes casts out his baby daughter to die in the wilderness, but as an adolescent maiden she returns to effect the reconciliation of the parents. Pericles, driven to despair by his ill-fortune, is brought back to life by the ministering angel Marina. And Prospero comes to realise that his only salvation will come by forgiving his enemies and giving his beloved Miranda away in marriage. Regeneration is the common theme enacted by these wonderful girls, all of whom are about sixteen years old. Mothers are curiously absent in most of Shakespeare's plays but feisty daughters (Juliet, Cordelia, Desdemona, Katharina, Hermia) are often in conflict with their fathers, who come to regret their tyranny. How much this reflects Shakespeare's own relationship with his daughters Susanna and Judith must remain a matter of conjecture, but whether he was drawing on personal experience or simply mining the dramatic potential of father–daughter relationships, they certainly feature heavily in his plays. The challenge he set himself is all the more remarkable in that all these crucial roles were to be played by boy actors. How much easier it would have been to focus on father–son conflicts (these occur too, but not as extensively).

Whether or not he saw himself as a great magician is also open to question. Prospero's lines can be interpreted as Shakespeare's claim to theatrical mastery:

> . . . I have bedimm'd
> The noontide sun, called forth the mutinous winds
> And 'twixt the green sea and the azured vault
> Set roaring war; to the dread rattling thunder
> Have I given fire, and rifted Jove's stout oak
> With his own bolt; the strong-based promontory
> Have I made shake, and by the spurs plucked up
> The pine and cedar; graves at my command
> Have waked their sleepers, oped and let 'em forth
> By my so potent art.

He had indeed created tempests, forests, oceans and deserts on an empty stage, and caused the dead to walk and talk again: Julius Caesar, Henry V, Antony and Cleopatra . . . And when Prospero decides to lay aside his art, he seems to be making direct references to the theatre:

> . . . These our actors,
> As I foretold you, were all spirits, and
> Are melted into air, into thin air;
> And like the baseless fabric of this vision,
> The cloud-capp'd towers, the gorgeous palaces,
> The solemn temples, the great globe itself,
> Yea, all which it inherit, shall dissolve,

> And, like this insubstantial pageant faded,
> Leave not a rack behind.

The references are more explicit if 'globe' has a capital G, and if by 'rack' he meant the scenery racks that stored the painted panels used in pageants.

But elsewhere a self-portrait is not very plausible. Prospero is a scholar, a dreamer who becomes engrossed in his books to the detriment of his efficiency as ruler. Shakespeare shows no such abstraction. He was essentially pragmatic, a man of business and eminently practical. His picture of Prospero is that of the humanist scholar gone wrong: one who is steeped in love of learning but only for its own sake. As a ruler he should apply that knowledge to good governance for the sake of his subjects. But instead, he to his state 'grew stranger, being transported and rapt in secret studies'. This phrase has a sinister ring, suggesting Prospero may have crossed the line of legitimate study and, like Faustus, begun dabbling in black magic. This obsession leads him into serious errors of judgment—not just neglecting his duties but appointing his easily corrupted younger brother, Antonio, as his deputy. Given such status and responsibility, it's little wonder that Antonio begins to imagine himself the rightful ruler who has to somehow get rid of his useless older brother. Prospero is full of rage and resentment at his brother's perfidy, but it's not hard to see Antonio's point of view.

The good humanist should also abhor slavery, but that is the only way Prospero knows to control people. He starts out with good intentions but botches it every time. He finds Caliban who, because he is 'different', a so-called monster, must be made to conform to Prospero's image of civilisation. Like a grammar-school pedant, he teaches Caliban his language and ideas of astronomy and natural law. This despite the fact that Caliban already has his own language, a finely tuned sense of natural beauty and musical sounds, the craft of subsistence in a wilderness and an initial trust and obedience. But the colonialist insists that the native be recast in his own image. When Caliban's natural impulses assert themselves he is cruelly punished, tortured, enslaved and abused. Similarly, Ariel is released from imprisonment by Prospero only to be immediately indentured to a new tyrannical master whose promises of freedom are somewhat rubbery. When Ferdinand refuses to surrender he is immediately disempowered and, like Caliban, enslaved as a beast of burden. Instead of proper nurture Prospero reverts to force, to punishment and magisterial control of his subjects on the island.

This humanist scholar has to learn about forgiveness, tolerance, letting go of jealousy, revenge, resentment and even art when it stands in the way of genuine human intercourse. But it's a mighty struggle for him, he is so locked in the role of the magus. Almost to the end he is intent on torturing and punishing all his enemies. Ariel, the airy spirit, is employed as his minister of justice; but even Ariel begins to feel compassion for his victims, and this wonderful transforming exchange takes place:

Ariel: . . . Your charm so strongly works 'em
That if you now beheld them your affections
Would become tender.
Prospero: Dost thou think so, Spirit?
Ariel: Mine would sir, were I human.
Prospero: And mine shall. Hast thou, which art but air, a touch, a feeling
Of their afflictions, and shall not myself,
One of their kind, that relish all as sharply
Passion as they, be kindlier moved than thou art?
Though with their high wrongs I am struck to the quick
Yet with my nobler reason 'gainst my fury
Do I take part. The rarer action is
In virtue than in vengeance. They being penitent
The sole drift of my purpose doth extend

Not a frown further. Go release them, Ariel.

I have played Prospero three times (so far). The first time was in Neil Armfield's production at Belvoir in 1990. I played it for Bell Shakespeare in Jim Sharman's production of 1997 and again in 2006 in a production by Peter Evans. I do love the role but admit that the first three acts don't yield much return for the actor. Right at the top of the play you have the longest exposition scene ever written, telling both Caliban and Ariel heaps of stuff they already know and then you tell Miranda your and her life story. Gielgud never liked this scene (Act I, Scene 2) and found it a terrible bore. But you have to remember that it's all new for the audience and this exposition is meant for them more than Ariel or Caliban. With Miranda it's a different story, because it's all new to her too. Because Prospero keeps peppering his exposition with remarks like 'Dost thou attend me?', 'Thou attend'st not!' and 'Dost thou hear?' some Mirandas take this as a clue that she must be drifting off and is bored witless. Nothing could be further from the truth: this is all absolutely riveting stuff—discovering that her father is a duke, that she's a princess, that they were betrayed, nearly drowned at sea, saved by divine intervention and that their enemies have just now arrived on the island! How could she be *bored*? She speaks the simple truth when she asserts, 'Your tale, sir, would cure deafness.' Prospero's interjections are markers as to the importance he places on the tale and how essential it is that she follows every twist and turn.

The scene can be as dry as dust unless it is fuelled by passion—and that is all written into the text. Prospero can barely contain his rage, grief and vengefulness as he addresses all three of his auditors. Besides, he is racing the clock. The ship has just been beached, his deadly enemies have disembarked and are on their way. This is no time for Prospero to sit down and indulge in reminiscence. He must not sit down at all. The scene should be played white hot with agitation and urgency—at the same time making sure that the other characters (and the audience) absorb all the information. As well as Prospero's fury, what drives the scene is the resistance offered by Ariel and Caliban—where there is conflict there is drama.

Nevertheless, that scene is something of a challenge for the actor playing Prospero, and then for the next three acts he just hovers in the background tossing in the odd sage observation. His pay-off doesn't come till Act IV, but what a pay-off it is! From that turn-around moment when Ariel prompts Prospero to forgive his enemies, a wonderful feeling of blissful release settles over the performance, at least for Prospero. All the rage and tension is gone, he is able to deliver those two magnificent arias and, one by one, bestow love and forgiveness on all. He is able to let go, at last, of his creative ambitions in the figure of Ariel and, perhaps most importantly, admit to himself the dark and destructive side of his nature. Confronting Caliban he says, 'This thing of darkness I acknowledge mine.' Caliban is the brutish, incestuous part of himself that Prospero hates, fears and tries to suppress. Once admitted, the danger is gone and Caliban can reply, 'I'll be wise hereafter and seek for grace.' I finished every performance of Prospero in a state of euphoria, feeling cleansed and unburdened. It's a great feeling to let go of jealousy, possessiveness, resentment, vengefulness, ambition, hatred, paranoia, status, control . . . even by proxy!

The Tempest is a fascinating play—so many ways into it, so many levels of understanding and interpretation, such a mix of clowning, magic, satire and social commentary. Shakespeare was, like most of his contemporaries, excited by the discovery of a New World, of uncharted seas, islands and possible civilisations. He devoured Montaigne's essays about governance and responsibility, especially the one dealing with cannibals—hence 'Caliban'. Through the homely character of Gonzalo he gently mocks the idea of a utopian existence; he was too much of a realist to believe in utopia. And his survey of English history finds a satirical end point in

The Tempest. He'd begun his career with a successful blockbuster about the Wars of the Roses—brothers, fathers, sons all killing each other to obtain possession of the isle of Albion. Now the isle is shrunk to a desert island but people are still plotting to kill for possession of it. What greater parody of the history cycle than the sight of a clown, a drunken butler and a monster swaggering about in robes of state, plotting to kill Prospero and bestowing regal and vice-regal titles on themselves! It's delicious satire.

Of the three productions I felt most at home in Armfield's, even though that was my first go at the role. The staging was reassuringly simple—a sandy beach backed by a huge pile of driftwood, the detritus of many wrecks. Alan John's music was whimsical and ethereal.

I have been fortunate with my Ariels—all three played by women. Gillian Jones was the first—febrile, quirky and tormented. In Jim's production Paula Arundell played Ariel like a cheeky cherub. The Peter Evans version featured Saskia Smith as a Nordic beauty with a gorgeous voice.

The moment of parting between Prospero and Ariel calls for a directorial decision. Some directors overplay the pathos—others go too far the other way: in an RSC production Simon Russell Beale's Ariel spat in the face of Alec McCowen's Prospero. I found the most satisfying interpretation the last time I played it: Prospero bade farewell with great regret. Ariel looked frightened for a moment, unsure of what to do with her newfound liberty, but then seized it ecstatically.

20

The Bell Shakespeare Company

I shan't reiterate the origins and first years of the Bell Shakespeare Company; I covered that in my previous book, *The Time of My Life*. Anyway, when the time comes a proper history of the company should be written by a qualified and more objective historian than myself.

As I write this, the company is celebrating its twentieth anniversary and the most common question I am asked is: 'Did you think, twenty years ago, the company would be where it is today?' and the answer is no, I had no idea where it would be or if it would be here at all. The only thing I knew was that I wouldn't let go of it. It was too important a project, or mission, if you like, and too many people, like my friend the late Tony Gilbert, had invested an enormous amount of money, effort and hope in it, and in me. The company's vision and mission statement today are very much in line with what they were twenty years ago:

> The Bell Shakespeare vision is to create theatre that allows audiences of all walks of life to see themselves reflected and transformed through the prism of great writing.

Shakespeare's legacy to successive generations is his firm faith in human potential. His writing challenges us to reach beyond our grasp and gives us the wherewithal to imagine our future. If we can learn anything from Shakespeare and the great writers of our past, it is that we hold within ourselves the power to make choices about who we want to be.

Bell Shakespeare believes that our greatest resource is our capacity to imagine and to transform: to picture a different world, to know that it can be one of our own making—and that we can be both its creator and a character within.

It's remarkable to think of Shakespeare walking around with all those characters inside his head, all clamouring for attention and begging to be let out. He can hear their voices, feel their energies, their rage, happiness or despair. And by making marks on a piece of paper he enables actors to bring to life these very characters, these same emotions and actions in exquisite detail—the hellish imagination of Macbeth, the calm heroism of Hermione, the infectious buffoonery of Falstaff, the ecstatic ego of Cleopatra... As we roam the galaxy of Shakespeare's characters we cannot help but compare and contrast ourselves with them, study their mistakes, their inherent flaws, the choices they make. At times we share Hamlet's bafflement and sense of impotence; we are powerless to stop Antony in his hedonistic rush towards self-destruction; we long to share and prolong Rosalind's ecstatic experience of first love...

It was this early experience of transmigration, of feeling my spirit merge with another, that drew me to Shakespeare as an adolescent. I was not only transported to different eras, different historical landscapes, but I could enter into the very minds and souls of amazing people and feel their emotions pumping through my veins, all through the marvellous use of language—violent, witty, bawdy, sublime. Shakespeare became an instrument through which I could meditate on myself as well as the world around me—a lodestar and personal guide. Reading the words on the page was thrilling enough, but to actually stand up and deliver them aloud, to inhabit and personify them—this was true fulfilment. This sense of wonder, of discovery, of fulfilment is what I have always wanted to pass on to others—to audiences, to the actors I direct and to school students toiling over their Shakespeare texts in the classroom.

From our first season in 1991 through to the present, the education (or, as we prefer to call it, learning) arm of the Bell Shakespeare Company has meant an ever-increasing and significant activity. We began with one team of Actors at Work performing in schools, then two, then three: one based in Sydney, one in Melbourne and one working out of Adelaide and Perth. Each team had three different one-hour shows built around the themes and ideas in particular plays. They performed up to three shows a day and drove themselves from school to school with a minimal stock of set pieces and props. They also conducted workshops for students and teachers and visited remote Indigenous communities, sometimes taking up a fortnight's residence there. All in all, the teams were playing to some eighty thousand school students a year.

The scheme has worked well and enjoyed enormous popularity over the last twenty years. It is a great apprenticeship for young actors to play Shakespeare for a whole year as well as being a steep learning curve in life lessons: travelling and performing every day with the same small bunch of people, being on the road, living and eating together. You have to learn to get on, respect each other's private spaces and mood swings. Many of the actors who started with us as Actors at Work have gone on to major roles with the company. But we are aware that it's probably time for a change and we need to find ways to make the job less gruelling, more attractive. From 2011 we are creating an ensemble of eight actors to be known as The Players. They will still continue the Actors at Work programs but will also have the opportunity to play their own main stage productions in capital cities and spend less time on the road. We will trial this model in 2011 and weigh its effectiveness against the previous one.

Some people may question what we are doing in the Indigenous communities, especially the long-term residences, but this is some of our most rewarding and satisfying work. It's not a matter of foisting 'white fella culture' on unwilling victims. Shakespeare is still on the curriculum for many of these kids and they have as much right to see a performance as anybody else. But our work in these communities has a wider agenda. We engage our audience in retelling the stories in their own languages and re-setting them in a familiar location. Our workshops focus on the kids performing, overcoming shyness and realising their creative potential. School attendances increase quite noticeably when the actors arrive and we try to return to the same communities every year to consolidate the work.

Not so long ago I was visiting a Sydney school where the kids were presenting their annual Shakespeare Festival. A journalist asked one of the teachers, 'Don't you think it's a bit elitist teaching these kids Shakespeare?' The teacher replied, 'I think it would be elitist *not* to.'

We do our best to help teachers all over Australia with the difficult task of communicating Shakespeare to adolescents (especially in those schools where English is a second language) by running regular workshops and seminars for teachers as well as students. And we do our best to seek out and encourage the talent of students nationwide. Our actor-teachers audition kids wherever they are on tour and give scholarships to two each year to spend a week with the company in Sydney. I guess most of the actors who come to audition for us these days first encountered Shakespeare through Actors at Work.

A typical example is a young man we auditioned a few years back. We put to him the usual question: 'Why do you want to audition for this job?' And he responded, 'When I was at school, Actors at Work came to perform for us and my class was pretty rude and unruly. I felt very embarrassed and went up to the actors afterwards to apologise. One of them said to me, "Don't worry about it; we know that in every show we do there is someone there who appreciates it, and today we did that show just for you!" That's the day I decided to be an actor. Now I've graduated from NIDA and I want to join Actors at Work.' That's when you know you're doing some good...

As we come to the end of our first twenty years, the company seems to be in good shape. We've had our flops and our successes. We never please everybody and I guess we never will; everyone feels they own Shakespeare and knows how it should be done!

The company is on as sure a financial footing as any arts company can hope to be in the face of low-level government funding, an unpredictable marketplace and degrees of corporate sponsorship and private philanthropy that are vastly underdeveloped. The supporters we do have continue to demonstrate a long-standing loyalty.

I am excited by the possibilities of constantly expanding and upgrading our education work—the possibilities are infinite and the results are so gratifying.

I am excited by the expansion of our Mind's Eye research and development arm with thirty new submissions received this year alone. It means that we have the chance to explore and encourage new writing and leave a legacy of Australian work alongside our dedication to the classics.

I am excited by the emergence of so much talent from our drama schools—actors, designers and a new generation of directors who seem truly interested in making theatre and making it in Australia.

I've never had any interest in trying to develop a 'house style' for Bell Shakespeare. I think such a concept is stultifying. It's far more interesting to employ a range of directors with very different approaches and aesthetic values. Over the twenty years my directors have included Steven Berkoff, Michael Bogdanov, Carol Woodrow, Jim Sharman, Peter Evans, Lee Lewis, Marion Potts, Elke Neidhardt, Barrie Kosky, David Freeman and Michael Gow. I never interfere with their aesthetic decisions, reserving my comments to the clarification of the storytelling and honouring the language. In my own directing, especially if it's a play I've not done before, I try to start with a clean slate and wipe out memories of past productions: what does this play need now—at this time, in this space, for this audience?

As I sign off I am excited by the prospect of the work that lies ahead. I am fortunate to have in Peter Evans, my new associate artistic director, an exemplar of that talented next generation of theatre-makers that promises some years of stimulating collaboration to come.

Conclusion

> For what we lacke
> We laugh, for what we have, are sorry, still
> Are children in some kind. Let us be thankfull
> For that which is, and with you leave dispute
> That are above our question: Let's goe off,
> And beare us like the time.
> THE TWO NOBLE KINSMEN

What is it that still appeals to me about Shakespeare's theatre? Its exultation in language, its broad sweep, its outrageousness, its lack of pedantry and its wild fancy, its use of music, colour and action, its robustness, its naivety and unpretentiousness in establishing a simple contract with its audience: 'On your imaginary forces work... once upon a time...' The fact that it played so much *to* its audience, shared their space and had a vital physical contact with them; that it set out to give pleasure and yet dealt with momentous issues... These are just a few of the factors that have made Shakespeare's theatre the most vital and important since Sophocles and Aristophanes. It's a writers' and actors' theatre. It encourages a freewheeling mix of styles and conventions and is the antithesis of the well-made drawing-room drama. It's fantastically liberating, and modern audiences can still respond to that and thrill to high-flown rhetoric as long as it's made comprehensible.

There is no worldwide conspiracy to keep Shakespeare alive. He survives because actors want to go on performing him and audiences want to listen—no matter how often the plays are trotted out and no matter that most productions fall short of excellence. Indeed, a great many performances and productions of Shakespeare (including a fair number of my own) have been mediocre if not downright woeful. But we keep coming back because there is so much worth grappling with.

A few years back I read about a judge somewhere in the United States who gave young first offenders the option of so many hours' community service or doing a Shakespeare workshop. Many of them opted for the latter, seeing it as a soft cop. When quizzed by a journalist as to the wisdom of this course, the judge explained: 'Most of these kids come from poor, depressed areas. When they do a couple of weeks in the Shakespeare workshop they learn a lot about empathy, about team spirit, about creating something. They can be transformed by it.' When the same journalist went on to interview a couple of the kids in the program, one said: 'When I go out there in front of my teacher, my folks or my probation officer and I'm doing Mark Antony or Julius Caesar, I feel I'm doing something big, something classy . . . you learn a bit of self-respect, and once you start to respect yourself, you start to respect other people.'

Something big, something classy . . .

I guess that's what I responded to at about the age of fourteen and why I go on responding nearly sixty years later. Judi Dench says her family used to speak of Shakespeare as 'the gentleman who pays the rent', and I guess I too have a lot to thank Shakespeare for; not just all those years of transport and delight, but a career, a living and a goal in life culminating in my own Shakespeare company. Despite the many ups and downs and scary patches, it has been a most thrilling and satisfying adventure.

Bell Shakespeare continues to be a happy and inspiring place to be, and I look forward each day to stepping into the office or the rehearsal room. I count myself extremely fortunate in the friends and colleagues who have shared the adventure with me so far and equally privileged to devote my time and energies to exploring and performing the works of the greatest dramatist who ever lived. I hope the preceding pages have succeeded in conveying something of Shakespeare's continuing fascination for me, the mystery and power of his works.

I can finish on no better note than by quoting the words of his dear friends and publishers of the *First Folio*, John Heminges and Henry Condell:

> Read him, therefore; and againe, and againe: And then if you doe not like him, surely you are in some manifest danger, not to understand him.

Appendix A

What Shakespeare's contemporaries said about him

Shakespeare was one of the best known and successful men of his day, despite the fact that the still-evolving theatre was regarded by many as disreputable and its practitioners no better than rogues and vagabonds. But Shakespeare and his fellows succeeded in turning that perception around. They attracted the patronage and protection of eminent noblemen and, finally, Queen Elizabeth and King James. Many theatre practitioners became wealthy men and some, including Shakespeare, were granted a coat of arms and the title of 'Gentleman'.

There are over fifty documents relating to Shakespeare, his family and his acting company in the London Public Record Office alone, and there are many references to him by contemporaries—friends, colleagues, other writers—and by those who came shortly after. Here are just a few of them:

> . . . he was a handsome well-shaped man . . . a very readie and pleasant smooth wit.
>
> John Aubrey (1681)

Everyone who had a true taste of merit, and could distinguish men, had generally a just value and esteem for him ... a good-natured man, of great sweetness in his manners, and a most agreeable companion.

Nicholas Rowe (1709)

This William being inclined naturally to poetry and acting came to London I guess about 18 and was an actor at one of the playhouses and did act exceeding well.

William Beeston (1610) (actor in Shakespeare's company)

The sweet witty soul of Ovid lives in mellifluous and honey-tongued Shakespeare, witness his *Venus and Adonis*, his *Lucrece*, his sugared sonnets ...

Francis Meres, *Palladis Tamia: Wit's Treasury* (1598)

As Plautus and Seneca are accounted the best for comedy and tragedy among the Latins, so Shakespeare among the English is the most excellent in both kinds for the stage. For comedy, witness his *Gentlemen of Verona*, his *Errors*, his *Love Labour's Lost*, his *Love Labour's Won*, his *Midsummer Night's Dream*, and his *Merchant of Venice*; for tragedy, his *Richard the 2.*; *Richard the 3.*, *Henry the 4.*, *King John*, *Titus Andronicus* and his *Romeo and Juliet*.

Francis Meres

The younger sort takes much delight in Shakespeare's *Venus and Adonis*: but his *Lucrece* and his tragedie of Hamlet, Prince of Denmark, have it in them to please the wiser sort.

Gabriel Harvey (1610)

to our English Terence,
Mr Will Shakespeare ...
Some say (good Will) which I, in sport, do sing,

Appendix A

> Hadst thou not played some kingly parts in sport,
> Thou hadst bin a companion for a King.
>
> John Davies (1610)

From 'In remembrance of Master William Shakespeare. Ode':

> Beware, delighted poets, when you sing
> To welcome nature in the early spring,
> Your num'rous feet not tread
> The banks of Avon; for each flower
> (As it ne'er knew a sun or shower)
> Hangs there the pensive head . . .
>
> Sir William Davenant, *Poems* (1637)

'Upon the Lines and Life of the Famous Scenic Poet, Master William Shakespeare':

> Those hands which you so clapped go now and wring,
> You Britons brave, for done are Shakespeare's days.
> His days are done that made the dainty plays
> Which made the globe of heav'n and earth to ring . . .
>
> For though his line of life went soon about,
> The life yet of his lines shall never out.
>
> Hugh Holland, in *Comedies, Histories, and Tragedies* (1623)

'To the Memory of the deceased author Master William Shakespeare':

> Shakespeare, at length thy pious fellows give
> The world thy works, thy works by which outlive
> Thy tomb thy name must; when that stone is rent,
> And time dissolves thy Stratford monument,
> Here we alive shall view thee still. This book,

When brass and marble fade, shall make thee look
Fresh to all ages. When posterity
Shall loathe what's new, think all is prodigy
That is not Shakespeare's ev'ry line, each verse
Here shall revive, redeem thee from thy hearse ...

Be sure, our Shakespeare, thou canst never die,
But crowned with laurel, live eternally.

Leonard Digges, in *Comedies, Histories and Tragedies* (1623)

'To the memory of Master W. Shakespeare':

We wondered, Shakespeare, that thou went'st so soon
From the world's stage to the grave's tiring-room.
We thought thee dead, but this thy printed worth
Tells thy spectators that thou went'st but forth
To enter with applause. An actor's art
Can die, and live to act a second part.
That's but an exit of mortality;
This, a re-entrance to a plaudity.

James Mabbe, commendatory poem in the *First Folio* (1623)

'An Epitaph on the Admirable Dramatic Poet, William Shakespeare':

What need my Shakespeare for his honoured bones
The labour of an age in piled stones,
Or that his hallowed relics should be hid
Under a stary-pointing pyramid?
Dear son of memory, great heir of fame,
What need'st thou such dull witness of thy name?
Thou in our wonder and astonishment
Hast built thyself a lasting monument ...

John Milton (1630)

Appendix A

'An Elegy on the death of that famous Writer and Actor, Master William Shakespeare':

> I dare not do thy memory that wrong
> Unto our larger griefs to give a tongue;
> I'll only sigh in earnest, and let fall
> My solemn tears at thy great funeral,
> For every eye that rains a show'r for thee
> Laments thy loss in a sad elegy.
> Nor is it fit each humble muse should have
> Thy worth his subject, now thou'rt laid in grave . . .
>
> . . . Sleep, then, rich soul of numbers, whilst poor we
> Enjoy the profits of thy legacy,
> And think it happiness enough we have
> So much of thee redeemed from the grave
> As may suffice to enlighten future times
> With the bright lustre of thy matchless rhymes.
>
> Anon (1640)

'Upon Master William Shakespeare, the Deceased Author, and his Poems':

> Poets are born, not made: when I would prove
> This truth, the glad remembrance I must love
> Of never-dying Shakespeare, who alone
> Is argument enough to make that one . . .
>
> . . . but O! what praise more powerful can we give
> The dead than that by him the King's Men live,
> His players, which should they but have shared the fate,
> All else expired within the short term's date,
> How could the Globe have prospered, since through want
> Of change the plays and poems had grown scant . . .

... And on the stage at half-sword parley were
Brutus and Cassius; O, how the audience
Were ravished, with what wonder they went thence,
When some new day they would not brook a line
Of tedious though well-laboured *Catiline.*
Sejanus too was irksome, they prized more
Honest Iago, or the jealous Moor ...

... when let but Falstaff come,
Hal, Poins, the rest, you scarce shall have a room,
All is so pestered. Let but Beatrice
And Benedick be seen, lo, in a trice
The cockpit galleries, boxes, all are full
To hear Malvolio, that cross-gartered gull.
Brief, there is nothing in his wit-fraught book
Whose sound we would not hear, on whose worth look;
Like old-coined gold, whose lines in every page
Shall pass true current to succeeding age.
But why do I dead Shakespeare's praise recite?
Some second Shakespeare must of Shakespeare write;
For me 'tis needless, since an host of men
Will pay to clap his praise, to free my pen.

Leonard Digges (1640)

Gullio: O sweet Master Shakespeare,
I'll have his picture in my study
At the court ... I'le worship sweet Mr Shakespeare and to honour him will lay his *Venus and Adonis* under my pillowe.

Anon, *The Return from Parnassus* (1600)

Let this duncified world esteem of Spenser and Chaucer, I'll worship sweet Mr Shakespeare.

Anon (1599)

Appendix A

The following well-known anecdote was recorded by Sir John Manningham in his diary in 1601. It may be apocryphal but even so, it attests to the interest in gossip about theatre folk of the day and implies that the names of both Burbage and Shakespeare were well known. It also assumes that both were well enough known as 'ladies' men' for the story to have some credence:

> Upon a time when Burbage played Richard III, there was a citizen grew so far in liking with him, that before she went from the play she appointed him to come that night unto her by the name of Richard the Third. Shakespeare, overhearing their conversation, went before, was entertained and at his game ere Burbage came. Then, message being brought that Richard III was at the door, Shakespeare caused return to be made that William the Conqueror was before Richard the Third.

Let's give the last word to Shakespeare's greatest contemporary, friend and rival, Ben Jonson:

> ... Yet must I not give nature all, thy art,
> My gentle Shakespeare, must enjoy a part.
> For though the poet's matter nature be,
> His art doth give the fashion; and that he
> Who casts to write a living line must sweat—
> Such as thine are—and strike the second heat
> Upon the muses' anvil, turn the same,
> And himself with it that he thinks to frame;
> Or for the laurel he may gain a scorn,
> For a good poet's made as well as born.
> And such wert thou. Look how the father's face
> Lives in his issue, even so the race
> Of Shakespeare's mind and manners brightly shines
> In his well-turned and true-filed lines,

In each of which he seems to shake a lance,
As brandished at the eyes of ignorance.
Sweet swan of Avon! What a sight it were
To see thee in our water yet appear,
And make those flights upon the banks of Thames
That so did take Eliza and our James!
But stay, I see thee in the hemisphere
Advanced, and made a constellation there!
Shine forth, thou star of poets, and with rage
Or influence chide or cheer the drooping stage,
Which, since thy flight from hence, hath mourned like night
And despairs day, but for thy volumes' light.

         Ben Jonson, the *First Folio* (1623)

Appendix B

The sequence of the plays

Scholars disagree as to the exact date of authorship of some of the plays. We know when many of them were first published and we know when many of them were first performed, but the exact date of their composition cannot be proved in every case. Here is a reasonable conjecture based on recent academic research... Alongside the list is another of significant events that coincided with the works' composition.

Play	Year	Contemporary events
Love's Labour's Lost	c.1590	Galileo publishes results of experiments with falling bodies. Edmund Spenser publishes *The Faerie Queen*.
The Comedy of Errors	c.1591	Sir Philip Sidney publishes *Astrophel and Stella*.
Two Gentlemen of Verona	1592	Christopher Marlowe writes *Dr Faustus*.

Play	Year	Contemporary events
Henry VI: Parts 1, 2 and 3	1592	
Richard III	1593	Henri IV of France embraces Catholicism.
Romeo and Juliet	1593	Marlowe writes *Edward II*, Marlowe murdered.
Titus Andronicus	1594	Thomas Kyd writes *The Spanish Tragedies*.
Richard II	1594	Henri IV of France crowned at Chartres.
King John	1594	
A Midsummer Night's Dream	1594	
The Merchant of Venice	1595	Father Robert Southwell (poet) executed for saying Mass.
The Taming of the Shrew, Sonnets	1596	English sack Cadiz. Peasants in Oxfordshire rebel against bad conditions for workers. Tomatoes introduced from the New World.
Henry IV: Part 1	1597	Tyrone leads Irish rebellion against England. England makes begging illegal and starts transporting convicts to its colonies.
Henry IV: Part 2	1598	Ben Jonson writes *Every Man in His Humour*. Sir Thomas Bodley builds library in Oxford.
Henry V	1599	Essex fails to put down Irish rebellion. He is arrested.
Julius Caesar, Much Ado About Nothing and The Merry Wives of Windsor	1599	The Globe Theatre opens.
As You Like It	1600	Elizabeth I appoints Lord Mountjoy governor of Ireland. He starves the rebels into submission.
Twelfth Night	1600	Giordano Bruno burned for heresy. English East India Trading Company founded.

Appendix B

Play	Year	Contemporary events
All's Well That Ends Well	1602	Elizabeth I dies. James I crowned. Sir Walter Raleigh imprisoned for treason.
Troilus and Cressida	1602	Ben Jonson writes *Sejanus*.
Hamlet	1602	Severe plague epidemic in London.
Measure for Measure	1604	Lope de Vega writes *Comedias*. Strong measures in England to repress Catholics.
Othello	1604	Silk manufacture begins in England.
King Lear	1605	'Gunpowder Plot' discovered; Guy Fawkes and conspirators arrested. Tsar Boris Godunov dies. Cervantes writes first half of *Don Quixote*.
Macbeth	1606	Fawkes and friends executed. Ben Jonson writes *Volpone*.
Antony and Cleopatra	1607	Jamestown, first permanent English colony on American mainland, settled. Claudio Monteverdi writes *Orfeo*.
Coriolanus	1608	Thomas Middleton writes *A Mad World, My Masters*.
Timon of Athens	1608	Protestant Union founded in Germany.
Pericles	1608	Invention of first microscope and telescope.
Cymbeline	1610	Henri IV assassinated, Louis XIII succeeds.
The Winter's Tale	1610	English colony founded in Virginia.
The Tempest	1611	George Chapman translates *Iliad*. 'Authorised' version of the Bible published.
Henry VIII	1613	Galileo agrees with Copernicus and defies Church teaching. Globe Theatre destroyed by fire.

Recommended reading

I cannot begin to calculate how many books and articles I have read over the years about Shakespeare. Here are some I recommend highly:

Peter Ackroyd, *Shakespeare: The Biography* (Chatto & Windus, 2005)
W.H. Auden, *Lectures on Shakespeare* (Faber & Faber, 2000)
Jonathan Bate, *The Genius of Shakespeare* (Picador, 1997)
Jonathan Bate, *Soul of the Age: The Life, Mind and World of William Shakespeare* (Penguin, 2009)
Harold Bloom, *Shakespeare: The Invention of the Human* (Faber & Faber, 2000)
Graham Bradshaw, *Shakespeare's Scepticism* (Cornell University Press, 1990)
Jonathan Dollimore and Alan Sinfield (eds), *Political Shakespeare: Essays in Cultural Materialism* (Manchester University Press, 1994)
Declan Donnellan, *The Actor and the Target* (Nick Hern, 2005)
Marilyn French, *Shakespeare's Division of Experience* (Abacus, 1983)
Stephen Greenblatt, *Will in the World: How Shakespeare Became Shakespeare* (Jonathan Cape, 2004)
John Gross (ed.), *After Shakespeare: An Anthology* (Oxford University Press, 2003)
Anthony Holden, *William Shakespeare: His Life and Work* (Abacus, 2000)
Frank Kermode, *Shakespeare's Language* (Penguin, 2001)
Frank Kermode, *The Age of Shakespeare* (Weidenfeld & Nicolson, 2004)
Laurence Kitchin, *Mid-Century Drama* (Faber & Faber, 1960)
Jan Kott, *Shakespeare Our Contemporary* (Methuen, 1964)
George Henry Lewes, *On Actors and the Art of Acting* (Grove Press, 2004)
A.D. Nuttall, *Shakespeare the Thinker* (Yale University Press, 2007)
Garry O'Connor, *William Shakespeare: A Life* (Sceptre, 1992)
Fintan O'Toole, *Shakespeare Is Hard, But So Is Life. A Radical Guide to Shakespearean Tragedy* (Granta Books, 2002)
James Shapiro, *1599: A Year in the Life of William Shakespeare* (Faber & Faber, 2005)
René Weis, *Shakespeare Revealed: A Biography* (John Murray, 2008)
Ian Wilson, *Shakespeare: The Evidence* (St Martin's Griffin, 1999)
Michael Wood, *In Search of Shakespeare* (BBC Books, 2003)

Index

accents
    Australian 81–6, 99
    British new wave 84–5
    Elizabethan 22, 52, 68–9
    mock Italian experiment 162, 240
    'proper' English 52, 81–2, 99, 103, 161–2, 239–40
Ackroyd, Peter ix, 45, 205, 214, 295, 349
acting 66–96, *see also* Bell, John; casting; *names of plays*
    action flow 87–8
    and costume 107–8
    and directing 104–5
    and proximity to audience 5, 78, 87, 107, 197
    and Shakespearean language xvi–xvii, 83–90, 92–3
    audition criteria 96
    bad acting 88, 92–3
    Bell's training at RSC 12–18
    best books 94
    big acting 79
    body language 81, 92
    challenges of Shakespeare 85–8
    cultural variations 83
    dictionary work 88–90, 95
    elements 37–8
    Elizabethan 1–4, 305–8
    emotion 95
    good acting 189–90
    Hamlet's acting lesson 8, 67, 71–4
    in Australia 81–5, 98–100
    interpretations of 'Ah, soldier!' 50–1
    mobility 5–7
    particularising 91–2
    playing a parody 161
    playing a person 295
    playing comedy 222–3, 243, 369
    playing Hamlet 180–6
    private corners 189–90
    qualities of best actors 36–7
    research 37–8, 163, 236–7, 367–8
    silences and pauses 86–8
    sonnet/speech exercises 227
    subtext 86
    transmigration 379–80
    verse stress 93–4
    voice 13–14
    what ifs 38, 183–4
acting companies, *see names of companies*
acting styles 174–6, *see also* Burbage, Richard; Olivier, Laurence
    amateur troupes 66–70
    British new wave 84–5, 185
    Burbage revolution 3–4, 56, 70–7, 79, 181–2, 184
    Garrick 77
    generational change 77, 80–1, 174–6
    grand acting 79, 174–6, 199–200
    Kean revolution 77–9, 236

acting styles (*continued*)
    Olivier revolution 79–81, 84, 185, 201, 211
    screen acting 14, 85–7, 175, 176, 200
acting troupes 28–9, 48, 54, 56, 60, 66–70, 299–309
Actors at Work 380–2
Adelaide Festival 12, 160
Admiral's Men 122, 300, 304
Aldwych Theatre 16
Alexander, Robert 233
All Is True, see *King Henry VIII*
Allen, Giles 302–3
Alleyn, Edward (Ned) 3, 71, 74–5, 121, 269, 299, 300, 306
all-female casts 218, 219
all-male casts xiii, 102, 248, 271
All's Well That Ends Well 49, 215, 249, 253–4, 262, 399
    RSC production 253–4
Anatomy Titus Fall of Rome xiii–xv, 269–72
animal improvisations 162, 163
animal shows 28, 44, 54, 269, 368
animals 43–5, 216, 329
Anne, Queen 307
Anne Hathaway's Cottage 26
anti-Semitism 121, 231–2, 236–7
Antony and Cleopatra xvi, 268, 283–90, 358, 399
    'Ah, soldier!' interpretations 50–1
    Cleopatra 49, 130, 241, 285–8, 305, 359
    Enobarbus 288
    love theme 41, 49
    productions
        BSC 106, 289
        RSC 288
    v. *Julius Caesar* 283–4
Arabian Nights 363
Arden, Edward 25
Arden, Mary 21, 24, 25, 117
Arden family 25, 187
Aristotle 117–18
Armfield, Neil 375, 377
Armin, Robert 243, 247, 301, 369–70
Armstrong, Chloe 334
Arundell, Paula 289, 377
As You Like It xvii, 124, 240–5, 253, 310, 318
    characters 48, 241–3
    productions
        BSC 240, 244, 282
        Nimrod 240
    sex and love 38–9, 215
    sources 24–5, 243–4
    stricken deer speech 44
Ashcroft, Peggy 80, 158, 216, 218
Aubrey, John 28, 389

audience 385–6
    19th century 77–8, 236
    and comedy 74, 223–4, 243, 247, 368
    as mob 281, 283
    BSC mission 378
    bushfire victims 249
    comprehension 101, 106, 129
    Elizabethan 1–5 *passim*, 53, 55–6, 69–70, 158, 203–4, 262, 360
    and everyday experience 174, 199, 272
    expectations 232–3
    proximity 5, 78, 87, 107, 197
    taste for bloody spectacle 269, 368
    expectations xiv–xv
    fourth wall 86–7
    Hamlet on audiences 72–4 *passim*
    interaction 92, 164, 283, 342
    Jacobean tastes 210–11
    participation 220, 239–40
    reactions 181, 205, 207, 224, 269–70
    responsibility to 105–6
    Titus Andronicus 269–71
    Troilus epilogue 343–4
    young 181, 338, 357–8, 386
auditions 96
Australia 81–5, 98–100, 107, 129, 137, 138, 145–6, 205, 220, 222, 230–1, 294, 332, 352–3
authorship 30, 51, 130, 299, 300
    and Bacon 154, 311, 324
    and Earl of Oxford 22, 310–11, 324
    and Marlowe 119–20, 324
    Cardenio 265, 309, 370–1
    Pericles 252, 360–1, 362
    Timon of Athens 350

Bacon, Francis 52, 154, 202, 311, 324
Badger, George 23
Baines, Richard 121
Baker, Stanley 159
Bandello, Matteo 262, 338
Barbour, Lyndall 82
Barton, John 13, 109
    All's Well That Ends Well 253
    Coriolanus 291
    Henry V 145
    Love's Labour's Lost 15, 226
    Twelfth Night 13, 103, 248
    Wars of the Roses 16, 103, 157–8
Bassano, Emilia 38, 318
Bate, Jonathan 33, 128, 154
Bath Shakespeare Festival 5, 222
BBC TV series 218, 230, 364
Beale, Simon Russell 377
Bear Garden 44, 368
bear-baiting 44, 54, 269, 368

Index

Beckett, Samuel 211
Beeston, William 390
Bell, Hilary 20, 254
Bell, John 130, 382, *see also* acting; directing
  Bristol Old Vic Theatre School 12, 200–1, 226, 333
  childhood 11, 178–9, 273–5
  children 20, 30, 193, 246, 254, 332, 366
  inspired by Olivier 8, 11, 12, 79–81, 178–9, 200–2, 203, 291
  marriage 12, 19–20, 254
  NIDA 230–1, 333, 367
  Nimrod 17, 161–2, 180–1, 194, 205, 224, 239–40, 246–7, 250, 334
  Old Tote 12, 179–80, 219–20
  one-man show at Genesian Theatre 12
  performs at Duntroon 273
  research for roles 37–8
  return to Australia 17–18, 98, 230–1, 332–3
  RSC 12–18, 19–20, 98, 145, 153, 157–8, 193–4, 245, 291, 332–3, 339, 349
  Russian tour 194, 253–4
  school years 8, 11, 178–9, 193
  Stratford-upon-Avon 19–20, 29, 332
  Sydney University Players 246, 290–1
  university 11–12, 179, 224, 246, 290–1
  visits new London Globe 1–5, 8, 87
Bell, John, director xvi–xvii
  Antony and Cleopatra 106, 289
  As You Like It 240, 244, 282
  The Comedy of Errors 282
  Coriolanus 291
  Edward IV 158–9
  Hamlet 178–9, 181
  Henry IV 137–8
  Henry V 141–2, 145–6
  Henry VI 158–9
  Julius Caesar 106, 279–80, 282–3, 289
  Love's Labour's Lost 226
  Macbeth 193, 194–5, 197–8, 334
  Measure for Measure 250, 251
  A Midsummer Night's Dream 230–1
  Much Ado About Nothing 162, 224, 239–40
  Pericles 358, 359–60, 362–4
  Richard III 161–2
  Romeo and Juliet 334
  The Taming of the Shrew 217–18, 220–1
  Twelfth Night 246–7
  Wars of the Roses 158–9
  The Winter's Tale 367
Bell, John, roles 130
  Antony 279–80
  As You Like It 244
  Berowne 226–7
  Coriolanus 291
  Eisenring, *The Fire Raisers* 179–80

Hamlet 12, 14, 178–81
Henry V 12
  in Brook's *The Investigation* 17
  in *The Government Inspector* 14
  in *Henry V* 145, 244–5
  in *Love's Labour's Lost* 226–7
  in *Timon of Athens* 349–50
King Lear 79, 199–200, 205–7, 212–13
Lennox 14, 193–4, 254
Leontes 37, 367
Macbeth 37, 193, 195–6
Malvolio 246, 291
Nicanor 291
Paris 339
Pericles 364
Petruchio 98–9, 217, 219–20
Prince Hal 132–3
Prospero 375, 377
Richard II 153
Richard III 37, 161–4
Romeo 333
Rosencrantz 14
Shylock 37, 233, 236–7
Titus Andronicus xiii–xv, 269–72
Trofimov, *The Cherry Orchard* 179–80
Ulysses 341–6
Valentine 14, 245
Bell, Lucy 20, 30, 246
Bell Shakespeare Company (BSC) 378–83
  20th anniversary ix, 378, 382
  Actors at Work 380–2
  directors 382–3
  education function 100–1, 222, 380–2
  first UK venture 222
  funding 382
  Indigenous work 381
  Mind's Eye 382
  modern v. original versions of plays 100–1
  The Players 380–1
  vision/mission 99, 100–1, 378–80
Bell Shakespeare Company (BSC), productions
  Antony and Cleopatra 106, 289, 399
  As You Like It 240, 244, 282
  The Comedy of Errors 5, 222–3, 282
  Coriolanus 291–2, 295
  Dance of Death 222
  Hamlet 162, 181, 233
  Henry IV 137–8
  Henry V 141–2, 145–6, 244–5
  Henry VI trilogy 158–9
  Julius Caesar 106, 279–80, 282–3, 289
  King Lear 101, 206–7, 212–13, 270
  Long Day's Journey into Night 82
  Macbeth 37, 195–6
  Measure for Measure 250, 251
  The Merchant of Venice 162, 233

403

Bell Shakespeare Company (BSC), productions (*continued*)
  Othello 205
  Pericles 356, 359–60, 362–4
  Richard III 160, 162, 163–4
  Romeo and Juliet 334
  The Taming of the Shrew 217–21
  The Tempest 375, 377
  Titus Andronicus xiii–xv, 269–72
  Troilus and Cressida 341–5
  Twelfth Night 246, 249
  The Two Gentlemen of Verona 216
  Wars of the Roses 158–9
  The Winter's Tale 367
Belvoir Theatre 375
Bergman, Ingmar 193
Berkeley's travelling players 28
Berkoff, Steven 109, 291–2, 382
Berliner Ensemble 237
Betty, William Henry West 181
Bible 22, 37, 52, 264, 399
Birthplace Trust 20
black actors 85, 201–2
Blackfriars Theatre 197, 304, 312, 357, 368
Blair, Wayne 205
Blanchett, Cate 94
Bloom, Harold 184
Bodley, Thomas 299, 398
body language 75, 81, 92, 161
Bogdanov, Michael 102, 109, 219, 341–5, 382
books and book trade, *see also* libraries
  Euphues 224
  First Folio 27, 32, 34, 155, 224, 297–9, 316, 323, 360, 387, 396
  Richard Field 47, 257–65
boy actors 216, 303–5, 323, 334, 335–6, 372
Brady, Ian 37, 195
Branagh, Kenneth 140, 141, 204, 228
Brando, Marlon 94, 175, 202, 284–5
Brecht, Bertolt xvi, 55, 71, 153, 161, 176–7, 291, 371
Brenner, Nat 12
Brenton, Howard 344
Bristol Old Vic Theatre School 12, 200–1, 226, 333
British Council 12
Brook, Peter 9, 16–17, 109, 240
  Antony and Cleopatra 288–9
  King Lear 211
  A Midsummer Night's Dream 16, 101–2, 230
  Titus Andronicus 269
Brooke, Arthur 261–2, 338
brothels 38, 54, 252–3, 269, 360, **362–3**
Brown, Bille 98, 342
Brown, Tom 179–80
Browne, Robert 308
Bryson, Bill ix
Burbage, Cuthbert 56, 116, 302
Burbage, James 54, 56, 61, 302–3, 304
Burbage, Richard 48, 50, 56, 116, 258, 300, 302–6 *passim*, 316
  Burbage revolution 3–4, 70–1, 75–7, 79, 181–2, 184–5
  Richard III anecdote 38, 395
Burghley, Lord, *see* Cecil, William, Lord Burghley
Burton, Richard 217, 293–4
Bury, John 193
bushfires 249

Cairnmillar Institute 368
Campion, Edmund 25
Cardenio 265, 309, 370–1
Carpenter, Kim 161, 246–7
casting 106–7
  auditions 96
  race issues 201–2
  Romeo and Juliet 333–4
Catesby, Robert 199
Catholicism 22–3, 25, 54, 122–3, 152, 156, 166, 171–2, 187–8, 199, 265, 340, 398, 399
Catiline (Jonson) 118, 275
Cecil, Amber May 82
Cecil, William, Lord Burghley 54, 203, 315
censorship 4, 104, 160, 185
Cervantes, Miguel de 265, 371, 399
Chamberlain's Men, *see* Lord Chamberlain's Men
Chandos painting 34
Chapman, George 318, 399
Charlecote Manor 28, 30
Charles 1, King 266
Chaucer, Geoffrey 101, 264
Chekhov, Anton xvi, 55, 179, 245, 359
The Cherry Orchard 179
Chettel, Henry 63
child actors 181
child murder 37, 43, 195–6
children 42–3, 366
children's companies 303–4
Chimes at Midnight (film) 137
Chkhikvadze, Ramaz 80, 83, 103–4, 160, 164
circus 12, 240
Ciulei, Liviu 109
Clark, John 179, 333
classical literature 22, 37, 55, 57
classical unities 117–18, 256, 283
Cleese, John 218
Clopton, Hugh 29
clowns 42, 67, 74, 243, 253, 300–1, 369–70
Coleridge, Samuel Taylor 77, 202, 356

Index

Comedies 38–9, 215–55, *see also names of plays*
   overview 215–16
comedy 218–19, 245, 306–7, 368
   in-jokes 247
   playing clowns 369–70
   playing comedy 74, 92, 105, 222–3, 243
   v. farce 222–3
   v. funny 215, 223, 238, 243, 255
The Comedy of Errors 53, 118, 221–4, 397
   Ephesus location 361–2
   productions
      BSC 5, 222, 282
      Nimrod 224
   themes 221, 357, 361
Complicite 104
Condell, Henry 48, 54, 56, 297–312, 316, 360, 387
Conference of the Birds 17
Cook, Adam 367
Cook, Alexander (Sander) 50–1
Coriolanus 268, 290–5, 399
   Coriolanus xvii, 171, 293–4
   mob 282, 293–4
   productions
      BSC 291–2, 295
      RSC 291
      Sydney University Players 291
   Volumnia 49, 294
costume 83, 153
   and production design 100, 107–8
   and roles 163, 193–4
   Elizabethan 5–6, 306
   Japanese references 363–4
Cottam, John 25
Cottam, Thomas 25
Courtyard Theatre 29–30
Coward, Noël 85
Cowley, Dick 301
Cremorne Theatre (Brisbane) xiii–xiv
Curtain Theatre 61
Cymbeline 46, 47, 356–7, 364–6, 399

Da Vinci, Leonardo 91
dance 243, 300–1, 363
Daniel, Samuel 318
Davenant, William 38, 391
Davies, John 310, 318, 391
Davies, Lindy 89–90
Davies, Richard 82
Davis, Essie 217, 334
Davis, Judy 205
Davison, Francis 318
Day-Lewis, Daniel 14
de Chirico, Georgio 282–3
de la Tour, Francis 13
De Niro, Robert 175

De Vere, Edward, Earl of Oxford 22, 310, 324
Death in Venice (film) 246–7
Debdale, Robert 265
Dench, Jeffrey 15
Dench, Judi 15, 80, 103, 196, 248, 386
Deveson, Anne 368
Dickens, Charles xvi, 236
dictionaries 52, 68
dictionary work 88–90, 95
Digges, Leonard 238, 275, 392, 394
Dignam, Arthur 291
directing xvi–xvii, *see also* Bell, John; *names of plays*
   and Australia 98–100
   BSC directors 382–3
   costume 107–8
   director's role 105–7
   hardest parts 109–10
   lessons from good directors 108–9
   list of don'ts 104–5
   no 'correct' method 100–1
   stand-out productions 101–4
Domingo, Placido 203
Don Quixote (Cervantes) 265, 371, 399
Donnellan, Declan 83, 94, 102–3, 248
Dr Faustus (Marlowe) 120, 317, 397
Droeshout, Martin 32, 34
Drummond, William 117
Dudley, Robert, Earl of Leicester 156, 306–7
Dumas, Alexandre 127
Duncan, Alastair 82
Duntroon Military College 273
Dvorokovsky, Marian 162

Eastwood, Larry 161
Edgerton, Joel 138, 146
education 22, 358
   BSC learning arm 100–1, 380–2
Edward II (Marlowe) 121, 398
Edward III 130
Edward IV 158–9
Edward VI Grammar School (Stratford-upon-Avon) 21–2, 25, 28
Eisenstein, Sergei 196
Eliot, T. S. 294
Elizabeth I, Queen 51–2, 56–7, 121, 130, 144, 153–7, 203, 231–2, 237, 247, 267–8, 290, 293, 307, 310–11, 315–16, 389, 398, 399, *see also* Queen's Men
Elizabethan Theatre Trust 291
Ellis, Bob 246
English Shakespeare Company 341–5
Ephesus 118, 221–2, 361–3
Essex, Earl of 54, 144, 153–4, 174, 311, 316, 398
Euphues (Lyly) 224, 264
euphuism 224

405

Evans, Peter 216, 375, 377, 382, 383
Every Man in His Humour (Jonson) 116, 300, 398
Every Man out of His Humour (Jonson) 116
Ewing, John 205
The Famous Victories of Henry V 57, 156

farce 222–3, 357
father-daughter relations 207–8, 357, 361, 371–2
father-son relations 132, 134–5, 137, 371
Fawkes, Guy 25, 122, 199, 399
Fellini, Frederico 110
feminism 217, 219
Fenton, David 195, 246
Ferdinando, Lord Strange 156–7, 299
Fiddler on the Roof 237
Field, Richard 47, 56, 257–65
Field, Sue 162
Fig Tree Theatre 179
film and television 68, 187, 196–7, 270, 360
    screen acting 14, 85–7, 175, 176, 200
Finney, Albert 84, 230
Fiorentino, Giovanni 262
The Fire Raisers 179–80
First Folio 32, 34, 155, 224, 297–9, 316, 323, 360, 387, 392, 396
Fishburne, Laurence 204
Fitton, Mary (Mall) 247, 316
Fitzpatrick, Neil 180, 201
Fletcher, John 130, 165, 309, 361, 370–1
Florio, John 260, 264
fools, *see* clowns
Forbes-Robertson, Johnston 181
Forest of Arden 24–5, 78, 292–3
Forman, Simon 318
Forsythe, Drew 217, 227
Fortune Theatre (Perth) 217
Fox, Louise 206
Freeman, David 382
Friels, Colin 205
Frisch, Max 179
Fuller, Thomas 115, 318

Gaden, John 138, 217, 246, 291
Garner, Julian 244, 334
Garnet, Henry 199
Garrick, David 20, 77, 79, 223
Gaskill, Bill 226–7
Gastrell, Francis 23
Genesian Theatre (Sydney) 12
Georgian Theatre Royal 5
German theatre xiv, 200
Gielgud, John 16–17, 79, 84, 152, 153, 350, 375
Gilbert, Tony 378
Gilkes, Denne 19

Gilshenan, Darren 217, 246
Global Financial Crisis 352
globalisation 99
Globe Theatre 1–9, 44, 48, 54–5, 78, 87, 107, 116, 144, 153–4, 166–7, 210, 269, 275, 279, 302–12 *passim*, 357, 371, 373, 391, 393, 398, 399
Globe Theatre (London) 4–8
gloves and glovers 20, 28, 258, 370
The Godfather (film) 239
Goethe, Johann Wolfgang von 256
Gogol, Nikolai 14
Goodman, Henry 80, 236
The Government Inspector 14
Gow, Michael xiii–xv, 163–4, 205, 271, 382
Gower, John 264
Graham, Marcus 204
Greenblatt, Stephen ix
Greene, Robert 35, 47, 57, 58–64, 70, 121, 265, 268
Greer, Germaine 217
Grooms of the Chamber 57, 267, 311
Grotowski, Jerzy 109
Guild Chapel 23, 188
Guild Hall 28, 29, 56, 155, 188
Guinness, Alec 202
Gunpowder Plot 25, 122, 199, 399
Guthrie, Tyrone 250–1

Haddrick, Ron 14, 81–2, 217, 274
Hall, John 25, 31
Hall, Peter 14–17, 108, 344–5
    Hamlet 14, 16
    Henry V 145
    Macbeth 14, 193–4, 253–4
    A Midsummer Night's Dream 229–30
    Wars of the Roses 16, 103, 157–8
Hall, Susanna 25, 27, 31, 42, 371–2
ham actors 28, 66–7, 79, 200, 291
Hamlet 15, 47, 64, 85, 86, 106, 130, 136, 175, 178–91, 242, 245, 264, 272, 276, 359, 399
    acting Hamlet 178–86, 189–90, 200, 284–5
    autobiographical content 187–9, 327
    Bell's performances 179–81
    Elizabethan performance 1–4
    gravedigger scene 30–1, 182, 183, 369
    Hamlet and the players 28, 67, 71–4, 94, 186, 304
    Hamlet and women 40, 189
    Hamlet's age 180–2
    nihilism 171–3, 188–9
    Olivier 11, 178
    productions 99–100
        Brook 17
        BSC 162, 181, 233
        Elizabethan 1–4

Index

Nimrod 180–1
Old Tote 12, 179–80
Peking Opera Company 83
RSC 14, 16
soliloquies 76, 84, 190–1
time scheme 182–3
Hamlet (film) 11, 178–9
Hardy, Robert 230
Harris, Richard 84
Harsnett, Sam 265
Harvey, Gabriel 64, 390
Harvey, William 317, 322–3
Hathaway, Anne 26, 27–8, 31
Hathaway family 27, 265
Hay, Alexander 227
Hazlitt, William 97, 149, 202, 294
Hedley, Phillip 333
Heminges, John 48, 50, 54, 56, 155, 297–312, 316, 360, 370, 387
Heminges, Rebecca 155, 300
Heminges, Thomasina 301–2
Henry IV 74–5, 130–8, 188, 398
 emotional triangle 132, 135, 137
 Falstaff 64, 130–1, 135, 136, 148–9, 159, 237, 300, 307
 Prince Hal 132–6
 productions
  BSC 137–8
  Nimrod 132–3, 137
  Orson Welles 137
  Shanghai Shakespeare Festival 83
Henry V xvii, 69, 74, 83, 85, 139–49, 188, 275, 398
 alternative readings 139–41
 Falconbridge 150–2
 Harfleur scene 167–8
 Olivier 11, 80, 139–41
 orations 146–8
 productions
  Adelaide Festival 12
  BSC 141–2, 145–6, 244–5
  Old Vic 80
  RSC 145
 war theme 43, 139, 141–4, 149, 267
Henry V (films) 8, 11, 139–41
Henry VI trilogy 16, 48, 53, 62, 70, 80, 93, 103, 121, 154–9, 164, 167, 231, 300, 398
 commissioning 155–7
 mob 276, 282
 productions
  BSC 158–9
  RSC 157–8
Henry VIII, see *King Henry VIII*
Henry VIII, King 67, 174, 328
Henslowe, Philip 54, 61, 63, 113, 158, 269, 350

Herbert, William, Earl of Pembroke 56, 261, 315–16, 323
Hero and Leander (Marlowe) 124, 264
Heywood, Thomas 317
high art xv, 8
Hilliard, Nicholas 315
Hindley, Myra 37, 195
Histories 128–68, *see also names of plays*
 overview 129–30, 167–8
Hitler, Adolf 37, 161, 163, 176
Hoffman, Dustin 236
Holland, Hugh 391
Holm, Ian 14, 15, 80, 145, 147, 230, 245, 339
Holy Trinity Church (Stratford-upon-Avon) 30–1
Horace 261
Horler, Ken 246, 290, 291
Howard, Alan 18, 288
Howard, John 205
Hunsdon, Lord 318
Hunt, Thomas 25

iambic pentameter 74, 86, 93–4, 119–20, 322
The Ik 17
Iles, Paul 222
Indigenous Australians 205, 380–1
infanticide 43
The Investigation 17
Irving, Henry 48
Isle of Dogs (Jonson) 113–14
Italy 119, 120, 216, 239–40, 260, 262, 339

Jackson, Glenda 14, 288
Jacobean theatre 210–11, 250
Jaggard, William 317
James I, King 57, 167–8, 199, 210–11, 250, 267, 292–3, 300, 307, 316, 322–4, 357, 389, 399, *see also* King's Men
Jenkins, Thomas 22
The Jew of Malta (Marlowe) 121–2, 124, 203, 221, 231–2
Jewish actors 200, 201, 236
Jews 37, 121–2, 231–3, 236–7
Johns, Alan 138, 377
Johnson, Samuel 68, 169
jokes 38, 53, 223, 243, 247, 306–7, 368
Jones, Gillian 194, 205, 377
Jones, Inigo 307
Jonson, Ben xvi, 32, 47, 55, 56, 57, 61, 71, 112–26, 184, 199, 221, 242, 260–1, 275, 283–4, 298–300, 306, 307, 309, 311, 318, 351, 357, 370, 395–6, 398, 399
Julius Caesar xvi, 111, 118, 135, 268, 273–83, 296, 301, 398
 and Jonson 275–6, 283
 Antony 279–81

407

Julius Caesar (continued)
   Brutus 148, 275–7
   Caesar 278–9
   Cassius 277–8
   mob 279–83
   productions 291
      BSC 106, 279–80, 281–3, 289
      radio 274
   time scheme 182
   title 275–6
   v. *Antony and Cleopatra* 283–4
   women 281
Julius Caesar (film) 274–5, 284

Kabuki theatre 162
Kean, Charles 79, 200
Kean, Edmund 77–8, 236
Keats, John 313
Kemp, Robert 163, 271
Kemp, Will 71–4, 76–7, 243, 300–3, 369
Kenna, Peter 162
Kermode, Frank ix
Kiefel, Russell 247
Kierkegaard, Søren 10
King, David 363
King Henry VIII 130, 149, 165–7, 370, 399
King John 42–3, 130, 135, 149–52, 165, 231, 398
King Lear 49, 135, 150–1, 205–13, 264, 265, 282, 358, 399
   father-daughter relations 207–8, 357, 371–2
   first scene 208–9
   King Lear 79, 147, 171, 173, 186, 199–200, 267, 353
   Lear's Fool 67, 301, 369
   Lear's sexual revulsion 39–40, 330
   nihilism 211–12, 270
   productions
      BSC 101, 206–7, 212–13, 270
      Jacobean 210–11
      Nimrod 205
      RSC 211
King's Men 57, 166–7, 199, 210, 267, 299, 300, 307–8
Kingsley, Ben 18
Kiss Me, Kate 217, 220
Kitchin, Laurence 80
Knell, Rebecca 155
Knell, William 155
Knight, Ted 299
Knollys, William 247
Kohler, Estelle 339
Kosky, Barrie 109, 382
   King Lear 101, 206–7, 270
Kott, Jan xvi, 103, 152–3, 159–60, 196, 211
Koun, Karolos 339
Kozintsev, Grigori 99

Kurosawa, Akira 83, 99
Kurzel, Justin 138
Kurzer, Edie 362–3
Kyd, Thomas 57, 123, 268, 398

Lanier, Emilia 318
Lapaine, Daniel 334
Laughton Charles 229–30
lawyers 53
Leicester, Earl of, *see* Dudley, Robert, Earl of Leicester
Leicester's Men 28, 155, 304
Leigh, Vivian 29, 269
Lennox, Duke of 316
Levin, Bernard 354–5
Lewes, George Henry 77–8
Lewis, Lee 249, 382
Lewis, Wyndham 293
libraries 37, 260–1, 299, 398
Limbourg brothers 139
Lincoln's Theatre Royal 333
literacy 21, 51, 53
Lodge, Thomas 24–5, 61, 243
Long Day's Journey into Night 82
Lopez, Roderigo 121, 231–2
Lopez conspiracy 121, 231–2
Lord Chamberlain's Men 122, 300–2, 303, 306, 318
Lord Strange's Men 28, 156, 157, 299–300
love, *see* sex and love
Lovejoy, Robin 98–9, 217
Lovell, Nigel 82
Love's Labour's Lost 27, 43, 55, 224–8, 397
   and *Euphues* 224, 264
   Berowne 219, 221, 224–8
   language 26–7, 45–6, 224–5, 227
   Nine Worthies 47–8, 53, 225
   productions
      Bristol Old Vic Theatre School 226
      Old Tote 226–7
      RSC 15, 226
   sex and love 215, 216, 241, 326
Lowin, Jack 301
Lucy, Thomas 28, 30
Lyly, John 61, 224, 264
Lynch, Julie 363–4

Mabbe, James 392
Macbeth 106, 135, 191–200, 359, 399
   acting Macbeth 88–9, 199–200
   curse 194
   directing challenges 197–8
   Lady Macbeth 120, 194–6
   Macbeth 36, 43, 88–9, 165, 171–2, 177, 186, 191–2, 199–200, 267, 273, 329
   nihilism 36, 171–2, 177, 191–2

Index

porter 198–9
productions
    BSC 37, 195–6
    Nimrod 194–5
    RSC 14, 193–4, 196–7, 253–4
    Sydney Theatre Company 195
    Zulu *Macbeth* 83
research for roles 37–8, 195–6
time scheme 182
witches 68–9, 198
Macbeth (films) 196–7
MacLiammoir, Michael 203
Macnab, Francis 368
Macready, William 200, 204–5
Maher, Jonathon 363
Mamet, David 82
A Man for All Seasons (film) 350
Mankiewicz, Joseph L. 274
Manningham, John 38, 395
Manson, Charles 194
Marat/Sade 16
Marlowe, Christopher 1, 57, 61, 63, 70, 71,
    74–5, 94, 119–25 *passim*, 203, 221, 231–2,
    264, 268, 299, 306, 309, 317–18, 324, 397
Marowitz, Charles 219
Marston, John 114
Mason, Brewster 158
Matisse, Henri 282
McBurney, Simon 104
McCallum, Joe 179
McConnochie, Rhys 244
McCowan, Alec 377
McDonald, Garry 251
McKellan, Ian 161, 196, 292
McQuade, Kris 205
Measure for Measure 129, 215, 238, 249–53,
    267, 343, 399
  characters 250–2
  interpretations of Isabella 251–2
  Jacobean 250
  low-life world 38, 250, 252–3
  productions
    BSC 250, 251
    Nimrod 250, 251
Mellor, Aubrey 205–6
Mendelssohn, Felix 102
Menzies, Robert 205
Merchant, Vivien 193, 194
The Merchant of Venice 48, 120, 231–7, 245,
    262, 398
  acting 80, 91, 93–4, 236–7
  and *Jew of Malta* 121–2, 231–2
  love triangle 234–5
  productions
    Berliner Ensemble 237
    BSC 162, 233

  racism and materialism 232–4, 235
  research for Shylock 236–7
Meres, Francis 390
The Merry Wives of Windsor 47, 83, 237–8, 262,
    398
  classroom scenes 22, 55
  commissioned by Queen 130, 237
  productions 98
    RSC 237–8
Michell, Keith 289
Middleton, Thomas 47, 350, 399
Midland Rising, 1607 292–3
A Midsummer Night's Dream 214, 215, 245,
    304, 398
  humour 306–7
  original work 228–9, 262
  productions
    BBC TV 230
    NIDA 230–1
    RSC 16, 101–2, 229–30
  Pyramus and Thisbe 8, 21, 47, 67, 102, 230
Miller, Arthur 71, 175–6
Miller, Jonathan 218
Milton, John 392
Mind's Eye 101, 382
Mirren, Helen 17, 18
mobs 276, 279–83, 292–3
Molière xvi
monarchy 129, 137–8, 148, 152, 159, 267–8
Montaigne, Michel de 257, 264, 376
Morality Plays 70
Morality plays 165
More, Thomas 21, 174, 361, 370
Morris, Mary 289
Moshinsky, Elijah 230
Mountjoy, Mary 38
Mountjoy family 258–9, 263, 360
Mozart, Wolfgang Amadeus 229, 245, 354
Much Ado About Nothing 48, 150, 216, 238–40,
    253, 398
  Nimrod production 162, 224, 239–40
Müller, Heiner, *Anatomy Titus Fall of Rome*
    xiii–xv, 269–72
Myers, Bruce 17
Mystery Plays 28, 53, 57, 67, 70, 72, 162, 167,
    198

Nashe, Thomas 61, 63, 70, 71, 158
National Institute of Dramatic Art (NIDA) 179,
    230, 333, 367, 382
National Theatre 16–17, 201, 226, 236
  Romans in Britain 344–5
Neeme, Aarne 217
Negro, Lucy 38, 318
Neidhardt, Elke 382
Nevin, Robyn 195

New Place 23–4, 29
'new men' 135–6, 148, 151, 288
NIDA, see National Institute of Dramatic Art (NIDA)
nihilism xv, 35–6, 171–4, 191–2, 211–12, 270, 343, 356
Nimrod Theatre 17, 290
  As You Like It 240
  The Comedy of Errors 224
  Hamlet 180–1
  Henry IV 132–3, 137
  King Lear 205
  Macbeth 194–5
  Measure for Measure 250, 251
  Much Ado About Nothing 162, 224, 239–40
  The Resistible Rise of Arturo Ui 161
  Richard III 161–2
  Romeo and Juliet 334
  Twelfth Night 246–7
Nunn, Trevor 17–18, 196, 197, 236

obscenity charges 344–5
O'Casey, Sean 82
O'Connor, Gary 338–9
Oedipus (Seneca) 16–17
Old Tote Theatre, *The Resistible Rise of Arturo Ui* 161
Old Tote Theatre Company 12
  formation 179
  Hamlet 12, 179–80
  Love's Labour Lost 226–7
  The Taming of the Shrew 98–9, 217
Old Vic 12, 80, 201
Old Vic Theatre School, *see* Bristol Old Vic Theatre School
Oldham Rep 153
Olivier, Laurence 84, 226
  Coriolanus 291, 293
  death 350
  great Shakespearean actor 12, 79–81, 185, 200–2, 203, 211, 291
  Hamlet 11, 178
  Henry V 8, 11, 80, 139–41
  Olivier revolution 79–81
  Othello 12, 79, 80, 200–2, 203
  Richard III 11, 43, 159, 162
  screen performances 8, 11, 80–1, 139–40
  Titus Andronicus 269
Orwell, George 273
Osborne, John 84–5, 152, 185
O'Shea, Sean 251
Ostler, William 301–2
Otello (film) 203
Othello 48–9, 200–5, 358, 399
  acting Othello 199–200, 203
  casting issues 201–2

Iago 67, 135–6, 202–3, 205, 369
Kean 77–8
nihilism 171–2
Olivier 12, 79, 80, 200–2, 203
Othello 47, 171–2
productions
  BSC 205
  Old Vic 12, 201
race issues 201–2
sources 37, 67, 204, 262
Othello (films) 80, 201, 203, 204
Other Place 29, 196, 197
O'Toole, Peter 84, 185
Ovid 22, 37, 57, 77, 264, 265
Oxford, Earl of, *see* De Vere, Edward, Earl of Oxford
Oxford's travelling players 28

Pacino, Al 236
Packer, Kerry 353
Pageant of St George and the Dragon 28
pageants 6, 28, 53, 166, 373
Painter, William 262
Pandosto (Greene) 64, 265
Parnassus plays 76–7, 116, 394
The Passionate Pilgrime by W. Shakespeare 317
Peele, George 61, 63, 70, 300
Peking Opera 83
Pembroke, Earl of, *see* Herbert, William, Earl of Pembroke
Pembroke's company 307
Penrith Panthers Club 205
Pericles 38, 340, 356, 357, 359–64, 367, 371, 399
  authorship 252, 360–1, 362
  BSC production 358, 359–60, 362–4
  Ephesus 118, 221, 361–2
  final scenes 359–61
  sources 264
Petrarch 322, 326
Philip II, King of Spain 204
Phillips, Augustine 154, 301
Pinter, Harold 84–5, 193, 359
plague 20, 60, 259, 305, 307–8, 399
Plautus 22, 119, 221, 264, 390
Pliny 204
Plutarch 22, 37, 57, 106, 261, 280–1, 289, 293
Poets Laureate 38, 126
Polanski, Roman 196
Polson, John 181
Potts, Marion 212, 217–18, 219, 382
Pram Factory (Melbourne) 98
Pratt, Richard 353
propaganda 54, 139–40, 156–7, 159, 231
proscenium arch 6, 7, 78, 107
psychiatry 37, 367–8
psychopaths 37, 163, 194, 195, 367–8

Index

publishing 297–312
  Elizabethan practices 298–9
  Elizabethan scripts 2, 7–8, 60–1
  First Folio 27, 32, 34, 155, 224, 297–9, 316, 323, 360, 387, 396
  Green's pamphlet 62–3
  Heminges and Condell 56, 297–312
  Jonson's works 117, 126
  Richard Field 47, 56, 257–65
  sonnets 316–17
puns 68–9, 243, 322
Puritans 54, 188, 246, 266, 335–6

Queen's Men 29, 54, 56, 57, 68, 155–6, 158, 304, 306–7
Queensland Performing Arts Centre xiv
Queensland Theatre Company
  Anatomy Titus Fall of Rome xiii–xv, 269–72
  Long Day's Journey into Night 82
  Richard III 163–4
Quentin, Robert 179
Quiney, Judith 24, 25, 27, 42, 371–2
Quiney, Thomas 25
Quinn, Anthony 202

race 201–4 *passim*, 231–3, 236
radio actors 82
radio drama 82, 274
The Rape of Lucrece 56, 259, 315, 390
Raymond, Andrew 363
The Recruiting Officer 226–7
Redgrave, Michael 82, 84
Redgrave, Vanessa 230
Reformation 23, 28, 53, 166, 188
refugees 203, 232, 249, 282
rehearsals 108, 223, 226, 227, 240
republicanism 266–8, 274–7, 284
research
  by Shakespeare 37–8, 120
  dictionary work 88–90, 95
  for roles 37–8, 163, 236–7, 367–8
  Mind's Eye 101, 382
  Shakespeare's books 257–65
The Resistible Rise of Arturo Ui (Brecht) 161
Restoration 78, 211
Revenge plays 187
The Revenger's Tragedy 17–18
Richard II 79, 121, 130, 152–4, 167, 171, 231, 311, 398
  RSC production 153
Richard III 150, 159–65, 177, 282, 300, 398
  and *Tamburlaine* 121–2
  productions
    Bell 161–4
    BSC 160, 162

    BSC/Queensland Theatre Company 163–4
    Georgian 83, 103–4, 160, 164
    Nimrod 161–2
    Old Tote 161
    RSC 104, 164
  Richard III 36, 43, 148, 155–8 *passim*
    Bell 37, 161–4
    Burbage 70–1, 75–6, 79
    Chkhikvadze 80, 83, 103–4, 160, 164
    in *Henry VI* 155, 164
    Kean 16, 79
    Olivier 79, 159, 162
    origin in The Vice 67, 70, 75–6, 165
    psychology 37, 163–4, 165
  Shakespeare/Burbage anecdote 38, 395
Richard III (films) 11, 159, 161, 292
Richardson, Ian 14, 145, 238, 291, 350
Richardson, Ralph 29, 80, 350
Rigg, Diana 14, 245
Rodway, Norman 339
Rogers, Paul 351–2
Romances 356–77, *see also names of plays*
  overview 356–9
Romans 266–95, *see also names of plays*
  overview 266–9
Romeo and Juliet 7, 21, 216, 326, 332–40, 398
  balcony scene 333, 334–5
  casting 333–4
  directing challenges 333–8
  love theme 41, 334, 335–6, 338–9
  nihilism 171–3
  Nurse 49, 219, 336, 339–40
  productions
    BSC 334
    Lincoln's Theatre Royal 333
    Nimrod 334
    RSC 339, 344
  sources 261, 338
  time scheme 182, 336–7
Romeril, John 98
Rosalynde (Lodge) 24–5, 243
Rose Theatre 61, 158, 269, 300
Roundhouse (London) 104, 160
Rowe, Nicholas 390
Royal Shakespeare Company (RSC) 19, 29–30, 82, 98, 332–3
  Bell's training 12–18, 20
  new wave 17–18
  Russian tour 194, 253–4
Royal Shakespeare Company (RSC), productions
  Antony and Cleopatra 288
  Coriolanus 291
  Hamlet 14, 16
  Henry V 145

Royal Shakespeare Company (RSC),
   productions (*continued*)
   King Lear 211
   Love's Labour's Lost 15, 226
   Macbeth 14, 193–4, 196–7, 253–4
   The Merry Wives of Windsor 237–8
   A Midsummer Night's Dream 16, 101–2, 229–30
   Richard II 153
   Richard III 104, 164
   Romeo and Juliet 339
   The Taming of the Shrew 219, 341, 344
   The Tempest 377
   Timon of Athens 13–14, 349, 351
   Titus Andronicus 29, 269
   Twelfth Night 14–15, 103, 245, 248
   Wars of the Roses 103, 157–8
Royal Shakespeare Theatre 29
Rush, Geoffrey 98
Russia 83, 99, 102–4, 160, 164, 165, 185, 194, 248, 253–4
Ryan, Damien 244
Rylance, Mark 5

Sadler, Hamnet 38
Sadler, Judith 24
Saint-Denis, Michel 13
Schlesinger, John 13, 349, 351–2
Schofield, Leo 341
Scofield, Paul 13–14, 153, 193, 194, 211, 351–2
Scott-Mitchell, Michael 342
screen acting 14, 85–7, 175, 176, 200
scripts 159, 302, 309
   Elizabethan scripts 21
   published by Jonson 117, 298, 299
   sold by Elizabethan actors 2, 7, 60–1, 298–9
Sejanus (Jonson) 118, 275, 399
Seneca 16–17, 22, 57, 261, 264, 272, 282
sex and love 38–42, 186, 215–16, 228, 241, 243, 288–9
   Romeo and Juliet 334–9
   sonnets 314–31 *passim*
sexual deviance 246
sexual politics 215–19, 228, 281
sexual repression 251–2
sexual revulsion 39–40, 189
Shakespeare, Edmund 21, 264, 305
Shakespeare, Gilbert 21
Shakespeare, Hamnet 24, 42, 187, 249
Shakespeare, John 20–3, 28, 47, 48, 56, 117, 187, 258, 306
Shakespeare, Judith 24, 25, 27, 42, 371–2
Shakespeare, Richard 21
Shakespeare, Susanna 25, 27, 31, 42, 371–2
Shakespeare, William 34–57, *see also names of plays*
   and Burbage 38, 56, 70–1, 75–7, 258, 395
   and Essex rebellion 153–4
   and Greene 35, 47, 61–3
   and Heminges and Condell 297–312 *passim*
   and Jonson 114–19, 125–6
   and Marlowe 74–5, 94, 119–25 *passim*, 231–2
   and women 38, 48–9, 228, 260
   as actor 2, 28–9, 36–7, 47–9, 56, 57, 116, 199, 299–300, 310–11
   as playwright 55–6, 124–5, 311–12
   at Titchfield 259–60
   business interests 48, 54–5, 57, 187–8, 309–10, 371
   Catholic connections 22–3, 25, 187
   character 35–6, 309–10
   childhood 20, 21–2
   children 25, 27, 31, 38, 42–3, 248–9, 371–2
   coat of arms 24, 48, 116–17, 324, 389
   conditions for emergence
      opportunities 57
      right family 55–6
      right people 56–7
      right place right time 51–5, 266
   country values 43–8, 187–8
   death of brother Edmund 305
   death of son Hamnet 42, 187, 249
   education 21–2, 53, 118, 310, 371
   family 20–4
   greatness xv–xvii, 51
   joins Queen's Men 29, 56, 155
   later years 361, 370–1
   love of common folk 281–2
   love of theatre 259–60, 308
   marriage 27–8, 38, 57
   move to London 27–8, 38, 57, 155–7, 259
   New Place 23–4, 29
   patrons 56–7, 261, 315, 323–5
   political views 266–8, 282, 294
   portraits 32, 34
   Prospero as self portrait 370–3
   research 37–8, 204
   sexuality 38–42, 216
   tombstone and memorial 30–2
   use of books 257–65 *passim*
   views of contemporaries 389–96
   youth 49
Shakespeare Birthplace Trust 20
Shakespeare memorial (Stratford-upon-Avon) 30–2
Shakespeare Memorial Theatre 81–2
Shanghai Shakespeare Festival 83
Shapiro, James 111
Sharman, Jim 375, 377, 382
Shaw, George Bernard 51, 253, 371
Sheldon, Tony 247

Index

Sher, Antony 164, 236
Shoreditch theatre 302
Shostakovich, Dmitri 360
Sidney, Philip 55, 144, 264, 316, 397
Sieff, Percy 233
Sincler, John (Sinklo) 302
Sinden, Donald 15, 103, 248
Sir Thomas More 361, 370
Slye, Will 301
Smith, Hilary 20
Smith, Maggie 227
Smith, Mike 20
Smith, Saskia 377
soliloquies 76, 87, 94, 138, 164, 182, 190–1, 196–7
Somers, Will 67
sonnet exercise 227
sonnets 39, 314–31, 398
   content 318–22
   Dark Lady 38, 260, 315, 318, 322–6, 330
   dedication 316–17, 323
   examples 317–22, 328–31
   form 322, 326, 330
   identity of protagonists 315–18
   lovely boy 315–17
   manuscript/publication 316–17, 322, 324
   rival poet 317–18
   W.H. 316–17, 322–3
Southampton, Earl of, *see* Wroithsley, Henry, Earl of Southampton
Soviet Union, *see* Russia
The Spanish Tragedy (Kyd) 123, 398
Spencer, Gabriel 113–14, 122
Spinning Out (TV documentary) 368
Spriggs, Elizabeth 339
Stables Theatre (Kings Cross) 194
Stanley, Thomas 156–7
Stanley, Dr Tom 367–8
Stanley, William 156
Stanley family 156
Stephens, Robert 227
Stewart, Patrick 18
Stollery, Chris 217, 218
Stratford-upon-Avon 19–32, 332–3
Stratford-upon-Avon Cemetery 30–2
Street, Peter 303
Suchet, David 34, 35, 236
Sussex's Men 155
Swan Theatre 29, 61, 350
Swift, Clive 104
Sydney Festival 103
Sydney Olympics Festival 341–2
Sydney Opera House 226–7
Sydney Opera House Drama Theatre 195
Sydney Opera House Playhouse 342–3
Sydney Theatre Company 195

Sydney University 11–12, 224, 333
Sydney University Dramatic Society 290
Sydney University Players 246, 290–1

TaikOz 363–4
Tamburlaine (Marlowe) 71, 74–5, 121–2
The Taming of the Shrew 46, 48, 217–21, 300, 398
   directing approaches 218–21
   Kate's final speech 218–19
   productions
      BBC TV series 218
      BSC 217–21
      Marowitz 219
      Old Tote 98–9, 217
      RSC 219, 341, 344
   sexual politics 216, 217, 219
Tarlton, Richard 156, 300–1, 307
Tate, Nahum 211
Tate, Sharon 194
Taylor, Elizabeth 217
Tearle, Godfrey 80
television, *see* film and television
Tell Me I'm Here (Deveson) 368
The Tempest 118, 220, 268, 356, 357, 366, 369, 370–7, 399
   acting challenges 375–6
   nihilism 173–4
   productions
      Belvoir Theatre 375, 377
      BSC 375, 377
      RSC 377
   Prospero 372–6
   self-portrait issue 370–3
   sources 262, 373, 376
The Theatre 56, 61
Theatre for the Deaf 240
Theatre of Cruelty 219
Theatre of the Absurd xv, 153
Theatre Royal (Sydney) 160
There Will Be Blood (film) 14
This Sceptr'd Isle 12
Thorpe, Thomas 317, 322
Throne of Blood (film) 83
time schemes 117–18, 182–3, 256, 283
Timon of Athens 129, 173, 238, 343, 349–53
   productions, RSC 13–14, 349–50, 351
Titus Andronicus 37, 48, 156, 203, 231, 268–73, 300, 398
   horrors 35–6, 268–72
   nihilism 35–6, 173, 270
   productions
      AnatomyTitus Fall of Rome xiii–xv, 269–72
      BSC/Queensland Theatre Company xiii–xv, 269–72
      Elizabethan 6
      RSC 29, 269

Tolstoy, Leo 65
Tooley, Nick 50–1, 304–5
Town, John 155
Tragedies 170–213, 356, see also names of plays
   nature of Tragedy 170–7
Tree, Herbert Beerbohm 78
Troilus and Cressida 56, 129, 238, 249, 341–8, 369
   BSC production 341–5
   humour 343–4
   modern translations 84, 101
   Ulysses 345–6
   Ulysses's speech 346–8, 350
Troilus and Criseyde (Chaucer) 264
The Troublesome Reign of King John 57, 156
The True History of King Leir 57
The True Tragedy of Richard III 156
Twelfth Night 48, 53, 67, 245–9, 262, 301, 369, 398
   jokes 247, 306–7
   love and sex 41–2, 215, 216, 235, 245, 247, 248
   productions
      BSC 246, 249
      Donnellan 83, 102–3, 248
      Nimrod 246–7
      RSC 14–15, 103, 245, 248
      Sydney University Players 246, 291
   structure/themes 221, 245, 357
   title 247
The Two Gentlemen of Verona 300, 397
   BSC production 216
The Two Noble Kinsmen 309, 361, 370, 385
Tynan, Kenneth 203
Ubu Roi 17

unities 117–18, 256, 283
University Wits 47, 59, 61, 62–3, 70, 76–7, 303–4
U.S. 16

Vautrollier, Jacqueline 258–9
Vautrollier, Thomas 258–9
Vautrollier family 258–9
Venus and Adonis 38, 44–5, 56, 259, 308, 315, 323–4
Verdi, Guiseppi 203
Vice (character) 70, 75–6, 165
Visconti, Luchino 246–7
Volska, Anna 12, 17, 19–20, 37, 195–6, 217, 227, 233, 240, 253–4, 332, 349
Voss, Gert 237

Walsingham, Francis 54, 122–3
Walton, William 159
war 132, 272–3, 289, 292–4, 343–6
   Henry V 139–49

war crimes 43, 267
Wardlaw, James 162
Warner, David 14–15, 16, 80, 158, 185, 245
Wars of the Roses (BSC) 158–9
Wars of the Roses (English Shakespeare Company) 341
Wars of the Roses (RSC) 16, 103, 157–8
weather 46
Weaver, Jacki 227
Weever, John 279
Weis, Rene 45, 177
Welles, Orson 137, 196, 203, 236
Wesker, Arnold 84–5, 152
West Side Story 340
What You Will, see *Twelfth Night*
Wherrett, Richard 132, 137, 161, 181, 195, 233, 333
Whitehouse, Mary 344–5
Whittet, Matt 206
Wilde, Oscar 82, 153
Wilkins, George 252–3, 360, 361
Williams, Clifford 14, 245
Williams, Fred 282
Williams, Tennessee 175–6
Williamson, David xiv, 98
Williamson, Nicol 185
Wilson, Frank 132–3
Wilson, Ian 296
The Winter's Tale 26, 37–8, 43, 49, 356, 359–60, 366–70, 399
   bear stage direction 368
   clowning 369–70
   productions
      BSC 367
      Complicite 104
      NIDA 367
   psychiatric research 367–8
   sources 64, 265
witchcraft 198, 199, 221–2
Wolfit, Donald 79
women 22, 189, 196, 281, see also sex and love; sexual politics
   all-female casts 218, 219
   Cleopatra 285–8
   father-daughter relations 207–8, 357, 361, 371–2
   roles 48–9, 120, 150, 216, 241
Wood, Michael xi
Woodrow, Carol 233, 382
Wotton, Henry 129, 166–7
Wroithsley, Henry, Earl of Southampton 56, 154, 261, 315–17, 322–4, 399

Zappa, Bill 289
Zeffirelli, Franco 203, 217